THE
PACK
A JONATHAN CROWLEY NOVEL

JAMES A. MOORE

Chapter One

I

Stan Long and Dave Pageant stared at the drive-in's screen, mesmerized all over again by the movie they had already watched twice this week, which had been filmed several years before the man became a politician. The drive-in was not exactly known for having new fare, but it was always good and, man, there was NO ONE who could kill 'em as well as Arnold; goofy accent or no, he was the very best.

The celluloid hero threw another man half his size through a window, following after him with what looked like a bazooka held in one arm. This was where the story really started to pick up; this was where he took on the whole gang of cyborgs with an attitude problem. Stan stared at the dusty screen, ignoring the raindrops that gave his hero running acne scars. The rain was getting heavier, and Stan was dreading the sound that would inevitably come along to ruin everything: the sound of his mother calling out for him to come in out of the rain.

Beside him, round face covered with a Phillies baseball cap to stop the worst of the drops from hitting his bespectacled eyes, Dave Pageant reached under the plastic bag that covered their goodies and snatched another Dorito. Most of the nacho cheese flavoring seemed determined to stick to Dave's fingers, but he didn't care. Nothing ever seemed to bother Dave. Stan sighed under the sounds of multiple explosions and screams, wished once again that he could just live for the moment like Dave always did. Without any conscious thought Stan allowed his eyes to move toward the lights of the city in the far distance. Tonight the city was all but hidden by clouds, the underbellies of which captured the gleaming lights and held them as closely as Stan longed to hold the city. Sometimes Stan hated looking at the city; it reminded him of how far away from any place with real people he was, stuck in the boondocks with a bunch of trees between him and the rest of the world.

Just before he could get truly depressed, he heard the sound of his mother's voice, made shrill by distance and exasperation, calling for him to come home. "Better get goin', Stan. Your mom's gonna peel the skin off your butt otherwise."

Stan stood up, looking desperately at the screen of the drive-in, wanting to stay and knowing he could not. "Yeah. I'll see you tomorrow, Dave."

Stan turned morosely away from his best friend and started up the steep hill that stood between him and his destination. Rain-slick and thick with unmown grass, the hill almost proved too much for Stan to handle until he finally broke down and used his hands to grab piles of grass between his fingers for the extra leverage needed to hoist himself up the hill. Over to the other side, sliding, wishing desperately for a firm handhold, Stan slipped in the wet, well-maintained lawn and slid all the way to the bottom of the hill. He just managed to keep the profanity from his lips as he saw his mother standing before him.

Adrienne Long tried to be upset with her son, but watching him slide down the hill, watching the look of shock on his face as he finally landed with bright green stains covering most of his backside and loose grass in his hair, she forgot to be angry. How could anyone be upset with a skinny little wet puppy who was trying so desperately to behave and always failing so miserably? He wanted to fit in, but somehow Stan normally managed to be off in another of his dreams when the best opportunities came around.

With a grin breaking through her scowl of disapproval, she started her motherly tirade. "Stan, dinner was ready an hour ago." Lie; she had just finished setting the table. "Now we have to wait while you get cleaned up. Move it, kid, before I decide to let your father handle this mess." Yep, that got him moving. Through the entrance normally blocked by a glass sliding door and into the kitchen, where he meticulously wiped his muddy shoes before bolting upstairs to the bathroom.

Once there, Stan fairly leaped out of his clothes and into the shower. Icy cold water switched to scalding hot and then finally to lukewarm as he lathered and rinsed himself. Stan wrapped the thick blue towel around his narrow waist and rubbed his body dry vigorously. He could never stand the water from the shower or bath on his body; a good rainstorm, or even a romp through the creek, that was one thing, but the shower? Somehow it just never felt right.

Mad dash to the bedroom, quick change into fresh underwear, shorts, and a heavy cotton T-shirt. Dash back down the stairs, and there was his whole family, waiting with varying degrees of patience for him to sit down. April was looking at her watch, no doubt thinking about her date with whichever high school jock she was seeing this weekend. Dad was sitting in his chair, shaking his head and grinning. Mom was looking at Dad with something like relief; things hadn't been real great between them lately, and when he was happy, she was happy. And, of course, Beauregard. Beau was Stan's best friend, the only one who never yelled and never got upset. Weighing in at just under two hundred pounds, Beauregard the Saint Bernard was also his number-one protection from any possible threat. One look at Beau, and people decided that maybe now wasn't the best time to bother good ol' Stan Long. To date Stan had not told anyone that Beau was all bark and no bite. Why make life harder than it already was?

Beau sat at his normal spot next to the kitchen door and started sucking in his cheeks. The only dog on the planet that was forty pounds overweight and trying desperately to look like he was starved. Sad, chocolate brown eyes regarded Stan as he sat down. Beau waddled forward and slapped a massive paw against Stan's bare thigh, leaving red marks as he displayed his affection and desire for a few treats during the family's dinner. Naturally, Beau's bowl was filled with fresh food, both wet and dry, but it wasn't the same as people food; it never quite tasted as good as the stuff people ate. Having smelled wet dog food, Stan could understand his dog's desires for something fit for consumption.

Stan lifted the huge paw away from his thigh and scratched behind his best buddy's ear. There were tiny scabs where the fleas had made their presence known. "Hey, Beau. Hi, everyone, sorry I'm late."

Dad put on his serious face, mostly for Mom's benefit, and pointed a meaty finger at him. "You want to watch that. You need to be where you can hear your mother calling for you, you understand me?" Even with the stern look, Stan knew his father was hardly worried about waiting a few minutes. If anyone was actually upset, it was April. No way did she get out for her date until dinner was over. Stan made certain that his parents were both busy grabbing food before he stuck his tongue out at his older sister. April just rolled her eyes and sighed, obviously *so* bored with her little brother.

Stan knew better. April was just going through one of her *I'm sixteen years old and don't have time for a little brother* phases. In a week's time she'd be right next to him, watching TV and wishing that the jock du jour would just please call her already.

Mom noticed his little interplay with his sister and halfheartedly smacked his hand, mumbling something about keeping his tongue where it belonged. Stan put on his best innocent son look and started grabbing at the bowl of spaghetti noodles. Meatballs no less, the good stuff. Almost too good, downright boring. Stan pushed the thoughts away as he started noisily slurping up long strands of spaghetti.

Dinner passed with casual conversation and April checking the hands on her watch every ten minutes. No big problems, no major arguments, just that cold distance that Stan wasn't even consciously aware of, growing between his parents. Stan wanted his life to change, wanted things to be as exciting in town as they simply had to be in the city. Anything had to be better than being stuck out here, anything at all.

Before the night was over Stan's wish was well on its way to coming true. The storm carried Stan's wish into town, and the wishes of others as well.

II

The following day started so well that most people could almost imagine Mother Nature was apologizing for the weather of the night before. The air was cool and a good deal drier than it had been only twelve hours ago; the ground was almost dry, having drunk deeply of the waters that fell the night before. The sky was free of clouds, and already the sun was beaming golden light into the windows of houses that faced toward the east.

Charlene Lyons was bored, her normal state of mind these days. Her father refused to let her go out on school nights, and since it was only Thursday, she still had one more night of prison to go through. The day hadn't even ended in school, and already Charlene was imagining the drudgery of yet another night at home.

Math. Charlene hated math. She hated math, and she hated Mr. LeMarrs, her math teacher. Never had one man believed so heavily in the curse of homework. It seemed the year had only just started, but school was almost over, and the endless days of homework would fade away. Already the days were growing longer, and the heat outside the air-conditioned building was doing a gradual slide toward inferno level. Charlene loved the summer best of all, loved when she could go out into the darkness with her friends and not have to worry about homework or any other facet of school.

"I see I've started boring you again, Ms. Lyons!" The voice was bright and cheery, overly loud, and designed, Charlene was certain, to grate on her nerves. Mr. LeMarrs's huge body was over her, practically leaning across the desk as he waited for her answer.

"Nossir. I was listenin'." She saw his thick eyebrow rise in amusement, wanted desperately to disappear from the room, or better yet to make him disappear.

"Well then. Can you give me the answer to my last question?"

Charlene drew a complete blank. Zip, nada, nothing. "I-I forgot the question."

Around the room she heard several people start to snicker. She was pleased to note that Stan was not among the guilty.

LeMarrs was getting that look on his face, the one that was always followed with something like *Perhaps you could learn to pay attention if you spent the afternoon after school writing all the questions and answers on the board*, when another voice chirped, "Forty-seven."

Charlene and the teacher both looked at Dave Pageant the same way, with a small O of shock planted on their mouths. NO ONE interrupted LeMarrs when he was making an example of another student. It was almost certain to cause grief. Dave had planted a look of complete innocence on his face, no doubt certain that he was caught, and just as likely willing to tough out another detention. Charlene hated to think of what his dad would say if he was stuck after school again. Dave somehow managed to keep a straight A average in all of his classes, and managed simultaneously to stay in the doghouse in conduct.

"Was I talking to you, Mr. Pageant? I don't recall actually calling your name at any point during my discussion with Ms. Lyons."

Dave smiled serenely in response, his look of innocence compounded by his blameless grin. With almost any other teacher, it would have worked.

"You can knock that little smirk off of your face this instant, Mr. Pageant. Perhaps you'd like to explain to Principal Wortham why you have decided to interrupt my class."

That was another thing Charlene hated about LeMarrs, he sounded like a little old lady, prim and proper despite his youthful appearance. He didn't look a day over thirty, and if he was five years older than that, Charlene would kiss his fat face. He'd been a teacher when her older sister, Nancy, had graduated, but that didn't mean he should act like he was someone's grandmother.

Dave Pageant said nothing, simply stared and smiled.

LeMarrs continued to stare for a few more seconds and finally turned away from the boy in disgust. "I think that perhaps we should continue this discussion after school, Mr. Pageant." The man glared at Charlene for a few seconds, letting her know that he had not forgotten about her dreaming in his class. As much as Charlene wanted to do as Dave had just done, the man before her was too intimidating in his own prissy way. Sometimes she wished he'd just drop dead.

When the man's back was turned, Charlene turned and mouthed her thanks to Dave. Without any noticeable change in his expression, he lowered one eyelid in a slow wink and then turned back to the front of the classroom.

LeMarrs continued his boring speech in his boring voice for another endless fifteen minutes before the bell released them from his little section of the school. Ten minutes until the next class, Charlene had just enough time to thank Dave again. But, as usual, Dave was halfway through the door by the time the bell finished its ring. Off, no doubt, to wait for Stan by his locker. When Charlene thought about the two of them, she had trouble understanding how they could be best friends. Dave was so flamboyant, so full of life, and next to him, Stan seemed, well, kind of geeky. Stan was a great guy, and she thought he was just about the cutest boy in school, but he was also very quiet and very studious. Like Charlene, he had to really study when he got home, just to finish the homework. Dave never had that problem. Dave was calm and relaxed around everyone and about everything. Stan was pretty calm all the time, especially around her.

"Charlee!" The voice was almost too friendly, and even when only spoken at normal volume had a shrill nasal sound that drove into Charlene's head like steel spikes. With a grimace turned into grin, Charlene turned to face her best friend, Jessie Grant.

Jessie was a little shorter than Charlene, but only a little. She just seemed a lot shorter, as in dwarflike. Jessie came all but skipping down the hallway, her smile darned near bright enough to blind, and her eyes with that normal slightly haunted look. Jessie was great to be around, but not at school; not where her always-nervous smile seemed to stick out twice as much as it did anywhere else. Much as she loved being with Jessie, Charlee thought the girl looked like a whipped puppy in class. No backbone worth mentioning.

"Hi, Jessie. How's things?" If Jessie heard the forced friendliness, she hid the knowledge well. That was good; she was Charlee's best friend after all.

"Charlee, I heard you got into some sort of trouble with Mr. LeMarrs." The girl's blue eyes grew incredibly wide behind her eyeglasses, almost matching the lenses' perfect roundness. "You're not gonna be in Dutch are you?"

"No way. All I did was daydream. LeMarrs can be upset about it, but what's he gonna do, have me suspended for being bored?"

"I heard it was Da-ave that kept you outta the principal's office." There it was, that damned smirk that made Charlee want to swat her best friend in the head almost every time she saw it. What her dad always called a "Shit-Eating Grin." Despite her best efforts to prevent it, Charlee felt the red flow of blood into her cheeks as she started blushing.

"It wasn't like that. You know Dave, always trying to crack up the whole school." She tried for the casual sound, a quick dismissal of the subject, but Jessie wasn't going for it.

The smile on Jessie's face grew even broader, eyes almost vicious behind her glasses. The light freckles on her face seemed to grow darker, but Charlee was convinced that it was only her imagination. "Uh-huh. Su-ure that's all it was." Her voice grew into a sing-song tone as she continued, "Dave's gotta crush on Char-lee... Dave's gotta crush on Char-lee."

Charlee was getting just about ready to pop her friend in the nose when the warning bell erupted through the noise of the crowded hallway. *One of these days...*

Jessie's grin became almost normal for a second, and then off she went with a "seeyalater," all but skipping down the corridor. It didn't look like anyone had overheard their conversation, and Charlee was grateful. She made a promise to herself to give Jessie the silent treatment later. Nothing ever bothered Jessie as much as the silent treatment.

III

Joey Whitman stared intently at his wristwatch, waiting for the moment when the final bell would ring, and he would be allowed to go home. He felt another headache coming on, and he just knew if he didn't get some Advil into his system that he would suffer for it. He felt as bad as Lawrence Grey looked, and Lawrence Grey looked horrible. In the seat next to him, Lawrence was dutifully writing down notes on tomorrow's assignment. Lawrence's handwriting was almost as pinched as his face. Lawrence was a born lemon sucker if there had ever been one.

Lawrence glanced over and smiled and, for just that brief second, he almost looked human. Lawrence was pale, almost white, even after most of the summer had come and gone. His hair was thin and dark and just sort of sat there on the top of his head, looking like dried-out grass, lifeless. His uneven features shared only a certain gauntness to associate them to each other—thin nose, thin lips, and narrow little eyes—his features seemed like they would have all been more comfortable on different people. His face just did not look right. As a result, Lawrence looked even worse than he should have with his pallid complexion.

Except when he smiled. When Lawrence smiled, his whole face lit up. His cheeks looked almost healthy instead of being so fleshless, his dark muddy eyes gleamed, and even his undersized teeth looked good when Lawrence was happy. Not that Lawrence smiled very often. Not that he ever had reason to.

Lawrence was the only kid in school who was never allowed to go out and play, even on the weekends. With the way his bedroom faced the ballpark, it was even worse for him. He'd be sitting in his room, a lonely hangdog look set in place, and he'd be watching all of the other kids playing ball. If he was lucky, his mom let him open the window, let him hear the happiness out there instead of just seeing the other kids playing.

Lawrence was hardly Mister Popularity, but Joey liked him just the same. The clanging of last bell finally came, and Lawrence waved a sad good-bye, weak smile in place. Joey knew that his mother was waiting outside, probably timing how long it took him to get from the room to the car, ready to take him back to his prisonlike home. By the time Joey got to his locker and grabbed the necessary books, he'd forgotten all about his desire for an Advil.

IV

And life went on in Serenity Falls. Most of the schoolchildren went home and then out to play for a while. Except for Lawrence, stuck at home again, Charlene suffering from the same fate, but not as seriously as Lawrence, and Dave.

Dave was having yet another talk with Principal Wortham. The man was balding, slightly pudgy, and as jovial as Santa Claus. Dave almost felt sorry for him, being in charge of meting out punishments; the poor man just wasn't the type to enjoy it.

Instead of his normal smile, Principal Wortham was looking slightly exasperated. "Now, Dave, how is it I just knew you were going to be in my office again before the day was out?"

Dave's eyes sparkled, his face amused and friendly. "Well, I figure I'm about three days overdue for our weekly visit. I'm normally here no later than Monday."

Wortham allowed himself to smile at that, because it was true. Sometimes Dave sensed the man was ready to throttle him for being so amazingly annoying, sometimes he sensed the man would be lost without their regular little visit of the week. "What is it this time, Dave?"

Dave Pageant sucked in a huge lungful of air, scrunched his face into a reasonable facsimile of Mr. LeMarrs's features, and proceeded in a high-pitched whine that was incredibly close to the teacher's own voice: "I can't have you disrupting my class, Mr. Pageant. It's not your place to answer questions directed to another student." Dave let the remaining air out of his chest with a whoosh, and Wortham found himself chuckling, even though the last thing he wanted to do was encourage the boy.

Wortham forced himself to look stern, knowing full well that it had absolutely no impact on the fifth grader before him. "He's right, you know. You really shouldn't interrupt his class."

Dave actually managed to look guilty for all of half a second. "Yeah, but it just comes so easily with him." Then he grinned ear to ear, that natural charisma shining out from him in almost visible waves. "I just can't resist watching his whole face turn purple like that; it's better than cartoons."

Wortham shook his head to hide the smile on his face. He tried to stay somber in appearance, but the little kid inside of him related too well with what the boy was saying. "I'm gonna have to give you the usual punishment, Dave. Two days. After school. You can start today, if you like."

Dave nodded, his face growing serious for a moment. "Why don't we make it four days?"

Wortham looked at him for several seconds, again having to force himself to remember that Dave Pageant was just a boy. "What on earth for?"

Dave's grin came back, mischievous and honest. "Down payment on next week?"

Wortham looked back at his young friend with a smile. "Incorrigible, Dave. You are absolutely incorrigible."

"Yeah. Isn't it great? What would you do without me?"

V

Tom Lassiter hated working nights, but the money was decent, and that was a bonus. The Quik-Mart was a dead-end job, absolutely no chance of promotion or advancement, but it did help pay for the computer courses during the day. The absolute worst part of working as the "night manager" was fighting off almost continuous bouts of boredom. There were a few comics in the stand, but the first night after they arrived he had read them all. There were a few books, but they were all romance trash, nothing really worth noticing. The girlie magazines grew old within hours, and Tom could only look at them for so long without suffering from terminal blue balls anyway.

If there had been any better propositions, Tom would have jumped at a career change. *Oh well, such is life. Or as my momma likes to say, "C'est la pool."* Tom was just reaching for the latest *Gallery*, one he'd only looked through about seventeen times, when he heard the bell above the front door make its little tinkling noise. Tom looked up and smiled. Any company was better than none.

Upon seeing his customer, Tom changed his mind about that. Mike Blake stood blinking in the glare from the neon lights, unclean, unshaven, and wearing the same clothes he had been wearing for at least the last two weeks. Tom groaned inwardly; Mike had only come for more Thunderbird, and Mike knew that Tom was an easy mark.

"Hey Tom. How's it hangin', man?" Flash of a nervous smile, he was half expecting Tom to kick him out already.

"Hi, Mike. It's been better, it's been worse. What can I do for you today?" Tom did nothing to keep the frost out of his voice. The more he saw of Mike, the more disgusted he grew. Two years ago Mike had been going somewhere, there was talk of him replacing Rich Waters as the manager of Serenity Falls' First National Bank. Now look at him: a hopeless, useless waste of space. Tom tried to calm those thoughts down. After all, if his wife had been murdered, he'd have probably taken it poorly, too. Of course, he'd have to have a wife first, and there was little chance of that as long as he was looking as soft around the middle as he did now. Maybe he'd cut back on the Ho Hos.

Mike looked around for a while, nodding to himself and beating a nervous tattoo on his thighs with both of his hands. He reached into a pocket of his stale jacket and pulled out a fistful of paper scraps and loose change. Meticulously placing each scrap of paper back in his jacket, Mike started counting his change out loud. Satisfied that he actually had the money, Mike walked over to where Tom sat and poured the large handful of change onto the counter. He methodically sorted quarters, dimes, nickels, and a large quantity of pennies into dollar portions and into the fifty-six cents he'd need in addition, walked away, and collected a packet of Oscar Mayer bologna and a bottle of Thunderbird. The change was slipped back into his pocket with a whimper, not with the rattling of money striking money.

Tom barely managed to keep the sneer off of his face as a waft of Mike's body odor hit him. Jesus, thirty-seven years old, and the poor bastard was a has-been. Tom promised himself, again, that he would never end up that way, a promise that he made whenever he saw Mike Blake. Mike's freckled bald spot fairly gleamed in the cold white light of the store, and for half a second, Tom would have sworn that he was looking at a bleached skull. The image shook him deeply. Mike looked up then and smiled, exposing gums that had started to show the effects of longtime neglect, and even teeth that had not been brushed with more than a finger in over a year. "We'll see ya later, Tom. Keep on those books, okay?" Dirty fingers plucked at threadbare fabric, lifting the jacket that Mike wore closer to Tom, allowing him a close inspection of the dirt-stained wool. "I'd hate to see you wearing this sorta shit."

Tom watched his only regular nighttime customer head toward the door and raised his voice. "Hey, Mike!"

"Yeah?"

"Um. Listen, you can hang around here if you want. At least until the boss comes around." Tom had a strong sense that if Mike left, he'd never see him again. He just knew that Mike would be dead if he walked outside. The feeling swept over him, leaving waves of gooseflesh crawling over his arms and back.

Mike looked at him for a few seconds with a skeptical expression of curiosity. Then a slow smile spread across his face as he reached for the glass door. "Thanks, but I'll be okay." He gestured with one hand, indicating the pleasant if humid night beyond the Quik-Mart. A quick wink flicked from his eye. "Ain't like I'm gonna freeze." A sad expression covered Mike's face. "I gotta go say hi to Amy anyway." Mike pushed the door all the way open and stepped across the threshold, blocking the door's closing with one foot. "You keep studying. Make ol' Mike proud." Mike walked away.

Tom stayed where he was, stayed seated behind the counter. Mike's last words echoed in his head. Shit, it was like Mike had felt the same thing, and maybe was saying his good-byes. Tom Lassiter shivered in the well-lit Quik-Mart, watching as Mike Blake faded into the night.

By the time Perry and Andy Hamilton came into the store, trying to buy cigarettes and beer with yet another false ID, Tom had forgotten the strange experience. He'd have reason to remember it when he read the paper the next day.

VI

Tom Lassiter was closer to being right than he could have possibly known. The truth of the matter was that Mike Blake intended to commit suicide. Mike had made the ultimate effort during the last week to stay sober and to reflect on just where his life was going and where it had been. He found his life to be very wanting.

When Amy had passed away—*Murdered! Some sick bastard murdered my Amy! Not "passed away," you pathetic loser! She was MURDERED!*—Mike had lost his only real reason for caring about anything. He'd never been much of an overachiever until Amy came into his life. He'd been perfectly content to work at the bank and collect his barely adequate little paycheck every two weeks, until he met her.

Really met her. He'd known her most of his life—just about everyone at least knew everyone else's name in Serenity Falls—but that did not mean that they *knew* each other. Oh, Lord, when he'd met her, his whole life had turned around. His normally dour personality became friendly, outgoing. His self-esteem skyrocketed; obviously Amy saw something in him, or why would she bother? His entire life went from dull to fascinating. When they needed more money for their wedding, he asked for a promotion at the bank. Maybe it was because they had seen the changes that had come over Mike, but the powers that be actually gave him the promotion and a substantial increase in his finances.

Mike had become interested in the stock exchange and had made a decent amount of money playing the market. Oh, certainly not enough to live on, but enough to start building a comfortable little nest egg. Life had become more and more dreamlike with Amy at his side. And it was a helluva fine dream at that. Enough money to live in relative comfort and a wife that loved him as much as he loved her.

Then someone took her away. Some sick fuck had come into town, just passing through, a drifter that a few people had seen the night she died, and taken his Amy away. Tom Norris had found her body at the edge of the town limits. Mike would never forget the look on Tom's face when he had been obligated to ask him to come to the morgue below the police office to identify the remains. Mike would also remember staring down at her cold, lifeless form for as long as he lived.

Amy, so beautiful in life, nothing but a hollow shell, broken inside and out. The transient hadn't just killed her; he'd made it hurt, and he'd made it last. The psychopath had violated Amy in every way imaginable. Rape, sodomy, and knives—many, many knives. He'd left her face alone, but there was little else about Amanda Watson Blake's body that had not been sliced into ribbons of tattered flesh.

That was it, finding out that Amy was dead, finding out that she had been brutally tortured and murdered, well, it just sort of took away everything that was important in Mike's life. He'd tried for a while, tried to make himself get up every day and go to work, tried to convince himself that Amy would have wanted him to continue on. Nothing worked. There was no longer any motivation. Mike had been getting downright pudgy right before Amy died. With her gone, it was seldom that he could make himself choke down food. The bank had been very understanding: Mr. Waters had even let him slide on being unshaven and wearing the same suits constantly, he'd tolerated Mike's sullen refusal to participate in office meetings, and his perpetual tardiness. He'd even given of his own personal time to try to help Mike out of his grieving stupor. But when Mike came in ripped on whiskey after two warnings, Waters let him go. He might have kept him on even then, if Mike hadn't tossed his cookies in the lobby.

Mike didn't blame the man. He'd have done the same thing, and probably a good deal sooner than Waters had. From there it was an easy slide into the life he lived now. No home, they'd been forced to repossess, and Waters had done his best to avoid that, too. No job, Serenity Falls wasn't exactly a town with a booming job market. No one to care about or who cared about him. He slid deeper and deeper into poverty and depression, a broken man.

And so it was time for a last good-bye to his Amy. Time to die. Mike walked along Dunhaven Street, past the junior high school, all the way down to the Powers Memorial Cemetery. The gun in his pocket was loaded, and the Thunderbird would numb him enough to let him avoid a panicky run to the clinic in order to save himself.

Mike walked with his head down, lost in his memories and heartbreaks. He stepped past the cemetery gate, ignoring the twin marble lions that guarded against trespass. The lions had the decency to ignore him as well. Mike had stepped past the first clean row of headstones before he saw the grave markers in Powers Memorial. He stared around him, taking in every detail his mind could accept, and feeling his rage burn away the fog of deep depression. All thoughts of suicide left him, replaced by a crystalline anger like none he'd ever known before.

Monuments to the memories of the dead, headstones, placards, tombs, even a few crypts, everything in the cemetery was devastated. Not a single piece of granite was left untouched by the hands of vandals. The bottle of Thunderbird slipped from Mike's hand, shattering on the sidewalk they'd added to the graveyard last year. Mike stared at the remains of his beloved Amy's headstone, broken into as many tiny fragments as his heart, and something inside of him just snapped.

Mike walked stiffly over to the pay phone at Dunhaven and Fourth, slid a quarter out of his pocket, and dialed a number that he'd forgotten until a few moments ago. Jack Michaels answered the phone on the fourth ring.

With a voice that was amazingly calm, Mike Blake talked to Police Chief Michaels about the scene at the cemetery. Jack didn't recognize the voice at first, almost asked who was calling before he realized that the voice was familiar, just sober for the first time in forever. He asked Mike to wait for him, Mike said that he had something to do first, but that he'd meet him there in fifteen minutes.

Mike Blake left the cemetery after hanging up. He now had something more important in his life than fading memories and a fractured will to live. Suddenly he understood for the first time since his wife's death what it meant to have a reason for living.

Mike Blake walked quickly to his small efficiency apartment and rummaged through his closet for clothes to wear—clean clothes, preferably not too musty. After laying out old jeans, a T-shirt with a snarling wolf and a Harley-Davidson logo, and his cleanest tennis shoes, Mike Blake took a short but furious shower, scrubbing vigorously at his skin with Lava soap and scalding-hot water. He looked in the mirror and shaved, finding a razor that was relatively sharp. The razor burn would no doubt assault his skin in a few minutes, but that was all right. Pain was good for the soul, and it helped him focus on what needed to be done.

Mike Blake had finally found a reason for living. Had Amy Blake been alive, she would have cried out in grief. The man who'd been ready to end it all only twenty minutes earlier decided that if nothing else worked, revenge was a worthy excuse for not killing himself.

Chapter Two

I

The solitary figure stared out from his window, smiling down on the commotion outside of his house overlooking the graveyard. From his lightless room the view was perfect. And he doubted that anyone could honestly see him. Not that it mattered if they could. They'd find no evidence of wrongdoing, excluding the obvious violation of moral decency. No fingerprints on the stones, nor footprints in the dew-dampened grass. He was nothing if not meticulous.

In the strobing flashes of red and blue, he smiled, tight-lipped and vicious. He started rocking back and forth on his heels. Step one had been taken; now it was only a matter of gauging reactions before he made his next move:

Still smiling, still rocking on his heels, the man started humming tunelessly. "It's a good start. Now, now the fun can begin."

II

Stan Long took a good look at the cemetery's remains before being ushered along by Tom Norris. Tom understood where he was coming from, understood the powerful curiosity involved in such a major event, but he couldn't let Stan stay around for more than a few minutes. Any longer than that and Tom would get himself in trouble.

By the time Stan got to school, most everyone was talking about the cemetery and the vandalism that had occurred there. Those who were not were talking about the sudden change in Mike Blake. Literally overnight, the man had changed back into the Mike Blake everyone remembered. He was sleepy, certainly not in his best shape ever, but he was sober, clean, and capable of rational thought. Several people noticed him right away, before they even noticed the broken headstones. Stan just noticed the headstones; they were much neater to look at, and besides, he hardly knew Mike Blake except as the resident town bum. Without the facial stubble and dirty clothes, he was just another grown-up and thus hardly worth the effort of noticing.

By second period the furor had run dry, and by lunchtime it was back to the important business of the weekend ahead. Stan and Dave had plans for the usual Friday night, provided they could both skip out on their parents after dinner—not much of a challenge, as normally both sets of parents were ready for a night out on the town themselves. Neither of them knew what was playing at the drive-in, but they knew it was bound to be spooky. Nary a Friday went by when there wasn't a monster movie at the drive-in, and it had become tradition to meet there and eat munchies while listening to Dave's boom box whenever there was a horror flick, even if it was something dorky like *Frankenstein Meets the Wolfman*. It took a little finagling to figure out the exact frequency the drive-in's signal came in at, but Dave was a master.

The final bell of the day blasted its good-bye to the students and, as usual, the student body poured forth from the doors of the school in an especially chaotic stream. It was Friday after all, and that meant that the next two days were theirs alone, save for the chores meted out by their parents and maybe a few hours at the church or synagogue.

Stan waited in the customary spot for Dave, behind the gym, not too far from the back streets that led over to the cemetery. All thoughts of what had occurred there only the night before were already gone, removed by the more pressing matters at hand. There was little thought for anything, save the drive-in.

If he had been thinking of other things, he would have noticed the appearance of the Hamilton boys behind him. Perry and Andy Hamilton had a long history with Stan, a history that normally revolved around their insatiable need to do him harm on a regular basis. Nothing serious, just a little pushing around and maybe a wedgy if he wasn't already looking at them. Wedgies were best when done by surprise, at least as far as the Hamiltons were concerned. Today, Andy and Perry were going for a slightly different tactic; today was ideal for the patented ear pull. The premise was simple enough: each of the boys grabbed one of their chosen victim's ears, and they had a tug of war.

The ear pull was an all-time favorite with the two, because it allowed them to both win, while the only loser was their victim. No one in Serenity Falls could miss the rivalry that ran between the two Hamilton brothers, least of all any of their victims.

The two moved with clockwork precision and, a few seconds later, Stan was trying his best not to cry out at the burning pain that lanced through his head from both sides. "Hey, Perry, maybe we should let 'im go. He looks like he's gonna cry." Andy was looking at his brother but mostly facing Stan, a deliberately overemphasized pout on his face.

Perry looked over at his brother and gave another savage twist to Stan's ear. He had a grin on his zit-crusted face, and his brown eyes were crinkled with laugh lines. Stan noticed that his hair had been freshly bleached; the roots were not showing as badly as they had the last time the duo had decided to target him. "C'mon, Andy, look at him. I'd say he was holdin' up pretty good. I don't see any tears." Stan winced as Perry started dragging his ear up and down, forcing his head to make a nodding motion. "See, little Stanley even agrees with me. Don'tcha, kid?" The question was rhetorical, or so Stan had assumed until Perry pulled his head around with enough force to almost crack the cartilage in his earlobe. "I said you agree with me, *don'tcha?*" Perry was in his face, spittle wetting his thin lower lip, sneering in Stan's direction.

Stan started to feel the burning at the base of his eyes that signified tears and angrily tried to shake them away. Perry decided that his motions meant that Stan disagreed, and pushed hard at Stan's face with his free hand, knocking him on his ass. "Are you calling me a liar, Long?" Perry landed with one knee on either side of Stan's rib cage, scraping his knee down the left side of Stan's torso in the process. Stan started crying in earnest, more from fear than from pain. Only then did he remember that Dave had to stay after school again, stuck in detention for at least a half hour. Perry started slapping Stan lightly on each side of his face. "C'mon, Stanley, you don't want to call me a liar, do you?" Andy was watching his brother and had apparently decided that it was time for him to get in a few good licks. While Perry continued to slap lightly at Stan's face, Andy placed one foot on each of Stan's shins and started lifting himself off of the ground, balancing by his toes with his full weight on Stan's lower legs.

Stan let out a yelp of pain as he heard the bones in his legs start to creak, had visions of the bones snapping and each of the brothers taking a leg to pull or bend as they pleased. Stan went from a yelp to a full-scale scream of fear. His right arm had broken a few years back after a nasty spill from his bike, and all Stan could see was spending his entire summer in bed, waiting for the bones to mend and feeling the fiery itch run rampant under the heavy casts.

The scream took both of the brothers by surprise. Perry started to stand up, and Andy slipped off of the shinbones he'd been balanced on, only to land on the soft meat of Stan's calf muscles. Stan howled even louder than before, loud enough that his throat would be sore for the rest of the night, and lashed out at the pain in his legs. Stan missed Andy Hamilton by a mile; the swing was wild and without any discipline.

"Shit, Perry, looks like the little prick's trying to get even." Andy was laughing, but the laugh sounded a little off, like maybe he realized that he'd pushed Stan too far. Andy stepped away from Stan, eyeing the smaller boy warily. Perry saw his brother back up and laughed.

Perry stepped toward Stan with his hands held up, as if Stan had a gun to his stomach. The look on his face was jovial, almost friendly. Stan didn't trust the look one damn bit. Stan glared at Perry between wiping the humiliating tears from his eyes and the snot from his nose. He hated crying, always had and always would. He crawled quickly to his feet, his eyes never leaving the older boy. At least he could try to run if he was standing. "Hey, kid. Relax. I'm not gonna hurt you." Stan backed away just the same, unwilling to trust the older boy. Perry's hand moved too quickly for Stan to dodge, but instead of hitting him, simply slapped him lightly on the shoulder. Perry smiled, a cocky, arrogant expression that did nothing to make him look any better. Except for the wealth of zits, the smile was just like his brother Andy's. Stan hated him.

"Yer okay, got more balls than I thought." Perry said the words as if they were meant to be a compliment, and maybe coming from him they were. "See ya round, Stan." Perry turned and walked away, and a very confused-looking Andy followed. Red-faced and runny-nosed, Stan sat down in the grass. His body shook with adrenaline release, the kind that makes you sort of nauseated and hyperactive all at once. His ears were still burning, but the flame was lesser. His face was red and lightly welted from where Perry had been slapping him, and his legs sure as hell felt broken, even if they weren't. In some way he felt as if he'd passed a test, but he was damned if he could understand what the purpose of the test had been.

III

A good deal later in the night, when the sun had set and Stan and Dave had once again managed to sneak off to the drive-in—another college sorority being stalked by a supernatural killer movie, but neither of them were complaining, the girls sure did look good in their underwear—April Long started walking home from her latest date.

The nerve of Jerry Cahill, thinking he could put his hands up her skirt just because he'd paid for dinner. They hadn't even made it to the drive-in before he was trying to grope at her privates and stick his tongue in her ear. April had given him a solid slap across the face for his troubles, and Jerry had told her to walk home if she was going to be a stuck-up little tease.

The word hurt. April had never thought of herself as a tease; she was only willing to go so far was all. She'd really begun to like Jerry, too. If he'd been willing to wait, to not push her so hard, he might have even gotten what he was after. April stamped her feet as she walked, trying, like her brother, to avoid the tears that wanted to come.

The air was cooler than she had thought it would be, and April had gone out without even a sweater. The chill in the air brought goose bumps to her arms and brought on what her mother liked to call the "CT's," cold titties. Not that April had much to get cold, mind you. April hated the lack of development in her chest region almost as much as she hated her period.

April's shadow started to grow, stretching away from her body as the headlights from a car grew brighter behind her. April's fast pace slowed as the cat pulled up next to her. She fully expected to see Jerry Cahill's battered old Mustang when she turned. Instead, she saw Mike Blake's gray Mercedes. No one had seen his car on the road in a long time, but there it was, still in desperate need of a good wash and wax.

April looked through the window of the Mercedes-Benz and stared long and hard at Mike Blake. Mike was clean, his hair was cut to a respectable length, and even his cheesy mustache had been shaved off. Whatever had happened to make Mike change, April approved of the transformation. Mike smiled, leaned across the car seat, and pushed the door open.

"C'mon in, you look like you're about to freeze to death."

April only hesitated for a second, then she slid into the relative warmth of the car and closed the door. "Thanks. I really appreciate the lift."

Mike smiled, and April noticed the deep lines that had been etched into his face. He must have been handsome once, but the last two years had been harsh. What should have only been character lines looked more like scars from a bad accident. Still, despite the lines, he had a nice smile. "Well, I couldn't just let you walk home..." The sentence was unfinished, and that was just as well. Everyone in town knew what had happened to Mike's wife. Maybe not the full details, but they knew just the same. That kind of secret could not be kept in a town the size of Serenity Falls.

They drove in silence, neither really knowing what to say. Mike wasn't used to talking to people while sober, and April hardly recognized Mike as the bum she saw almost every day. Despite years in the same community, they had nothing in common, no basis for conversation. After only a few minutes, Mike pulled in front of the Long home and waited in his car until April had reached the door. April waved her thanks and watched as Mike drove away.

IV

Terri Halloway was having a night that was almost remarkably like April Long's. There were a few differences, but most of them were almost negligible. Terri's boyfriend, Terry Palance—and wasn't it just too cute, Terri and Terry? Couldn't you just die?—had also done his best to convince his date that it would be okay if they went farther than a little hugging and kissing. Like April before her, Terri did not hesitate to let him know when enough was simply too much.

And just like Jerry Cahill—Jerry and Terry, wasn't it just too much?—Terry Palance felt no obligation to escort his date home. That was pretty much the extent of the similarities. The biggest difference between the two's night came only a few minutes after Terry had dumped Terri on Old Farm Road, about three miles from where she lived. The biggest difference was that Mike Blake wasn't there to save Terri's life.

Terri had managed about a third of the distance to her home when she realized that the sound of her footfalls on the old, cracked asphalt didn't sound quite right. Her footsteps sounded instead as if they were being duplicated, mimicked from a distance of about ten feet behind her. She did not actually think of the sound's change in a conscious way; she simply realized that she was no longer alone with her thoughts.

Terri turned around without thinking and noticed the solitary figure that was behind her. The figure was masculine and heavily shadowed in the night's darkness. Even with her brown eyes now adjusted to the absence of light, Terri could not identify the shape that followed her. "Who's there?" she asked, even as her mind berated her: *Oh good, just like in the slasher movies. And when he doesn't answer, please don't forget to run straight into the woods and trip over the first convenient log... We wouldn't want to disappoint our viewing audience, would we?*

Terri waited for a few seconds for an answer, and when none was forthcoming, decided that there was no time like the present for hauling ass down the road. Grateful for the Reeboks on her feet, Terri started sprinting toward home. She ignored her mind's advice and stuck to the main road; no convenient logs suited for tripping over on the pavement, nosiree.

Terri risked a look behind her and saw the shadowy outline start following her. Despite the speed and length of her strides, the man seemed to be keeping up, even though he was only walking. The voice behind her caught Terri off guard. The voice was familiar, one that she knew. "Terri? There's no reason to run, I just wanted to make sure everything was okay."

Terri applied the brakes to her running legs and slowed to a walk as she circled back the way she had come. Her heart was already doing a jig in her chest, and she berated herself for giving up on the aerobics classes at the youth center. "Sorry, you spooked the heck out of me. I thought maybe you were Andy Hamilton or one of his friends. I don't like them. They look at me like I was meat."

The figure walked slowly forward, a smile flashing white across the shadows that buried his face. "No, I'm not one of the Hamiltons or a friend of the Hamitons, for that matter. Are you all right? You had me a little worried, too. Young ladies shouldn't walk home by themselves at this time of night. Certainly not on a road as dark as Old Farm. Didn't I see you earlier with Terry Palance?"

Terri felt herself blushing and was glad for the darkness that surrounded them both. "Well, we had a fight. He told me to walk home."

The figure nodded to her as he approached, and Terri felt a chill as the wind picked up again. "Well, maybe I should have a talk with Terry's parents. I don't think much of a young man that would leave a nice girl like you out in the cold like this." The shadow man reached put and touched Terri's hand. The chill was worse than she had thought, or her protector had been out in the night too long, because the touch of his hand was like ice. "Yes. Why don't you give me Terry's number. I think Frannie Palance needs to know what sort of stunt her son pulls when he's out on a date."

"Oh no, I don't think that's a good idea. Terry'd be awfully upset if I did that."

"Terry would have no right to be upset. Terry should be shown the error of his ways. I think his mother should be told. What if I were a rapist, or worse? Then where would you be?"

Terri was touched by the level of concern but still was not convinced. "Well, I don't think he meant for anything to happen to me. We just had an argument, is all. Just you wait. I'll let him know what a mistake he made."

"Tell me his fucking number, Terri. I don't want to get angry."

Terri was taken aback by the tone of the man's voice, doubly so by his use of profanity. He NEVER used profanity, not ever. Without another second's thought, she blurted the number out.

"Thank you, Terri. And I'm sorry about the language. I haven't been feeling myself lately."

"Oh, that's okay. I know how that goes." That was better, more like what she expected from him. Terri let herself relax a bit.

"I'm sure you do." The freezing hand clutched hers a little tighter, and Terri squeezed back in response. It was nice to feel safe and protected.

The two walked in silence for a few minutes, companionable silence, the kind that you can share only with someone you trust. Then her benefactor spoke again. "Terri?"

"Hmm?"

"It was nice knowing you."

Terri pulled out of her silent comfort and looked at the man. He smiled as his hand locked onto hers with enough force to make the bones crack. Seeing the smile on his face, Terri tried to pull her hand away and failed. The cold that had been assaulting her hand started in on her stomach, freezing the hot dogs from her early dinner in place. She yanked hard at her hand, still having trouble believing that this could be happening.

The shadow man's free hand wrapped across her mouth as Terri started to draw in a breath for screaming. A sudden odor rose from him, a smell as foul as a backed-up sewer. "Don't worry, Terri." He whispered in her ear, cold breezes that carried his word straight to her and froze her gold-stud earring to her face. "It only hurts for the first few hours; then the pain starts to fade."

Terri struggled as best she could, thrashing and kicking at him, to no avail. He seemed completely immune to pain. If anything, he seemed to enjoy her struggles, seemed to almost thrive on her frantic and futile attempts to defend herself. He moved his hand from her mouth and let her scream. The sound echoed through the woods, but if anyone was around to hear it, they didn't do anything to show themselves.

Terri continued to fight back, nonetheless. What else was there for her to do? Her labors increased again as the man reached into his jacket and pulled something from the depths of his pocket. Whatever it was, it was moving, pulsing and reaching for her. The thing's touch sent waves of nauseated repulsion through her, and Terri opened her mouth to scream a second time. Her screams were blocked by his hand and the thing he held in it. The few cars that passed them, Terry

Palance's among them, saw nothing at all after the man had finished dragging her into the deep woods.

He had lied to her. The pain was still going strong when the sun rose. By then they had moved several miles down the road. He'd dragged her through the woods and even across a couple of streets that were dark and abandoned. Her body was a nest of abrasions by the time they finally stopped, but the scrapes and friction burns were soon the least of her worries.

She'd always heard that pain could be blocked or become so overwhelming that it could no longer be felt. Another lie. She was still feeling the pain when she finally expired just after noon.

V

He washed himself carefully, meticulously removing four of Terri Halloway's long brown hairs from between his fingers. It was still too early in the game for him to be leaving clues behind. The water that ran down his body from the shower was almost painfully cold, leaving gooseflesh wherever it touched. Just the way he liked it.

He whistled as he showered, pausing between tuneless little songs for a brief smile of anticipation. The girl was well hidden, and it would take a fair amount of time for her body to be found. The girl was only the beginning, naturally, but she was a good start.

He lathered himself more vigorously, scouring away a full layer of flesh as he showered, washing away the dead cells on his body with a passion that most people saved for times when they were with their spouse or regular lover. The best part started tomorrow. Tomorrow he would begin playing with the children.

In the house where he showered, his family slept. None of them was aware of what he had done, and none of them was likely to find out. Right now they were all too busy struggling with the nightmares that assaulted their unconscious minds. He smiled about that, too. He loved giving the children nightmares.

Chapter Three

I

Stan and Dave started out for the quarry about five minutes after the sun had broken into the sky. For what had to be the billionth time, both groups of parents quietly lamented that the boys were never quite as eager to rise when it was a school day.

The Blackwell Granite Quarry had been closed for over fifteen years, ever since Joseph Blackwell, his wife Clarisse, and their three children turned up dead. Most people claimed that Blackwell had been murdered, but there was absolutely no proof and, frankly, little for anyone to gain from killing the man. With no known heirs, save those who died with him, and more money than God—money he was more than glad to spend in town—there was simply no real motive. If anything, the town of Serenity Falls had suffered when the man died.

No one really knew what had happened to the family, but the Blackwell house had long since taken on the stigma of being haunted, and no one in their right mind went anywhere near the place. Not too surprising, really. Take an unsolved murder case, place it in a big old house worth more than most people in the town could ever hope to make, and the stories of strange sounds and lights coming from the place were almost inevitable.

Naturally enough that meant the place was very appealing to all of the kids in town. Put any curious preadolescent in the same area as a haunted house, and there was bound to be a magnetic attraction, just as there was for anything that was forbidden or any place that had secrets. Many were the stories of what had happened to a local foolish enough to spend the night in the Blackwell house. Just thinking about it covered Dave Pageant with a fine sweat of anticipation.

The catch would be convincing Stan to go with him to the old house. Not that there would be much of a problem. Dave knew very well that Stan looked up to him as some sort of role model, but he never took advantage of the knowledge. Well, not often at any rate. Today would definitely be one of the days when he did. There was simply no other way to convince Stan to go with him to the old Blackwell place.

"Stan?"

"Yeah?"

"Why don't we go over to the Blackwell place first?"

"Hunh-uh. No way"

"What? Are you chicken?" Dave smiled with the words, a big shit-eating grin that challenged his friend to prove that he was not, indeed, a chicken.

"Up yours. There's probably a lot of stuff out there that's dangerous."

Dave watched his friend closely behind the grin, watched the gears in his head move to find the best responses to stave off Dave's challenge.

"'Sides, my mom says I got to stay away from there, says that most of the boards are all rotted out, and that it's dangerous."

Not a bad excuse for a quickie, Dave acknowledged, *but not a good one either.*

"Why should that stop you? You never listen when your mom says not to go swimming right after eating."

Stan fumbled for words, looking at Dave and obviously fighting for an appropriate response. Dave stared back, a tiny smile playing at the corners of his lips. Dave waited; Stan thought hard. Finally, Stan admitted defeat with a mighty sigh, and they turned a little on their path.

Ten minutes of fumbling through the woods led them to the Blackwell house. The place was huge, and in its prime it must have been the pride of Serenity, but its prime was long past. Fifteen years ago, a very successful family had died a bloody death in that house, and even from a distance, there was little doubt that Blackwell and his family still walked the rotting floors. The house was three stories tall and surrounded by trees that had been saplings when Serenity Falls was still a part of the forest primeval. The Georgian architecture was lost to most, hidden in the depths of a small woodland retreat, hidden even from the rest of Blackwell Road by the trees that surrounded it and the shrubs growing out of control around them. There was something almost chilling about the landscape, even in the light of early morning. The oak trees seemed not so much to stand as sentinels around the building, as to lean over the house, demanding their space, almost crowding the house out of existence. The house itself seemed almost bitter, as if it resented the loss of a family to keep it. The ornate windows were mostly intact, though a few had been shattered over the course of time, either by vandals' stones or the forces of nature. The holes left by the absence of glass had been boarded over a long time ago, likely with the intention of keeping kids like Dave and Stan from doing what they were now planning.

On the low wall that surrounded the estate, a tarnished brass plate stated simply the name that Blackwell had given his home: Havenwood. The wall had once been stuccoed, but the outer coating was mostly gone in some places, peeling away like the flesh on a corpse, exposing the brick layer beneath, the skeleton that held the structure together. Fifteen years had not been enough to destroy that wall, but Dave imagined the time when the wall finally fell. Beside him, Stan was looking at the building with something akin to religious fear. Dave felt only the compelling need to get inside, to see the interior for himself and to stand in the spot where Joseph Blackwell had died.

Stan looked ready to run, but Dave tapped him on the shoulder and pointed with his chin. "Come on, let's go see if Blackwell's ghost is there." Stan shook his head but stepped forward with him just the same.

The boys walked slowly, mingled feelings of excitement and dread coursing through their bodies. The day was already warm, up into the eighties, and it wasn't anywhere near noon. But damn, there was a definite chill, either in the air or in their blood. Neither could have said which it was.

Up close, the house's state of disrepair was more blatantly obvious. Dave was having second thoughts, and Stan hadn't liked the idea to begin with. Still, neither would have dared back out. Dave's earlier comments had seen to that very nicely.

The wind moved past one of the ancient oaks, rattling the leaves and sending a sinister moan through a breach in the base of the trunk. Neither of the boys jumped. Much. The air was oppressive near the house; it seemed somehow heavier, pregnant and full of sinister possibilities. Exactly thirteen stairs led to the wraparound porch, each built from granite stones cemented together. The years had been cruel to the grout between them, turning it a dark gray and painting it lightly with green mold. The exterior of the house smelled of mildew and decay, and neither of the boys wanted to think about what the inside smelled like.

Dave silently cursed himself for his sudden inspiration, knowing full well that Stan was probably cursing him as well. In Dave's own opinion, he really was his own worst enemy. No one could get Dave Pageant into more trouble than he could. It was a curse, much like his easy manners and way with schoolwork was a blessing. Everyone seemed to think he was something special, but he knew better. He was just lucky. His parents were well off, just the draw of the cards. He was okay-looking, not a real stallion or anything, but that, too, was simply genetic poker giving him a winning hand. He was strong and tall for his age, but that could change given time, if puberty was less than kind.

In Dave's eyes, the lucky one was Stan. Stan had the natural good looks that would certainly turn heads, and already did, though Stan would never believe it; Stan had a family that at least talked, at least communicated with each other, even if the communication often came in the form of arguments. And Stan Long was allowed to have a pet. Those were the things that mattered most to Dave: a loving family or, at least a pet. They mattered the most because he had neither. At least not in the way he felt he should.

Dave's family was…unique. His parents, his brothers and sisters, and his cousins were all gathered together in a collective of farmhouses that seemed almost too large to qualify as a family. They were more like a commune. And while there were animals in abundance, Dave couldn't quite bring himself to think of the chickens, goats, and cows as pets. They were livestock, and there was a difference. Any illusions he might have had about that were shattered the first time his father took two hens to the chopping block just outside of the kitchen window. After that, they were just animals. It wasn't like he had a dog or even a cat. The closest he came to a pet was his little sister, and she was more annoying than amusing. Dad wasn't exactly the stay-at-home type. He left most of the communal management to his wife and to his older sons. Mom had too many things to do, too many little social clubs to play with, for her to bother overly much with her son. That shouldn't be taken to mean that he had no family, because Dave actually had a very large collection of siblings and cousins living with him and his parents. But they were mostly a good deal older than he was, and even the ones closest in age to him were often far too busy leading their own lives to bother with him. Not that he allowed that to stop him from enjoying his life to the fullest. If anything, it made him want to find new challenges all the more. Sooner or later, he would make his parents notice him, but in a good way, not because he'd been thrown in jail or anything stupid like that, just because he was their son and had made them proud.

He shook the thoughts away, focusing on what he was here for and concentrating with special force on making sure that Stan had fun, even if it killed him. Dave was pretty certain that Stan would stay locked away in his house, if not for his own intervention. Stan wanted to spend too much time daydreaming or reading books on any place but where he was, any place that had even the hope of excitement. Life in Serenity Falls just bored Stan Long to tears, and Dave meant to change that, meant to prove to Stan that even The Falls had excitement, if only Stan would take the time to look. It had become something of a challenge to Dave, and along the way he had become friends with Stan, which was all the better.

Stan was pale, and sweating; he looked ready to bolt and to just fall down in a dead faint at the same time, like a rabbit caught in the path of a Mack truck. Dave dry-swallowed, trying to get spit back in his own mouth, and slapped Stan on the back. Stan damn near ran but stopped himself just in time. "You ready to see a ghost?"

"Ready as ever, I guess." Stan's reply was hardly enthusiastic.

"Good," Dave chirped cheerily. "Let's go in." And together, close enough to brush their shoulders, they pushed at the door. The door should have at least been warped shut, possibly stuck as a result of too many years without being opened, but it slid open as if it were on well-oiled hinges. Both boys hesitated a moment longer and then stepped past the threshold.

The interior of Havenwood was buried in a caul of shadows, and the air smelled of too many years trapped in the same closed space. Dave licked nervously at the sweat starting on his upper lip and stepped deeper into the house. Even with the curtains open, the boards nailed in place over the empty window frames kept all but the faintest light out. The boys paused for a minute more, letting their eyes adjust to the nearly total darkness. As Dave stepped forward again, with Stan on his heels, the floorboards beneath his feet made cries of protest that were amplified by the utter silence in the house.

Something moved on the second floor, and Dave felt the hairs standing on the back of his neck. He was assaulted by cold goose pimples as the sound was repeated. Footsteps, and they were coming closer. Dave let out an involuntary moan; beside him, Stan whimpered.

Both of them looked up toward the wide staircase above them, following the shadowy carpeting as it hugged each individual stair. The steps were closer now, approaching the end of the hallway at the top of the stairs. Dave felt Stan's hand clamp down on his arm, and let out a tiny scream, just loud enough to echo off the barren walls. A dark form grew from the top stair, a black silhouette against the gray shadows above.

A voice came floating down toward them, faint and friendly, but filled with menace just the same. "I hadn't expected visitors."

Both boys started walking backward, stumbling slightly, with shaking knees. Dave's foot settled on something soft and slippery and, whatever it was, it shrieked its outrage. Dave leaped forward, smacking into Stan and knocking them both sprawling on the ground.

The figure stared down at their prone forms and threw something through the air. Stan and Dave watched as a smaller shadow separated from the larger one at the stairs' pinnacle and rolled through the blackness, spinning and falling toward them, even as they scrambled madly to their feet. Behind Dave, the rat that he had stepped on flopped feebly on its way, one leg injured and its tail shifting brokenly like a snake that was too stupid to know it had been hurt. It chattered angrily and snapped its jaws in their direction.

The smaller shadow rolled through the air and descended in an arc. It hit the stairs with a solid thud about halfway down the long carpeted flight. It rolled awkwardly, careening off the wall and then bouncing twice before finally stopping at the base of the stairway. Twin pools of light burned in the withered, severed head of Joseph Blackwell, and the drawn, putrefying mouth opened in a twisted grin and spoke: "Welcome to my home."

No one was close enough to hear the boys' screams.

II

Charlee and Jessie were not alone at the quarry; they shared the waters with Joey Whitman and Becky Glass. For all anyone heard out of her, Becky could well have not been there. That was pretty much the norm; Becky almost never spoke. She seldom did anything but smile and nod her head.

As long as she smiled and hugged close to the walls, no one ever really noticed Becky, and if they did not notice her, they could not hurt her. It was a safe philosophy but not one that she enjoyed living by. Still, so far she had avoided most of the worst parts of growing up, she avoided getting spanked, and she avoided getting into trouble. And she avoided the names. That was the worst part, always, the names. If Becky had been a leper, at least then the reason for the abuse her classmates heaped on her would be more obvious. Not that the reasons weren't obvious enough, just that they really weren't very fair.

To begin with, Becky was large; not really fat, but large and sturdy. She looked almost like she was on steroids. Her hair was an impossible mop of tangles that could never decide if they wanted to be curly or just plain frizzy, and a flat light brown in color to boot. Her eyes were very pale, almost hazel, but not quite. Her nose was too small, and her mouth was too large. Most embarrassing of all, she was already developing breasts. All of that would have been enough of a curse as far as Becky was concerned, but she was also clumsy. She could trip over a small rock and, in fact, she had on more than one occasion. Becky seldom wore shorts simply because they would show the almost endless collection of scabs on her knees.

Becky, much like Stan Long, wanted away from Serenity Falls, wanted to leave and never come back, unless she could get some major plastic surgery first. The difference was, she planned to do something about her desires. Just down the street from her house, the main entrance to the highway stretched off into the distance. She had her backpack ready and was fully prepared to leave in a heartbeat...just as soon as she built up the courage to take the first step.

In the shade of the quarry's deep end, where the sun had not yet managed to touch the chilled waters, Becky paddled back and forth, hating that she looked much like a killer whale in her black-and-white one-piece. She didn't know if she'd ever have the guts to actually run away, but she wanted to, she almost physically needed to, because she was afraid she would just explode if she stayed in The Falls any longer.

Becky seldom thought anything; more often, she knew things, if you can see the difference. She knew, for example, that she was a huge disappointment to her parents: to her father because he had wanted a boy, and to her mother because she had wanted a girl. Becky really didn't seem to fit into either category very comfortably, and in truth, the most feminine thing she owned was the atrocious bathing suit she was now wearing. Becky looked at Joey as he walked to the ledge of rock that served as a diving board for the quarry, preparing to pull another flawless dive into the waters, like the last dozen he had managed. She'd have given anything to be that dexterous, or even half as pretty as Charlene, or half as rich as Jessie's family—for all she knew, Jessie's family was filthy stinking rich with their big old house, but the truth of the matter was, Jessie's father hadn't worked in several months, and the only thing keeping them afloat was a lot of money taken from the savings accounts they'd built up over the years. The little nest egg the Grants had amassed through the course of their marriage was almost gone, not that Becky or anyone else had the vaguest notion about that. Keeping up appearances was very important to the family.

Instead, she was just Becky Glass, last in a long line of losers. And she hated it. She hated being Becky the same way some people resented being born with a deformed arm or with a spine that curved into painful shapes.

She was just contemplating leaving the waters and slinking back home with her imaginary tail between her too-thick legs, when Dave Pageant and Stan Long came charging down the weed-choked dirt road that passed as access to the quarry. Both of them looked like they had a pack of demons snapping at their heels, and neither of them so much as looked where they were going, or even called out a warning, before they stormed the rock ledge above the waters.

Joey Whitman turned at a warning called by Jessie Grant, just in time to get a face full of Dave's torso. It was a good thing he was at the very edge of the diving rock, or he would certainly have sprawled across the ground and scraped the hell out of himself. As it was, both he and Dave did a graceless somersault into the green waters below, sending a plume of white spray high into the air, screaming all the way down. In comparison, Stan Long was like a gazelle. He hit the edge of the outcropping and soared through the air, his feet still trying to make contact with the land that had suddenly disappeared, and a look of comical surprise frozen on his features. He cleared a good ten feet, and if he'd gone any farther before gravity reached him, he likely would have smashed into the opposite wall of the quarry.

Stan didn't so much splash into the water as hit it. There was very little by way of waves as he impacted, and the stunned look on his face became an open expression of pain before he sank into the murkiness. Becky looked where he had gone down and started to worry. Dave and Joey came up sputtering and shocked, lifting out of the water like some sort of deep-sea charge had shot them to the surface. Joey's face was red, and he was coughing violently, his mouth making fishlike motions between hacking whoops. Dave's hand was wrapped around his bicep. Dave looked simultaneously worried and chagrined, Joey simply looked wet and in need of air.

Dave lifted his other arm out of the water, scissoring his legs fiercely to keep them both afloat. His fingers found purchase in the lines of the rock wall, and he all but lifted Joey out of the water. Charlee and Jessie swam over to aid him, and Joey continued to gasp and cough, pausing from time to time to puke water out of his gaping fish mouth. Jessie started smacking him soundly on the back, while Charlee yelled shrilly for her to thump him hard, not slap him silly.

And while everyone was watching the Joey Whitman Hack and Wheeze Show, Stan Long sank slowly down under the calming surface of the deep pond, taking water into his lungs.

III

Stan remembered the water rushing at him, remembered the girl looking at him, her mouth open and gaping, and he remembered thinking, *Hey, the ground's gone.* Then the water played dirty and punched him in the solar plexus. The air escaped from him in a cry that was muffled by the water jetting into his face, plowing up his nostrils and down his throat. Then the darkness came up and covered him in a warm shield of silence.

Stan's eyes were open, but they saw nothing of the world outside his own mind. Blurred images danced around the fringes of his mind's eye: Beau as a bungling puppy. The look on his sister's face when she came through the door last night, angry at her latest boyfriend. The graveyard with its headstones smashed to flinders. Old, drunk Mike smiling numbly from a bench in the park... Nothing of great significance, just moments from his own life. He wondered idly if this was what dying felt like, and he suspected it was.

Then everything changed. He saw the house again, Havenwood, with its faded wooden exterior, and the darkness inside the building, the darkness that wanted to suck away his soul. His scalp was assaulted with a fearsome stinging pain, and a feeling not unlike a dozen wasp stings crept across the crown of his head. Something grabbed his arm, and he knew that the darkness had come, he saw it smiling in the depths of his mind, a feral, vile grin, the sort of smile that promised nothing but sorrow and worlds upon worlds of pain.

Stan thrashed, trying to swing his free hand at the claw that clutched him, but his hands seemed frozen in molasses, held back by fibrous strands from some enormous spiderweb. He opened his mouth, tried to suck in air, and inhaled liquid death instead. Fire ran through his lungs, and his muscles spasmed in helpless attempts to expel the water. With every cough, the water came back, returning with a vengeance, and trying to bury him in its seductive coolness. The demon's claw kept pulling against him, and finally started to win the battle against his failing strength. The darkness crashed into him again, and Stan fell into a gray void, one filled with nightmares and worse.

IV

Becky Glass dove for the third time, maintaining her calm, and finally succeeded in grabbing a part of Stan's body. The water was too dark for her to really see anything, but the texture gave her find away. A thick hank of hair was the only purchase she could manage and, steeling herself against her repulsion at the feel of the water-slicked mass, she pulled. Beneath her hand, he moved and thrashed like a fish that had just discovered its capture. She reached out with her other hand, searched with her fingers and her eyes, and finally grabbed a limb.

Stan's struggles increased to a near frenzy, and she was afraid she'd lose her grip. She almost gave up, but she could hear the jeers in school, the cries of the people who already treated her as if she were less than human: "Hey, there goes Becky Glass. Didja hear? She let Stan Long die, couldn't even fight back against a drowned boy. Hey, Becky, catch anything fishing?" They would go on and on, as mercilessly as they ever had. Stan was one of the few who didn't give her grief for no reason, and she wouldn't let him down. Hell, he'd even attended her one attempt at a birthday party. Him and Dave and maybe a couple of others, but he and Dave were the only ones to bring a present. She owed him, and so she dug her nails into his forearm, and she pulled mightily.

Whatever he'd been fighting against, he'd finally stopped. Part of Becky was glad that he'd stopped. She doubted she could have held him any longer otherwise, nails or no. But, God, did that mean he'd drowned? What then? Too late, Becks, too little, too late! You should have grabbed him when you saw him hit the water, instead of watching Joey blow water like a whale. She felt the first nibbles of real panic and bit down on her lip to stop them from growing any larger. Her own lungs were burning now, and she realized that she needed to breathe, or she was never going to get him out of the water.

Becky broke the surface of the quarry pond, sucking greedily at the fresh air, and pulled Stan's head out of the dankness. Her hair was blocking most of her view, but from what she could see, Stan didn't look like he was breathing. She started kicking for the shallow part of the quarry, trying to keep Stan's head clear of the waves, and working her own lungs like a bellows. Through the water in her ears, she heard excited voices and then felt hands lifting the burden from her chest.

She swiped the hair away from her eyes and looked up as Dave and Joey half-dragged, half-pulled Stan to the rocky shore. Dave was pale and shaking, mumbling under his breath, calling someone an idiot. Joey looked like a stone statue given life; he was turning Stan on his side and pushing hard at Stan's stomach. Stan didn't move, but with every push, water leaked from his mouth. Charlene and Jessie were both looking on, dancing from foot to foot, like they had to pee real bad, and Becky could understand the urge; she desperately wanted to go pee, herself.

When he was done pushing at Stan's stomach, Joey rolled him onto his back and lifted his head, so that his mouth fell open naturally. Becky finally remembered to climb out of the water, and walked over, hating the feeling of the drops running down her legs and sending tiny splashes of mud back up to paint her ankles and calves.

Joey bent over Stan, whispering a quick prayer first, and began to breathe into Stan's open mouth. Stan's chest lifted, then slowly settled. Joey repeated the exercise. Again and again and again. Finally realizing what he was doing, Becky walked over and knelt with one leg on either side of Stan's narrow chest, and placed her hands on his rib cage, preparing to push. Joey looked up and shook his head, and Becky feared the words that would come from his mouth in that one frozen second: *"Too late, Becks, too little, too late! You should have grabbed him when you saw him hit the water, instead of watching me puke my guts out. Can't you ever do anything right?"* Instead he just said, "Lower, you'll break his ribs there." He pointed at his own stomach, at the area directly below the rib cage, and made an X to indicate the right spot. Without another word, he bent back down to force more air into Stan's lungs.

Following his directions, Becky pushed lightly at Stan's lower torso. Joey looked up again. "Four times, then pause, four times, then pause."

She did as he said; she kept counting four, waiting a few seconds, and counting four again. Just when she felt she could go on no longer, Stan bucked under her, throwing her to the side with the strength of his thrust.

Stan looked around wildly, his eyes wide and his mouth drawn down in an ugly grimace. His chest moved rapidly, lungs snatching at the air with a desperation born of deprivation and fright. He didn't seem to know anyone he was looking at; his eyes flicked anxiously from face to face, but no recognition came. But, was he really looking at them?

Becky didn't think so. He was frantically searching for something, but he was more looking through the group of nervous people, seeking something else…perhaps some danger that no one else could see. Then he cried out, and the words sent chills through Becky's body, the words, and the terrified tones that carried them. "It's coming back! It's coming back home!" And then Stan Long fell quiet, slumping to the ground like a deflating balloon. His eyes rolled into the back of his head, and his skull landed against the rocks with a solid thump. For a second, Becky thought he was dead after all, but then she saw the movement of his chest, the gentle flaring of his nostrils. For the first time since climbing out of the water, Becky Glass remembered to breathe.

V

Jack Michaels shifted in his seat, looking around at the people that populated Frannie's Donut Hut and nodding to the few that waved. He knew most of the faces, knew their stories and their histories. There were only a dozen or so people in all of Serenity Falls that he could honestly say he didn't know on a first-name basis. He'd grown up in The Falls, and he planned on staying through to his retirement in ten years' time, and beyond then as well. Jack was and likely always would be, small-town folk. That suited him just fine, because the big city scared the hell out of him. The big city had too many unknown faces and too many untold tales. He preferred the small-town security, and he absolutely loved the small-town crime rate.

The latter was no surprise, considering that he was the chief of police in The Falls. Jack peeled his latest toothpick free from his mouth and reached for another one, waiting for Frannie Palance to point a finger at him and start scolding him gently about the waste of good toothpicks. It was an ongoing joke, almost a tradition, and one of the many numerous small routines that filled his day with little joys. Today the chastisement wasn't meant to be; Frannie hadn't even cracked a smile since he'd come in. Frannie was normally easygoing, but when she was in a mood, everyone in town took the hint and gave her enough space to breathe. Besides, when she was ready to talk, Frannie would tell Jack about whatever was haunting her, and he'd look into the problem if it was a legal matter, or he'd offer a shoulder to cry on if she needed one, not that she ever did. More likely, she'd need an ear to bend.

But that time obviously wasn't now, so Jack continued scanning the booths and tables, seeking anything out of the ordinary or at least interesting among the lunch crowd that filled the diner every workday. He spotted Frannie's son, Terry, brooding in a corner, and knew the source of his friend's duress, if not the actual reasons for it. Terry was a good kid, but one with a temper and one who just couldn't stand the idea of having to listen to his mother's rules.

Two tables away, Mike Blake sat eating a thick steak with scrambled eggs and a pile of home fries that came dangerously close to spilling off of the plate. Jack was reservedly happy about the change that had taken place in Mike. On one hand, the man was more active and aware of the world around him than he had been at any point since his wife was murdered. On the other hand, Mike Blake seemed filled with too much energy, like a generator that was working at twice its safe limits and was ready to explode. Mike was definitely better for the change, at least on the surface, but he was constantly in motion, and Jack would have bet large sums of money that the man wasn't sleeping more than a few hours a night. He'd have gone double or nothing that those limited hours of downtime were hardly restful.

More than anything, it was Mike's intensity that worried him. The only people Jack regularly saw looking that way were normally the same ones that he ended up throwing in the can overnight for getting drunk and pounding their spouses into hamburger meat. Mike had pretty much stayed drunk for the last two years, but he was a friendly drunk, maudlin to be sure, but friendly.

Now? Well, Jack didn't want to be around when Mike finally blew his cool. He had no doubt that there would be hell to pay for the person who pushed Mike too far.

Jack was still contemplating Mike, who'd now moved on to the enormous slab of cherry pie that Frannie set before him as she refilled his coffee mug, when the first stranger of the day made his appearance. The man was grizzled, dusty from the long ride from God alone knew where, and positively mountainous. The Levi's he wore were almost skintight, and the hiking boots on his feet were scuffed and well worn. A red T-shirt that had long since faded to off-pink stretched to its limits in a vain attempt to cover a wide, muscular torso heading slowly down the road to flab. Written across the shirt in chipped, peeling letters was the simple legend, Why Not Smile? with a smiley face in broken yellow just beneath it. One eye of the happy face had peeled away completely, making the face wink secretively. A battered army surplus duffel bag was draped almost casually across the man's broad back, and Jack figured that even one more item in the green canvas would have split the bag like a piñata struck by a solid lead baseball bat.

Jack stared at the man's meaty biceps and forearms, watching in utter fascination as the muscles danced beneath the surface of the stranger's darkly tanned flesh, cording and shifting. There were several tattoos, the sort that were disgustingly intricate and must surely have taken several sessions each, running the length of those arms and stopping just above the wrists. Hands, each big enough to wrap completely around Jack's face, curled into fists, and the fists in turn settled on the square hips sheathed in tight, faded denim. Jack's mouth went slightly dry, and he reached for his Diet Coke, missing the first time and finally grabbing the sweaty glass as his eyes went up to the stranger's face. *Sweet Jesus have mercy*, he thought, *that man is as big as three of me.*

The stranger's face was a slight surprise, and a pleasant one at that, because the wide-open face looked cheerful, and that meant the man wasn't going to start anything that Jack couldn't finish. Pale blue eyes peered from beneath sun-bleached eyebrows as thick as caterpillars, resting above a slightly hawkish nose. The man's wide mouth was set with a faint smile. His broad, lined face was tanned to a dark copper and painted lightly with bronze freckles, that were, in turn, half-hidden away by several days' growth of thick reddish beard. Long red hair, bleached in some places to a strawberry blond, was tied into a ponytail that fell halfway down the man's back. Jack suspected that the hair looked better loose, more like a lion's mane than a pony's tail. The only things missing to make the man a flawless image of a Viking were the large battle-ax and the furs to take the place of his modern-day clothes. Despite the youthful vitality that practically flowed from the man, Jack guessed his age at close to forty.

The giant turned slowly, scanning the faces in the room much as Jack had done, and finally the pale blue eyes settled on Jack. The police chief knew a brief, hot flash of fear, and then the man's face opened into a bright smile, and he strode over to Jack with one massive paw extended. "Hi there!" the man's voice fairly boomed, a sound as large as the man himself. "You must be Chief Michaels."

"I must be." Jack was pleasantly surprised by how calm he sounded. "How can I help you? Mr....?"

"Barnes, Victor Barnes." He grabbed Jack's hand, completely engulfing it in his own, and pumped three times, solid motions with less force than Jack had honestly expected. "I'm here about the position in your department that I heard needed filling."

Jack squinted up at the friendly face and smiled, himself. "Got a criminal record?"

"Nossir."

"Know how to handle yourself in a fight?"

"Yessir."

"Any experience?"

"Six years with the military police in the U.S. Army, if that counts, and a few stints as a civilian." The man's voice was friendly and just a touch deferential. That was a good thing, too, because Jack liked his people to know he was the boss.

"If I look into your background, am I going to find out you have a problem with drugs or keeping your hands off the ladies or drinking? Any of that nonsense?"

The giant looked down at him and smiled. "If I had something to hide, I'd be in a big city. They have less time for close scrutiny, don't you think?"

Jack smiled in response. "You come on down to my office, just around the corner to the left, the third building, and fill out some paperwork. I imagine we might work something out."

Victor Barnes nodded his head, taking Jack's hand into his own again, and nodding. "Thanks. I appreciate the opportunity." He laughed, a sound that was warm and as big as the man himself. "I know I look like the sort of people most policemen don't want to see coming into their town."

Jack looked at him and nodded, smiling along with him. "No. You look like the sort of man I'd rather have on my side in a fight. Not that I'd expect too many of those around here." He started looking around the diner again, his eyes watching over everyone but never lingering very long in any spot. "I'm gonna finish my meal, then we can talk about what we can work out, deal?" Barnes nodded amiably and not so much walked as strode from the building. Jack shook his head in wonder. "Just what the hell does that boy eat to make him so big?"

Off in the corner, Terry Balance stood up impatiently, set his money down on the table—Frannie always made her son pay for his meals, she claimed it taught responsibility, and Jack couldn't disagree—and stormed out of the restaurant. Terry was normally friendly, but whatever was bothering him had stolen his manners away. Jack watched him go and decided it was about time to head to the office himself. Breakfast was all good and well, but when a man had a job to do, the man did it. He paid his own tab, nodding to Elmer Homesby and Walt Chambers, just coming in as he was leaving. Both of them did odd jobs around town and had been spending long hours over at the scene of the latest crime. They were covered in dirt and sweat marks and looked ready to fall into comas from the exhaustion of their labors.

The mess at the cemetery had been cleaned up, but there was still no solid evidence to be had when it came to finding the culprits. Most of the people in The Falls acted as if the entire incident was in the past, but Jack could see the stress on a lot of faces. Few things hit as close to home as the desecration of a graveyard; murder, rape, any violent crime, they all left their marks. But the graveyard left different marks, bitter wounds on the memories of dead family members and loved ones. Some of the folks were cracking jokes about the situation, some were mumbling threats, but almost everyone was still shaken by the atrocity.

Jack had little hope of finding the guilty parties. The amount of devastation told him that it had to be a large group that hit fast and hard, or somebody would have noticed the activity, even late at night. Without fingerprints, he was without even one solid suspect in the entire town. There were a few people, like Karl Banks and Joe Miller, who could have done the damage, were certainly disrespectful enough to do it, but they both were basically cowards, and damn near every family in town had kin buried in Powers Memorial, besides. If even one stone had been left unblemished, he would have had a lead. But the desecration had definitely been equal opportunity; nothing was left unscathed.

The only redeeming factor in the crime was that the assholes hadn't managed to exhume any of the corpses. Jack spat his latest wooden victim from between his teeth and slipped a fresh toothpick into his mouth. At times like this he almost wished that he still smoked. He was just starting up the stairs toward his office when Bill Karstens and Bob Steinman came peeling out of the station with the patrol car's sirens blaring and the red-and-blue flashers going off. Bill called out from the driver's seat, hollering at the top of his lungs. The only words that Jack could understand were "drowned" and "quarry." Jack bypassed the office and headed straight for his own car, visions of dead bodies forcing themselves into his mind.

From down the road, not half a mile away, he could hear the mournful cries of the emergency center's ambulance starting up, answered by the howls of a dozen dogs. Jack grimaced. Kids at the quarry and a possible drowning. He hopped into his own cruiser, and amid the sound of his siren, headed toward the old quarry and whatever might await him.

The roads were almost empty of traffic, and what little was there moved quickly out of his way. One van, an oversized Atlas moving truck, blocked his way for only a moment, not that it could be helped. The van was in the process of doing a laborious turn onto Blackwell Road, and Jack had to ride across the curb and over a portion of the lawn to get around the blasted thing. Must have been lost. No one lived out on Blackwell, not since the family had been murdered all those years ago.

Within ten minutes he was at the quarry, looking at the gathering of kids off to the side and looking at the one boy sitting up on the ambulance gurney and breathing in oxygen through a mask. Bill Karstens was talking with the group of youngsters, taking notes and asking questions. Bob Steinman was standing with his hands on his hips, looking for all the world like he owned everything in his sight and just knew somebody was out to rob him. Steinman was a cocky little bastard, and Jack genuinely didn't like him, but he did his best not to let it show. Next to Steinman, Karstens looked calm, and that was almost scary.

Jack slid out of the patrol car, noticing as he did the dusty Mercedes of Mike Blake sliding into the area behind him. Jack closed his eyes and prayed for patience. Mike was, no doubt, here to see if there had been any progress in the search for the cemetery vandals. He was sober now, and that was good, but he'd already made a nuisance of himself about the situation.

Jack ignored the man and walked over to see what was up with the Long boy, who was slowly getting his color back as he breathed in the oxygen. Walt Greene, the paramedic watching over the boy, smiled and nodded. "Just a scare this time, Jack. Nothing to fret over."

Jack nodded. "That's a good thing. Anyone know what happened?"

The question was answered by Bill Karstens, who walked up as the conversation started. "Looks like a couple of the boys were over snooping around at the Blackwell place. Dave Pageant swears he saw a ghost, and maybe something more."

Jack listened for a few moments, getting all the relevant details, and sighed. "I don't figure there's anything to it, but I'll check it out."

Bill looked disappointed. "Well, if you want, I could go look into it."

Jack knew the man was hoping for any sign of trouble. Bill Karstens loved trouble, especially the kind he could crush under his well-polished boot.

Jack shook his head. "Get on back to the station and go home, Bill. Your shift is already over. Not that I don't appreciate the offer," he added hastily. For a grown man and an officer of the law, Bill could get downright pouty.

Karstens looked at him for a second, a blank expression that stated very clearly he wasn't pleased, and then he nodded his head. A few moments later, he and Steinman were on their way back to the offices and, hopefully, out of Jack's hair for a few hours. He looked around at the chaos left in their wake and almost wished he hadn't sent them off. But only almost. The simple fact remained that the two of them together were just about more than he could tolerate. There was a reason that he worked a separate shift, and it had less to do with the hours than it did with the fact that they annoyed him to no end. If they weren't both competent, if they had ever given him any reason at all, he would have fired them a long time ago.

He sighed, heading back to his car. Mike Blake stood off to the side, not actually bothering him with questions about the cemetery desecration. Jack thought about it for all of three seconds, then went over to where the other man stood, looking down at the waters that filled the old quarry. Mike stared down at his own reflection, his face lost in deep thought.

Jack smiled and slid another toothpick into his mouth. "How are you doing, Mike?"

Mike seemed surprised by the interruption. Jack thought maybe he understood. During most of the last two years, it had been something of a rarity for anyone to ask the man how he was doing, without him actually starting the conversation. Town drunk was not a job that brought people running up to see how life was treating you. Quite the opposite in fact.

Mike smiled, an expression that his face seemed uncomfortable with. "Oh, I'm fine, Jack. Thanks..." He trailed off and looked around for a moment. When he spoke again, his voice was far softer. "I was just thinking back to when I was a kid. When I used to go swimming here on weekends." He looked at the constable and smiled wistfully. "Amy and I met here. Really met, I mean. Became friends, you know?"

Jack looked away. The depths of Mike's loss, even after two years, made him uncomfortable. Just as the fact that he'd never found any clues as to who had killed Amy, Blake left him feeling edgy and even angry. Amy had been a sweet kid. That anyone would even consider doing to her what was done made him want to scream.

Jack sighed and looked at Mike hard. "I know it isn't easy for you, Mike. But I'm glad to see you on the wagon."

The man looked at him, his skin glistening with a faint sheen of sweat from the rising heat of the day. "Well, I guess it's about time." He looked away, his eyes searching the water, as if looking for clues that were beyond Jack's scope of understanding. "It was get sober or get dead... I'm still not sure I made the right decision."

Jack looked into the reflection of Mike's face in the water. It was paler than the original, and the shadows made his face look almost spectral. "I think you did, Mike. I think it's what Amy would have wanted, don't you?"

Mike nodded, and his reflection joined in.

"I'm feeling a bit out of it right now, Jack. Most of me really wants another drink, like my lungs want another breath."

"You okay to drive?"

Mike nodded. "Yeah; but I'm probably gonna stay here for a while, anyway. Soak in a few rays and think for a while."

Jack returned the nod. "I'll come back later. If you need to talk, or need a lift, just say the word."

Mike smiled his thanks, and Jack went on his way. He left the other man sitting at the edge of the water, lost in his own reflection.

Getting back to the old Blackwell place was easy enough, but Jack sat outside at the edge of the driveway for almost a full minute before he finally left the confines of his squad car. It took him that long to collect his thoughts and fully comprehend what was going on.

The moving van was parked in front of Havenwood. A small army of men was moving about, pulling supplies from the back of the truck and moving them into precise stacks in front of the old house. Most of the men were familiar; they were locals who were ecstatic to get work in a time when there was little enough work to be found in the area. The only stranger was the one sitting on the edge of the porch, supervising.

The stranger was lean and well tanned, with dark brown hair and the sort of clothes that spoke of money. He was dressed casually, but the look was affected. He would have been just as comfortable in a custom-tailored silk suit as he was in the jeans and polo shirt he was wearing. He wore sunglasses that probably cost as much as Jack made in a week. The sort that bore a designer name and probably fell apart if you looked at them for too long. One look at him, and Jack knew he was probably richer than the entire town.

The man looked up from the clipboard he was holding and spotted Jack coming. The smile he flashed was filled with perfect, sparkling white teeth.

Jack returned the smile, at about half the wattage, and nodded slightly. "How are you today?"

"Too much better," the man replied as he rose and extended his hand, "and I'd have to worry about it." As he and Jack shook hands, the stranger slid a little closer, lowering the clipboard. "You must be Constable Michaels. My name is Steve Ferrier."

"Nice to meet you, Mr. Ferrier, but I have to ask, what the heck's going on over here?" Jack gestured at the house, the crew, everything.

Ferrier's smile grew even larger. "You mean to tell me no one informed you?"

"On a good day, I might hear a little news of what's happening in town. But I'm pretty sure I'd have remembered if someone told me Havenwood was getting a face-lift." Jack did his best to keep his voice calm and friendly, but it wasn't easy. Something about the man's smile annoyed him.

Ferrier laughed, shaking his head. "What can you do? You pass the information down the chain of command, you expect people to follow through with their part of the bargain, and then it all blows up." He looked around, and Jack had the very distinct feeling the man was working fast on a cover story of some sort. "I represent the Dunlow Natural Resources Corporation. We just bought the Blackwell Quarry."

Jack looked at the man as if he'd lost his mind. "You're kidding, right? No one's done anything with the quarry in over ten years. Last I heard, it was still up in the air if anyone could do anything with it."

Ferrier shook his head, his grin still in place. "It was still up in the air until about the middle of last week. The Dunlows have been eyeing the quarry ever since Blackwell and his family died. Now that the state finally decided on who owned the place, the Dunlows picked it up. Looks like there's going to be a few job openings in the area."

Jack nodded, allowing himself a little enthusiasm, despite the fact that he genuinely didn't like Ferrier—the man was smarmy, as cheap and falsely enthusiastic as a greedy televangelist and probably as sincere—God knew the town could use a few more jobs. As it was, most of the townies had to drive into the city to get any work at all. "I can't say as the idea breaks my heart, Mr. Ferrier. This town could use the boost to the job market."

Ferrier's smile grew just a little larger. "Well, wonderful! We've been looking at the quality of stone here for a long time and hoping we could get our hands on the granite. I've got to tell you, there's a heavy demand for quality stone these days, and the Blackwell has top-notch materials."

Jack nodded, looking toward the house. "Any chance you were inside about an hour ago?"

Ferrier frowned in concentration. "No, can't say as I was. I got here with the truck."

"Well, we had a couple of local boys who got themselves a good scare. They're swearing up and down they had a run-in with someone inside. Is it all right with you if I take a look around, Mr. Ferrier?"

"Not at all, Constable. None of the children were hurt, I hope?"

"Not so badly as anyone should be too worried, I suspect. More of a scare than anything else. One of the boys almost managed to get himself drowned when he fell into the quarry runoff, but he'll be fine."

Jack slid past the newcomer, heading for the front door of the old house. And Ferrier moved with him. "That's good to know. The Dunlows would be upset if anything happened on their land. I suppose I'll have to get a few signs warning of the risks and all that, hunh?"

Jack nodded. "It can't hurt, I suppose. Most of the kids are smart enough to stay out of trouble, though." Jack moved into the darkness of the house, reaching for his flashlight automatically. The clear white beam of light cut through the darkness of the foyer and all the way to the great staircase beyond it. The rooms were dark and dirty, and even from a distance, he could see the wood rot in a few of the floorboards. "Might want to tread carefully, Mr. Ferrier. This place has definitely seen better days."

Thick coatings of dust and mildew covered the floor and the lower portions of the walls. The furniture that had once probably been grand was now showing the signs of fifteen years of neglect and rodent infestation. He guessed most, if not all, of the furnishings would have to be scrapped.

"The Dunlows figuring on making this their offices?"

"No, not at all. Amelia Dunlow intends to move in here when it's been restored. Which might take a little longer than I'd originally guessed..." Ferrier's voice softened a bit, faded, as he started really noticing the level of decay in the old manor.

Jack chuckled. "Well, let's just say I hope she isn't planning on moving in tomorrow."

"Next week, actually."

"You're kidding, right?"

"No sir. She's got her heart set on it. Looks like there'll be some fellas making overtime, to me."

"You ain't kiddin.' Looks like you could probably use a few more men, too. I could pass the word around if you wanted."

"That would be highly appreciated, Constable."

Jack nodded. "Consider it done. I can think of a lot of people who'd be happy for the work around these parts."

Jack noticed the footprints on the floor, just around the right size for the boys who'd been in earlier, and followed their path through the foyer. Not far from the base of the massive staircase, he saw a small patch of blood and the trail of something that had run off with a bad leg. The markings in the dust led to a corner of the room and vanished into a hole in the wall. Looked like one of the boys had stepped on something and hurt it in a bad way. He hoped if it had to die, it did so quickly. While Jack was hardly a fan of rodents, he didn't like to think of anything suffering that much.

His eyes moved back to the kids' footprints and then over to a spot where it looked like something had hit the ground and bounced a few times. But despite looking around carefully, he saw no sign of whatever had made the markings in the patina of mildew. He shrugged lightly to himself and moved toward the stairs. Whatever it was, it had to come from somewhere.

He almost jumped out of his skin when Ferrier spoke again. The man continued to walk with him, standing close enough to just miss being annoying. "I'd be careful on the steps, Constable. Who can guess what shape they're in or how much they'll hold."

Jack breathed deeply of the stale air and waited a few seconds for his heart to calm down. He'd completely forgotten the man was even with him. "Nothing I can't handle, I figure. I'll walk lightly." He managed to reach the top of the rise without incident and saw no signs that anything larger than a medium-sized rat had been on the second level of the house in a long, long time. His footsteps and Ferrier's set the wooden stairs to creaking and groaning. The place was creepy, and thinking about the fact that a family had been murdered within its confines did nothing to make the fluttery feeling in his stomach any weaker. It had been years since Jack had really given any thought to Havenwood, but being on the grounds, in the house itself, was unsettling. He scanned the hallway in both directions briefly, then turned to head back down the stairs, narrowly avoiding a minor collision with his new personal shadow.

For just the briefest of instants, he thought he saw a man heading toward him on the stairs. An older man, slightly portly, with blood on his hands and a savage, ugly grin on his face.

Jack blinked, and the image was gone.

He didn't actually run down the stairs and out the front door back into the light of day, but he thought about it with every step he took in reaching the exit. When he was outside, Ferrier still next to him like a vigilant guard dog, Jack inhaled deeply, enjoying the fresh breath of air that cleared the must from his sinuses and lungs. "Looks like those boys managed to get scared by a rat."

Ferrier smiled. "Sounds about right. Just as well, I'd have hated to run across a stranger in there. Or a ghost."

Jack nodded. After a few pleasantries, he was on his way and glad of it. Havenwood, despite its previous grandeur, was an uncomfortable place. Being around the house for too long made the hairs on his neck stand up and sent shivers down his arms like a cold breeze on sunburned flesh. As long as he could remember—and that was long before the Blackwells were murdered—the land had felt wrong. Like the house was holding its breath and waiting for something to happen. Jack allowed himself a brief shiver as the car moved down the long driveway, back toward Blackwell Road.

"No sir, I don't like that house at all."

VI

Charlee and Jessie spoke almost no words as they headed away from the quarry. For Jessie the incident of the near drowning had brought back to her every fear she had about mortality. The idea that life could end so quickly was not only unpleasant but also depressing. And terrifying. Just like when she came home from school a couple of years back to find her Grandmother Murphy dead. The old woman, who had always scared Jessie a bit despite being one of the sweetest people she'd ever encountered, was sitting on the love seat, staring blankly at the TV, when she found her. She looked alive, but pale. The only indications that she was, in fact, deceased were the complete lack of movement, and the way her eyes looked dried out. Jessie had tried for several seconds to rouse the old woman, but had finally called it quits and bolted over to the Johnson house next door to call the police. Her grandmother had died in her sleep, but that didn't make Jessie feel any better about the situation. "Died peacefully" still meant she'd died. It took Jessie almost a month before she cried over the loss. It took her that long to get over the revulsion of touching a dead person.

For Charlee, the silence merely hid her mind's activity. She kept seeing it again and again in her personal instant replay, the way Becky Glass had hauled Stan out of the water, like a fisherman snagging his prey. She wondered if she'd have had the wits to notice Stan drowning or the strength to pull him back up. That in turn made her feel like a pile of dog poop for the way she'd always treated Becky. Or rather, the way she hadn't treated her. Becky Glass was a nonentity. She always had been. It wasn't that Charlee had any ill will toward the girl, it was merely that she seldom noticed her. And most of the time when she did notice her classmate with the bad hair and freckles, it was only in passing or because Becky had done something really stupid again. Well, not stupid, maybe, but clumsy. Becky was almost always falling over herself, or tripping or running into someone when she was just *walking*, for godsakes. Charlee tried not to laugh, but she wasn't always a hundred percent successful. And for the first time in her short life, she wondered if she'd done something wrong by simply being who she was.

The notion wasn't pleasant, and the feelings the idea brought were downright miserable.

They cut across Blackwell Road about thirty yards from the front of Havenwood. Normally they would have never given the place a second thought—unlike Stan and Dave, the idea of actually going into that creepy old house was never really considered an option by the two of them; they had a better sense of self-preservation than either of the boys—if they hadn't heard the noises.

The sounds of men grunting under heavy strains and the echoing crack of wooden boards being forced away from the places where they'd been nailed were too enticing to be completely ignored. Without a word, the two girls headed up the road, away from their final destination, to see all of the activity.

It wasn't really much to see for most people, but there are exceptions to almost every rule. They watched the men in silence for several moments, before Charlee nudged Jessie and pointed to one of the men climbing out of the big Atlas truck full of supplies. Walter Grant was not a big man in a physical sense, but to his daughter Jessie, he was a giant. At the moment, Jessie's dad was hauling several very long planks of wood out of the truck, hefting them on one shoulder and walking in time with the man behind him, who supported the rest of their weight. His thinning brown hair was matted with sweat, and his slight potbelly seemed more pronounced because of the weight he strained with. Jessie called out to him, and her father looked in her direction and smiled.

And then the man behind him missed a step, and both men stumbled under the weight of the wood. There was a moment when Jessie was certain, as certain as the sun was shining down on her sandy hair, that her father would fall from the truck's ramp and break his neck. He wobbled, and the man behind him did the same, and then they managed to right themselves. Not that all went well. The lumber they were hauling slipped and scraped down the right arms of both men before falling away to the ground a few feet below. The wooden boards fell, and two of them broke like fragile glass, despite their being good, sturdy oak.

It wasn't funny, but the look of shock on Walter Grant's face was so much like his daughter's that Charlee had to bite her lip to keep from laughing. The feeling went away a second later, when a well-dressed man with a clipboard started screaming at the two men. Jessie and Charlee watched as the man yelled, all but throwing a tantrum. They watched as he called both of the men before him names and pointed an accusatory finger.

And Jessie watched her father take it. Just stand there, shamefaced, and take all the name-calling. Charlene watched, too, her mouth hanging open in shock. Her father would have knocked the man through a wall or two before he would have just stood there like that. Her father would have used the man calling him names to sweep the hallways of the big old, nasty house behind them. She might have said as much, too, when she turned to look at Jessie, but the expression on her best friend's face made her think before opening her mouth.

For all of her life, Jessica Elizabeth Grant had looked upon her father as a sort of god, beyond reproach and impossible to hurt. He was her father, after all, and that was to be expected. She hadn't yet reached the point where she doubted that her father was the best man in the world, and exactly the sort of man that everyone else should look up to. But now, watching him look down at the ground while the man in front of him—the man in the sissy clothes, with the sissy haircut no less—ripped into him, Jessie felt that image of her father begin to fragment and break. Charlee, almost always an observant person if not nearly as often tactful, noticed this in the look on Jessie's pretty face, and kept her mouth shut.

"Come on, Jessie," she whispered. "Let's go get a soda or something."

Jessie looked back at her in complete silence, her face warring between anger and tears and the need to hide what she was feeling, and nodded numbly. For the first time in her life, Charlee felt awkward around her best friend. She imagined it was even worse for Jessie. Without a word, she wrapped a companionable arm around Jessie's shoulders and felt the girl stiffen for just a moment before she relaxed. They walked on in silence; there were no words that either could figure to say.

VII

Stan Long rode in the ambulance across the town of Serenity in a daze. He knew that he'd almost drowned, knew that *Becky Glass*, of all people, had pulled him out of the water, but beyond that, his mind was filled with strange thoughts and images that made no sense. He saw an angry group of people dressed in the funny clothes that belonged to another era running toward him. He saw the palatial Blackwell house as it had looked long before he was born, in its heyday. There seemed to be a few hundred people in formal attire moving around on the lawn alone, and he knew there were more still inside the house. He felt himself standing on the ground where he *knew* the quarry was supposed to be, but where no sign of man's intrusion into the granite could be seen. He heard laughter and anger as if they were leaves blowing in a hurricane-force wind.

And above it all, he heard the sound of the ambulance's sirens screaming through the air as he headed toward the medical center that served as a hospital for the area. *Dad is gonna skin me alive. Mom is gonna yell at me, and April's gonna laugh and laugh and laugh…* The worst part was, he deserved any trouble he got into for listening to Dave in the first place. Dave was always coming up with stupid ideas that would almost guarantee he got into trouble. Unlike Dave, Stan was not designed for getting into grief with his folks. Stan hated being busted for doing the wrong things; Dave almost seemed to thrive on the idea. *Hey, Dave didn't exactly twist my arm…* He wanted to be mad at Dave, but it never stuck very well. In truth, Dave hadn't had to work hard to make him come along. His friend just had a knack for coming up with stupid ideas and then surviving them.

Stan tried to open his eyes, but the bright flashes of light erupting behind his closed eyes were enough to change his mind. Cool, dry hands were working at his wrist, checking his pulse presumably, when he drifted away into darkness and sleep again.

In his dreams, he could see them coming: a small army of shadowy figures moving toward the town of Serenity Falls like there was something urgent that had to be done. They were silent, and they were grim. He could see no faces, but he could sense their need to be in the town. In the silence of his mind, he could hear their impatience at being delayed. And for just a second, a nauseating wave of stench came from them. The only time in his life he'd smelled anything like it was when he stumbled on the bloated, rotting flesh of what had once been the neighbor's cat. The odor was exactly the same but intensified by the sheer numbers of shadows heading his way.

Stan whimpered in his sleep.

Walter Greene looked down at the boy with his fitful, troubled brow, and checked to make sure he was getting enough oxygen. The kid was young; the last thing he needed was to suffer permanent brain damage or worse from lack of oxygen in his blood. All was well as far as he could tell.

Chapter Four

I

The man watched from a park bench as Jack Michaels walked from his offices with a slightly defeated stride. The poor constable looked…distraught. It was a start. He allowed himself a faint smile as he looked away, examining the people in the small open park. Over to his left, Greg Randers was sitting with Nona Bradford. Greg had blond hair and blue eyes, the all-American boy. Nona, four years older than him, was a brunette with a delicate body and a sweet, pretty face. Girl-next-door pretty. Even from a distance it was obvious how much they liked each other. Not a bad-looking couple, but a serious pity that Nona was married. Carl Bradford was a bit of a pig, really. Not in his body, but in his mind. He expected his wife to be a servant to him, and if the rumors were true, had forced the issue on a few occasions.

At their feet, a bungling little dog sat on its leash, looking at them expectantly. After a few seconds of being ignored, it started chasing its own tail. Above him, the two leaned forward for a stolen kiss. It was a very passionate kiss, nothing shy or coy about it. Only the puppy and the man noticed. Only the man cared. His face stretched into a broader smile as he watched.

The two of them were practically like schoolkids, and that was going to prove bad for them. He doubted they could even cross on the street without making cow eyes at each other. If Carl ever found out, there would certainly be hell to pay. But they were safe for the moment at least; Carl was working on the rebuilding of Havenwood. The man knew, because Nona had mentioned it.

The thought of Carl Bradford discovering his wife kissing another man was amusing. He made a note to make sure it happened but not just yet. In the meantime, there was work to do. It was work he loved, but it was still work.

While the two lovers kissed, completely caught up in each other, he focused his attention on the little puppy. It looked to be a mutt but at least partially German Shepherd. It would do. He was merely grateful it wasn't a Chihuahua. Greg got daring, his hand moving up Nona's arm to her shoulder, almost brushing her breast, and the puppy, completely forgotten, wandered toward the street. He rose from his place on the next bench, his warm, friendly voice calling out with mild alarm. "Look out, little fella."

His warm, strong hands scooped the puppy out of the road mere seconds before there would have been a bloody mess instead of a young dog. The pup wagged its tail vigorously, looking at him with the same carefree abandon it had shown to the approaching vehicle. He smiled back, nuzzling against its face. The dog licked and nipped in response, and finally, Greg Randers noticed the dog was gone. His face screwed up with concern for a second, until he saw who the dog was with.

The man breathed out, a fine silvery spray that couldn't be seen from more than a few inches away. The puppy, unawares, drank in the breath.

Randers came closer. "I was wondering where he'd gotten off to." His voice was nervous, afraid he might have been caught in the act of kissing his secret girlfriend.

The man smiled, his eyes full of a sincerity he simply wasn't capable of feeling. "Not to worry. I saw him as he started toward the road. He's perfectly safe." Greg was still looking nervous, and that would never do. The fun would only happen if the boy was allowed to throw caution to the wind. "Lucky for you, I looked up from my crossword puzzle when he ran over my shoe."

The boy relaxed noticeably and took the puppy into his hands. "Thanks for the save."

"Oh, my pleasure. I'd hate to think of a little guy like that getting squished." He looked at his watch and feigned surprise. "Lunchtime is over, back to the day job."

"You have a nice day."

"You, too, Greg. You, too." He turned away without a second glance at the boy. Greg Randers was young and stupid, letting his hormones think for him. He was exactly the sort of person the man liked to meet. He was the sort who made the job so very much easier.

II

Mike Blake barely made it home before the real shakes began again. He could almost live with the strange visions brought on by his body detoxing itself, but damn, the shakes were bad and ugly. His whole body felt like it was being wrung out in the hands of a giant with an attitude problem. And he was soaking through his clothes from the sweat that seemed determined to erupt from his every pore.

He knew the bugs were in his mind, but that didn't make the way they crawled on him any less repulsive. He closed the door and let himself fall on the floor, his mind and body racked by hideous waves of sensation.

The good news, as far as he was concerned, was that this one seemed less intense than the last few. Two years of pickling himself had not been good to him. Getting clean was, the more he thought about it, almost more effort than it was worth.

He managed to crawl all the way to the bathroom before he threw up the breakfast he'd had earlier. For a week, he'd practically gone cold turkey, sipping just enough to take the edge off of the shakes when he was sober, before he really decided to quit. Before he saw the violation of the cemetery and found an anchor, something to stop him from blowing his own skull wide open. He didn't want to imagine what this would have been like if he hadn't given himself that week of almost sobriety before starting this.

The dry heaves stopped after a few minutes. By then he'd finished emptying his stomach. The shakes lasted a lot longer. Mercifully, his mind let him drift into a state of unconsciousness after only an hour or so.

Mike Blake drifted into a fitful sleep on the cold tile floor of the bathroom, completely unaware that someone was watching him. Even if he'd known, he'd have been in no shape to defend himself.

III

The giant was still waiting when Jack reached his office. Jack had to look carefully to make sure his eyes weren't deceiving him. Damn, but the man was enormous. The idea of breaking up another bar fight with Victor Barnes beside him as backup had a certain appeal. The huge man was sitting in one of the patently uncomfortable plastic and steel chairs, his legs out in front of him and his huge hands on his knees, when Jack came in. Jack smiled apologetically and moved in his direction.

He was walking toward Barnes when Gene Halloway popped into his view, looking for all the world like a man who'd just swallowed a live, squirming toad. "Constable? I have a small problem."

Jack wanted nothing to do with Halloway, a man who at his best was still a bastard, but he was the constable, and if the man had a problem, it was his job to deal with it. He looked at the graying, curly black hair on the man's head, and then into the dark eyes beneath them. The eyes were filled with fear and with a touch of actual disgust at having to speak with Jack. Years ago, they had been friends. That was before Bethany McNeil—now Halloway—had stepped between them. Gene had been a good friend in his time, but when Jack started dating Bethany, that all changed. They went from friends to blood enemies in the span of roughly two months. That was when Gene proved just how far he would go to get his way. He didn't just tell a lie or two to win Bethany away; he started an all-out war of slander against Jack Michaels that ended only when he had convinced Bethany that Jack was the lowest form of pond scum. Jack became a pariah with Bethany and her friends as a result of accusations that he bought sex from whores, chased little girls, and had performed oral sex for the coach to become the halfback of the high school football team.

The man he'd once called his best friend had ruined him to win the girl both had vied for, and now here he was, looking at Jack with desperation in his eyes and asking for help. Jack wanted to spit on him, even after over twenty years, but he didn't. Instead he took a deep breath, tried to think of other things, and forced himself to be civil.

"What can I do for you, Eugene?"

Halloway didn't even bristle at the use of his full name, which made Jack feel bad about using it. "It's my daughter, Terri. Jack, she's missing. She never came home last night." Gene Halloway's voice cracked, and for the first time, Jack could see beyond his own bitterness to the fact that the man was truly, deeply afraid.

All thoughts of past betrayals fell away instantly. He nodded and led the man to his office, looking over at Victor Barnes and asking for patience with his expression. Barnes nodded silently.

"Tell me everything you know, Gene." Jack felt his brow knit with concern and led the man who had long been his—if not enemy at least unpleasant acquaintance—to a seat.

The office was cluttered with unfiled reports and the last few weeks' worth of the *Serenity Falls Sentinel*. Jack sat down behind his desk and pushed the piles away until he could find a blank pad of paper and a pen.

"She was with Terry Palance last night. They went out on a date, just like they have every Friday for the last two months…" Gene's voice drifted away as he looked around the room desperately, trying to avoid having to look Jack in the eyes. Michaels felt oddly sympathetic toward the man at that moment. His world was falling apart, and the only person he could turn to was someone they both knew he'd done wrong a long time back. A man he'd done his best to avoid over the last two decades rather than confess to having resorted to smear tactics. Gene had always hated being caught at being less than perfect. Admitting to having lied and cheated to win the heart of his wife would be like deliberately swallowing burning gasoline to the man.

Jack had mercy on him. "Look, Gene, the past is done. Don't sweat it. Let's us just worry about your daughter right now."

Eugene Halloway flushed slightly but nodded his gratitude. "Jack, she's *never* missed curfew. *Never.* And I tried getting hold of Terry Palance all day long, but no luck. He isn't at home, and I missed him by a few minutes at the diner. I-I don't know what the hell to do, Jack."

Jack forced himself to smile consolingly. "I know, Gene. But I promise you I'll get right on it. Just don't go worrying yourself too much until you have to. Maybe she just ran off to a friend's house and forgot to call." He held up a hand to stop the man's protests. "I know she never does it, but you'd be surprised how many times I've dealt with youngsters who never do anything stupid or never forget to report in until the one time their parents get worried and call me."

He stood up and walked over toward his office door. "I'll make you a deal. You head on back to work, and I'll get on this straightaway. Try not to cook yourself up more trouble than you need. Like I said, if this goes the way most cases do around here, Terri's probably just fine and trying to figure out how to explain herself to you and Bethany."

Gene looked over at him, then looked down at the ground, his face getting flushed and red. "Pr-promise me you won't hold what I did against her? Please?"

Jack Michaels looked levelly at the man, wanting to scream at the very notion, but once again held himself in check. "I swear it on my mother's grave. Like I said before, the past is the past."

Gene nodded his thanks as he was escorted from the office. Jack picked up his hat and headed toward the front door of his office. Victor Barnes looked back with endless patience and a slight smile on his face. As Halloway walked away, Barnes spoke up. "Having one of those days, Constable?"

Michaels smiled ruefully. "That would be a fair statement. Can I make you a deal? Maybe meet you at the diner for dinner, my treat?"

Barnes stood up, seeming almost to swell in size as he reached his full height. "That's not a problem, sir. I suspect I can keep myself occupied for a few hours."

"I appreciate your patience, Mr. Barnes."

"There's one condition to this arrangement, Constable." The man looked down, his face inscrutable.

"What might that be?"

"You call me Vic. My old man was Mr. Barnes."

Jack smiled, liking the giant a little more. "You have a deal, Vic. My name is Jack."

Jack pivoted on his heel and headed toward the door again. The day was not going well, but he kept telling himself it could only get better. Quite naturally, he was very, very wrong.

IV

For his part, Terry Palance was having a pretty foul day, too. For one thing, he was pretty damned sure that Terri was never going to speak to him again. He'd changed his mind five minutes after he'd kicked her out of the car. And even he had to admit he'd acted like a complete asshole by telling her to walk home in the first place.

That was the night before, and even though he'd gone back after only a few minutes, there'd been no sign of her.

They had what could best be described as an adversarial love relationship. Easily half the time they spent together was spent arguing. Fighting about one thing or another. Never loud screaming matches—well, rarely—but fighting just the same. The worst part was he liked it that way. The idea of being with Terri without the spats and quarrels seemed almost boring. *Besides...* He allowed himself a small smile. *Making up is always fun.* The thought was nice, but this time he got the impression making up wouldn't be as easy as it had in the past. This time he'd maybe pushed all the wrong buttons. The fighting was fun, true. But the time when they weren't fighting was even better. What good was the seasoning if the stew was absent?

He'd called her three times, and each and every time he'd gotten a busy signal. When the hell were her parents going to figure out what call-waiting meant, anyway? Just to make matters worse, his mom was being a complete hard-ass of late. If he wasn't in trouble for bad grades—well, okay, abysmal, really—then she was ragging on him about working at her damned diner. Besides, working in a restaurant was for girls. Not that he'd ever dare tell his mom that. She'd knock his teeth down his throat.

He didn't want a job at the diner. He didn't want to study all damned night, and he sure as hell didn't want to screw things up with Terri. What he wanted, simply put, was to have a little fun for a change of pace.

He flopped on his bed, narrowly avoiding a collision with his electric guitar. The bed groaned in protest, sounding all too much like his mother when she came home from a long day of work. Above him, James Hetfield and the rest of Metallica were sweating and screaming on a poster that had seen better days. Cigarette smoke and several holes made by tossing pencils at the ceiling had long since ruined any gloss the old picture once had. There was a time he'd given a damn about the picture above him and the guitar at his side. These days, after finally accepting that he was about the worst guitarist he'd ever met, both were just more reasons for him to be bitter.

Terry wanted more than anything to be creative, to be an artist. He didn't really care what sort of artist, as long as he could have the admiration of the people around him and get paid for playing instead of getting a real job. The problem was—and he knew it, which just made matters worse—that being creative and being an artist was work. Work was the last thing in the world he wanted to think about.

He turned over on the bed, ignoring the sounds of the mattress complaining as easily as he ignored the sounds when they came from his mother. On the nightstand to his right was a picture of him and Terri taken a few months earlier. He looked at her long brown hair, the soft brown eyes, and her easy smile and felt his stomach turn in on itself again. Why had everything seemed simpler even just that short time back? Terri wasn't giving him grief about college, and his mom hadn't been bitching so much about him working and his guitar.

He reached for the phone, ready to call her again. His hand never quite made it to the receiver. *What if she's still pissed? What then? How do I apologize for being a dick?* The thoughts made him want to curl up and die. Terri was a sweetheart, but when she was angry, the whole world knew it. God above, if she told his mom, his life was as good as over.

He let himself lie back on the bed, his nerves, already wearing thin, breaking before he could make himself dial her number. He started to reach again, scolding himself for his cowardice, when the phone rang. The shrill scream of the damnable device almost made his heart leap out of his throat.

He grabbed the phone quickly, annoyed by its noise and by the interruption of his plan to call Terri. At least that's what he told himself. It was easier than admitting his cowardice. If his voice was a little higher than usual, it wasn't by enough to make him feel any worse than he already did. "Hello?"

The connection was bad. There was a heavy rain of static and white noise creeping in through the earpiece, and it took him a second to realize who was speaking to him. Terri's voice came over the receiver, and the depth of the sorrow and loss he heard in her tone was enough to send shivers of cold through his entire body. "Terry?"

"Uh…hi. I tried calling you earlier, but the line was busy." He felt his face flush with guilt, the thought that he'd actually hurt her with his stupid act had never even crossed his mind until he heard her speak.

"Terry, how could you? You said you loved me…"

It was a primal thing, instinctual, really. But the tone of her voice, the way that she spoke to him, made it hard to breathe. Terri had never, not ever, sounded so miserable, so completely lost and deeply wounded.

"Oh, God, Terri, I'm so sorry! I never should have done that! I came back, I did, but you were already gone by then." The words sounded lame, even to his own ears, and he *knew* he was being sincere. Still, there was something in her voice, a sort of desperation that carried over to him. He spoke quickly, trying to get the words out before he could lose his nerve. "Are you okay? I've been wanting to talk to you ever since I pulled that shit. Please, please tell me you forgive me, Terri. I love you, I really, really do."

"Terry, you left me there!" Her voice fell into sobs, deep racking cries of grief and pain, and Terry Palance felt his entire body grow cold and numb. "Terry…he took my eyes with him when he was done with me…"

The phone made a clicking noise, and the sound of her agonized accusations disappeared. Several seconds later, the mechanical words of a recorded operator started speaking. "If you'd like to make a call at this time, please hang up and try again."

Terry held the phone until the message had repeated seven times, his mind whirling in a depth of fear and remorse the likes of which he'd never imagined was possible. When he was finally able to speak again, he whispered into the phone, speaking the only words that would come to him. "Who took your eyes, Terri? Terri? Are you there?" The angry beep of a phone left off the hook was his only answer.

He left the house a few minutes later, taking his secret stash of vodka with him. He needed to think. He needed to get away and work everything out if he could. Terri's words haunted him as he left.

V

Constable Jack Michaels looked at the house in front of him with something akin to complete terror. The house itself was not spectacular, nor was the neighborhood anything special. It was all upper middle class, and it was all well-kept.

What made his stomach do slow rolls while the butterflies inside of it beat their wings against him was the woman he knew was on the other side of the door. He'd done everything he could to avoid even thinking about Bethany since the breakup. He cursed silently at his own cowardice and knocked on the door, praying desperately that she either wouldn't be there or that he wouldn't make a complete ass of himself.

She answered the door on the third knock.

Jack looked at her and kept his face as calm as he could. His knees, on the other hand, turned watery the second their eyes made contact. "Hello, Bethany."

For her part, Bethany McNeil Halloway looked at him as if the last person she ever would have expected had just viciously slapped her. Maybe he had. "H-hello, Jack."

"Gene told me you've got a missing daughter. I just wanted to check in with you, find out what you know about what her plans were for last night." He could have patted himself on the back. That sounded downright professional, and at no point did his voice crack.

Bethany looked at him with those big eyes of hers, and he forced himself to look back, forced himself not to burn up at the very thought of being this close to her again. "Of course… Come inside."

Jack moved carefully, making good and damned sure that his body made no contact with hers. He stepped into the cool interior of the house and did his best to stop his traitorous legs from trembling. *Look at her. How the hell does she stay so young, so damned pretty…*

"Can I get you anything to drink, Jack?"

"No, but thanks."

The two of them stood awkwardly in the foyer. Finally, just for something to say, she suggested they move to the living room. He nodded, and they settled in, on the comfortable sofa for her, on the edge of a chair for him. He did his best to talk to her and never really look at her. "What were Terri's plans for last night? Gene said something about a date with Terry Palance."

Bethany nodded. "They've been going out for around two months. Nothing too serious, but they were almost always together on the weekend nights."

He flipped open his notepad and jotted the name down. "Any idea what they were planning to do?"

"S-she said something about a movie."

"At the drive-in, or over at the dollar cinema?"

"At the drive-in..."

"When did she leave the house?"

"A-around six thirty. They were going out for dinner first."

"What was your daughter wearing?"

"Jeans, dark, I think, and a green blouse, short-sleeved."

"Do you have any recent pictures of her?"

Bethany nodded silently, her face struggling against going into understandable tears. Without a word she rose and walked away from the room. Jack sat just as silently while he waited, looking around the room and seeing all the signs of a family life. He resented the hell out of every one of them. Each little sign, from the pictures on the mantel of the fireplace, down to the dust bunnies under the edge of the sofa, should have been in his house instead. The pen in his hand creaked under the pressure of his squeezing. He made himself relax.

Bethany came back a few moments later, holding a picture in her hand. He nodded his thanks and looked carefully. She was beautiful, just like her mother. Same dark hair and dark eyes, same full lips and wide, friendly smile. "May I hold on to this?"

"Of course."

"I guess that's all for now. I'll keep you posted of any developments." He nodded and moved toward the door. His legs still felt like turning traitor, but he forced them to behave themselves by walking stiff-legged.

Bethany called out, her voice soft, so very much like he remembered it from years ago that for a second he half expected her to be looking at him, her face lifted and waiting for a kiss on her perfect lips.

For an instant he almost allowed himself to think that was possible. He turned, and there she was, still almost ten feet of distance between them. She looked at him with those amazing eyes of hers, and her expression said a kiss was the furthest thing from what she wanted at that moment. He kept his face impassive. "What can I do for you, Bethany?"

"Find her for me, Jack. Find her whole and alive. Please."

He nodded. "I'll do my best." He left without saying another word. Most of him was fine with that decision, but a small voice in the back of his mind called him a coward and repeated the accusation a hundred times or more during the course of the day. Sometimes he hated his job.

With his mood as foul as it had been in a very long time, he headed toward the diner. It was time to have a talk with Terry Palance, and he suspected whatever words they exchanged would do nothing but make his day worse.

VI

Serenity Falls settled in for the evening with few incidents of note, save one. After much conversation and a very long delay, Victor Barnes and Jack Michaels sat down over a very late dinner and talked about the job prospects in the local law enforcement department. Jack was once again taken aback by the sheer size of the man. Sitting across the booth from Barnes at the diner, he felt like a ten-year-old kid sitting across from his father. It wasn't just that he was taller by over half a foot, it was the man's width as well. Both of Jack's forearms placed together would have maybe equaled one of Victor Barnes's. Frannie had set the place up for comfort, with wide booths big enough to seat six, and the giant still looked cramped on his side of the table.

"So, tell me about yourself, Vic. What are you hoping to get from working here?"

Victor Barnes smiled over his cola as he sipped. "What does anyone look for? I'm looking for a better life." He hesitated, going back to the burger on his plate and taking a small bite. When he was done chewing and swallowing, he looked Jack in the eyes. "I'm not as young as I was even two years ago. I've seen and done a lot in my life, and I want to settle down. I'll be honest, Constable, I'm getting too old for wandering around the country and looking for anything new and exciting. I've been across the country twice now, and it's time to settle down in a place where I can be comfortable and maybe even find myself a place where I can take root."

Jack thought about that, covering his tracks by sinking his teeth deep into a burger. "So why here?"

"Excuse me?"

"Why here, why in Serenity?"

"Hell, have you looked around? You've got a nice little place here, and close enough to a major city that I can actually go out and do things if I get too bored. Why not here?"

"Well, to start with, the economy has gone to hell since the quarry closed, and that was over a decade ago. If you're looking for work, this isn't a place known for great opportunities."

Barnes looked at him and smiled. "There are always opportunities for a guy like me."

"How do you figure that?"

"Got a bar here in town?"

"Several."

"Anywhere there's a lot of fighting?"

"Sure. What's your point?"

"How much fighting do you think goes on in bars where I'm the bouncer?"

"Probably a lot, if there's gunplay involved."

"There's almost never gunplay involved when I'm a bouncer. I'm not just a bouncer, I'm a deterrent."

"Is that so?"

Victor Barnes looked at the constable and smiled. "Let's not kid ourselves, Jack. I'm not big, I'm huge. Most people look at me and wonder whether or not one bullet will stop me. It has nothing to do with physical prowess, it has to do with body mass and pure intimidation."

Jack nodded. "How often have you had to fight?"

"More times than I care to remember."

"Why?"

"Why the fights, or why the not wanting to remember?"

"Both."

"Because no matter how big I am, there's always someone out there who figures he can take me if he's had enough to drink. And because, much as I may not like it, I have lived in the sorts of places where there's always someone who drinks too much for his own good."

"Ever lose a fight?"

"Plenty."

"Ever win a fight?"

"More than I lost."

"Do you have a record?"

"Yes."

"What for?"

"Disturbing the peace."

"Why were you disturbing the peace?"

"My girlfriend left me. I got drunk. I lost my temper."

"Did anyone get hurt?"

"Only my car. I took to it with a sledgehammer until I felt calmer."

"Why your car?"

"It seemed like a nicer idea than taking my bad day out on a person."

Jack nodded and took a bite of his burger again. He liked Victor Barnes. The man was straightforward—at least on the surface—and he was friendly. He also didn't take his size as an excuse to cause mayhem, which was a tremendous relief to the constable. His papers said he'd been a military policeman for six years before going into the private sector. After that, he'd worked as a beat cop in several cities, with long spans where he was apparently unemployed.

"Okay, Vic. Here's the deal. I'm going to look over your criminal record and do a background search. If it all comes out as clean as I'm hoping, we can talk about a job."

Barnes looked at him and nodded as he chewed on a small pile of catsup-drenched fries. "That sounds fair to me." The man grinned, washing down his food with a massive gulp of the cola in front of him.

"If all goes well, we'll have you working in a few days. In the meantime, the meal's on me."

Ten minutes later, Victor was on his way to the rooming house where he was staying. Jack stayed in the diner for a while, wondering if he'd made a good move or a bad one. Frannie remained almost silent throughout the entire meal. Jack watched her as she cleaned the counters and waited patiently for him to finish. When he finally realized what time it was, he turned the sign on the door to Closed himself and then helped with the last of the dishes.

Chapter Five

I

It didn't take long for word of actual WORK to spread through Serenity Falls. The mining company set up a trailer near the old Blackwell place, and by the morning's light, there was a line of willing would-be employees. One of then was Mike Blake, who had long since drained away most of his savings and was in need of a solid job.

The interview was perfunctory at best. The man behind the desk was overweight, sweating like a virgin in a room full of rapists, and in a very foul mood. He asked all of four questions, and then he dismissed Mike back into the glaring heat of a day that promised to be a true scorcher.

Mike left the trailer in a bad mood and foresaw nothing but more bad mood in the future.

He wanted a drink in a desperate way. Instead, he started walking. Walking didn't do much to keep his mind from wandering, but it allowed him to keep his body busy, and that was half the challenge anymore. If he could keep himself away from the booze, he remained convinced that he could avoid drinking it.

But damn, it was tempting. The very thought of kicking back with even a light beer was enough to make his mouth water. He didn't think he was going to get the job, and that bothered him a lot. He needed work, something to pay the bills and something to keep him occupied. Without them, he was certain he would falter.

So Mike walked, lost in his thoughts and sweating almost as much as the bastard behind the desk at the temporary site for the quarry. And every step he took was one more step that kept him away from one of the bars or the Qwik-Mart's perpetually well-stocked refrigerators.

Half a mile down from the quarry, Mike saw a puppy. It was a cute little bundle of energy that was far too young to be out on its own. It looked like a Shepherd of some sort, but mixed with other breeds as well. It was a mutt, and he liked mutts best of all. They had the best temperament, in his limited experience. Mike's parents had never let him own a dog. They said they were too dangerous, too unpredictable for anyone to trust.

Mike reached out to the puppy, seeking companionship for the moment, even if it only came from a stray who had wandered away from his home.

The sharp little teeth didn't quite break his skin, but they came damned close. One second the animal was looking at him with bright puppy eyes, the next it was trying its best to gnaw through his wrist. Mike pulled his hand away with a hiss and a curse, as the puppy ran from him, shaking its head as if it were either disgusted with itself or with him. Either way, the feeling was mutual. Had he been feeling more energetic, Mike might have kicked the little shit out of pure spite.

More depressed than he had been before seeing the dog, Mike went on his way with the sun beating down on him. He could feel the tremors of another bout with the DTs trying to set in, and walked faster, hoping to burn them away with sweat and effort.

II

By eleven in the morning, while Mike Blake's best efforts to avoid the DTs were failing miserably again, Stan Long was heading through the doorway of his house and was grateful to have escaped from the hospital. He'd barely even crossed the threshold when Beauregard, barking and shaking with excitement, sent him to the ground. The massive dog was beyond ecstatic to see him, and Stan felt the same way in return. For Stan it had been a night of bad dreams and strange images that ran through his head. For his dog, it had apparently been far too long without the pleasure of his master's company.

Stan laughed as Beau licked his face, one massive paw on either side of his head, barking excitedly as if trying to tell his best friend in the world everything that had happened in his absence. Behind the gigantic face that licked at his own, Stan saw his sister calling out to the dog, her face one part worry, one part confused laughter, and one more part that seemed to be happiness at seeing Stan himself alive and well.

Stan found the idea of April worrying about him and being glad to see him almost as unsettling as the near-death incident he'd gone through. Both notions seemed better suited for a TV fantasy than for reality.

April screamed shrilly at Beau, who stopped lapping at Stan's face and looked over his shoulder at her with a puzzled expression.

"Get off of him, Beau! He's been hurt, you silly bear!"

Beau sighed mightily—as dramatic a sigh as anyone in the family had ever heard—and wandered over to the corner of the room to sulk, while Stan sat up on the carpeted floor.

April did the unthinkable and gave her brother a hug that left him feeling slightly embarrassed.

"Hey, April. Did ya miss me?"

She hugged him again, and for lack of anything to do with himself, he hugged back. "Thank God you're okay. You had me worried almost to death!"

"Geez," he stammered. "All I did was suck in some water."

Behind him his parents looked on, smiling faintly, glad that their son was in fact unscathed by the entire incident. Jason Long looked at his son and sighed as deeply as Beau. "Well, let's make sure it doesn't happen again, all right? You had your mother worried sick."

Adrienne Long looked over at her husband, her mouth set in a way that said she was ready for an argument, but kept silent instead. The smile she flashed her son was tight and as sincere as the sympathy offered by an ambulance-chasing lawyer. He looked from his mother to his father three times and felt a cold dread fill his stomach just as the water from the pond had filled his lungs before.

April sensed it, too, and like him seemed unable to quite grasp what it meant. They shared a quick look, and then their father stepped into the house, heading toward his office in the spare bedroom. Stan's mother watched him go, and her eyes were unreadable. Then she looked at him and forced that plastic smile back onto her face. "Let's get you settled back in, and then it's time for dinner. Pizza tonight, from over at D'Angelo's."

Stan forced a smile of his own, puzzled by what wasn't being said and by the tension he felt between the two grown-ups who meant the most in his world. "Mmmm. Great!" The cheer in his voice, like everything else that was going on around him, seemed very, very forced.

Moments later his parents had both left the room. April looked at her brother, and he returned the look. Neither knew quite what to say. In the end, they said nothing. Stan went to his room instead, and April went to hers. Life in the Long household went on, but that would change soon enough.

III

Dave Pageant and Joey Whitman walked at the leisurely pace that only kids can really manage for more than a few minutes at a time. They were going to see Stan, who had not been in school that day. Dave had a long stick in his hand and was using it to prod whatever struck his fancy. At the present time he was pushing a small rock down the side of the road, a challenging prospect, as the branch was thin green wood and bent easily.

Joey had waited for Dave after school, waited until his latest bout of detention was finished. Joey couldn't understand Dave. The boy always had good grades and normally behaved himself, but he seemed to have a personal need to get himself in trouble in classes. Almost daily there was at least one teacher who warned Dave to keep his mouth shut. Sometimes the warnings were affectionate, more of a reminder that other kids had to have a chance to answer the questions, but sometimes the warnings were anything but kind. Dave just didn't seem capable of listening to them.

"Dave?"

Dave looked over at Joey and raised one eyebrow. "Yeah?"

"Why are you always mouthing off in class?"

"Why not? It passes the time, doesn't it?"

Joey thought about that for a while as Dave finally flicked the round stone he'd been pushing across the road into the trees on the other side. "Well, yeah, but don't you worry about getting in trouble?"

"Nah. The most they can do is keep me after for a while, and that just gives me time to read."

"What do you read?"

"Books, nimrod."

"You mean like novels?"

"Sometimes. Mostly I just read the schoolbooks."

"Why?"

Dave looked at him and stopped walking. "Because there's lots of information in those books. There's all sorts of stuff you can learn from 'em."

"Yeah…but isn't that what the teachers are there for?"

"No. They like to think that's what they're there for, but really they're just babysitters."

Joey blinked at that. *"BABYSITTERS?"*

Dave looked over at him and smiled. "Babysitters. Mr. LeMarrs is a great big babysitter. He just likes to think he's there to teach us stuff."

"That's crazy."

"Maybe," mused Dave. "But have you ever learned anything from him you couldn't have learned from the book?"

"No… But still…"

"Babysitters. That's all."

The conversation ended as they reached Stan's house. Like all of the houses in the neighborhood, it was clean with a well-groomed lawn. There was little to separate it from any of its neighbors beyond the number on the mailbox in the front. Joey looked at the front of the place and shook his head. He'd always hated the newer subdivisions. They were generic. No one seemed to want a place that was different from everyone else's home, and he couldn't understand that.

Dave walked up to the door and knocked. His whole body looked ready to spring if the door opened, but then, Dave almost always looked that way. Like he was ready to run or attack. It was just the way he carried himself. He looked like a man who had to get somewhere, anywhere, immediately. Despite that impression, Dave never seemed to be in a hurry.

After almost a full minute of waiting, Stan's sister April opened the door. She was dressed in only a towel; spots of moisture still glistened on her skin. Four years of age separated them from her, but it may as well have been a few lifetimes. April was very, very pretty, even with that little pout on her full lips, and both boys felt both awkward and excited looking at her. Seeing her in a towel was almost more impressive than seeing her in a thong bikini would have been. Both of the boys looked at her with embarrassed faces, but Dave at least had the ability to speak. "Uh… Hi, is Stan here?"

April looked down at the two of them and smiled slightly, amused by the nervous stutter in Dave's voice. She'd known Dave for years and had never made him flustered before. It was nice in a weird way. In a few more years she might appreciate the power of that effect on men, but for now, she was fairly harmless about it. "Yeah, guys, come on in. I'll get him for you."

Dave and Joey watched April walk up the stairs, very aware of the difference a few years could make in the opposite sex. For once, Joey didn't even think about being sick.

Only a few minutes later, Stan came running down the stairs, looking as healthy as he did before he took his plunge into the deep waters and almost drowned himself. If he was at all angry with Dave for what had happened, he didn't show it. "Hey, guys! What's happening?"

Joey just beamed, glad that Stan was okay. Much as he wished that he himself would get a cool illness, he didn't want that for his friends. Besides, Stan had enough weird shit going on in his life already. There were endless rumors that his parents were getting ready to separate. At least if what Joey's own parents kept saying was true. By the way they talked—and apparently half of the other parents around the school district—it was like the Longs had already divorced and just forgot to mention it to their children. Heck, the only person who didn't really seem to know it was Stan himself.

Joey blushed slightly when he realized both Stan and Dave were waiting for a response from him. "Hunh?"

"I said, 'What are we doing today? Movie? Video games?'"

"Oh. Well, we could go look at what's playing, I guess…"

Dave rolled his eyes, grinning a stupid smile. Stan shook his head. "I'm the one that gets brain damaged, he's the one that can't think… We already went over what's playing. That's the reason for the newspaper in my hands."

Joey was about to make a smart-ass comeback when Stan looked at him for a second and then fell backward like a toppling statue, his eyes rolling into the back of his head. Joey didn't even consider that it might be a joke. He dropped down next to him and felt at his neck, afraid there would be no pulse. Behind him Dave called out for April.

April came running, the tone of Dave's normally calm voice convincing her that something bad had happened. She was barely dressed, only a T-shirt and panties on her body, but this time around neither of the boys bothered to look at her body. Both were focused completely on Stan, who was starting to twitch, his body writhing across the floor like a snake with a stomach cramp.

April's voice was about an octave too shrill when she called out. "Stan? Stan! Stan, stop it!"

Joey looked at his friend with the eyes of a doctor, forcing himself not to consider who was having a problem, but rather focusing on what could be done about it. He noticed the flushed skin, the rapid eye movement, and the spasmodic nature of the writhing Stan did. He saw the tightly clenched teeth and heard the sounds coming from Stan's throat. The sounds were completely wrong, more like what should have come out of an adult than a kid.

Joey looked at Dave and spoke very calmly. "I think he's having an epileptic seizure…call nine-eleven." Dave nodded, reaching for the phone on the end table near the sofa. Joey thought hard about what a person was supposed to do to treat an epileptic. He drew a complete blank. He knew the symptoms well enough; he'd seen his cousin go into a fit once at the family reunion and had read up on it. But nothing he could remember reading had said what was supposed to be done now.

They waited in near silence as Stan's episode slowly wound down. The sounds he made calmed, and his voice went back to normal. In a matter of a few minutes, Stan was lying unconscious on the living room floor, softly snoring.

April remembered to run upstairs and pull on some jeans, coming back down just as the ambulance arrived.

Joey watched Stan carefully all the while, pondering the strained, garbled words his friend had been muttering as the seizure hit him. He wouldn't have bet money on being right, but Joey could almost swear he'd heard Stan talking about something in a coherent stream, muffled only by the strain of speaking past clenched jaws. But the words didn't make any sense. "Every solace green… Every solace green…" The same words over and over. It meant nothing, but just the same, the words sent shivers through him.

IV

Jessie and Charlee watched the older kids as they slowly formed teams and prepared for war. Both groups were dressed in civilian clothes, and the strongest weapons they had were their own bodies, but there was no doubt there would be violence. That was what football was all about.

They didn't even know half the names of the kids playing, but that didn't matter. There was something primal about watching each group get ready, planning their strategies as they prepared to kick the old pigskin around. Still, to Charlee it felt wrong. It was too early in the year for football. She looked across the field to where the older teens were crouched in their circles, and then she looked past them to the brooding house that sat like a cancerous lump just past the park's field. Sure enough, looking back down at her was Lawrence Grey.

Poor Lawrence. His mom never let him out of the house. He just sat in his room and watched, and even though she couldn't really make out his face at this distance, she could imagine the expression was the same as always: wistful and tragic. She couldn't imagine what it must be like, stuck in the house all the time like a prisoner. Of all the kids at school, she felt sorriest for Lawrence. Even Mikey Chambers in his wheelchair had it better as far as she was concerned. Mikey at least knew how to be happy.

Lawrence looked on from his window for a moment more, and then he faded from view.

On the field, the groups of boys were lining up for their game. If it went like all of the others, it would disintegrate into a free-for-all in about half an hour. In the meantime, she would decide which team had the cutest guys and bet on them.

Jessie always agreed with her though, so the bet didn't count for much. She looked over at Jessie, who was in turn looking over the guys on the field and trying to decide who she liked best. Charlee knew her friend's decision would change within the hour. *Nothing new there,* she mused silently. Jessie changed her mind as quickly as a bank teller counted dollar bills. The only part of that she found disturbing was that her best friend always seemed determined to agree with whomever was actually speaking their mind at the time.

"Who do you think'll win, Jessie?"

Jessie looked over at her with an almost comically blank face. She was caught off guard by the question, which was normally hers to ask Charlee. "Umm... Maybe Jeff Ordun's group?"

Jeff Ordun was a big boy who had more muscles than brains and normally managed to win from sheer ferocity. But he was up against John Chambers, Mikey's big brother, who was faster than the wind when he tried. It was almost like John had stolen all of the speed Mike should have had and left his brother with wheels to make up for it. "Okay. I've got a dollar that says Mike's team wins."

Jessie blinked, her face almost panicky. Charlee could see her trying to figure out how to get on the same side as her best friend in the bet. Before she could speak, Charlee interrupted. "You already picked, so even if there isn't a dollar in it, it's my team against yours."

"Oh... okay." Jessie almost sounded like she'd heard her favorite doll had been crushed under a car.

"Relax. One way or the other, we're still friends when it's done."

That seemed to help. Jessie almost managed to relax and enjoy the game. Thirty-seven minutes later, the game fell into chaos—a record for the length of time it took—and Jessie's team had the upper hand. Charlee reached into her jeans and pulled out a crumpled dollar bill.

Jessie took it, almost as if the money would bite her. "Y-you don't have to give me the money, Charlee..."

"Sure I do. You won." She smiled her brightest for Jessie and nodded her satisfaction when Jessie took the bill and put it in her own jeans. A few minutes after that, they were headed on their way into town to go window-shopping. For Charlee the incident was forgotten. For Jessie it was all but a major event in her life. She'd never bet against Charlee before—not really bet against her, she just took whatever team her best friend didn't, but this was different, this time when her team won, it was *her* team, not the leftovers—and she'd certainly never won a real bet before. She rather liked the feeling.

V

Jack's day was only going from bad to worse as time went on. First he'd had to fill out several stacks of papers he'd been deliberately ignoring, and now he had to spend time seeking any information he could get on the disappearance of his high school sweetheart's daughter. Almost two days without a sign of the girl, and that wasn't a good thing. He had seen enough in his time to know that much for certain.

To make matters worse, he hadn't had any luck at all finding Terry Palance. The boy wasn't at his house, he wasn't at the diner, he wasn't in any of the places where Jack expected to find him. He had no intention of involving Frannie unless he had to. Frannie had enough on her plate without making her worry about whether or not her boy had been doing things he shouldn't. As it was, she was almost constantly lamenting not being able to spend enough time with him when he was growing up. Jack knew for a fact that she'd paid good money to keep him in day care and to see to his needs. It wasn't like he'd been abandoned somewhere along the way. Frannie just kept thinking that she could have done more.

To his way of thinking, if you did too much for your child, you risked at least as much as if you did too little. But then, he wasn't a parent, and he doubted he ever would be. That required a willing partner—under any but the sort of circumstances he didn't even consider as an option in jest—or at the very least the money to adopt.

He shoved those thoughts out of his head as quickly as they had risen. Best not to think about what would never be. Best to pretend that all was right with his world and forget about... *Bethany...* the women he'd met and passed along the way. Best to focus on what he could make right in the world, like finding a lost little girl. Jack frowned in thought, but the frown grew deeper when he saw Terry Balance's car on the side of the road. Terry was never far from his car, and that meant he was somewhere nearby.

A dark little part of his mind whispered that the boy might be hiding evidence of a crime—a crime against a girl that could have been his daughter if the world had been a little kinder—and he did his best to shut it away. Until he knew otherwise, he had to assume the boy had done nothing wrong; innocent until proven guilty was something he believed in, or at least tried to believe in. But that didn't make it an easy thing to handle.

Jack slid out of the cruiser with one hand on the butt of his revolver. He wasn't much in the mood to take chances with anyone or anything today. Something in the air felt... wrong. He moved toward Terry's souped-up muscle car as casually as he could, but his eyes were snapping everywhere, soaking in details of the lay of the land.

He found Terry Palance almost a hundred yards off the road, sitting with his back against a tree and drinking down a fifth of vodka. The bottle was mostly empty, and judging by the sweet smell of the boy's sweat, he'd been drinking almost nonstop. Jack looked at the way the kid's head swayed from side to side in a drunken stupor and eased his hand off the butt of his revolver. Even if Terry decided to get combative, it wouldn't do him one lick of good in his current state.

As Jack approached, Terry Palance looked up at him with eyes that refused to focus, and did his best to look remotely sober.

"Hi, Officer Jack."

He had seldom heard anyone sound so rough and raw. Jack sat down beside him in the dried vegetation at the base of the tree. "Hi, Terry. I've been looking for you. Do you know why?"

Terry looked at him. Despite being seventeen, despite the stubble on his face and the reek of booze-sweat coming from his every pore, he looked all of twelve with that tragic expression on his face. Terry's lower lip trembled, and his eyes watered slightly. Much as Jack Michaels wanted to comfort him right then, that wasn't in his job description. "Because Terri Halloway is missing."

"That's right. And the way I hear it, you were the last person who saw her."

Terry nodded, his face finally collapsing under the weight of the tears that fell freely from his eyes.

Jack waited for almost two minutes before the crying jag faded. "Want to tell me what happened?"

"I got stupid, Jack." Terry swung his hand up in an arc and pounded himself in the forehead with his own palm. "I got fucking stupid..."

"How stupid did you get, Terry?" His voice was soft, but he felt twinges of fear jolting through his own stomach at the thought of what the kid might have done to his girlfriend. Kids his age did stupid things all the time, and he knew for a fact that very few of the really stupid acts ever came out in the open.

"I dropped her off on the road late at night, and I made her walk home, and she never got there." Terry collapsed into tears again, his face a tortured mask of grief the likes of which no one his age should have to endure.

"Tell me everything, Terry. Tell me every last detail. Can you do that for me?"

Terry could and did. By the time he was finished, Jack's skin felt chilled in the hot afternoon, and Terry himself seemed almost sober.

VI

Waking was painful. Every part of her hurt in ways she had never imagined possible in her entire young life. The endings of her nerves screamed in protest against the feel of the sun on her bare skin and the gentle kiss of the breeze that moved across her form.

Still, she moved. She dared the agonies of the flesh as she slowly crawled back toward consciousness and the realization that she had been changed in some fundamental way.

In time she managed to stand and remembered to breathe and to open her eyes. As she gathered her wits, she felt the searing pains slowly fade from her body, sliding down into a level that didn't threaten to shatter her mind any longer.

How long, she wondered, *have I been here? How long since I could feel anything at all?* There was no one to answer her. With careful, deliberate steps, she moved from the place where she had lain and headed toward the house she could see through the break in the trees. There, in the window that peeked between the branches of the trees, she saw a face through the reflection of the sky that covered the glass. The face was long and angular, with dark hair and eyes that blazed with energies that seemed to her as bright as the sun. She closed her eyes as she walked, and when she looked again, that face was gone, replaced by another. The new face was unknown to her, but that hardly mattered. It was a disguise, after all, a mere mask to hide the presence that had called her forth.

That presence was dark and wild and filled with an unnatural hatred for all that it saw, but the mask it hid behind smiled serenely to her and beckoned her to come forth, into the light of her first day in her new life.

The mask she wore smiled back, and she moved more quickly, eager to meet the force that had freed her from the silence of the grave.

VII

Adrienne and Jason Long sat next to each other in the hospital's waiting room, the silence between them as cold and unfeeling as outer space. Somewhere in the vast, sterile building their only son was being treated for his unexpected seizure, a dilemma that should have pulled them together, united them in this time of crisis, and yet they could barely look at each other. Their daughter April sat nearby, flipping through the same magazine she'd been looking at for the last two hours, her face as blank and lost as both of them felt.

Jason wanted so desperately to take the two of them in his arms, to hold them both tightly and make all of the pain go away, but he just couldn't. The gulf that separated him from Adrienne was too great, and these days it stretched out to interfere with his love for his daughter as well.

He looked at Adrienne as she started searching through the magazines for anything that might work as a distraction from the fear and frustration of waiting for the doctors to come back and tell them—please, God!—that everything was all right. She was as beautiful now as she had been on the day they were married. Her light brown hair and deep brown eyes, her faintly olive skin and her full, sensuous lips were all as flawless as ever, and even after two children and almost twenty years of marriage, she still had a body that made men look twice. And deep inside, below the cold vacuum he'd allowed to grow, he knew that he still loved her.

But that didn't change anything. He couldn't reach out, he couldn't pull her close and hold her and give her strength even as he took strength from her. He couldn't get past the barrier that stood between them.

It didn't matter anymore, none of it. Because he didn't think he'd ever be able to trust her again. And that hurt so very much. To the point where it was easier to be numb than to let himself think about it.

It was just a letter, just a note he found in the mailbox, returned to sender because the man it had been sent to had moved away. He knew the handwriting of his wife as surely as he knew the wrinkles on his own face and the laugh lines around her beautiful eyes when she smiled. Despite every part of his mind that told him to put the letter down, he'd opened it. He'd read her words of love to another man, and he'd felt his heart die from a thousand cruel cuts.

If Adrienne knew what he'd found, it was not because he told her. He'd put that letter away in his briefcase and buried it in his office files the next day. He'd hoped that by hiding the evidence he could make himself forget the words she'd written to another man. But they were still there, just hidden.

"*I love you, Stephen. I love you, I miss you, and I will never be the same without you*"

Such simple words, direct and to the point. Such easy words on the eyes, and if the name had been Jason instead of Stephen, the world he lived in would not have begun to crumble.

Jason shoved the thought out of his head and made himself think of Stan, his son, who even now was lost to him. Or at least he tried. It didn't work, it never worked. No distraction could take his focus away from the damned words that had been written on that stupid piece of paper and folded into a crisp envelope and sent to someone who was no longer even in town, to the best of his knowledge.

Stephen Wilkins was dead. He'd killed himself almost a year earlier. Jason remembered reading about it in the papers and hearing about it at work. It wasn't every day the head of the town council committed suicide. Two days later the letter had come back in the mail. She'd sent a letter to a dead man, and it had come back to her, but he had intercepted it and damned himself and their marriage. Whatever had once been between Jason and Adrienne Long had been destroyed by a letter to a man who would never respond, because he could not. And all Jason could think about was where his wife would be if Stephen hadn't died.

Funny in a sad way, to be haunted by the specter of a man he had only ever met in passing. Even in a town the size of Serenity Falls, there were faces that were familiar that had no real connections. To feel that ghost's touch push him farther and farther away from the woman he'd married and not be able to stop it.

Dr. Evan Marsh came into the room as those thoughts washed over Jason again and again in an endless litany of grief, and then he added a new level to the burdens that clutched at Jason's heart.

After beating around the bush for ten minutes, the good doctor told them he didn't know what was wrong with their son, but that he suspected epilepsy. There would be more tests, of course, and it was possible that with medication, if he were right about the nature of the problem, Stan would be able to live a relatively normal life.

Relatively normal. Jason looked at his wife's face as she crumpled into tears and forced his arm around her shoulder. He felt nothing but numb. *Relatively normal.* He could understand that feeling, and he wanted so much more for his son.

VIII

Arnold Holiday had no interest in the new company moving into town, except for the fact that it meant jobs for some of his friends who'd been out of luck or working odd jobs for the last few years. He was already happily employed by the Melmouth County Power Company. He had been since he was only nineteen, and he was already almost that long on the job. At the present time he was doing what he did on most days, reading the meters on the homes in The Falls and watching people spend money they could probably find other ways to spend if they had any choice in the matter.

Still, unless they wanted to live like old Simon MacGruder on the edge of town, they had to pay for the power in their homes. Simon had a wood-burning stove and a fireplace for the winter. In the summer he was forced to sweat through the really hot days. Or maybe he had a generator. Either way, he didn't have a meter to read and so was not really a part of Arnold's life. He never seemed to mind very much. Arnold checked the meter on the Randers place and made notes in his little notepad. When the run of houses was over with, he would write the numbers down on the proper forms and make his comparisons.

He walked toward the side of the two-story house, pausing long enough to wipe the sweat from his brow and give a moment's consideration to what Nona Bradford's little Corolla was doing parked next to Greg Randers's beat-up old Cadillac. People would talk if the two of them weren't careful, and Carl Bradford would do more than just talk.

Arnold and Carl went way back, all the way to when Carl's father had been in charge of the power company and Arnold had worked under him. He knew from the stories the old man had told before his heart attack dropped him into an early grave that Carl had a mean temper. He knew from personal experience just how mean. Carl had put his fist through the door of one of the houses where he was reading meters back when the younger Bradford was still in high school. Seemed he'd heard a few stories about the skirt he was dating back then having a taste for older men, just like Burt Weldon, the man whose door he punched out. Arnold had called the police in time to stop Carl from beating the man to death. Carl, being only sixteen at the time, got a slap on the wrist, and his old man had to pay Weldon's medical bills.

Carl had grown a lot since then. About the only man he'd seen who was bigger was the stranger hanging around the police station looking for a job. He figured Carl could probably break Greg Randers over his knee without working up much of a sweat.

Well, whatever the case, Arnold Holiday didn't figure it was any of his business. He decided it was best to just let the matter alone and watch where the cards fell. He sighed to himself, idly wondering if Nona was half as good in the sack as she looked like she'd be. He was just contemplating whether or not she would be worth facing the wrath of Carl when he heard the growl.

Arnold looked down and saw the puppy he'd spotted when he arrived. It was baring its teeth at him and doing its very best to look fearsome. The whole thing might have worked better if it were old enough to walk without looking like an inchworm trying to wiggle sideways. He smiled and squatted down until he was closer to the level of the dog. "Hey, that's the spirit, little guy. I bet in a few months I'll have to ask your daddy to lock you away so you can't tear me up." He figured by then the dog would know he wasn't a criminal and would let him do his job. That was the way it almost always went. And if the dog didn't catch on quickly enough, there was always the pepper spray. He didn't like to use it, but he had on a few occasions.

The puppy heard his words and snarled even more. Arnold shook his head and stood up. Much as he loved dogs, he couldn't possibly spend the day trying to get this one to like him. He made a mental note to bring some peanut butter with him the next time. Not only would the dog love him for it, he'd have the pleasure of watching the critter try to clean the paste from the roof of his mouth.

As Arnold slid his notebook into the pocket on the left side of his Melmouth Power shirt, he heard the tone of the dog's growl change. The high, almost humorous, growl was replaced by a deeper bass sound. Confused, Arnold looked back at where the puppy should have been. Instead of the little bumbling pile of fur, he saw a much bigger dog, almost the size of a Saint Bernard.

The power man's eyes grew wide, and he felt the adrenaline produced by his fear kick into overdrive. "N-nice doggy... good boy..." He spoke in the placating tones of a man who desperately wanted peace, which was exactly what he wanted. The dog looked big enough and mean enough to bite through a good-sized tree limb. And, frankly, it looked bigger than it had a few seconds ago. That was crazy, of course, but it seemed to be growing. He did not want to think about what it could do to, say, his throat or his arm. He reached for his pepper spray and started backing away. The dog watched him, its hackles rising as its muzzle peeled back to reveal teeth the size of steak knives. Even as big as the animal was, its teeth shouldn't have looked quite that terrifying.

Arnold felt the pepper spray canister in his hand and carefully thumbed off the safety. By feel alone he aimed the muzzle at his unexpected visitor and did his best to stay calm. Losing his nerve could mean losing a pound or two of flesh if Rover over there decided to play nasty.

The dog crouched low, its eyes burning with hatred for him, and Arnold Holiday shot liquid pepper into its face even as it started to leap. His aim was perfect. The stream ran into the eyes, nose, and mouth of the leaping animal, and he felt a momentary flash of satisfaction as he watched the dumb beast start snapping at the air. The dog jerked hard, almost as if poleaxed, and landed roughly on the ground, shaking its head and half growling, half whining.

Being a man who knew an opportunity when it arose, Arthur took to his heels and, performing a fine impersonation of an Olympic athlete doing a hundred-yard dash, headed for the truck that also served as his office. He didn't think he had it in him to move anywhere near that fast, but fear was a powerful motivator.

From behind him, he heard the change in the sounds the big dog made, and then he heard the sound of paws scrabbling for better purchase as the animal started its pursuit. As fast as he was running, he knew, just *knew* by God, that he would never make the truck. He could hear the sounds of the damned dog getting closer at a pace that just had to be tearing up the distance between them. He didn't dare turn around to find out.

"Damn me...damn me...damn me..." The words that spilled from his mouth were as involuntary as his heartbeat, but they were taking away his breath at a rate that had him worried. He ran faster than he ever had before, and still he heard the beast getting closer. He clenched his hand on the all-but-forgotten pepper spray and swung his arm behind him, determined to blind his attacker and get away.

His plans changed radically when he felt the teeth of the animal sink into his wrist and tear through flesh and muscle all the way to bone. Arnold Holiday cut loose with a scream that almost stripped his vocal cords as the massive black dog shook its head and damn near bit his hand off. All of the energy he thought he had was gone in an instant, and all that remained in his world was an endless stream of shrieking nerve endings.

Arnold fell to the ground as the dog jerked and dragged backward on his arm, a fisherman reeling in the catch of the day. Desperate in a way he never would have imagined possible in all of his thirty-eight years, Arnold twisted himself around as much as he could and kicked hard at the side of the massive head encasing his arm. The blow was grazing at best. He tried again with more success, and the dog let go as the meter man's heel slammed against its nose and dragged all the way to its eye and then its thick, brutal skull. Holiday felt a half second of victory before the dog snarled deeply and lunged, baring teeth that were now colored crimson by his blood.

When the dog bit down again, the massive fangs sank into his forehead and his chin before meeting at the place where his nose came free from his skull. His second scream was very short-lived, and Arnold himself only lasted a moment or two beyond the end of the noise he made.

If anyone within the confines of the Randers house noticed the noise, they managed to ignore it. The dog stared at its victim for several seconds before it started pulling him toward the woods behind the house he was guarding. Deep within the primitive brain of the beast a silent command rang out. It listened, and it obeyed.

Chapter Six

I

*E*pilepsy.

Stan Long looked in the mirror and saw his own face. It hadn't changed any, except that he knew it was the face of a person with a stupid disease. *Epilepsy.* He snorted toward his reflection and watched while the face looking back at his sprouted a small grin. *This has just got to be eating Joey alive. He'd love to have something like this. Me? I think I could do without.*

It was not the sort of thing he wanted to dwell on, this new and unusual illness, but it seemed that at least part of his mind all but insisted on sticking to the idea and mulling it over with all of the possible implications. The doctors didn't want to give him any antiseizure medications yet, but they put him on a sedative, something to keep him calmer. Because, apparently, getting excited could cause a seizure. His reflection rolled its eyes toward the heavens, and he felt a mild bubble of hysteria building in his chest. *Oh, the day I go on my first date should be interesting... and just imagine what sex will be like. First base, not a problem; second base, just fine; third base, everything's looking great; and then fourth base, pardon me while I do a fish out of water dance all over the floor.*

He did his best not to dwell on the idea. As it was, he felt enough like crying without thinking about it. What the hell chance was there that any girl in the world would want to go out with a spaz who started twitching when they got to heavy petting?

He spun away from the mirror over his nightstand and flopped bonelessly on the bed, as only a preteen could ever manage. He was beginning to understand how Lawrence Grey must have felt about his life, locked away from any possible harm and all but held prisoner in his own home.

Somewhere downstairs, his parents were doing their best to ignore each other. He was up here, in his room, doing his best to ignore the both of them. Even Beau was feeling the tension in the house, and not nearly all of it was because of the new medical troubles in the Long household.

April was out, doing her best to not worry about her own problems, like her best friend Terri's disappearance. He felt sorry for her. He also hoped everything was all right, because he'd long since developed a healthy crush on Terri, even though he knew the girl looked at him like an adopted little brother. The fact that she found him uninteresting did not counter the fact that he thought she had about the best legs on the planet and hair he could stroke through his fingers for hours on end.

As he understood, it, Terri had disappeared after Terry Palance dumped her on the side of the road. That same night, Jerry Cahill—official persona non grata at the Long residence, and desperately trying to get back into April's good graces with absolutely no luck—had dumped April on the side of another road for not letting him cop a feel. Stan hoped he never got that stupid.

The end result was that April was out checking all of the favorite haunts for her best friend, hoping to find her somewhere along the way. She'd taken Beauregard with her, an extra precaution to avoid ending up on the missing cute girl list. That meant that Stan was by himself, and for once he didn't really mind all that much. It gave him a chance to think about everything going on and to try to regain his mental balance.

So far, he hadn't had any luck. The strange dreams he'd been having weren't helping, but at least they weren't as bad since he'd started on the sedatives to keep him calm. Or, if they were, he wasn't really noticing. The dreams were doozies though, with all sorts of creepy shit that left him feeling shaky and cold when he woke up. Dark figures moving closer to town, though he couldn't really figure where they were supposed to be coming from. Wherever it was, they weren't thrilled about being there in the first place, and they all seemed to have a serious hard-on for coming to Serenity Falls.

He shivered at the thought and closed his eyes, ready to try resting again. Rest, however, was not to be. Just as he thought he could drift away, he heard the sound of his father storming up the stairs and into his private den again. Dad liked locking himself away whenever the pressures between him and Mom got to be too big. Stan wanted to know what was wrong, when, exactly, everything had blown up, but he didn't dare ask. He might get an answer he didn't like.

II

Mike Blake settled into the routine of working with a passion he didn't think himself capable of anymore. The sheer pleasure of actually making money and doing something other than drinking himself into a stupor almost made him feel giddy. Oh, after only two hours of lifting supplies and carrying them into the various rooms of Havenwood, he was already sore, and his muscles were almost vibrating from the exertion, but he didn't care. It was honest work, even if it didn't come close to paying what he had grown accustomed to only a few years ago. After years of working himself like a dog, he'd let himself slide into a nasty depression and then compounded the error by trying to drink away his sorrows. He'd felt less like himself with every passing day and never even tried to correct the problem. It had been easier to just wallow in his own misery.

Not again, he promised himself. Tom Hardwick was working with him, and between the two of them they'd hauled more lumber and stone than he'd ever imagined a house could need. He was tired, but he was satisfied in his exhaustion, and Mike hadn't been satisfied about anything in a very long time.

Hardwick was a big man, with muscles that held up better under the struggle than Mike's were managing to do. But he was patient enough with Mike. A few years back, when money had been very, very tight around the Hardwick house, Mike had let him slide for six months without foreclosing. There had been arguments with Rich Waters, but in the long run, Mike's estimation had proved true, and Hardwick had started paying again. Tom had never forgotten that kindness and wasn't likely to, either.

When they'd finished moving the last of the lumber from the truck onto the ground just outside the front door, they sat for five minutes and recovered, drinking down cold water from one of the massive coolers filled with ice and liquid. Mike had never tasted water that was sweeter. It revitalized him and made him feel almost human again.

Hardwick lit a cigarette and settled his butt against the side of the stack of boards they moved last, squinting into the morning sun and enjoying the moment. Several of the men were taking quick breaks, and so far the foreman hadn't gotten annoyed about it. It was too damned hot for as early in the day as it was, and everyone had been doing heavy work.

Mike wanted a beer in a bad way but forced the thought from his mind with thoughts of the first paycheck and what he would do with it.

Marty Fulton, the foreman, was not from town. He came with the money behind the renovations. His hair was almost bleached white from too long in the sun, and his skin had the look of well-tanned leather. His teeth were stained brown from too much chewing tobacco, and his smile looked more like a challenge than anything friendly. Aside from all of that, however, he seemed like a decent enough sort. He wasn't too pushy, and he did as much work as any of the men he had under him. He walked over to where Hardwick and Mike sat and pulled a wad of papers from his back pocket. "You two... Tom and Mike?" They nodded to let him know he had the names right. "I've been over the house, and a lot of the floor is for shit. I want you guys to look for the orange marks on the floor and use a couple of crowbars to peel the bad wood out. Do it right and be careful. I mean some of the wood won't hold much more than a mouse, and I don't want anyone breaking their legs. If there's orange paint on the wood, it has to go."

Hardwick nodded, and Mike followed his lead. Hardwick spoke in his usual clipped tones when he replied. "Where do you want the old wood taken?"

"There's a spot on the side of the house that's been cleared already, off to the right of the big maple tree. Throw it there."

Both men got up, Hardwick throwing his cigarette butt into the gravel at the edge of the driveway. Mike rolled his shoulders and felt the tendons groan in protest. Marty Fulton was a bit anal-retentive when it came to supplies, so finding the crowbars was easy enough. They each grabbed one, and Hardwick slipped a pair of heavy leather gloves over his hands. Mike hadn't thought that far ahead and was stuck using bare skin. They got to work on the floor in the foyer and soon discovered that what Fulton had told them was true. Most of the boards were dry-rotted and desperately in need of replacement. A good number of them broke into pieces rather than lifting up when the pair started prying. The taste of moldy wood soon filled Mike's mouth, and judging by the look on Hardwick's face, he was having a similar experience.

Mike stepped around the worst of the boards and remembered to step damned carefully when he watched Tom Hardwick's bulk drop through the floor only a few feet away from him. One second the man was six inches taller than he was, the next he was half a foot shorter. Hardwick got lucky; the floor under the rotted boards wasn't quite as weak. All he got for his troubles was a severe scraping along both shins. Mike saw the blood that ran lightly from the wounds and winced in sympathy.

Tom started to try pulling his right foot from the ruined wood and almost succeeded before the plank holding his weight underneath the flooring gave out. His left leg sank fast, and Mike heard him scream as the weight of his body shifted awkwardly. Mike reached out, grabbing both of the bigger man's arms, and pulled hard. With the added support, he managed to climb the rest of the way out of the hole he'd punched in the floor.

Tom grunted his thanks and hobbled across the boards he knew were safe, until he could get outside and look at the damage done. He'd scraped several layers of skin away where he fell through the floor. His shins were a mess of bloody flesh and ruined jeans. Mike looked at the floor where he'd walked and saw the pooling crimson stains on the wood. It was not pretty.

Marty Fulton came running when he was called, and he looked at Hardwick's legs and shook his head in disgust. "Damn it all, didn't I warn you about stepping on those boards?"

"He listened, Mr. Fulton. He was standing on the unmarked boards when it happened."

Fulton turned and looked at Mike as if he were looking at a particularly unpleasant bug. "Well, I guess maybe a few more boards are rotted than we thought."

Mike considered just who might have inspected the boards and thought that maybe it had been Fulton himself. "Well, sir, I just guess the boards didn't hold up with all the wood we'd pulled around it. I don't think it would have given out as quickly if we hadn't already stripped away so much."

Fulton nodded at the quick save. It might not have been a very good explanation, but he apparently liked it better than the idea that he might have screwed up. He looked toward Hardwick, who nodded his agreement. He and Mike were in the same boat, and they all knew it. Hardwick needed the job, and so did Mike. Fulton was in a position to cost them those jobs if he felt inclined, and they wanted to make good and damned sure that didn't happen.

Fulton pulled his cellular phone from his utility belt—a thought that made Mike want to grin, the idea that anyone in construction would need a cellular phone was amusing to him—and dialed a number. When someone on the other side responded, he ordered one of the medics they had on the site over to look at Hardwick's legs. He then called for Walter Grant to help Mike with the flooring.

Until a few years ago, Walter had been in the landscaping business. Tough times in Serenity Falls had put an end to that. Mike had watched what had been a solid business fade slowly and had been on the scene when Walter had to give it up completely. He was glad to see the man working again. Walter was a good guy.

As they walked back into the site, Mike's eyes trailed along the ground, seeking out and avoiding the pitfalls where the boards had been and the ones that were still too dangerous to stand on. He had an unpleasant feeling in the pit of his stomach, and it took him a moment to realize what the source was. Tom Hardwick's blood had been spilled on the wood, and now it was gone. He thought about that for only a moment before brushing it aside. Best not to dwell on that thought or on the ghost stories about the old place. Besides, there was work to do, and he needed the money. There was probably a good explanation...someone came by and cleaned it up while he wasn't looking, or maybe the old wood was just very dry and soaked it up.

And that thought lingered in the back of his mind and sent a shiver through him before he bent back to the task of prying up the rotted wood. *Thirsty…maybe the house is thirsty.*

III

Jack Michaels welcomed the newest constable to Serenity Falls with gusto. The paperwork was done, and the reports he'd received had all been favorable. Victor Barnes would be a welcome member of the town's small police force, doubly so since the workers at the construction site were already celebrating without having received their first paycheck. They'd already broken the record for drunk-and-disorderly arrests and citations since the work had begun only a week earlier. He couldn't be surprised. It had been a long time since most of the men in the town had even had a hint of a real job that didn't involve driving into Utica, and that was a substantial haul for anyone to have to make.

Barnes must have known that things were going to go well. He'd been to a barber since the last time Jack had seen him, and his hair was now little more than a red crew cut with silver shot through it. The biggest problem he looked likely to have was finding a uniform large enough to fit the giant in front of him. He'd already ordered the largest size available for the man, but he doubted it would fit him comfortably. The other three men on the police force looked at Victor Barnes as if he were an approaching mob. Michaels understood how they felt. Even after three interviews and a meal with the man, he was still overwhelmed by the sheer size of him. For his part, Barnes took the appraisal in stride. Doubtless he'd been through similar situations many times in his life.

"We're gonna make this an easy day for you, Victor. Today you get to play my shadow and ask questions." Simply put, Jack had too much to do to even consider leaving the new guy by himself, and there wasn't a chance in hell he'd leave him with one of the others. They were all good guys in their way, but none of them was exactly a supercop.

Barnes nodded his assent. "Seems like a fine idea to me, Jack. I can't think of a better way to learn my way around the town." He carefully pinned his badge to a blue button-up work shirt as he spoke. It was the best he could do until the uniforms came in. Jack watched as the man partially removed his belt and slid the holster to his service revolver onto it. "Ready when you are."

Jack nodded and grabbed his hat. "Let's get on the way then. We still have a missing girl out there, and I want to make sure she gets found." Terry Palance had been more than worried about his girlfriend; he'd been absolutely terrified. When Jack heard about the phone call, he decided then and there to get busy with the search. There were already over thirty volunteers lined up to help comb the woods, and he'd gladly take more if they offered themselves. As it stood, Karstens was going to head up the search parties. He had a great deal more experience in the woods than Jack did, and most of the men in town respected his abilities as a tracker and a hunter. As he turned to leave, he looked over his shoulder and called out to Bill Karstens, "Bill, would you let me know what Elway has to say about using his dogs to try tracking her?"

"Will do, Jack. I don't think it's gonna be a problem." Karstens grinned. "He still owes me a favor or two for not nailing him to the wall for hunting out of season."

"Good, just please get on that. I don't want her trail getting any colder than it already has."

The two men left the building, striding toward the patrol car and looking as official as possible with only one of them in anything remotely like a proper uniform. Barnes slid a pair of reflective aviator-style sunglasses onto his face, and Jack grinned and laughed. When Barnes looked at him quizzically, he chimed in, "I figure you're scary enough just because of your size. First time a person speeds and sees you climbing out of the car with those on your face, they're going to piss their pants."

Victor laughed easily. "You should have seen the looks I got when I used to do the biker thing. I swear I had people ready to hand their wallets to me when I walked into about half the places. Luckily for them, I'm a nice guy."

Jack nodded at that. He could just imagine what the man must have looked like duded out in leather and chains, with that mane of hair spilling behind him. It seemed strange, even after only a few days, to see the man without the ponytail trailing behind him.

"So, where to, boss?"

"I figure we're about ready to make a run around town. We'll start at Havenwood and swing past the cemetery, then through the different neighborhoods. I want to make sure you get a proper feel for the size of Serenity."

Victor nodded and settled himself as comfortably as he could into the passenger's seat. Jack remembered watching a Porky Pig cartoon as a kid where a very large man climbed out of a very small car, his body seeming far too large to have ever climbed into it in the first place, and wondered idly if they actually made cars for people the size of the man next to him. They were in a Ford Crown Victoria, a car made to seat five or more comfortably, and the man was still all but crowding him in the front seat.

Jack slid smoothly onto the road and started toward the old quarry and Havenwood. Barnes looked over at him and spoke softly. "Do you think there're going to be changes in Serenity because of the quarry being reopened?"

"God, I certainly hope so. This town's needed a little new life in it since the quarry closed the first time around. If it goes well, we might even get a few new businesses around here. That would be something to see."

"I don't know. I sort of like it."

"Well, I'm fond of Serenity myself, but half of the stores in town are closed except during the tourist season, and only open then out of desperation. No one in this town's had money to spare in a long time, except the lot that drive to other places for work. And believe me, most of them are just barely getting through the month. Rich Waters and me had a talk a few months back. He told me over half the houses here would be the property of the bank right now if there was the slightest chance that any of them would sell. Almost everybody is a few payments behind where they should be."

Victor Barnes looked out the window of the squad car, his eyes absorbing everything they saw.

Jack could almost imagine a child looking with the same intensity. The look made him think of what a young man's face looks like the first time he sees the woman he intends to marry: it was wistful, sad, and just a little filled with awe, all at the same time.

"Damn shame how that works. I've been all over the country a few times, and I've seen towns that were as pretty as could be where everyone was working and happy, and I've seen just as many where there's not a job to be found for miles, and the only thing that keeps the towns alive is a stubborn streak half a mile wide in the people living there."

"Yeah." Jack nodded as he turned onto Blackwell Road. "I can see where that makes all the difference in some cases. It hasn't gotten quite that desperate here, but I'm guessing it's closer than anyone likes to think about."

"You'd think there'd be a way to balance it all out, but if there is, I haven't read about it or seen it on the news."

Jack slowed as he saw something big go moving through the woods off to the left of the car. Whatever it was disappeared before he could get a good look. He might have stopped completely, but just then the radio squawked into life. "Jack, you there?"

"I'm here, Bill. What do you have for me?"

"Elway Deveraux says it's all good on using the dogs. He'll have them over here within the hour. You want me to start the search, or do you want to handle it?"

"I'll get back to you on that."

Bill hesitated, and Jack knew, just knew, that he was fuming at the thought of playing second string again. Like as not, Jack would let him run the show, but why let him assume he would? Sometimes Bill needed reminding as to exactly who was in charge. "Ten-four."

Michaels sighed and set the radio back in its caddy. Victor looked over at him without turning his head much and grimaced. "Not all quiet on the western front, hunh?"

"What do you mean?"

Barnes chuckled. "I mean I could hear the tension between you two over the radio, Jack. That's not a good sign for two people carrying guns."

"Oh, it's not nearly that bad. He just wants my job is all."

"Doesn't like being second in command?"

"Something like that." Jack sighed again. "Bill Karstens can't stand the idea that somebody like me is his boss."

"What do you mean, somebody like you?"

"Somebody who doesn't feel the best way to run a police force is by setting up roadblocks and speed traps to catch the unwary doing stupid things. As far as Bill's concerned, the job is to arrest people whenever possible. As far as I am concerned, the job is to keep the peace…to protect and serve."

"I can see where that would be a problem."

Jack shook his head as he turned down the long driveway to Havenwood. "No, it isn't a problem really. I just have to let him know from time to time that we're playing under my rules, and he has to listen."

"Has he had trouble listening?"

"A few times. But he normally catches the hint after I've thrown it his way a few hundred times."

The conversation ended as the massive house poked up through the woods. Jack looked at it in awe. There were literally dozens of men working, and most of them were locals. But it had been so long since Jack had seen so many of them together that he'd practically forgotten just how many people actually lived in the town. He looked at the small army moving and shook his head.

Victor Barnes apparently felt the same way. "Kind of hard to imagine that many people working on one place, isn't it?"

"You don't know the half of it. Most of these men haven't had real jobs in years. Now look at all of them. Hellfire, even the ones I threw in the drunk tank last night are working like dogs, and I didn't figure half of them for making it home without losing their breakfasts first."

The two men climbed out of the car—Jack almost heard the sigh of relief from the vehicle as Barnes's weight was removed and the McPherson struts were allowed to go back into their usual position— and Victor planted his massive hands on his hips, his eyes scanning everywhere at once. "Any of these boys regular troublemakers I should know about?"

"A few. But don't worry about that right now. I just wanted to see how the place was shaping up." He looked carefully, seeing the piles of rotted wood that had been peeled away and the mostly depleted stacks of fresh lumber that had replaced them. "So far I have to say I'm damned impressed."

"It sure doesn't look like the place I saw when I was coming into town…" Barnes's voice trailed away as he saw another vehicle coming up behind theirs. It was a very large limousine with a glossy silver sheen and windows tinted to the point where nothing could be seen of the interior beyond the driver's seat. "Looks like the new owners might be here."

Jack turned to face the limo and watched as the immaculately groomed chauffeur climbed from the front and moved with machinelike precision to open the back door. The woman who stepped out and took the offered hand of the driver was enough to make both men very aware of the fact that they were, indeed, male and heterosexual. Her hair was jet black, her eyes were hazel, her skin was the color of cream, and her body belonged in the centerfold of a men's magazine. Despite the fact that she wore jeans and a man's white work shirt—a look that Jack had always found incredibly sexy on women, though he couldn't have said why—the way she carried herself and the very look of her spoke of money and breeding far more effectively than a dozen Miss America crowns could have. He had to resist licking his lips and leering at her.

The lady moved away from the massive vehicle, and two others crawled out behind her. One was the man he'd met when he discovered that the quarry would be reopened, Steve Ferrier. This time around he was dressed in a charcoal-gray business suit that had very obviously been tailored to fit him. Ferrier looked over his way and smiled brightly. Jack nodded back, allowing a small smile of his own. From behind the man handling the affairs for the Dunlow family came another man. He was tall and lean and looked enough like the woman that Jack guessed they were probably related. His hair was just as dark, but with a little gray showing at the temples, and if his smile was lower in wattage than Ferrier's, it seemed more sincere.

Ferrier pointed to Jack and spoke softly to the other two. The three of them came toward him, though he noticed that they all looked at Victor with the same sort of mild shock he'd felt himself the first time he saw the man.

"Constable Michaels, so good to see you again." Ferrier shook his hand with that same strong grip and then gestured to the two people with him. "I'd like to introduce you to Vernon Dunlow, the president of Dunlow Natural Resources Corporation, and his daughter Amelia Dunlow." Vernon Dunlow shook his hand with a paw that had seen plenty of heavy work over the years. There was muscle and callus aplenty in that steely grip. His daughter's hand in comparison seemed almost ethereal, but no less surprising; her touch left him feeling pleasantly tingly. Jack introduced Victor to all three of them and watched him greet each of them pleasantly. Even Dunlow, who had workman's hands and muscle enough to make him formidable, looked tiny next to him.

Amelia was the first of them to look away from Jack and Victor, her eyes going to the house behind them. "It's even prettier than you'd told me, Stephen!" Her smile was as pleasant to look at as the rest of her. Jack liked the laugh lines around her eyes and the way her wild spill of hair bobbed in its ponytail as she looked the place over. "How long before it's finished and I can move in?"

Ferrier smiled. "For once, a project is on schedule. We should be done by Friday, and the decorators have already been preparing for when the rebuilding is finished."

"Wonderful! I can't wait to get inside and look around." She started toward Havenwood with a solid, eager stride, and the men followed.

"I'd be careful, Ms. Dunlow. There's been a lot of boards torn out and replaced, and I suspect there might be a few spots where it wouldn't be healthy to slip." Victor's words were softly spoken but also just a little urgent. "I wouldn't want to think of the lady of the house getting herself hurt before she's had a chance to move in."

Vernon Dunlow chuckled deep and low in his throat, his voice rich and cultured. He spoke with a voice that was rather like Vincent Price's. "I don't think you need worry too much on those lines, Constable Barnes. Amy is not known for being clumsy."

Amy, thought Jack. *I rather like the sound of that.* He watched the eyes of the men on the construction site as they in turn watched the couple. Ferrier, who had almost looked ready to go in with them, turned away abruptly, heading toward a stocky man with a clipboard, who was looking at him with a faint smile in place. They had obviously worked together in the past.

Amelia spoke directly to Jack, and he had to concentrate to avoid just watching her lips move. She had very kissable lips. "Is it true that Havenwood is supposed to be haunted, Constable?"

"First, call me Jack. Everyone else does. Second, yes, if you listen to the kids who were in here a few days ago and ran out like Satan had lit a fire under their butts." He was immensely grateful for the fact that he wasn't a teenager. If he were still that young, he'd likely have been stuttering while he looked into her eyes. She was almost magnetically attractive. He could have spent hours looking at her.

She smiled at his answer and placed a hand on his shoulder. Her fingers felt wonderful in an almost adolescent way. "Oh good! I've been wanting to see a ghost my entire life."

"Honestly, Amy," her father chided with amusement. "Your endless need to find something unnatural never ceases to amaze me. If you weren't so damned efficient, I probably wouldn't have given you this job." There was no venom of any sort in the comment, and Jack suspected it was an old game between the two of them. Just one of those little pet sayings that was basically expected between father and daughter. He guessed they were close and more like friends than most parent-and-child combinations he'd seen in the past.

"Father, you are far too involved with the mundane. You probably wouldn't even notice if a ghost bit you on your ass."

He swatted her backside and made tsking sounds. "Language, my dear. Your mother would certainly be offended." Again the words lacked any venom.

They stepped past the threshold of the house and looked around, clearly impressed with what they saw. From the floor to the ceiling, most of the wood had been replaced, and the brass fixtures that had looked so ancient had been meticulously polished and restored. Jack looked around in genuine shock. Even with the supplies outside the house mostly gone, he hadn't really expected to see so much of the interior refinished already. The wooden boards on the floor were clean and level, and even as he watched, several men were sanding the wood to perfection.

"Daddy, make sure I remind Stephen to let the decorators know I want the floors bare, won't you?"

"Of course, dear. How could you possibly go skating otherwise?"

Victor looked at the two of them skeptically. "Skating?"

Amelia looked at him with amused eyes. "Yes, Constable Barnes. I like to get into a good clean pair of socks and use them to slide as much as possible on a well-polished wooden floor. I know it sounds juvenile, but I find it entertaining."

Barnes laughed lightly. "I suspect most floors would rather me walk as carefully as possible, but it does sound like fun."

Amelia looked ready to make a comeback of her own, but just then Mike Blake looked up from where he was polishing the wood and damn near had a heart attack as he looked at the woman. The power sander he was using with fine-grain sandpaper dropped from his hands, and he made a noise rather like the squeak of a mouse. The sander, on the other hand, made a sound rather like a heavy power tool slamming into expensive wood while still engaged, and scraped a gouge into the oak floorboard.

Jack half expected one or the other of the Dunlows to explode. The damage could be repaired, but it was still very noticeable. Instead, Vernon looked puzzled, and Amelia moved over to him, her eyes concerned.

"Are you all right?" Her voice sounded almost panicky.

Mike looked at her and nodded his head, his eyes wide and his face paler than should have been possible with his deep suntan. "I—Yes, ma'am. I'm fine. I just..." He looked away from her, gulping in air as quickly as he could and still not seeming to breathe.

Jack looked at him for a second and then looked at Amelia Dunlow and felt the gears click in his head. *Damn me for a fool. She looks enough like her to be her sister.* Amelia Dunlow bore a powerful resemblance to Amy Blake. Enough of a resemblance that he could easily understand Mike's being a little shocked when he saw her walk into the room.

Mike stood up abruptly, shaking his head like a fighter trying to recover from a vicious blow to his skull. "I thought you were someone else for a minute." He flashed an embarrassed grin. "I thought I was seeing a ghost." Mike stepped away from her as if she might catch him on fire. "Excuse me, please." He walked very quickly out of the room, and while one or two men looked at him quizzically, most of them looked on with sad understanding in their eyes.

"Well, that was rather peculiar." Vernon Dunlow looked after Mike's retreating figure with that same vaguely puzzled amusement on his handsome face.

"Did I do something wrong?" Amelia sounded ready to go after him and apologize for anything she might have done.

Jack looked at her and shook his head. "No, Ms. Dunlow, you didn't do anything. You just look a little too much like Mike's wife for his comfort."

"Oh. Well, it should be interesting to meet her. I don't think I've ever met my own twin before, but they say everyone has a double." She was smiling, relieved that she hadn't actually caused the strange outburst.

Jack shook his head again, lowering his eyes. "Unfortunately, you still won't get to. She's been dead for around two years now."

Amelia and Vernon Dunlow blanched slightly. "Oh dear," Vernon said with a sigh. "I hope this won't become a problem for the poor man."

IV

Bill Karstens looked at the man climbing from his battered old pickup truck and smiled tightly. Elway Deveraux was as ugly as his hound dogs and even leaner, but if anyone or anything on this planet could get a scent on Terri Halloway, it was the pack of bloodhounds he brought with him to the police station. The dogs looked around them from the bed of Elway's pickup and wagged their tails lazily. Elway lowered the John Deere baseball cap he wore a bit to block the brightening sun, and then he ambled over to where Bill was waiting. He nodded a greeting and spat a stream of tobacco juice from his mouth. "Figure I'm about ready when you are…"

Karstens nodded his head. Jack Michaels had cleared him to start the search without him. Mighty decent of the chief constable, or at least Karstens was sure the chief felt that way. "We've got a load of people down near Freshing's Point, where her little boyfriend dropped her off, and we've got some clothing samples that haven't been washed and haven't been touched. Think your boys can do the job?"

Elway squinted his eyes as he looked up at the sun. "Ain't rained since she disappeared. Reckon they can find her."

"Good. Let's get on the way. I want to get this done and find out if the girl's still alive or if this is gonna be a murder case."

Elway moseyed back over to his truck and started it back up. It looked like crap, but the man knew how to keep an engine in good shape. The battered old wreck practically purred when the engine turned over. When Bill climbed into the squad car and started down the road, Elway followed him. Ten minutes later they were at Freshing's Point, and Elway was pulling the dogs from the back of his truck, all but cooing to them like they were babies. The hounds ate it up, and Karstens, who had once ridiculed the man about babying his dogs, watched as they captured the scent. He didn't make jokes about Elway Deveraux or his hounds anymore. He'd been witness once to the animals' tracking skills when Todd Hornsby got lost in the woods. Two days of searching had produced nothing, but the hounds located the boy in under an hour, alive and suffering from exposure. And that was after it had been raining.

Elway held onto the leashes on his hounds and nodded his head to Karstens. Then he whistled sharply between his teeth, and the dogs took off, all but dragging their master through the woods after their prey.

Bill Karstens walked after them, his legs pumping faster than he was used to in order to keep up. Behind him a baker's dozen more men followed, many of them wondering: If the girl was dead, who in town was to blame?

V

Mike Blake walked out of the house and straight over to one of the men he knew smoked, and bummed a cigarette. He sat pale and shaken, his face still a little wild-eyed, and killed the cigarette off in around four huge breaths.

That woman had caught him completely off guard. He hadn't thought it possible to be that completely shocked, not by anything, not since Amy had been murdered. It was a damned strange feeling having his heart in his throat and his blood pressure soar through the roof, then plummet until he felt like he'd faint. It was not a feeling he ever wanted to have again.

But worst of all, he knew who she was, knew that his stupid fuckup had probably just cost him the only job he was likely to find. Walter Grant walked over to him and sat down beside him. Without a word the man handed him another cigarette and just sat there.

"Looks like I've probably screwed myself out of a job, Walter."

"Nah. I just had a talk with Marty. He's cool with it. Said you could have the rest of the day off if you wanted." Walter lit his own cigarette after watching Mike light one. "Said if it had happened to him, he'd have probably pissed his pants."

"Thanks, Walter. Really. I appreciate it."

"Are you okay, Mike?" Walter's hangdog eyes looked at him with a concern that was almost embarrassing. Would have been embarrassing, in fact, if Mike hadn't already done such a fine job of making an ass of himself. "Are you gonna be okay with this?"

Mike looked at the ground and sighed deeply. "I think so. I just wasn't expecting to meet someone who looks that much like my Amy, you know? I mean, damn, Walt, she looks enough like her I almost had a stroke right then and there."

"Yeah. I saw her when she climbed out of the limo, and I thought she looked awfully familiar, but I didn't really give it any thought until I saw you coming out of the house. That's when I knew *why* she looked familiar." He laid a hand on Mike's shoulder for half a second and then moved it away. "I'm sorry, Mike. I know that had to hit like a ton of bricks." Walter sucked in on his Camel and blew out a cloud of smoke. "I'd offer to buy you a drink, but..."

"Yeah. But. And I could use a few drinks right now. God, could I use a drink." Even the thought of taking in liquor made his mouth water.

"Take my word for it, Mike, it ain't worth it."

Mike looked at him quizzically.

"I been there. I'm still there every time I look at my fucking bills and pull out my paycheck."

"I didn't know you had a problem."

"I never let it get to the level you did, Mike, but yeah, I like my hootch a little too much." He ground out his cigarette and smiled sadly. "Almost cost me my marriage, and I decided I'd rather stay with Mae. Hell, I figure any woman who can put up with me makes up for the lack of a twelve-pack now and then."

Mike thought of Amy and nodded his head. "Yeah, I know what you mean."

"I know you do."

"I miss her, Walter. Every minute of every day, I miss her."

"I know. I'd be lost without Mae in my life. Listen, I know you're down right now, and I know you're feeling about as low as you could, but believe me, no one in the house and no one in this town thinks any less of you for what just happened." Mike started to protest, but Walter shook his head. "We went to school together for twelve years, Mike. I know you well enough. You're thinking about going home and beating up on yourself like you always do. And you're thinking that maybe one little drink wouldn't hurt that much. But you'd be stupid to go home, and you'd be even dumber to knock back a beer. My advice to you is to take in another cigarette, contemplate how to make your face look properly neutral, and then get back in the house and get back to what you were doing before."

Mike looked at him for almost a full minute, studying the haggard face in front of him and wondering how it was that he'd never realized how wise Walter was. Finally he nodded his head. "Thanks, Walt."

"That's what friends are for, Mike. I gotta get back to work. Fulton might let you slide, but he'll chew my ass if I take any longer." That said, Walter Grant stood up, dusted off his butt, and walked back to the side of the house he was painting.

Mike smoked one last cigarette, worked on making his face stay properly neutral, and went back inside. There was a gouge in the wood that had to be repaired, and then it would be time to start putting down the sealant and waxing. There was work to be done, and if nothing else helped to keep him sane, he could concentrate on that.

VI

Becky Glass looked over at the quarry and sighed. She wanted to swim, she did, but swimming meant being around all of the others who had beat her there, and she did not want to be seen in her swimming suit. It wasn't an idea conducive to feeling good about herself. There was Dave Pageant, looking too cute to even talk to, and with him Joey Whitman, and Charlene and Jessie, and over on the edge, several of the older kids were sitting around trying to look cool.

In her book, there was nothing cool about Todd, despite his good looks. He was cute, even with the deformed right ear that looked like it had been added to his head as an afterthought. He was dark—not just in his natural coloration, but also in the way he had of looking at people. And Butch, well, Butch was okay as long as he wasn't feeling mean. At least he was confident enough to get into his shorts and walk around, even if he made her look slim in comparison. His hair was even redder than hers, and his skin was burned to a dark red. There were Andy and Perry, the greasy twins, two of the meanest and homeliest guys she'd ever met. And also with them, almost standing to the side as if they were too cool to be seen with the rest of the older kids, Marty, Derrick, and Marco. Marty was as skinny as a rail and had an overbite that was almost comical. But he was also meaner than the rest by a long cry. Derrick could almost have been handsome, but his teeth were a dentist's wet dream. They were all over the place in his mouth, and even after years of wearing braces, they didn't look like they had plans of straightening out any time soon. If you saw him with his mouth closed, he was kind of handsome, almost model quality. But when he smiled, it made people think of bad car wrecks. And then there was Marco. Marco actually *was* good-looking. He was downright handsome, but he was also kind of short, and he seemed to take his height as a challenge to prove that he was tougher than anyone else. She could have stared into his green eyes for hours, and his long black hair was almost like a frozen waterfall. It was always perfect, and even the wind couldn't seem to keep it out of place for long. Right now he was wearing cutoffs and tennis shoes, which meant he looked completely different than he normally did. Usually he was dressed in tight jeans and black T-shirts. And usually he looked like he was angry with the world. For once, he seemed relaxed and even managed a smile.

Yep, she thought to herself as her knees shook and tried to send her on the way back home, *that's a lot of people. Way too many for me to get out of my pants and into the water. Maybe I'll try later.*

She was still trying to build her courage when Dave looked over her way and smiled warmly. "Hey, Becky! Come on in, the water's fine." He looked right at her, and Becky thought for sure her face was going to catch fire, she flushed so warm. After a few seconds, she nodded her head and moved toward Dave Pageant and his group of friends. Even Charlee nodded to her and waved, and Charlene Lyons practically never even noticed she was there unless she was falling over herself again—Becky was, by her own standards, about the clumsiest person she'd ever met. She had even managed once to trip over her own shoes while they were on her feet. Graceful she was not.

She headed toward them and forced the butterflies in her stomach to calm themselves. Half of her expected a nasty comment from the bigger kids, but even they looked over at her and smiled. Perry opened his mouth and called out to her. "Hey, there goes the local hero!"

Becky blanched and looked his way. Next to him, Andy smiled and clapped his hands a couple of times. It was halfhearted at best, but it looked like he was almost serious about it. She felt herself blush even harder. Something very strange was going on here, and she had no idea whatsoever how to deal with it.

Dave climbed out of the water, lifting himself easily, and sat at the edge of the quarry. He looked at her with those blue, blue eyes and smiled again. "How are ya? How's fame treating you?"

"Fame?" She blinked, not expecting any sort of venom from Dave and not knowing if what he'd said was meant as some sort of mean joke.

"Yeah, fame. I've got the paper at home that talks all about how you and Joey over here saved Stan's life." He jerked a thumb at Joey, who smiled broadly and nodded.

Joey lifted his arms in a mockery of a bodybuilder and flexed his scrawny biceps. "Yeah, Becky, we're famous. Now I just need to get my agent to talk to Hollywood."

Becky pondered that for a second, and then she smiled. "We were in the paper?" She couldn't believe it. She'd never been in the paper for anything, ever.

Jessie pushed her glasses up a bit, smiling as prettily as she ever did—and despite what Jessie might think of herself, Becky thought she had the looks of a model—and then she spoke. "Yeah, Becky! You were in the paper. They got your picture from last year's annual, and there it is in full color on page three right next to Joey's ugly face." Her voice was light, and even Becky could tell she was joking about Joey being ugly. Heck, Joey was definitely one of the top five cute guys in their grade.

Charlene looked at her with one eye squinted against the glare from the sun up above and half-smiled. "You coming in or just standing there all day?"

Becky wanted to freeze. Going into the water meant actually taking off her jeans and T-shirt, revealing her flabby body to the world. Not at all an idea that appealed to her. But she had done it before, and she could do it again; it was just easier when she managed to get into the water before everyone else showed up. She made herself smile and nodded. "I-I'm coming in."

Charlee pushed away from the edge and backstroked through the water. Becky peeled off her jeans and pulled the shirt over her head, waiting for laughter or some nasty comment. She held her breath, ready to run at the first sign of it, even if that meant falling down and scraping the hell out of her legs on the coarse ground of the quarry.

She was rather pleasantly surprised when the laughter didn't come. She was even more surprised when everyone started talking to her, like it was just a normal day, and she was just one of the gang.

It was a wonderful feeling, and she hoped it would last forever.

VII

Jack Michaels and Victor Barnes had joined the rest of the search party around noon. They searched deep into the woods, actually moving well away from the town proper as they let the bloodhounds do their thing. They moved past the remains of the railway that existed solely to move the granite from the Blackwell Quarry to other places in the country. Along the way the men learned a lesson most of them had forgotten, namely that dogs have much greater endurance for hiking through the woods than the average human does. Within two hours, they were covered with heavy sweat and had been gnawed on by every insect known to live in the state. They were tired, irritable, and almost ready to quit by the time they met with success.

They found Terri Halloway at four in the afternoon, with her clothes torn and dirtied but intact. She was in the woods, roughly seven miles from where she'd entered them, and the hounds who found her were going absolutely crazy, barking and snarling at each other and the people around them by the time she was located. Elway Deveraux had to separate them by force, something he swore had never happened before. Around the third time one of the dogs tried taking a chunk out of his arm, he started swatting them with his belt and screaming bloody murder himself.

After the fighting was over, it took them a few minutes to realize that the Halloway girl was still alive, and as soon as they did, they called for the ambulance. By four fifteen, she was on her way to the medical center that served as a hospital in less extreme cases, and her parents were on their way there after a quick phone call from Jack Michaels.

Bethany and Gene Halloway were both ecstatic to find that their little girl had beat the odds. Their excitement faded a little when they discovered that she was at the wrong end of comatose from her time in the woods, but they were assured she would likely make a full recovery.

Both of them knew that finding Terri at all would have been impossible without Jack's efforts. Neither of them really wanted to think about it, however. Bethany was grateful, and seeing him, interacting with him, was doing bad things to her heart and mind. Like reminding her that she'd always had very strong feelings about the man who was now the chief constable for the town.

And Gene... Well, Gene Halloway was feeling about as good as a viper after it realizes it maybe went overboard with the venom. After all he'd done in the past—and he wasn't overly proud of the stories he'd made up about his one-time best friend, though he wouldn't have changed much, Bethany was far too important to him—the man he'd hurt more than he ever imagined he could hurt another was now responsible for saving his daughter's life.

Gene looked at Jack Michaels and forced himself not to sigh. The man was as tall and lean as he had been in high school, and if there was a little gray in his hair, it worked to compliment his features, not detract from them. For all of that, he could see that Michaels was under a lot of strain, and more than that, he could see the way the man kept looking at Bethany when he thought no one else was watching.

Gene couldn't really blame him. After all, once upon a time they had gone steady and talked wistfully of going off to school together and getting married. He looked down at the ground, anywhere that wasn't facing his old chum Jack. Guilt was an awful feeling, and one he'd done his best to avoid over the years.

But there it was, like an old enemy just lurking around the corner. He rubbed a hand across the back of his neck, barely even aware of the woman he'd married next to him. Oh, he loved Bethany dearly, there was no denying that, but at the moment she, too, was a source of guilty feelings. There had been a time, long ago, true, when he hadn't been in love with her, had barely even noticed her existence. She'd been just another pretty face, and one that he honestly didn't find all that interesting, truth be told. She was giggly and happy and so full of good vibes that it made him sick to be around her.

It was right around the same time she started dating his good friend Jack that she became interesting to him. She liked Jack, and Jack was obviously head over heels for her, and that was all it took to make Eugene Vincent Halloway decide it was time to win her heart.

Gene smiled at Bethany and walked outside to grab a cigarette. He was trying to quit, but it wasn't easy, and the stress of the day, of his feelings, was like an anvil sitting on his head. He hoped the nicotine would make it a little better. He lit his smoke and dragged in deeply, holding the cloud of burnt tobacco like it was marijuana. The better to get the full effect from one of the five cigarettes he would allow himself that day.

Jack Michaels was on his mind and had no intention of letting him go. Jack had been his best friend, and he'd stabbed him in the back, spreading truly ugly rumors about the man that he knew for a fact still came back to haunt him from time to time. He knew, because people still brought them up in conversation when they were talking to him about the glory days of high school. "Hard to believe he ever made it into law enforcement. I mean, what with the drugs and the hookers and all." Those were the very words out of Neil Martin's mouth only a few weeks ago. Back when Gene and Bethany and the rest of them had been in high school, the very notion of dealing drugs was a serious stain. But the addition of prostitutes…well, folks, that was just the right stroke of genius to ruin Jack in Bethany's eyes. Before he knew what the hell was happening, Jack Michaels was all but a pariah in Serenity. The rumor mill started small and grew. Gene had actually laughed about it back then, like it was just the funniest thing he'd ever heard. The notion that Jack had performed sexual favors for the coach had him chuckling for days. And if the rumors that the whores he saw were all under the age of fourteen was bad, well, he knew they'd fade in time. Gene had really outdone himself, especially because he never once said a word about it to Bethany himself. He let the gossipmongers take care of spreading the bad news. It was just a matter of knowing who to say the words to in order to ensure that they got to Bethany's ears.

All Gene had to do was be there to comfort her, and seeing how she'd gotten to know him through Jack, it was easy to manage that. But the best lies, the ones that really do their job, they tend to linger for a while. Jack Michaels's fictitious escapades in the land of dangerous drugs and loose women had gone on to haunt him for years afterward. It had taken a lot of effort on his part to even find a college that would take him in. None of the good universities wanted anything to do with him. Somehow, and as God was his witness, Gene had no idea how, his alleged illicit behavior had managed to get onto his school records. With one simple lie placed in the right ear, Gene had not only gotten the girl, he'd also knocked the academic feet out from under a man who should have had no trouble at all getting into Harvard.

Back then Jack had wanted to be a lawyer. True, he still worked for the law in a way, but the salary difference alone was enough to twist Gene's stomach with guilt when he let himself think about it. He hadn't allowed himself that luxury in a long time, but at the moment, it was damned hard to ignore.

Because his best friend from years and years back had just saved his daughter's life, and while few things could actually get under the emotional armor Gene Halloway wore, his daughter and his wife were both weak points. It was hard feeling as small as he felt right then and still looking anyone in the eye.

Victor Barnes came out of the clinic a few minutes later, just as Gene was crushing the cigarette out and contemplating a second one. The giant looked down at him and smiled. "Mr. Halloway? Constable Michaels wanted me to tell you that your daughter is awake." As Gene started forward, the man put a hand gently on his shoulder. Part of him was very glad the newest member of Serenity's finest was being gentle. Even through the excitement he felt at hearing that Terri was awake, he was very aware of the fact that the man could probably break his arms as easily as he could open a car door. "It will be a few more minutes before the doctors let anyone see her. But Jack wanted to make sure you knew."

"Thank you," was all he could manage to get out. Jack wanted to make sure he knew… Jack, the hero of the day, and the one man in the world he couldn't stand to be around. He forced the petty thoughts out of his head and composed himself. He had his daughter to see, after all, and she was more important than words could ever hope to convey.

VIII

"Day's done, Mike. You can go home now."

Mike looked over at Marty Fulton and smiled tightly. Despite his fears, the man had proved to be a good foreman, if a bit rough around the edges. Then again, he couldn't think of very many construction workers who weren't lacking in social skills. It almost seemed to come with the territory. Work hard, play hard, and never hesitate to show your lack of upbringing.

"I appreciate that, Marty. But to my way of thinking I still owe you for a floorboard, so I'm gonna do a little extra to make up for it." The workday was twelve hours long. Every man working was already making overtime, and not a one of them was complaining about it, but at the end of the shift, no one was exactly volunteering to do a few extra hours.

Fulton looked at him for a second and shook his head, his lips pursed almost like he was ready to lean down and kiss Mike on the lips. It wasn't an image that made Mike hot and bothered. "I already told you, accidents happen. You don't have to do this."

Mike smiled. "I know, and I know you mean it, but I'll feel better if I make up for the extra effort."

Marty leaned down and slapped him on the shoulder with a friendly hand. "Yer a bit of all right, Blake. Don't get so tired you can't work tomorrow, okay?"

"Not a problem, Marty. Have a good night."

Fulton looked back over his shoulder as he headed for the stairs down to the main foyer. "You, too. See you bright and early." Mike watched the man amble down the stairs with a tread that sounded like he should break right through the boards, and shook his head. Making up for the damaged flooring earlier in the day was only part of his reason for staying behind. The more significant cause was simply that he had no desire to give in to temptation. He wanted a drink badly, and he knew if he left now, with everyone else heading off and the usual offers to join them, that he would weaken. He couldn't allow that to happen.

For the first time in two years he felt like he had some semblance of control over his life and, damn it, he liked the feeling. He didn't want it to go away, not now, not ever. Mike leaned back on his haunches and looked at the boards he'd been sanding for the last three hours. The floors in the master bedroom were as smooth as glass, and he was pleased with the work. Manual labor was something he never expected to enjoy, but at least here there was an automatic sense of accomplishment. He could look at what he'd done over the last few days and feel a sense of pride at a job that he had helped do right. When they'd started in the master bedroom just that morning, the boards were still rough and had gaps between them big enough to drop a quarter through. Now they were ready for staining, and the difference was obvious.

It felt good. It felt damned good to have done something other than mope and drink the day away, even if the voice in the back of his head kept telling him that a beer or two would be a wonderful way to celebrate the accomplishment.

He was just allowing himself a real smile when he heard the voice behind him. "Wow… This place looks great."

And just like that, the butterflies nesting in his stomach exploded into activity. He knew the voice, even after only having heard it once. And he knew that if he turned around, he would see Amelia Dunlow. A woman who looked so much like his own Amy that it ripped into him like a rabid wolverine to even think about her face.

Mike swallowed hard and nodded. "Thanks. It's been a lot of work, but I think it's gonna turn out all right." There, that didn't sound nearly as stupid as his first reaction to seeing her had. With a little effort, Mike supposed he could make it through this encounter without making a complete ass of himself. He'd done a good enough job of that earlier, thanks just the same.

She moved closer to him, and Mike closed his eyes, made himself calm down. She even wore the same perfume as his Amy. Or at least something that smelled enough like it to make his heart beat faster when he caught the scent. Even from a few feet away, he could almost swear he felt the heat of her body radiating toward him.

He dared a look at her and saw the shape of her hip, the length of her thigh in the jeans she wore. Even that was too much. He wanted to run screaming from the room.

She leaned forward a bit and looked past him, her profile moving into his field of vision and sending a flash of heat through him, followed by a chill. He watched her face as she looked carefully at the wall and then squinted her eyes just a bit. And that look, too, made him think of Amy. She did the same thing when she was concentrating.

"Is it my imagination, or do the floorboards keep going?"

Mike forced himself to concentrate on her words. His eyes moved reluctantly from her face to look where she was focusing all of her attention. "What do you mean?" He spoke just to hear her voice, hating the jittery feeling her presence generated, even as he reveled in her proximity.

She pointed with her index finger to the edge of the floor. "Right there, the boards keep going, right under the wall." Mike looked more closely and saw that she was right. At the present time all of the trim along the floor had been taken up, the better to complete the refinishing of the floors. He hadn't really noticed it before, but the boards didn't stop as they should have; they extended under the wall. He shook his head, making himself concentrate on what he was seeing. The boards only continued their progress in a small area, about five feet wide. Most likely an entrance of some sort.

"It looks like they walled in something." He shrugged, curious, but not overly so. "Might be an extra closet they didn't want, or a doorway into another room."

Next to him, Amelia Dunlow smiled broadly and all but danced in place. "Oh, goody! A mystery! I love mysteries." He looked at her face, her smile, the laugh lines around her perfect eyes, and managed a smile himself. She was beautiful, and her energy was almost infectious. He thought about what he was starting to feel—attraction for a woman that looked anywhere near that much like his dead wife couldn't possibly be healthy—and then shook his head angrily at himself. *Stupid! I have got to get the hell away from here, get away from her! I don't need this, not now, not ever.* He stood to go, trying to make his mind forget how desperately he wanted to get drunk and ignoring the part of him that was aching to stay near the woman next to him.

He was in the process of turning toward the door and leaving when she called out to him. "Would you help me see what's on the other side?"

Mike froze. Every single brain cell in his head that was capable of logic told him to run, but there was that annoying voice in the back of his brain—the same one that kept suggesting a tall, cool beer as the best way to relax after a hard day of strenuous labor—that said he should stay. Like a fool, he listened to the little voice. What harm could there possibly be? It wasn't like he was addicted to her, after all. Besides, technically, she was his employer. It couldn't hurt to do a few favors to make up for his screwup earlier in the day.

He looked into her expectant eyes and nodded silently. "How do you want me to do this? I mean, the wall is solid. If I break through, you're either going to have to put in a doorway or have the section replaced. Either way is going to cost money."

She smiled brightly and shrugged. "We'll figure that out afterward. Right now, I just want to see what's over there."

Mike nodded and reached for his toolbox. After a few seconds he pulled out a short pry bar and walked over to the wall. As he got closer to his destination, he let himself get carried along by Amelia Dunlow's enthusiasm. *What the hell,* he thought. *At least it keeps me away from the bars.*

The first board pulled away from the wall with a scream that sent shivers through his body. He shrugged the noise away and started on the second. Later, when he was lying awake in his bed and trying to remember how to sleep and remembering the treasure they found, he'd reflect on how odd it was that each and every one of those boards seemed to shriek in pain as it was unseated.

IX

Night came to Serenity Falls and brought with it the sounds of far too many people celebrating their employment. Most of them still had no money, but that didn't stop the parties from growing in quiet, unexpected ways. Allen Cavender wound up inviting a few friends over for dinner, and before the events were all said and done, he had close to forty people lounging around the place and drinking everything from cheap beer to saki.

Before it was over and done with, several people had wandered off to engage in illicit affairs with associates, acquaintances, and complete strangers who would never have been considered when they were sober. When the morning came, several people awoke with unexpected guests in their beds. For Allen at least, it was a pleasant experience. Amber Pageant was a very attractive young lady, and his memories of the night before weren't so fogged that he couldn't remember her being a damned fine lover. Better than he'd expected. True, she had a bit of a reputation, but he'd long since taken for granted that the stories he'd heard about her sexual prowess were the standard tall tales told by men who didn't want to admit that they hadn't had any success in making a physical connection. It happened all the time to girls who really didn't deserve the smear campaigns started by the terminally insecure. Happily, this time the reputation was well deserved.

That memory held him in good spirits until just after lunch, when the rumor mill ground through the workers at Havenwood and reached the ears of a married man who heard a few things he maybe didn't want to about his wife. Most of the people at the party the night before were content to just leave everything alone. A few people made mistakes and wound up where they shouldn't have, but that was all. It was water under the bridge for most. Someone, however, had been talking a bit too much about what happened at Allen's place. Perhaps that wouldn't have mattered all that much, if Nona Bradford and Greg Randers hadn't been so very, very obvious about their waltzing off together.

The whole thing had merely seemed amusing when it happened. Sadly, Carl Bradford didn't look at it that way. Carl Bradford could be said to be in a downright foul mood about the entire situation. This, too, would have bothered Allen very little if it weren't for the fact that Carl was now standing in front of him.

Carl wanted answers, and what Carl wanted, he normally got. Anyone who knew the man would readily agree that the best way to avoid a lot of unnecessary pain was to simply let the man have his due. He'd been a bully through every year of his public education, and he'd never stopped being a bully afterward.

He and Allen had a long, long history together. Carl would threaten, Allen would resist, and Carl would then beat him senseless. Later, as Carl mellowed and Allen learned his lesson, Carl would ask, and Allen would give, as long as it in no way, shape, or form proved inconvenient. It was a simple program that was effective. Allen was not a coward, but he was also not an overly brave man. He did his best to avoid trouble with Carl by taking the path of least resistance.

Common sense dictated he should tell Carl all about Nona and Greg. They were both nice kids, but they really weren't a part of his world. What happened to them meant little in the long run. In this case, Allen's stubborn streak won out.

He looked at Carl and shook his head. "No, Carl, I can't say as I actually saw the two of them together." He kept his face mild and calm, knowing that Carl could smell lies as surely as dogs could smell each other's butts.

Carl looked at him dubiously. "But they were both at your place, right?"

"Yeah, them and about forty other people." Allen shrugged. "After about nine thirty, I wouldn't have noticed if the pope and the president were buggering each other on my sofa. I had a bit too much to drink."

Carl apparently found the image amusing—it was his sort of humor, which was exactly why Allen used it as an example—and snorted a gust of laughter. "Well, thanks, Allen. You're a bit of all right."

Allen nodded and went back to work. That was the last he thought of the matter. Carl went back to work, too, but the idea of his wife and that twerp Greg Randers together didn't leave him alone. He gave it a lot of thought as he went through the workday.

Chapter Seven

I

He walked past the construction with a curious eye. The rebuilding of the house was impressive and worth noticing. In less than a week the crews working the site had all but rebuilt the place from the bottom up. If he were the type to honestly care about such things, he'd have been in awe. But then, through the course of his lifetimes, he'd seen many such marvels. The human spirit was breakable—he had more proof of that than most people could hope to imagine—but it was also very stubborn when it felt the need. Money, such as that being paid for the efforts going into the house, could normally add substantially to that stubborn streak.

Or put another way, money talks. And the money being brought into town was certainly enough to talk very loudly or even to scream. He allowed himself a vague smile at the thought. Money was a wonderful thing, especially in the right hands. With very little effort, he would make the sudden financial good fortunes of Serenity work for him. Another bonus.

Several of the workers saw him and waved or nodded; he returned the favor, calling to them by name. Most of them were ready to leave for the day. It was time to go home or out to the bars, whichever struck their fancy. Mike Blake, for example, wanted desperately to go to a bar. He could all but feel the man's desire. Of course, seeing the woman who looked so much like his dead wife had only made matters worse.

Speak of the devil and there she was, looking out the window of the master bedroom, her eyes scanning the rapidly dwindling crowd. He stopped and admired her. She was truly a striking woman. Full of life and energy, her smile was the sort that made men want to do anything at all to please her. Steve Ferrier was walking next to her, and he was a golden example of how men tried to make her life better. He all but bowed and scraped to her, though, in his defense, he did it subtly. He had likely been raised to know how not to make an ass of himself in public. With his looks and charm, he could pick and choose from the women in the town, and likely in almost any town. But, like so many people, he decided instead to aim for an unobtainable goal.

Amelia Dunlow had already set her sights on the man she wanted, and she would likely be able to get him with very little effort. Oh, she'd play it cool, avoid actually pushing herself at him, but only because that was part of the courtship ritual. She wasn't interested in a quick relationship. She never had been. It wasn't at all her style. He knew that the second he looked at her. Just like he knew things about most of the people he saw.

He walked a short distance away from the construction site and looked down the road that led to the quarry. For now at least, it still belonged to the children. That would probably change soon enough. The land would be needed for other things, like carving more stone from the earth to make coffee table tops and majestic flights of stairs for hotels that charged enough to feed a hungry family for a week in exchange for the privilege of staying within the elegant confines of the establishment.

The children would have to find other places to spend their time. He smiled affectionately in the direction of their distant laughter. It was just as well that the quarry was reopening. It was harder to make the children war against each other when they could have fun equally and for free. They were easier to manipulate when they were reminded of their differences.

He closed his eyes for a moment, letting his senses spread out and away from him. The puppy had begun its work, planting the seeds of destruction, and that was good. But just as importantly, sweet young Terri Halloway was awake at last and ready to do her work as well.

He opened his eyes and started walking.

Serenity Falls had promise, and he intended to see that it reached its full potential.

II

They were watching their daughter when she opened her eyes and looked up at them. Bethany and Gene Halloway looked into Terri's face, and both of them loved her. For the briefest second, Bethany thought she saw panic in her daughter's eyes, and then Terri smiled weakly. Her little girl smiled at her, and all seemed right with the world.

She reached out her hand and touched Terri's fingers. They were like ice, despite the heat of the day outside. Those cold fingers squeezed back with far less strength than they should have, and Bethany had to force herself not to cry. That would be for later, when the visit was over.

And visiting hours ended in only ten minutes. That was when Jack Michaels was due to show up. Despite her all but begging him to let her stay, Jack had made it clear that the interview with Terri had to be done in private. Bethany looked at her little angel and forced the irrational anger away. Jack was only doing his job, and she had no justification for the thought that he might be making her leave the room out of spite.

Jack wasn't that sort of person, even if she'd let herself believe he was back in high school. Gene reached out his hand and placed it over her own and that of their daughter. She felt the love she had for him wash into her in response to his obvious feelings for her. It was good to be loved.

She stopped herself from thinking for a few minutes and then sighed when Jack Michaels entered the room. He stepped in quietly, respectfully, and still she wanted to yell at him, to rant and scream and demand that he just let poor Terri recover from her traumas.

Instead she smiled weakly and took Gene's hand as they rose to leave the room. The constable waited patiently until they'd said their good-byes to Terri. He had that much decency at least. Then, as they left the room, he pulled out a tape recorder and set it on the adjustable stand that passed for a table.

Constable Michaels then moved back to the door, smiling apologetically, and closed it firmly.

Just a few hours earlier she had been ready to fall in front of him and apologize for everything that had gone wrong between them years ago, ready to even consider that they could be friends after years of not speaking to one another. She still was, but at just that moment, she hated him. They waited outside of the room for almost two hours, during which time almost no words were spoken.

They were both thinking about their daughter. Wondering what had happened to her and just what the lasting effects of her traumas would be. If they'd known the answers, their tears would have started much, much earlier. And while they waited, Jack Michaels listened to everything Terri Halloway had to tell him, his stomach filling with a cold, angry frost at the thought that he ever could have trusted Terry Palance to tell him the truth.

III

The day was over, and Terry Palance was lying in his bed when he heard the doorbell below. He'd heard about his girlfriend's retrieval from the woods, but the news did little to comfort him. All he could think about was the desperate sound of her voice when she called him on the phone, the torment and torture in her every word as she accused him—and rightly so—of abandoning her to a dark fate.

But she'd said things on the phone—"*Terry...he took my eyes with him when he was done with me...*"—that made him almost certain she had to be ruined for life, blinded and crippled at the very least, and that wasn't the case. Just how angry was she to put him through that sort of torment? Pretty pissed off, that was how mad. He'd apologized on the phone, but there was no way that was nearly enough. So, even though he had enough common sense to know that any chance of a long relationship was over, he still had to go see her tomorrow. *Flowers and chocolate at least, maybe even a stuffed animal.* He was still doing the mental calculations on how much all of it was going to cost him—money was tight, but he'd manage—when his mom walked into his room, her eyes teary and on the verge of a full-scale crying fit.

"Mom?" He rose fast. His mother didn't cry. She just didn't, unless it was something really, really serious. "Mom, are you okay?"

Frannie Palance looked at her son with eyes that were a thousand years older than they should have been. "Constable Michaels is here to see you, Terry."

Terry felt a flash of dread that was compounded by his mother when she lifted a small plastic grocery bag full of toiletries. Behind her, he could see Jack Michaels's face set in grim lines. His face looked wrong that way, like seeing the Mona Lisa with a scowl.

"What's up? Is this about Terri? Is she okay?" His mind wanted to go in all sorts of directions at once, and because he couldn't figure out what to do about that, he let it just sort of sit there in idle. Not that he exactly had a choice.

Michaels moved past Frannie Palance, and Terri saw her face warring with itself between grief, anger, and disgust. Before the constable could speak, his mother answered his question for him. She sounded almost cold when she finally managed to look him in the eyes again. "You're going down to the station to answer some questions, Terry. And if Jack isn't happy with your answers, you're going to be staying in the jail for a few days. I packed your toothbrush and some other things…"

His mother looked away from him, her face collapsing into tears. "Mom? What's this all about?"

"Stand up, Terry. It's time to go." Jack Michaels spoke with almost no inflection in his voice. He sounded like a robot from a bad fifties drive-in flick.

"What the hell are you talking about, Officer Jack?"

"We'll discuss that down at the station, Terry. Not here. Not now."

Terry felt the man's hand on his shoulder, felt the tension in the muscles of that hand, and then felt a wave of panic start in his stomach and blossom through the rest of his body. He yanked his shoulder free from the loose grip and was moving before he knew he was going to do anything at all.

"Terry! Get back here!" Michaels's voice was one of authority. Never in his life had Terry ever considered disobeying that voice, because he knew where it counted that it was wrong to do so. But right then, at that moment, he couldn't have cared less. Terry pushed past his mother, ignoring the shocked look on her face, and ran for all he was worth toward the stairwell. He took the steps in leaping bounds that should have caused him to fall and break his neck, never thinking of the risk involved. He pivoted on his left foot at the bottom of the stairs and was heading toward the foyer without a moment's hesitation. He opened the front door and was out into the humid night before conscious, rational thought had a chance to make him stop and think. Whatever the hell was going on, he had no intention of answering questions and then spending time in a jail cell. He hadn't done anything to Terri, not ANYTHING.

He managed around fifteen steps out past the threshold before the tree trunk reached out and stiff-armed him. Terry Palance hit Victor Barnes's outstretched forearm and might as well have run straight into a brick wall. His chest stopped moving, and the rest of his body kept going for as long as it took for his feet to leave the ground and then fly out almost level to the lawn and concrete. Terry had just enough time to scream in surprise before he dropped onto the ground on his back.

He hadn't even managed to catch his breath before Barnes had him flipped over with his face in the grass and his arms yanked behind his back. The handcuffs locked in around the same time Terry had his first rational thought since his mom had opened his door.

Should have just gone along peacefully. Should have just answered the questions and then gone home. Now what the hell have I gotten myself into?

He found out all too soon.

IV

Stan Long and Dave Pageant sat on the hill behind Stan's house and looked at the drive-in screen in the distance. It was daytime, and there were no movies to watch, but it was something to look at just the same. Both of them had seen many, many things on that screen, including great quantities of artificial blood and more naked breasts than they would ever be able to forget. The odds were good that if their parents ever paid attention to what they could see from the top of the hill, they'd have been banned from even sitting up there ever again. They'd been up there for almost two hours, slowly roasting in the sunlight and relaxing, just enjoying each other's company. And then Stan looked at Dave and finally asked him the question that had been on his mind.

"Dave," he said, his voice trying to be more casual than he felt. "Do you believe in ghosts?"

Dave looked back, squinting against the sunlight, and smiled that easy grin of his. "Sure, doesn't everyone?"

"I'm serious..." Stan didn't want to argue, but he needed to make his point clear.

"So am I."

"You are?" Stan looked over at Dave dubiously, not sure where the zinger would come from, but more than half expecting one anyway.

"Stan, what the hell do you think we saw at Havenwood? Swamp gas?"

"I hadn't thought about it..." A lie; it was almost all he thought about.

"If I can see it, touch it, hear it, smell it, or taste it, it's real. And even more of a guarantee if *you* had the same experience."

Stan nodded, his fingers pulling nervously at the grass between his legs.

Dave looked over at him, studying his actions as intently as he would study his hand of cards if he were in a high-stakes poker game in Vegas. He always studied everything around him. Sometimes it annoyed Stan, but not today. "So what's up, Stan? You seeing ghosts?"

"I dunno. I think so, maybe, but not when I'm awake."

"So maybe they're just dreams?"

"No... Not when I'm sleeping, either. When I'm having seizures..."

Dave frowned, his eyes getting worried instantly. "I thought you were over those..."

"I am. Mostly." It was a lie, but only a small one. "I just see them now and then."

"What do they look like?"

"Shadows, moving away from a bright light and moving like they're angry."

"Then how can you be sure they're ghosts? Do you recognize any of them?"

"No, not exactly..."

"Maybe you're seeing something other than ghosts. If you don't recognize them, they don't have to be ghosts."

"No...I can feel it. Does that make any sense?"

"Feel it how?"

Stan sighed, frustrated at his inability to convey what he wanted to. "I just know that they're ghosts, and that they're coming here from somewhere else. And I don't think they're really in a good mood or anything. I think they're pissed off."

"Okay, so you can sense they're ghosts, but how do you know they're angry?"

"Same way, I can feel it. And they're saying something, but they're still far away when I see them, and they sound like they're whispering or like they're halfway across a football field." He shrugged, pulling a handful of grass from the ground and looking at the torn ends. "If I could hear what they were saying, maybe I'd know what they wanted."

"So, next time you see them, listen real carefully."

"I've been trying to, I have…"

"What does it sound like they're saying?"

"'Every solace green.'"

"Hunh?"

"'Every solace green.'"

"You're right; that makes no sense." Dave looked away for a minute, his eyes searching the town in the distance, the drive-in screen, everything. "So what do you think it means?"

"What, the things I think I see, or the things I think I hear?"

"Yes. Both of them."

"That I got my brain more hurt than I thought, maybe. Like Denny Johnson after he got hit by that car when we were kids."

Four years earlier, Denny Johnson had been one of the gang, a funny kid with a great smile and more energy then the Energizer Bunny on crack cocaine. Then he zigged when he should have zagged during a game of kickball, and moved in front of a car. Both of them had watched along with a dozen other kids as Denny's body sailed through the air—the sound of screeching tires making a counterpoint to their screams—and hit the ground headfirst. He was in a coma for almost a week, but eventually he came back to school. The problem was, the person who came back was a stranger. He had all of Denny's memories, and he looked like Denny, but he didn't act at all like their friend had before. He was as different as Mr. Hyde was from Dr. Jekyll, and in just as negative a way. Denny became an absolute tenor around the recess field and after school. By the time his family moved a few months later, everyone was glad to see him go.

Dave snorted. "Tell you what, you start turning into the class bully, and I'll kick your ass for you. Until then, you get to remain unkicked."

"Yeah, like you'd even get a chance."

"I could take you with one shot." Dave grinned, flexing biceps that really were ridiculously well developed for a twelve-year-old.

"Yeah, and then you could get up and try again."

Dave reached out as fast as a striking cobra and wrapped an arm around Stan's neck. Half a second later, the two of them were rolling down the side of the hill in a wrestling match. And if Dave held back a bit, it wasn't very much. For the first time since his accident, Stan felt like a human being again instead of like a china doll everyone was afraid to touch for fear it would shatter. It was a wonderful feeling.

V

Jack Michaels spent most of the day grilling Terry Palance about exactly and precisely how and why and where he claimed he'd abandoned Terri Halloway. The answers he got didn't jibe with what the young girl told him, and that was bad for her ex-boyfriend.

Terri Halloway showed signs of being badly beaten and possibly raped. And she claimed he was the responsible party. She claimed he'd strangled her, and she'd played possum as he dragged her through the woods and dumped her body. She claimed he'd left her for dead.

And, unfortunately for him, he couldn't prove that she was lying. Life was not looking up for Terry Palance, and it wasn't looking all that special for Jack, either. He liked Terry Palance. He liked Frannie Palance, too, but neither of these facts could stop him from doing what he had to do.

And he just knew Frannie would never forgive him. She would act like nothing had changed, she would pretend that they were still friends, but he knew better. It was going to get very ugly very fast on the old home front. It wasn't that he and Frannie were intimate or had ever really considered the idea. It was more that Frannie was always there when he needed someone to talk to, and was just plain always there.

And now she wouldn't be, and that hurt.

To make matters worse, there was now another missing person being reported, and he doubted very seriously that it would turn out to be a case of someone just forgetting to call home. The missing person in this case was Arnold Holiday, and even on his worst day the man wouldn't leave his equipment and truck behind. Arnie was as dependable as they came, even if he did like to talk a bit too much about what didn't concern him. That Arnie had vanished was not a comforting thought. Just as he was finishing with one case of a person gone missing, he got saddled with another, and he just didn't need it. Not now.

The last few days had left his stomach twisted into ugly knots anyway, and he just wanted to take it easy for a change of pace. Things weren't supposed to get anywhere near hectic in Serenity, and when they did, he felt like screaming. There were already too many new faces in town, too many people he didn't know and couldn't make snap decisions on. One of the things he'd always liked about working as a constable was the easygoing relationship he managed with the people around him. A few new faces, sure, not a problem, but the only thing that could have had more people cruising into the area was someone striking it rich with a gold mining operation.

As was his daily routine, Jack hopped into his cruiser and went looking for trouble. He hoped not to run across any, but it was part and parcel of the job. Most of the time he got his wish, but just lately he'd had very little luck along those lines. So why should today be an exception?

He'd made it halfway through the subdivisions around Serenity when the call came in about Elway Deveraux's place. Seemed there'd been an incident out that way, according to Tom Norris, though whoever it was that called it in was too frantic to give any solid descriptions.

Jack called back that he'd take the scene and headed out to the area where Elway lived. It wasn't really a part of Serenity Falls proper, but it was connected and close enough. The Melmouth County Sheriff's Department was supposed to handle the calls out of the town proper, according to the way everything was supposed to work, but the closest outpost for the sheriff and his people was almost thirty miles away. Why put the sheriff's department through the extra effort when he was out on the road anyway? Besides, it never hurt to have the county boys owing him a few favors.

The trip wasn't a long one, but as he drove, a strong sense of unease started growing in Jack's stomach. He kept thinking about the hounds out on the property and wondering what the hell could possibly happen when all of them were there to protect Elway. Lord above knew the man was harmless enough and certainly not well off enough to justify anyone wanting to rob him. That didn't leave too many options for what could have happened, except a fire or something worse. He was still considering calling for more details when he pulled onto the property where Deveraux had his breeding farm.

The land was perfect for farming: rich, fertile ground and plenty of water from the creek that ran at the edge of the property. Elway Deveraux was not a farmer, however, and the fields were wasted on nothing more than weeds and grass. More than a few people in the area would have paid top dollar for the land and for the farming equipment that mostly went to seed sitting in a barn that hadn't been used in almost ten years. Jack had long since given up on the man ever doing anything more than raising his hounds. He knew better. Deveraux was happy, and in the long run that was all that mattered to the man.

One look around, and he made the call. He wasn't sure what was wrong, but he knew immediately what wasn't right. There were no dogs barking at his approach, none of the hounds moving alongside his car and baying for attention. Elway's dogs were universally friendly and always glad to see visitors. They were hell if someone was being stupid, as a few of the locals had learned way back when—like when those insanely dense brothers, Andy and Perry Hamilton, tried sneaking onto the property under the misguided belief that Elway had a lucrative business growing marijuana. About fifteen minutes after they'd managed to cross over the fences meant to keep the animals locked up and to keep strangers out, Elway had let the hounds out of their kennels. He'd heard noises and felt it best to be careful. The two boys damn near had their asses chewed off by the dogs before Elway got there and called his hounds off of them. It happened now and then, and when it did, the town got a reminder that Elway Deveraux's hounds could be mean when they needed to. What everyone in town had learned as a result of these little incidents was that the hounds were not exactly stealthy. They tended to bark a warning—or, arguably a greeting—to everyone who came within earshot.

Jack parked his car on the visitor's side of the lengthy chain-link fence and honked the horn a few times. He thought he might have heard the dogs off in the distance, but nothing beyond that. After waiting patiently and trying the horn again, he opened the gate and let himself in. Elway's truck was right where it belonged, and that just might mean that the man needed help.

Walking toward the farmhouse—a two-story affair that needed a family to be complete, and Elway the perpetual bachelor—he looked over the lay of the land and tried to figure out where the hell the man might have gotten off to.

"Elway!" He called out with hands cupped to his mouth. The property pretty much demanded nothing less than a bullhorn, but he would make do. "Elway? Where are you?" When no answer came, he headed toward the house, wondering idly how long it would take the ambulance to arrive. He'd just made it to the front of the house when he heard the sound of growling.

And as soon as he heard the deep, rumbling sound of a dog stating its displeasure, the world seemed to slip into slow motion. His eyes caught the open doorway, the shape of a hand lying on the ground, the red stain of fresh blood on the fingers—*And where the hell is his pinky finger? I know he had one just the other day*—and his ears heard the faint sound of something wet being chewed and torn, a sound that came from near the hand just seen at the edge of the doorway.

And then he turned and saw them.

Elway Deveraux raised bloodhounds, and at that moment, the name seemed painfully appropriate. Jack had never bothered counting the actual number of dogs on the property, but at a guess, it was something over twenty of the beasts that were coming his way from the other side of the barn. Even at a distance he could see the red on the muzzles and the gleam of wickedly sharp teeth flashing from within all of that red. But aside from the unbridled rage he saw on the dogs that had always seemed as laid back as any animal he'd ever known, something else was wrong. They weren't the right size. The dogs looked more like ponies in perspective to the barn, and he had never seen any hound get anywhere near that big.

Michaels looked to the gate he'd walked in from, then he looked to the dogs heading his way, and prayed very hard for a miracle. There was no way in hell he'd manage to get back to the car before they were all over him. He started running anyway, and he pulled his pistol from its holster as he moved. "Oh God…oh God…oh God!" He pumped his legs as hard as he ever had, moving with the grace and speed of an Olympic athlete and pulling muscles he'd long since forgotten were a part of his body. He'd pay the price for the blessing of adrenaline later.

Assuming there was a later. He felt the hot, rancid breath of the animals on his heels, and he risked the time it took to turn around and fire at the one closest. The damned thing was only a little over a foot away from him and looked determined to tear his ass clean off his hips. He pulled the trigger when it was doing its best to take the lead in their little race and felt the pistol kick hard against his wrist. The bullet punched a small hole in the muzzle of the hound and then kicked a big damned hole somewhere in its side. Jack kept going forward, the dog veered sharply to the right. Sadly, the rest of the massive pack following behind the brute just kept coming right at him, excepting only the two that fell when they ran into the ex-leader of the pack.

All in all, Jack Michaels figured he was screwed.

He headed toward the home stretch, ready to make a serious run for the fence and try to climb over it if he couldn't reach the gate. Behind him he heard the sounds of growls and scrabbling paws hitting the grass. Mostly though, he heard the thundering of his own heart and a whimpering noise he knew was coming from his own throat.

And then the sweetest sight he'd ever seen came into view as he looked past the chain links and over to where his squad car waited. Victor Barnes and Bob Steinman looked toward him and past him, and aimed their shotguns with the greatest care. And Jack Michaels threw himself the last few feet toward the fence and started climbing like his life depended on it, which, of course, it did.

He scrambled madly to get a grip on the fence, which bucked and shuddered under the impact of his weight. Just out of the corner of his eye he saw Barnes pull the trigger on the gun and heard the explosive

BOOM of a twelve-gauge going off only inches away from him. He heard it again as Bob Steinman fired away. Both of them managed about four more shots each with the pump-action weapons before he was over the top of the fence and hitting the gravel on the other side.

Jack slid himself across the ground in a belly crawl, barely conscious of the pistol in his hand, and gasped in an effort to regain his breath. He heard a few more explosions and the sound of a wounded animal screaming in agony—it was a sound he wouldn't forget anytime soon; it sounded far too human for his comfort.

And then he very simply started heaving. His stomach decided it was just about time to remove all that annoying food he'd eaten earlier, whether he liked the idea or not. He'd never been that scared in his life and prayed never to get anywhere near that scared again. He was still coughing harshly, trying to lose the nasty flavor left over after hawking up his last meal, when Victor Barnes put a paw on his shoulder and slowly helped him up.

"Hey, Jack, you all right?"

"Fuck NO, I'm not all right," he screamed, surprised in a distant way that he had the energy left. "I just about got eaten by a goddamn pack of dogs ! How the hell am I supposed to be all right with that?"

Bob Steinman looked at him as if he'd lost his mind, and then looked back into the field. Victor Barnes, on the other hand, looked at him with a strange half smile on his face and replied, "Yeah, but aside from that, how's your day going?"

Jack stared hard at the man for a few seconds and then started chuckling. He knew it wasn't laughter from a great joke, more likely a small hysterical fit, but it felt good just the same.

Victor laughed as well, and Steinman shook his head and managed a small grin before getting serious. "Jack? Did you find Elway in there?"

"Yeah, I did. At least I think so, I didn't really have a chance to get a good look."

"Dead?"

"I'd have to say so." He thought about the hand he saw and the sounds of something wet being torn, and shuddered.

Barnes walked up to the fence, looking at the unmoving forms of the dogs he'd fired on and killed. His expression said he wasn't thrilled about having to kill them, and Jack was grateful for that. Any man who liked killing animals—except maybe for the occasional deer on a hunt—wasn't a man he wanted to know. He watched the expression on the man's face shift from regret to puzzlement to a blend of curiosity and fear. Barnes shook his head slowly. "Guys? Is it me, or are those dogs getting smaller?"

Both Jack and the other constable walked over to where the giant stood looking through the fence and studied the remains of the animals. For all the world it looked as if someone had punched a small hole in a balloon shaped like a dog, and as they stared, the bloodhound...deflated. In less than thirty seconds, the animal was back to the size it was supposed to be, though not a one of them could say how it had happened.

Jack Michaels looked over at the other animals and saw that they, too, had shrunk. He had to fight off a serious case of hysterical giggles by biting the inside of his mouth. It just wasn't supposed happen, but there it was.

The three men stood in silence for several moments, and the only sound they heard was the wind rustling lightly across the edge of the house and barn in the distance. Finally Bob Steinman cleared his throat and looked at Jack. "Reckon we ought to call for backup before we go in there?"

"No. We got guns, and they die well enough."

They loaded themselves up with every firearm they had and passed through the gate. Jack ignored his body's endless demands for the bathroom, preferring not to try his luck against the side of the barn. It would be damned hard to fire his shotgun if he had his pants around his ankles. Aside from the dogs they'd killed and the body of Elway Deveraux, there was nothing to find. The dogs had escaped through a hole in the back of the fence. The hole looked freshly chewed into the wire that made the chain links.

It took the rest of the day for them to figure out even the beginnings of what had happened. None of what they found was pretty.

VI

While Carl Bradford was considering just what he would do if he found out his wife was cheating on him—almost a certainty in his eyes, but only almost—Mike Blake was working in the master bedroom of a woman who looked enough like his deceased spouse that the similarities still unsettled him. He was putting the trim on the door he had opened into a room filled with oddities that left him slightly boggled when he considered the contents.

And even as he worked on putting in the framework for the door, Amelia Dunlow was sorting through the collections she'd found when he tore through the wall. She sat on a musty old chair in a musty old room and held each of the carved figures in her hands as if they were the finest of treasures.

He had to admit that they were unusual, but hardly what he'd call treasures. He looked over at the woman for a moment, admiring her beauty and the simple smile that played on her features as she held up another of the wooden figurines.

Each was unique. Every one of the carved images was as detailed as anything he'd ever seen put into wood, with clothes that draped realistically and were so well painted that he half expected they could be removed from the dolls when he first saw them. Each was almost a perfect model of a real person, though he couldn't say that any of them had resembled anyone he knew very closely. But the eyes were all colored to closely mimic real eyes, with the blendings of color that one expected to see when looking into a living, breathing person's face. Some had receding hairlines, some had moles, a few had the sunken faces of elderly folks with too few teeth and their dentures removed for the night. Some wore jewelry, and others did not.

But what struck him the most about the figures Amelia Dunlow was looking over was the careful attention to physical scale. The largest of the wooden carvings wasn't but seven or eight inches in height, and the smallest, a baby barely able to crawl, was just over half an inch. He'd held the baby for several minutes the day before, looking at the craftsmanship with a sort of numb awe. Despite its amazingly small size, the creator of the work had given it minuscule fingernails and carved the seams of the baby jumper it wore into the piece. Mike couldn't imagine how steady the hand making the figures would have been, but he doubted most surgeons had that level of control.

He looked from the figure Amelia—*That's Ms. Dunlow, Mike, and don't you dare forget it*—held in her hands and back up to the woman herself. A few seconds later he remembered how to breathe and made himself concentrate on the work ahead of him.

It took a massive effort to start tapping the nails into the wooden trim and manage not to smash his fingers with the hammer at the same time. He almost managed anyway when he felt the long, delicate hand of his employer on his shoulder.

"Mike," she said, her voice enthusiastic and almost brimming over with excitement. "I think I've got a notion about these things."

Mike Blake turned and looked into Amelia Dunlow's eyes and smiled awkwardly. "What might that be, ma'am?"

She chuckled—not a giggle or even a laugh, a chuckle, and he found that disturbingly sexy—"You don't have to call me 'ma'am,' Mike. You can call me Amelia or Amy." Her smile made her whole face bright and beautiful and so very, very hauntingly like his own Amy's that he wanted to cry or kiss her. Instead, he nodded his head.

"All right then, what might that be, Amelia?" He forced a smile onto his face that matched hers...truth be told, it didn't take a lot of effort. As much as he didn't want to like her, Amelia Dunlow was very likable.

"That's better. Geez, between you and Steve Ferrier I can't decide which one worries about being formal more."

He nodded his head. "Sorry about that, but my dad always told me to be polite to your employers."

She frowned at that, a little playful pout. "Employer? Well, I suppose I am, but that doesn't mean we can't be friends, does it?" He looked at her face, studied the features there, and felt himself flush with warmth.

"Well, I don't know if that's such a good idea..."

She pulled back, her pretty features moving into an expression of surprise. And then into one of what looked like genuine disappointment. He spoke quickly to take the sting from his words. "It isn't that I don't want to be your friend, Amelia. I mean that." He reached out and put his hands on her shoulders very lightly, as if she might break, or as if the contact might burn him. "What I mean is... You look enough like my Amy to make me feel confused. I've had about seven times already where I almost called you by one of my pet names for her." He stepped back, trying to read her face without much success. "I don't want to make an ass of myself around you, and I'm almost certain I will." He held his arms out at his sides, lost for what to say to complete his thoughts.

And Amelia Dunlow looked at him for a few seconds in utter silence before nodding her head. "I'm sorry, Mike. I wasn't thinking." Those were about the last words he'd expected. Like as not he'd figured on getting himself fired or at least chewed up one side and down the other. She shook her head sadly. "See? I always do this. Constable Michaels even told me you about your wife, and it didn't sink in. I...I didn't mean to be such a pest. It's just, you and I were the ones who found this." She gestured at the room that had once been hidden, at the dolls and the rows of shelves to hold them. "And I thought it meant something, like it was our secret place...like when I was a kid and found something neat with someone else, it was special to both of us."

She blushed, obviously very embarrassed by what came across as a childhood recollection.

And quite unexpectedly, Mike felt for her in that moment. Two years' worth of drunken embarrassment had done a lot to make him feel for people in awkward situations. His hand went up and touched her face—so very like his Amy's, enough that it was frightening—and he smiled softly. "I kind of like the idea of you and me having a special place and a secret or two, Amelia. Don't misunderstand me. I just wanted you to know that I could fall for you fast and hard, and maybe give you a warning to knock some sense into me if I start being stupid, okay?"

She smiled softly, her eyes wide and warm and wonderful, and she moved her face and kissed the palm of his hand briefly. "I'll let you know if you cross any boundaries, Mike. But you have to do the same, okay?"

He nodded very solemnly and held up his little finger on his right hand. He kissed the tip and held it out for her. "I'll even pinky swear to it."

Amelia laughed hard at that one. "Oh my GAWD, I thought I was the only one that ever did that!"

"Just don't spread it around. I already have enough people in town who want to see if they can take me in a one-on-one..."

"Seriously? Why?"

"Because I don't fight, and I've certainly made a few comments over the last two years."

"Well, it's lunchtime. Why don't I treat you to a burger, and you can tell me all about it."

"I only have half an hour for lunch..."

"Mike, I'm your boss. I'll tell myself not to fire you."

"I'm not sure of the logic there, but what the hell." He shrugged. "I figure if I don't eat something soon, I'll shrivel up and die anyway."

And from there, Mike Blake's day just got stranger and stranger.

VII

April Long left school at the usual time, right around five thirty in the afternoon when cheerleading practice was finished, walking toward her house and her family and the problems she kept bottled inside. In addition to worrying about Stan—he was a weenie, true, but he was still her brother, and she still worried about him—she had the big *D* to worry about. It was obvious enough her parents were headed for a divorce. The only question was how much longer until it came to be a reality. Stan getting sick was the only thing holding them together as a couple anymore, and even that was already wearing thin.

Sometime in the last year or so, her folks had gone from being almost embarrassingly in love with each other to barely able to stay in the same room for more than a few minutes. Something had happened, and she truly wished she knew what it might be. Her world just kept going in screwy circles, and she couldn't seem to get it to stop.

A car pulled up beside her as she walked, oozing slowly in order to keep pace. She didn't have to look to know who it was. Jerry Cahill was still trying to win her back after he'd dumped her on the side of the road. Through the open passenger's side window of his father's Thunderbird, she heard the radio playing more of the hip-hop he insisted on listening to, as if he could somehow connect with it. She figured he was maybe able to connect with his hand on a deeply spiritual level, but not much beyond that.

"April? Hey, April… You need a lift?"

She rolled her eyes and shook her head. "Fool me once, shame on you. Fool me twice, shame on me. No thank you, Jerry."

"Come on, you're not still mad about that, are you?" The frightening thing was, he was serious. He honestly couldn't understand how she could be angry about being dumped on the side of the road after dark.

"You're kidding, right? After what happened to Terri you can even ask me that?"

"Oh, hey, I didn't have anything to do with Terri, and you know it." He managed to sound defensive and wounded at the same time. April turned and looked at him, her eyebrows knitted together.

"You think I didn't hear about the bet you and that pig Terry Palance had going? You think no one in the school is gonna tell me when you're pulling shit like that, Jerry?"

"What are you talking about?"

"I'm talking about you had a bet with Terry that you could fuck me before he could fuck Terri. What was it? Fifty dollars? A hundred?" Jerry looked away, his face flushing red, and she sneered as her anger rose to the surface. "What makes you think for one second that I'd ever want anything to do with you again?"

"It wasn't like that, April…"

"Then you tell me how it was!" She threw her books down, not caring that her notes from biology were scattering everywhere. Despite her resolve to never let him see her show any small sign of weakness, April felt her eyes start to sting as the tear ducts prepared to rebel against her wishes. "You tell me how it was, Jerry Cahill! Go on, make me see the light!"

"It wasn't a bet, April! We were joking around, and somebody overheard or told you wrong. We were just joshing, guy stuff, y'know?"

"No! I don't know! All I know is you dumped me in the middle of *nowhere* and left me to walk three miles back to my house!"

"I came back, but you were already gone…"

She laughed then, a short, bitter bark of a laugh that didn't sound at all like her own voice. "When? Around three the next afternoon? I waited there for almost an hour before I started walking, Jerry. I waited. You didn't show."

"I was stupid, I know that." His voice was soft, and she could almost believe him, but she'd fallen for his type before and didn't really want to make the same mistake a second time with the same guy.

"Yeah, you were. And now we have nothing to say to each other."

"April, don't be this way."

"Be what way? Smart enough not to trust you anymore?"

"Look, I made a mistake. Can't you forgive me one lousy mistake?"

"No, *you* look. Look at Terri, and what one lousy mistake did to her. How could I ever trust you not to pull that same sort of thing again, Jerry?"

"I wouldn't, I promise."

"Too late." She shook her head sadly. "I thought you were a nice guy, Jerry Cahill. I was wrong."

April turned her back to him and angrily gathered up her papers and books. He watched her in silence, but she could feel his eyes boring into her, and she hated him for even daring to look at her.

He was still sitting in the same spot in his father's car when she started walking again. He stayed there until she was almost a block away and then he gunned his engine and roared off down the street.

April Long got home only a few minutes later. She said a cheerful hello to her mother, made small talk, and then, feigning an exhaustion she only just barely felt in reality, went up to her room. Once there, she quietly broke into tears and cried herself to sleep. In her dreams, she was loved.

VIII

The day had long since faded to night. The sun had set on the workweek, and Mike continued looking at Amelia Dunlow, uncertain as to why she was wasting time with him instead of doing whatever it was very attractive women did these days.

Across the table from him, the very woman he was pondering was slurping at her chocolate milkshake and smiling in his direction. He had absolutely no idea how to handle it. So he did what came naturally and just smiled back.

"So, you were the assistant manager at the bank?"

"Yeah." Mike shrugged. "It didn't work out."

Amelia smiled at him. Her eyes were dark and amused. "What did you do? Try to embezzle all of the funds?"

Mike looked away, shook his head, and sipped at his own milkshake. "No. I just couldn't pull myself together very well after Amy died."

Amelia Dunlow groaned and looked down at the remains of her French fries, and hamburger. Except for getting up to go to the bathroom, neither she nor Mike had left the booth at Frannie's Donut Hut since they'd sat down just after one in the afternoon. This was their second meal, and it had been as good as the first. But if she ate another bite, she just knew she'd rupture.

"I'm sorry. I put my foot in it again, didn't I?"

"Oh, hey, no." Mike reached out and touched her hand softly, smiling at her. "No, not at all. It's been over two years now, and I've never really spoken to anyone about all of this. You haven't done anything wrong. It's just I always feel weird bringing up what happened. It's not exactly considered good dinner conversation."

"Well, I just don't like that I'm dragging up bad feelings for you, Mike."

"You're not. There's nothing to drag up. It's something I deal with every day."

"I can't imagine how you manage it."

"Well, for the last two years it was sort of easy. You drink enough, and you don't have to think about it. But I'm not gonna do that anymore. I made up my mind about it."

"So how do you deal with it now?" Her voice was soft, and Mike looked into her eyes and shook his head slowly.

"One day at a time, I guess. And by keeping myself so busy I can't dwell on it for too long. The pain is still there, but it's not overwhelming when I work."

"So, you're good with numbers?"

"You sort of have to be if you work for a bank. They might forgive a few screwups, but not when it comes to big money."

Amelia took a bite of her burger and chewed thoughtfully while she looked at him. When she had finished, she paused to wash her mouth out with Pepsi and nodded her head. "So why are you working construction?"

"Not a whole lot of jobs for bankers in town."

"Well, what about accountants?"

"Same problem. Serenity isn't exactly a booming town, give or take your arrival, and there aren't many openings. If there were, they'd choose someone with a reasonably valid track record."

"You have a valid track record. You were the assistant manager of a bank."

Mike smiled tolerantly. "I was also the town drunk. Tends to counter the possible good points from being an assistant manager."

"Nonsense."

"No, Amelia. Not nonsense. I was the local lush almost as long as I was in management at the bank. Hell, most of the people in town do a double take when they see me, because they're seeing me sober for the first time in two years or more."

"Well, I must be biased. I don't see you that way."

"You missed my performance by a few days."

Amelia looked him up and down, her face almost impassive, but a small smile playing at her lips. Finally she set down her burger and looked him in the eyes. "Okay, here's the deal. I need someone I can depend on to help me run things around here. I want you."

Mike looked back at her, his face impassive. "Why?"

"What do you mean, 'Why?'"

"Just what I said. There are a lot more capable people out there, and they don't have a record for drinking too much."

"Fair enough." She set her burger back on her plate and wiped her hands on her napkin. "How about because I think everyone deserves a second chance?"

"It's very nice, and it's even flattering, but you have a business to run..."

"Yes, I do. And I take that job very seriously, and I wouldn't even consider offering you the job if I didn't think you could handle it. But,

Mike, I've watched you. You're meticulous, you're motivated, and you're intelligent. In addition to that, you're likable, all of which is very important in someone I'd be working with almost daily."

"We've also discussed the potential pitfalls of that situation..." Mike's face flared red. He wasn't used to being anywhere near this direct with anyone, and it made him feel more than a touch awkward.

"Yes, we have." She reached out her hand and touched his lightly. There was nothing to be read into the gesture, it was merely human contact. "And I believe we came to an understanding about that. Mike, I'm young, and I do things my way. That's one of the arrangements my father and I came to when I decided to take this job. But one of the side effects of being young is that I tend to be frowned upon by a lot of people who would never consider frowning at my father. And that little condescending attitude only gets worse when you consider that I'm a woman. It might be a changing world, but a lot of the people I'd consider for the job would never be able to take me seriously as a boss, especially since I'm very hands-on in my approach to business."

Mike opened his mouth to speak, and she silenced him with a gesture.

"Now, in addition to that, I'm new in town, and I want someone local who can tell me what pitfalls to avoid. You are local. That's a plus in your favor. The fact that you and I just spent five hours talking and you never once made a lewd comment or tried to look down my blouse also works in your favor. But mostly, I think I can trust you to get the work done, and that's important to me. Because from time to time I'll be called away, and I want someone who will actually *do* things when I'm gone."

Mike shook his head with a very slight grin of his own. "Thought it all out, did you?"

"Yes, I did. If you want the job, it's yours, barring any objections I have after talking to the bank manager. Waters is it?" Mike nodded. "Unless he tells me a very different story than you just did, I can't see that you've done anything that can't be overlooked."

"But I thought you already had an assistant."

"Who? Steve? No, he's my father's assistant. Not mine."

"Well then, I guess we can work something out."

Amelia smiled and did that little trick where the day seemed brighter and his heart ached for his Amy again. "Good. We can discuss the details over breakfast tomorrow."

"Okay. Did you want to meet at the house or over here?"

Her expression was one that he knew he was misreading. It was an expression that said he could decide that for himself, depending on what happened next. "That depends on you, Mike."

Mike swallowed hard. "How so?"

"Well, a big part of the answer depends on where you are sleeping tonight, and whether or not you're sleeping alone."

Mike couldn't remember the last time he'd been that unsettled by a simple sentence.

Chapter Eight

I

Victor Barnes made his rounds through the small town, pleased with the way everything was going. The job was nice and respectable, two things his mother had sworn he would never be. And yet, here he was, making the most of an opportunity he almost let go past him. If he hadn't decided on a whim to check out the constable's headquarters, he would likely never have known what the town was like, and he certainly wouldn't have stayed around.

He was glad he did. He liked Serenity. Except for the dog problem that had popped up during the day, it was a nice place to be. Oh, Jack Michaels was a little worried about the way things were shaping up, but Vic liked the sudden influx of people. The growth spurt could only do good in the long run, and it wasn't like a massive flood of people coming into the area—he'd been in Atlanta back in '95 after they'd announced the Olympic Games coming into the area; *that* had been a flood, and it was still going on, more people moving into the area all the time and a crime rate that was nightmarish—it was more like a trickle. Trickles could be contained if you handled the matter properly, and he had no doubt Jack would manage it. Jack just worried too much.

He pulled up in front of the Quik-Mart and slid out of his car, which promptly groaned its relief as his weight left the suspension. Four other cars were there, despite the late hour. Inside, Tom Lassiter was moving faster than most would have thought possible, ringing orders and keeping his eyes on a group of teens who looked, frankly, like they were up to no good. The young man's face showed relief when he saw Vic.

One look around told Barnes why the kid looked so happy to see him. He didn't know their names, but he already knew their faces. They were high school age, and not a one of them was very threatening to him, but he suspected to someone like Tom Lassiter—short, round, and soft as a sponge cake—they would be. Lassiter probably wasn't more than a year out of school himself, and they were the sort who probably ate kids like him for lunch. As a whole, there were five of them, and they were looking at him from the corners of their eyes in the hopes that he would just go away. Naturally, he had no intention of doing anything of the sort.

Vic walked into the store and half expected to hear the theme music from *The Good, the Bad and the Ugly* as he entered. Tom Lassiter looked at him and jerked his head toward the kids, and he nodded in return, walking directly over to them. One of them hastily pulled something from his pocket—a candy bar by the looks of it—and put it back into the box where the rest of the same confection rested.

Vic nodded to the boy, a kid almost as flabby as Tom but with the worst case of carrot-red hair he'd ever seen. "That's all right. You just go ahead and pick that candy bar right back up, and then you walk over to the counter and pay for it."

The kid looked up at him, and up and up. His white skin turned even pastier. "I ain't got any money."

"Really?" Barnes arched one eyebrow and smiled slightly. "Why doesn't that surprise me?" He leaned down, one hand on the butt of his pistol—not in a threatening gesture, but simply because he didn't trust any of the five twerps—and bared his teeth in a wide grin. "And why are you even in this store? If you aren't buying anything, you have no reason to be here."

"I-it's a free country." The kid tried to look tough, but the two chins and the forest of freckles didn't help his halfhearted attempt.

Barnes shook his head, his eyes never leaving the eyes of his victim. "Nope. It's a free country within limits. There's a sign on the door that says No Loitering. Which is exactly what you're doing. Now get out of here, or I'll drag you out and you can discuss the law with your parents at the station."

The kid moved toward the door, angry, but unable to think of any other good arguments. Barnes crossed his massive arms and looked down at the rest of them. "Do any of you have money to spend?" Their silence was answer enough. "Fine. Get out of here and go home."

They filed out of the store, and the only one who looked like he might cause a problem—a dark-haired kid with eyes that were a very light green—only stopped long enough to glare at Lassiter on his way out the door. Barnes resisted the urge to plant his boot against the kid's ass and give a push. He wasn't working as a bouncer this time; he was working as actual law enforcement, and there was a difference.

He stood around for a few minutes, making sure the kids had gone on their way, though he doubted they were headed for their homes, and Tom said a silent thank-you as he rang through another couple of customers.

After paying for his coffee and grabbing up a Tasteeclair, he was on his way. He didn't see the six figures standing at the side of the building. Five of them he'd just dealt with, and the sixth spoke to them in a soft voice and made suggestions to them about how to handle the newest member of the town's constables. The man was immaculately dressed and well respected in town. Even if he had seen the group together, he'd have suspected nothing more than that the man was trying to explain why the kids shouldn't be out so late on a school night.

He would have been very wrong.

II

They looked at the man as if he'd lost his mind. But what could they do, except listen? Perry concentrated on each word, his face flushed oddly red with excitement.

"The thing is, boys, that he can only be so many places at once. All you have to do is break up and move to different parts of the store the next time he comes in. Oh, and carry at least a little cash, enough to pick up a candy bar or two. He can't kick you out if you're a paying customer taking your time."

Marco spoke up first. "Um, what do we do if he tells us to leave anyways?"

The man smiled warmly, his face almost hidden by the night. "Why, Marco, then you file a complaint against him with the office of the constables. He is a servant to the town, and that means he has to have a reason to give you grief." Much as the constable had done a few moments before to Butch, the man leaned forward. "If you are doing nothing wrong, he has no right to hassle you. That's called harassment, and it's not something the police of any city or state government take lightly. It's the sort of thing that can cause the government to lose money, especially if there was evidence that the constable had done something very stupid, like, for instance, hitting one of you."

Marco shook his head. "There is no way I'm letting that guy hit me. He's big as a house, dude."

"Indeed he is. Which is why any good lawyer would love to have a case where he did strike someone." The man shook his head and grinned. "Of course, if you had a bruise and several witnesses to agree that he'd hit you…why, I don't much suppose it would matter if he really was the culprit. It would be his word against you and four or so of your good friends."

Marco's eyes lit up, and the man nodded.

"I have to go, boys. Just something to consider the next time that ape is hassling you for no good reason."

They thanked him and watched him walk casually into the darkness. Perry shook his head. "He just doesn't seem the same as he used to."

Andy looked at his brother, shaking his greasy hair. "What? You're complaining about it?"

"No. Hell no, I'm just wondering what he's up to."

Marty leaned down. His gaunt frame was taller than anyone else in the group, but almost skeletal. Puberty had not finished fleshing him out, but none of them thought he'd get much taller than his current six and a half feet. "I don't fucking care, dude, as long as he's on our side."

They cracked up, laughing and chuckling to themselves. After a few moments, Marco sobered up. "Well, I guess we better give some thought to what he said, though. It sure would be nice to get that asshole off our backs."

Perry pulled the tin of mint candies case from his pocket and checked his supply of pot. "Let's deal with it later. Right now, I can think of something better to do."

All thoughts of retribution went up in smoke a few minutes later, after they'd found a nice dark place where they could get stoned in peace. It wasn't long before the group of them could do little more than giggle. Perry always got the best shit to smoke, even though sometimes it was laced with other things they probably didn't want to think about.

Marco squinted his eyes as he sucked in a big lungful of the heavy smoke, looking at the rest of his group with the same mixture of amusement and anger that seemed to mark his features. There'd been a time when he was not one of the gang. When he'd been the brunt of many of their pranks, but that time was long past. These days he was almost the leader of the group, though none of them could really have been said to be the true leader. Everything changed for the group around the same time that he kicked Andy's and Perry's asses for giving him trouble one time too many. It wasn't a case of him suddenly going off the deep end; he'd warned them each and every time they'd screwed with him that he was going to make them regret it. Then on a day like any other, he'd seen them coming, seen the looks on their faces, and instead of merely warning them off, had dropped his books at his feet and waited for them. True to form, the two brothers tried starting something with him. On that occasion, he let them start it and then he finished it with several vicious punches and a clear warning to keep away from him in the future. They kept their distance until all three wound up in detention for a week together, After that, they started hanging around. A big part of the reason for Marco was that Perry was generous with his dope.

"So what's up for the rest of the night, guys?" Marco looked at the rest of them and saw that they had no idea what was next. Hell, if he was lucky, he'd be able to get them to think about anything other than eating over the next two hours. Common sense told him to go to bed, it was a school night. Marco never listened much to his common sense.

Todd looked back at him and shook his head. "Shit, I dunno. Why don't we just get something to eat?"

Marco shook his head. "Not yet. I eat too soon, the high goes away."

They started debating what to do, with most of them leaning toward consuming food, and with an occasional suggestion to find a few willing women. The likelihood of the latter was, of course, comical. None of them had money, and despite their bravado, the only one of them who wasn't a virgin was Marco, who had the good sense to keep his mouth shut about who he'd lost his virginity to. If he told, she'd stop putting out, and he wasn't willing to risk that.

As they discussed what they'd like to do, if they could ever actually motivate themselves to do anything at all, the man who gave them advice an hour earlier made a slow circuit around them. He nodded to himself and smiled several times, moving without making a sound, as he was not actually touching the ground anywhere along the way. The light coat he wore barely moved, and the only sound that was truly within the human audible range was the sound of him whispering. The obscenities that came from his mouth would have seen him burned at the stake during the times of the witch hunts. In his case, the folk who would not suffer a witch to live would have been justified in their actions.

He took several deep breaths, drawing forth a bit of himself to fill the air before him. Though the air pulsed and glowed before his mouth, none of the boys noticed. Then he let the air out of his lungs in a *whoosh* and watched his essence move over the gang of youngsters in a pale, thin wave. They felt nothing, which was the way he wanted it. Some in the town were meant to suffer great pains; others, like the boys he worked his magic on, were merely meant to be pawns.

Five minutes later it was over. The group of friends rose from where they sat and blinked with exhaustion that hadn't been there before. They had a lot of work to do, and he wanted them rested for what he had planned.

When the group had gone on their way home, he moved slowly through the night, heading for the cemetery. There had been far too much fun for the people in Serenity. It was time to shake things up a bit. Time to let them know, once and for all, that something was wrong with their town.

III

Stan Long slept, and in his slumber he saw them again. The dark figures, shadows that moved in the night and whispered in unison about green solaces, whatever the hell they were. He didn't know, but the way they spoke of them gave him the shivers in his bed. On a deep level, he knew that if something didn't change soon, he was going to start suffering even more ill effects. There hadn't been a night since he'd half drowned himself in the quarry when he got a decent sleep without the benefit of tranquilizers, and even those didn't help with the nightmares. But those thoughts weren't very prevalent in his mind right then. The only thing he concerned himself with was the small army of silhouettes that kept creeping toward him.

No, not toward him, toward Serenity Falls, which he knew, in his dream, was somewhere behind him. He could barely make out the place where he was supposed to be in the dream. It looked familiar, but not in a way he could grasp. All he knew for certain was the town had a major-league problem coming closer. And there wasn't a damned thing he could do about it.

But then, what could he have done anyway? He was only twelve and not the wisest of children by any stretch of the imagination, at least as far as his own opinion went. That honor went to his best friend Dave, who seemed to be better at damned near everything than he was. Even in his dreams, he barely felt adequate when it came to Dave and often wondered why it was his best friend bothered with him.

He heard the whispered words of the small army coming toward him—a sound that, while unsettling, was almost familiar at this point—and then he heard silence. The lack of the words they whispered as they approached was almost more disconcerting than when they spoke, because the absence was a change and not really very welcome. It made him think that something new was being added to the equation, and that wasn't a very comforting notion.

Then they started speaking again, and this time their words were not a muttered oath said in unison, but a mass of different phrases, a conversation among all of them. He could not hear any of their words clearly, but they sounded…angry. Where before the figures in his dream had moved slowly, in an orderly fashion, they now moved at a greater speed and in a state of chaos. They no longer marched; they ran. One of the figures ran without seeing him and before he could move out of the way, ran into and through his dream self. Though the shadow showed no sign of even noticing the unexpected contact, Stan was not nearly so lucky.

A blast of cold the likes of which he'd never experienced pulsed through Stan's body, a shiver that stripped the warmth from him and left a bitter void where it had been. Every bone in his body felt like an iceberg, and his muscles locked, straining and twitching beneath his skin. He fell to the ground and felt his skin break against the gravel that he hadn't noticed before. His palms were cut, his knees torn and bloodied by the impact. The ground near his right hand crumbled slightly and he heard the sound of dirt and soil falling into waters he knew were even colder than the feeling already going through him. More of the shadows ran past, and more of them trod upon and through his body. Each impact seemed to last an eternity and tear a piece of the warmth inside of him away.

Even in the darkness, he could see the streamers of heat escaping his body with every breath he took and the pain he felt was making him breathe very hard and fast indeed.

Stan tried to rise, but every time he thought he could finally muster the strength, another of the shadows ran through him and pulled a piece of him away. His eyes flashed madly around, trying to find some way to escape the torment of their touch, but there was nothing, no escape, no retreat from the brutal, raping cold that flooded his being.

Stan reached with bloodied hands, trying to grasp one of the shadows, to make it see him and make it stop the torments. His hands found no purchase, and the wounds on his palms cracked and grew with the cold that he touched. Stan threw back his head and screamed as the pain finally overwhelmed him completely.

And fell from his bed as the scream erupted into his waking world, muffled down to nothing but a whimper. He hit the shag carpet of the bedroom floor with a light rumble and shook his head, astonished at the drops of moisture that fell from his sweat-soaked scalp.

Stan blinked in the darkness, the only light allowed him was what little the moon and stars cast through the window to the right of his bed. He settled his palms on the carpet, prepared to push himself up, and winced in pain. He moved his legs and felt the warmth running from his knees followed by a lightning strike of agony in the torn skin there.

Almost delirious, Stan half crawled to his nightstand and turned on the lamp perched in its center. His eyes protested the sudden illumination, but he squinted against the glare and looked at his palms, at the cuts and scrapes that bled freely and at the spots where his skin was almost chalk white and seemed close to frozen.

Stan Long crawled back into his bed, too tired to do more than fall bonelessly across the sweat-stained covers and into a deep sleep. He did not dream any more that night, and in the morning was grateful for the escape from his nightmares.

And in the morning he found himself still in pain and still wounded but wondering if nightmares could leave wounds in their passing. He hoped so. If not, something even worse than bad dreams was going on, and he wasn't sure he wanted to think about that possibility too much.

IV

Mike and Amelia woke up in the same bed, and Mike smiled as he opened his eyes. Two years since he had been with a woman, and the one next to him was, simply put, an amazing lover. There was a moment, just after he'd awakened, when he was certain he'd have a panic attack, and only partially because he wasn't used to the hotel room where they were resting. Amelia was not his Amy, but she still looked enough like his wife that it was disconcerting. Waking up next to her and seeing the face of the woman he'd slept with sent a brief flash of guilt through him, but it lasted for only a moment.

For the first time in as long as he could remember, he hadn't needed alcohol to stop him from dreaming. It was a wonderful feeling, waking up without a scream wanting to leap from his throat. With her sleeping next to him, her face shorn of the expressions that showed her personality, he could see just how similar and how different she was from Amy. They had the same facial shape, the same nose and the same eyes, but the mouths were different, the ears shaped in ways that were not remarkably similar, though in both cases they were delicate.

And both, he mused, *snore when they are sleeping.* Mike smiled softly to himself, his eyes lighting up with affection for Amelia. How could he possibly ever thank her for being so…nice? Everything about her—everything he knew at least, and he was the first to admit that there was a lot he didn't know—was wonderful. She was intelligent, witty, as pretty as...well, anyone he'd ever met. And for reasons he didn't understand, she was decent to him. Even without the whole sex thing, which was amazing to say the least.

He reached out his hand and moved a stray strand of hair from her face. She woke up the second he touched her, and she smiled brightly. She even woke up nicely. Mike pulled her hand to his face and kissed her fingertips, returning her smile.

They did not make love again, and while a part of him was disappointed, most of him acknowledged that he was sore in a lot of muscles that he didn't normally use. Mike sat in bed for a few moments while she showered, and then he moved through the suite and into the kitchen, where he brewed coffee for the two of them. There was no food in the refrigerator, or he likely would have made her breakfast. This morning he was actually hungry enough to eat.

He'd just finished pouring himself a cup of the strong brew when Amelia glided into the kitchen. She was fresh scrubbed and prettier than she had a right to be. He told her as much.

"I'm a morning person. I always have been," she replied, pouring herself a cup and adding in enough sugar to fire up an entire herd of preschoolers. She sipped the coffee, thought about it, and then added even more powdered energy.

"I figure you add any more sugar to that, and I'm gonna need a shot of insulin."

Amelia made a face and poked him in the ribs. "I like sweet things."

"No kiddin'." He feigned surprise. "I'd have never guessed."

"Keep it up, Mike. I'm sure I can find another assistant." She laughed lightly and kissed his cheek. He breathed deeply of her scent and willingly lost himself in her presence.

They sat at the kitchen table for another fifteen minutes, and then Mike used the shower himself, letting the water strike across his back and shoulders. She pulled a fast one and joined him under the stream of warm liquid. Whatever disappointment he might have felt earlier went away in a puff of steam, and muscles that were already overtaxed went to work again. Not that he was complaining.

It was the longest shower of Mike's life, and he was very grateful to the hotel's designers, who'd had the foresight to put in very big water heaters.

Afterward they dressed and enjoyed a comfortable silence until they reached the car. As they started heading for Frannie's, Amelia switched into work mode, and they discussed the job offer she had for him. The salary was more than kind, considering his recent history. He accepted it gratefully. It might well be a mistake—Lord above knew he barely knew Amelia Dunlow from Eve and that if things went poorly between them she could can him in a heartbeat, but he didn't sense she was that type—however, it was one he was willing to risk.

Mike was thinking about how strangely his life had turned in only a few weeks when they came upon the cemetery and the devastation from the previous night. Amelia stopped for the police cars that blocked the road, and Mike looked at what someone had done to the graves as his mind reeled. Somewhere in the carnage was his wife Amy's body, bared and torn for all to see.

It was hard to tell where the sirens ended and his scream began.

V

The sun rose brightly in the morning, casting rays of illumination all over Serenity Falls and washing away the night fears that haunted more than a few of the townsfolk. The air was colder than usual, almost autumnal. It was doubtful, if the harsh nip in the air was a sign, that there would be any more excursions to the quarry for the children who wanted to swim. A faint frost covered the lawns of the houses and municipal buildings, but it was hardly worth noticing and was gone within minutes of being touched by the sun. Charlee and Jessie met up and started the walk to school the same as they did on every school day, with Charlee moaning about how much she hated her classes and her best friend immediately agreeing with her assessment of the situation. It was not surprising, but Charlee kept to forming her own opinions. Hope, as the saying goes, springs eternal.

They walked past the cemetery as they did every school morning, and for the second time in the school year, they saw the violations of the monuments to the dead. This time, it was a far worse offense than it had been before. This time, someone went farther than merely disrupting headstones.

Someone tore the bodies out of the ground.

The smell alone was enough to make them sick, and Jessie proved the point by vomiting her breakfast all over the sidewalk. But worse than the smell was the sight of what had been done. Bodies had been pulled from their final resting places and posed like manikins for all to see. Some were barely more than bones and a few ligaments, but some were still rather disturbingly fresh. A few of the corpses appeared to be dancing; others merely rested against headstones or were draped on the benches set along the cemetery's perimeter. Some were posed in sexual positions or in the acts of different depravities. The sluggish buzz of flies and the stench of decay filled the air, mingled with the talk of others who'd already found the obscenity committed on their departed loved ones and the sound of sirens coming from the constables' offices.

She saw Mike Blake—Hobo Mike as some of the kids called him, but that name didn't exactly fit anymore—walking slowly through the grounds, his face white and shocky, his eyes burning with a rage that could light a house on fire if it managed to escape from him. Not far away, that dark-haired woman who'd opened the quarry sat in her car, her face showing deep concern as she looked at Mike. She wondered if the concern was for the man or for whatever actions he might take. Probably a little of both was her final assessment.

As Charlee did her best to comfort her friend without puking herself, Mary Walker's Ford Taurus screeched to a halt as she took in the carnage. Ted Cartwright's Chevy pickup truck behind it didn't stop in time, and the sound of metal meeting fiberglass was enough to snap most of the people halfway or more out of their shock. Cartwright climbed out of his truck, ready to start screaming, but he stopped when he caught a whiff of the odor coming from the cemetery. The old man looked toward the grounds and stared slack-jawed at the desecration. After a few moments of silent contemplation, his face started getting redder and redder as he looked at the spot where his wife had been buried only a year before. Her grave was empty, save for the ruins of her coffin. Just where her body had gone was not something he wanted to contemplate at that time. Mary Walker was far too busy screaming to notice. Her uncle's body was positioned over the skeletal remains of what was possibly a woman, and looked for all the world to be performing an unnatural sex act. Unfortunately, Mary had had the displeasure of being on the receiving end of his crude advances in the past, and the image brought up very unpleasant memories.

Charlee continued patting Jessie's back, hoping to bring her friend comfort in some way. She was pretty certain she failed, but at least she tried. Down the road, heading their way, she saw Stan and Dave and Joey coming toward the cemetery. She waved a hand, and Dave almost immediately came jogging over, his body moving with the same ease and fluid grace that she always noticed. His eyes cut to the cemetery, and he stopped for about two seconds, then ran the rest of the way to where she and Jessie waited.

"It happened again?"

Charlee nodded, her face wrinkled in disgust as the breeze shifted enough to bring the stench of death over in a thicker cloud. She blew out a breath and forced herself to breathe through her mouth, but it didn't really help.

Dave leaned down and helped Jessie to her feet. Jess's hair had fallen loose from her ponytail, and a thin trail of spittle ran from her mouth down to the ground. If Dave noticed, he paid it no attention as he led the girl farther away from the site. She mumbled something under her breath that might have been a thanks, and Charlee followed along behind them as Joey and Stan met up with them. Stan looked like he'd just seen the mother of all ghosts; his skin was white and pasty, and his eyes looked shocky. Joey was on him like a mother hen, all but clucking with concern and spouting advice.

The sirens from the police cars finally came to a halt as the constables—and it looked like all of them from every shift—climbed from their vehicles, their faces registering disgust and the same sort of shock that was so prevalent everywhere. The new guy, the one who looked like he ate tanks for breakfast, bellowed at the top of his lungs for everyone to clear the area immediately. Bill Karstens sauntered in the direction of Mary Walker and Ted Cartwright, asking questions in a low voice. Charlee and the rest moved on, but Stan kept looking over his shoulder, and she didn't like the way he was sweating.

Ten minutes later they were at the school, and Charlee was grateful for the chance to escape from what they'd left behind. Jessie had gone from being violently sick to resting her head on Dave's shoulder.

Charlee envied her that much but would have never admitted it in a million years. Dave was so nice, and the only one of them who didn't seem so rattled that walking was a chore.

The warning bell rang, shrilly informing one and all that they had five minutes to get to their homerooms. The group dispersed slowly, and Charlee sat at her desk, her eyes staring at the blackboard without really seeing anything. When the bell rang a second time, less than half of the seats were full. Many, it seemed, had decided to go home after passing the cemetery. Charlee was fine where she was. No one would be at home just then, and she had no desire whatsoever to be alone.

VI

Lawrence Grey sighed to himself as the last bell of the day rang. He was free from school, true, but not free from his mother. As he rose from his seat he looked over at Charlene Lyons and allowed himself the briefest of smiles. She was beautiful, and so very energetic. He always wondered if touching her would make his skin burn. He'd never had the balls to test the theory, but one day he just might. Charlene looked over his way, and he quickly averted his eyes. If she saw him looking at her, she might say something to him, and that was more than he could stand.

His face flushed from the close encounter with the woman of his dreams, Lawrence left the room quickly. Too quickly, it seemed, for his own good. With his eyes on the ground, he never noticed the older boys until it was too late. His lowered head ran straight into the back of Marty Hardwick and sent the older boy stumbling forward with a squawk of indignation.

Dave Pageant and Stan Long were there when it happened, and Dave burst into laughter at the sight of the older boy falling to the ground. Dave was like that; he laughed at almost everything, and he very seldom worried about the consequences. Hardwick fell to his knees, his long, gangly body running into Todd Hornsby. Todd, ever quick on his feet, pushed hard and sent Marty falling to the side. Todd was laughing, too, and so were the rest of his friends. Except Marty.

Marty was looking over his shoulder at the source of his fall, and his eyes pinned Lawrence with the accuracy of a surgeon's scalpel.

Lawrence started to stammer an apology, his face pastier than usual, and before the words reached his lips, Hardwick was in his face, standing up and pushing him backward hard enough to make him lose his balance and stumble. "What's your damage, Grey?" He shoved again as Lawrence tried to right himself, and Lawrence went down on the ground in a tangle of limbs and shattered nerves.

All his life Lawrence Grey had been forced to go home immediately after school. His mother picked him up, and there was no escaping from the woman. His mother—whom he loved as well as any son has ever loved his mother—did not take risks with his health. He had been a fragile child and born from a slow, painful birth that took almost two days. When he came out of the womb he was blue and almost cold, and the doctors had worked a miracle in saving him, his mother often told him. But that was the last time he was allowed the chance to get hurt. If he fell as a child, he was swept into her arms almost instantly and then tended to. If he cried out in his sleep, she was there to comfort him in a matter of seconds. When he was younger, his mother had arranged for a doctor she knew to write a note excusing Lawrence from strenuous physical activity. According to the doctor—a man who lived three towns away—Lawrence had asthma. It was a crock of doggy doo. He'd never had asthma. But that way his mother was certain that he wouldn't be hurt in group sports that required physical contact. On two separate occasions teachers had tried to get the boy doing some sort of exercise under the simple belief that anything was better than nothing, and both times his mother had nipped that notion in the bud with threats of lawsuits. Lawrence was sheltered and protected to the very best abilities of his mother. Simply put, Lawrence had absolutely no idea how to respond to the current situation. He'd never in his life been deliberately pushed by someone.

Marty grabbed Lawrence by his arm and pulled him to his feet roughly. "I said what's your damage, Grey? What, are you deaf now, too?"

Lawrence squeaked as the boy started shaking him. His vision went all funny with every yank on his arm, and his head snapped back and forth loosely. He was aware of someone calling for Marty to leave him alone, but far more loudly he heard the call for a fight and tried to focus enough to make sense of the words.

"I—didn't—mean to." He got the words out with great effort, and Marty stopped shaking him. Lawrence's ears were filled with the sound of his own heartbeat, and adrenaline coursed through him like water through a colander. His whole body shook from the physical encounter.

Off to his left, he heard Dave Pageant speaking. "He said he didn't mean to, Marty. Leave him alone." Dave, the laughing, joking voice of reason. Lawrence looked over at the stocky boy and begged with his eyes for help.

Before Dave could get closer, and judging by the expression on his face that was exactly what he intended to do, Marco DeMillio stepped forward and blocked his path. DeMillio smiled and shook his head. "No reason for others to get involved in this, Davey." His voice was a sweet singsong. "Let's let Lawrence handle this on his own. He's a big boy."

Marco DeMillio was fifteen, going on twenty. He was the only kid any of them knew who had to shave regularly. If he didn't, he had a shadow of stubble on the lower part of his face that made him look too much like his old man for anyone's comfort. DeMillio's father had been one of the most notorious hell raisers in town before he disappeared, and no one had been sorry to see him carted off to jail after he was accused of beating on Steve Wilkins—that was before Mr. Wilkins killed himself, a concept so unsettling that Lawrence did his best never to think about it—DeMillio's father had yet to come back to town, and that suited everyone just fine.

One look at Marco and Lawrence knew he was on his own. Though Dave didn't come any closer, he didn't back down, either. His blue eyes stared back into DeMillio's green eyes with a like intensity that obviously made the older boy a little uncomfortable. But only a little. Dave was big for twelve, but Marco was mature for fifteen. There was really no comparison.

Andy and Perry Hamilton were both cawing like crows at a harvest time in the cornfields, and beside them both Butch Carmichael and Derrick Brickman were calling out for Marty to "teach the geek a lesson." Todd Hornsby merely leaned against the wall and watched everything, his dark eyes glittering in the fluorescent light of the dingy school hallway. Lawrence, for his part, felt a strong urge to puke his guts out.

And then Charlene came into the hallway with her best friend Jessie. They took in the sight in an instant. Charlee's mouth set into a line and her eyebrows knitted over her pretty eyes. Lawrence felt he could tolerate almost anything, almost any humiliation, but the idea of her looking at him like a little kid was more than he wanted to ever deal with, and he could see already that the confrontation was headed that way.

More out of an urgent need to save face than because he really wanted to stop the conflict, Lawrence pushed his arms up between the arms Marty held onto him with and then swept them outward. One of his guilty pleasures—and one of the few his mother had never done anything about—was his love of bad Chinese martial arts flicks. He just did what he'd seen done in a few of those and swept his arms out and to his sides, knocking the restraining arms of Marty away from his collar.

Damn near every person in the hallway gasped. The last thing any of them actually expected was for Lawrence to do anything other than grovel. That fact, too, was embarrassing to Lawrence. He grimaced, felt his face flushing red, and forced himself to say something before he started crying or something worse. "I said I didn't mean to, Marty! I'm sorry! Deal with it!"

He looked at Marty, and Marty stared back. Lawrence knew that if he looked away first, he was going to get his ass kicked all over the place. Perhaps it was instinct, perhaps he'd read it somewhere, but he knew if he flinched, if he blinked, if he showed any sign of weakness at all, he was as good as dead. Marty continued to look at him for a few seconds and then backed off, his smile spreading slowly. "Long as we understand each other, Grey. That's all."

Lawrence nodded, stiff-backed, and moved down the hallway, never looking over his shoulder. He didn't want to know if he had been noticed. He just wanted to go.

It seemed like someone had set every muscle in his body on "vibrate," and his legs didn't want to go where he told them to, but he eventually made it out the door and into the sunlight. He endured his mother's usual questions about how his day had gone, knowing that in fact she was barely listening.

It didn't matter, because in the back of his head he was barely answering. He was lost in the exhilaration of what he'd just endured. Every part of him seemed more alive than it ever had before, and he felt an almost sexual excitement. *I stood up to Marty. I stood up to him, and I'm still breathing.* The idea kept cycling through his brain for the rest of the day, and Lawrence's mother had time to wonder why her son seemed so happy. She didn't ask him, however, but was merely glad to see her boy looking around with more interest than he had in a very long time.

VII

Jack Michaels was doing his best not to get ill, but it wasn't an easy task, and being around the corpses wasn't making his chances for not losing his three-egg omelet breakfast any better. He was, at the moment, surrounded by the bodies that had been torn from their final resting places and left by someone with a sick and twisted mind for all to see. They were unsanitary as all hell, and they smelled beyond hideous. And those were the nicer things he could think about the corpses that were still being bagged for identification.

Every last one of the constables and volunteers wore surgical scrubs, surgical gloves, and matching masks. In most cases they'd sprayed their facial coverings with Lysol to avoid having to deal with the reek of decay. It didn't help. Jack was breathing through his mouth to avoid the odor, and he could swear he tasted the corpses through the mask.

Someone needed to be hurt for this. Not just punished, hurt. Whoever had done the vandalism had taken their time and made sure they did as much damage as possible. Each gravesite had a shell of concrete around the coffin, and each was topped with a cement lid. The people responsible—and Jack didn't think any one person could have done the work without a bulldozer at the very least—had broken through the cement and then ruined the coffin in order to get to the corpse within. That took a lot of effort, and even in Serenity he had trouble believing that no one had seen a thing, regardless of the late hour.

Beside him, Tom Lassiter turned his head away as he helped pull another body into a bag. The kid's chest was heaving, and it was obvious he was close to vomiting all over himself. His already pale skin was looking particularly cheesy. He made a note to himself to, at the very least, write up a commendation for the kid. Just after he had that thought, Lassiter bolted from where he was and ran toward the edge of the cemetery-cum-crime scene, pulling his mask away. Victor Barnes moved over to where Lassiter was, waiting to offer his assistance.

Michaels looked around. They were almost done, and that was a good thing. School was out, and he didn't want any more kids hanging around and looking on. As it was, the people who'd come through the cemetery earlier had screwed up what could have been crucial evidence by seeking out their loved ones' remains. He couldn't blame them, but it didn't make his job any easier.

Bill Karstens was zipping up the last body bag when the first wave of kids came by. Most of them tried to linger, but one look at Vic Barnes—and the sound of his bellowing for them to get on home—and they were on their way. Having Barnes around was like having a traffic cop and a scarecrow at the same time. He kept things moving, and he intimidated the hell out of the local pests. It was a good deal in Jack's book.

He stood up, looking around at what remained of the Powers Memorial Cemetery. There were more emptied graves than full, and Jack wondered if they'd ever be able to put it all back together properly again. He had his doubts.

Karstens pulled the mask off his face, looking around him in a mild daze. He seemed less disturbed by everything than anyone else, but that didn't surprise Jack too much. Karstens was a prick, true enough, but he was also a good cop. Jack made himself a promise a long time ago that he'd always remember that fact, especially on the days when he wanted to just fire the man. Right now he wanted to give him a raise instead. Bill had remained calm and cool and reminded him of several procedural facts as they went through the investigative paces. He'd have likely screwed up the investigation if the man hadn't been there to guide him.

Jack looked over at Karstens and smiled tightly. It was the best he could manage with his stomach still considering an emergency evacuation. Bill nodded back, his eyes sharp and clear. He moved over to Jack's side and leaned in close. "I've got the coroner from Utica ready to come out here and look over the dental records we've got on file. With any luck, we'll be able to put every body back where it belongs."

"Which one are they sending?"

"Mmm...I think it's Muller. He's pretty good as I recall. Pays attention to details."

"Yeah, he's one of the better ones."

Bill Karstens looked him over and shook his head. "You look green, Jack. Go home. Get some rest. I'll make sure it all gets wrapped up."

And for once in his life, Jack Michaels listened to his second-in-command. "That's a deal, but only if you take tomorrow off. No one should have to work doubles around here unless it's me."

Bill nodded his head. "I figure I could take the family on a quick trip to the city. Do a little shopping and have some fun."

"Then it's as good as done. Give Maureen a hug and a kiss for me."

Bill nodded. "You got it. Now get out of here."

Jack said his good-byes and thank-yous to the crowd of volunteers and left instructions for a few people on the force. Then he went home. He was tired, and it was an effort to stay conscious.

Despite that, however, when he got to his house—it still puzzled him that he had a house; his family had always been in apartments, and the very notion of a house struck him as strange, but he was getting used to it and it would be his in only twenty-five more years—he stripped down and left a trail of clothes all the way to the shower.

He stayed under the heavy stream of water until the heat faded away and left a chilling wash to run over his body. The entire shower was spent alternately scrubbing his body and simply soaking under the current. By the time he was done, he felt almost human.

Jack dried off and walked back out to his living room, dodging the piles of clothes and debris that he'd left scattered throughout the place over the last week. He made a note to himself to take his uniforms to the cleaners. He was down to one at this point, and the situation would get dire if he didn't handle it.

He pulled on a pair of jogging shorts, flopped down on his sofa, and turned on the TV. He was asleep within minutes.

When he awoke, the sun was long down. The only light was the glare from the television, where Gilligan and his buddies were once again trying to get off the island. He blinked, not certain what, exactly, had pulled him from sleep. Then he heard the sound of someone knocking on the door and understood.

Bethany Halloway was not the last person in the world he expected to see. Elvis was maybe the very last. But she came in close. "Bethany?"

She looked at him with those eyes, damn it, those eyes that still made him weak-kneed and desperate to either kiss her or run away. "Hello, Jack."

He did his best to recover quickly, taking in her body under a light sweater and jeans that did nothing to hide her form. "What can I do for you tonight, Ms. Halloway?" He did his best to sound professional but knew he came across as bitter instead. He didn't mean to, but seeing her was not making him comfortable in the least.

Her face said so much. The way her eyebrows moved up and down told him that she wasn't sure how to take being called "Ms. Halloway," and that she probably didn't like it. The way she bit at her full lower lip told him she was nervous. It was a little gesture that had stayed with her over the years, and one he'd always found fetching. The way her chin just missed actually quivering told him she was at the edge of tears, and he found that, even after so long with her out of his life, he did not like to think of her close to crying.

Jack sighed and pulled the door open. "Come on in, Beth." He stepped back and let her move into the mess he called his home. "I was about to start some coffee. Would you like a cup?" She nodded her answer, and he pointed to the couch. "Make yourself comfortable, excuse the mess, and I'll be with you in a minute."

Jack put on the water for coffee and waited while the machine did its magic, turning the clear fluid into rich, dark brew. He tried not to dwell on Bethany in the next room. He tried not to think about her at all. But it was damned hard.

Mostly though, he tried not to let his anger at her come out. He still had strong feelings for her after all of these years, but a portion of those feelings were rooted deeply in the betrayal from so long ago. Anyone else he could have forgiven, or at least forgotten about. But Bethany? He'd told her he loved her, and she took someone else's word over his.

He shook the thoughts away, pushing them back down into their little prison, though they struggled to hang around. *Enough already. That was half a lifetime ago. Grow the fuck up.* He got the coffee, cream and sugar, and cups, and headed back into his living room.

Bethany was still there when he arrived. He almost wished she wasn't. Wordlessly, he poured the coffee and fixed his the way he liked it, with just a dash of cream and two sugars. Then he waited silently while Bethany made hers.

When he could take the silence no longer he sighed. "What can I do for you, Bethany?"

She did it again. She looked at him and gnawed her bottom lip, and he looked into her eyes and struggled to remember how to breathe normally. That she could have this effect on him was beyond annoying. It went almost to infuriating. Bethany Halloway kept looking at him for a few seconds, her eyes blinking as she fought back tears. He looked away from her, knowing if he kept staring he'd crack and try to do something completely moronic like offer her comfort.

"I don't know, Jack. I wanted to come over here and ask if you knew anything about what was wrong with Terri, if the way she's been acting was normal, and I wanted to come over here and thank you for everything you did and I wanted to come over here and apologize for being so damned stupid about everything when we were kids..." The words came out in a rush and he had to strain to interpret them into anything other than babble. "And I wanted to see if we could be friends, even though I've been a bitch to you for so long, because I think I need a friend right now, Jack. I really do."

And then she started crying. Jack looked back at her just in time to see the first tear spill from one of her eyes and felt the ice he'd built around his heart fracture and start to melt. And he hated her even more for that. But mostly, he hated himself for being weak enough to give in and pull her close and hug her to him as she started crying in earnest.

It was never easy being one of the good guys. If there was ever proof of that, Jack Michaels felt himself making the point as he comforted the woman who'd stomped his heart into the ground so long ago.

VIII

If there was ever a town without a make-out spot, Serenity wasn't it. Up near the quarry, on a piece of land that was of little value to anyone, there was a nice view of the town proper below. During the daylight hours it sat empty, devoid of anything but a few covering trees. But at night, the grass was crushed by the tires of cars, normally driven by teenagers, though there were exceptions, and the view of the rooftops in Serenity was seldom what brought any of them up there. The area was called The Point, and everyone in town knew it existed. Normally no one did a damned thing about it, and tonight was no exception. Oh, there had been a few occasions when the constables made visits, but after the day at the cemetery, none of them was up to it.

The violation or two of a graveyard was not, however, enough to stop young lust or young love or anything in between. Eight cars total were parked in the area, and all of them carried at least one couple. Glenn Harrigan's battered old van carried three couples total, all of which were engaged in the fine art of making out. Two others carried two couples each. And off to the side, near where the woods took over the clearing, Chris Parker's Ford station wagon, a hand-me-down from his father that had seen its best years a decade earlier, held Chris and his girlfriend, Eva Spinelli. The two of them had been dating for six months, and they were both firmly convinced that they were madly in love. Had anyone told them otherwise, they'd surely have scoffed at the notion. Though they had certainly never made any formal arrangements at the age of sixteen, they had already discussed their plans to attend college together and to marry and have kids. They were each the first love of the other.

So making out in the back of the station wagon was acceptable. They hadn't yet gone "all the way," but they were working toward it, and Chris had purchased condoms a few months earlier, just in case they got past second base. So far he hadn't managed that feat, but he was a patient soul. He had all the time in the world, and Eva was well worth taking it slow and easy.

Eva was, perhaps, ready physically to consummate their relationship, but she was still hesitant emotionally. It wasn't that she didn't love Chris, it was merely that she didn't feel the time was right yet. She felt she'd know when the time came.

The night was cool, and the car's interior was warm, and that led inevitably to fogged windows. The stunning view of Serenity that normally was only a few feet away was lost to the condensation, and Eva felt a little more comfortable with that arrangement. If she could not look out, no one else could look in, at least not without effort. Their mutual favorite band, 311, was playing on the radio, and playing their song—"Strong All Along"—no less. It was nice, being together. They seemed to spend eternities apart before they could sneak away and spend time alone. There was always something in the way. Her gymnastic lessons and the time on the girls' basketball team kept her busy most of the time. Also, he had a part-time job at Mercer's Grocery: the job sucked, but it paid for the car's maintenance and insurance and sometimes left him enough to buy something for Eva. He spent too much on her, but she couldn't really get upset about it. Whenever she protested, he got that pouty look on his face that was so cute and so frustrating at the same time. She liked to see him smiling, and the way his blue-green eyes lit up when he was happy, so she let him buy the stuff she just didn't really want or need, and he seemed to feel better for it.

The two of them had been lip-locked for what had to be a good ten minutes and, though she could run her fingers through his sandy blond hair for an eternity, breathing was becoming a bit of a challenge. Eva was trying to figure the best way to make that point known to Chris without hurting his feelings—sometimes he could be really oversensitive, and she didn't want him pouting—when an excuse came from outside the ancient land yacht. Something big and heavy slammed into the side of the car, and Chris pulled back fast, his bangs falling across his face in the darkness and his hand leaving her breast only reluctantly.

"What the fuck?"

Eva sat up quickly, readjusting her top. If it was one of the constables, there would be hell to pay. They weren't exactly understanding about the underage participants around here. And her folks would definitely not be cool with the idea, especially since she'd snuck out of the house after they'd gone to sleep. "Is it a person? Please don't let it be a cop. My folks'll skin me."

Chris shook his head. "I think someone hit the car..." His voice sounded tense, and more than just from the heavy petting. His lips pressed together, and he perched on his knees in the back area of the station wagon, his head hunched down so he could almost sit up properly. He half walked, half scooted toward the rear hatch, ready to at least roll down the window and see what was happening. His hand had just reached for the crank on the doorway when the sound came again, rocking the car hard enough to make him lose his balance.

"Dammit!" He didn't know if he should be scared or angry, and his voice reflected both emotions equally. He looked around the back of the car for anything that could be considered a weapon, even as his mind told him it was just a couple of the guys yanking his chain and trying to embarrass him in front of Eva. If that was the case, at least a couple of his teammates were going to be very bruised come the game tomorrow night. He'd personally kick their asses into the next time zone.

Eva pulled herself into a sitting position next to him, her head turning from one side to the other as she tried to see past the fogged windows. She'd heard about the desecration earlier in the day—and so had everyone else for that matter—and she couldn't help wondering if the people who'd done that were still around and maybe hanging out at The Point...

She shivered at the thought. If they'd do the things that had been done to dead people, what in God's name would they do to living people? "Chris? Let's just get out of here, okay?"

"I swear I'll kick their asses, baby. I'll beat the fuck out of them if they even come near you." Chris's voice was a blend of nervous energy and growing anger, but he had that look in his eyes, the one that made her worry sometimes. He'd never hit her, never even considered the idea most likely, but when he looked that way, she was scared of him just the same. "I just need to make sure the car's okay, and then we'll leave..."

"Chris, no! You can look at the car after we leave, but I don't like it here, and I don't like the way it sounds out there." There was a desperate edge to her voice, and normally she'd have been annoyed by it, but at the moment she was too scared to care. Eva knew what he was thinking, that as far as he was concerned, this was just another prank by his friends, but she didn't think so. It felt wrong out there, and besides, the guys on the football team would never have been able to keep from laughing by now.

Chris apparently didn't care, at least not until he heard the sound of breaking glass from one of the other cars, the sound followed almost immediately by screams.

And was that something growling out there?

Whatever the case, Chris changed his mind almost instantly. He scurried away from the rear hatch and pushed past Eva on his way to the driver's seat. His keys were already in the ignition, and 311 was fading away, replaced by an advertisement for the Dark of the Hills Haunted House. They had plans of hitting that next week; it was normally worth the long lines. Eva moved after him, veering off to her own seat, her eyes looking at the shapes that ranged near the car, blurred by the very condensation she'd been happy about a few seconds earlier.

Chris looked out the window, his face casting long shadows in the odd green light of the dashboard. He turned the key, and for a split second Eva knew—*knew* with every fiber of her being—that the car wouldn't start. They'd been in the back too long with the radio playing. It had surely drained the charge from the battery, and there was no way in hell she was going out to push the tank, not with the noises coming from outside. She giggled, the idea striking her as funny, and she was dimly aware that she must surely be sliding toward hysteria if she wasn't there already. The radio let out an evil cackle and scream as the commercial wound toward its end. Eva slapped the dials until she managed to shut the damned thing off.

The engine roared into life, and the only thing that stopped the ancient tank from leaping into the trees they faced was the fact that it was in neutral. Something outside roared back, taking the sound as a challenge maybe, or just knowing that the juicy tidbits inside the car were about to get away. Chris very calmly set the automatic transmission into reverse amid the sound of more screams and one voice—Eva thought it was Meg, her best friend for the last three years, but her voice was distorted by the sheer volume—calling out in prayer...or possibly just using the Lord's name in vain.

The tires on the old station wagon shrieked as they caught a firm hold of the ground, and Eva barely managed to avoid her head slamming into the dashboard as the Ford rocketed backward. Something a damn sight bigger than a football player let out a yelp of pain as the vehicle backed into and then over it.

Eva screamed. Chris screamed. Something under the car screamed, too, and it was much, much louder. Chris wiped at his window with his hand, trying to see what was outside. It was almost useless, the thick condensation smeared rather than clearing away, and the end result was a look at something dark and blurry with big white teeth coming at him through the glass.

Chris screamed again, but this time there was a note of terror that was much sharper than before. A black, furry face slammed itself against the driver's side window. Chris flinched back toward Eva, and she saw the daggerlike fangs buried between black lips. They both screamed again as the teeth scraped across the glass, leaving very noticeable marks.

The face in the window backed away and came again. This time the glass spiderwebbed, and the whole car shook when it hit.

Eva squealed in fright as another shape jumped on top of the station wagon's hood. "Oh God, Chris! Get us the fuck out of here!"

Chris made a keening noise that was not at all like his normal tone and slammed his foot onto the gas pedal. The car launched itself into reverse again, sliding in the remains of whatever Chris had run over, and backed all the way up into Glenn Harrigan's van. The dark shape on the front of the car staggered for an instant and then disappeared with a yelp. The sound of crunching metal overpowered everything else for half a second, and then Chris pushed the gearshift into first and gunned it again. Chris steered madly, the thing outside rolled to the side, narrowly missing the fate of one of its brethren a few moments before. The face rammed into the driver's side window again, and this time it came through the ruined glass, all teeth and slobbering lips, snapping madly, seeking something to bite into.

It found Chris's shoulder. Eva's eyes grew wide as she saw the muzzle of the thing—*A bear? A fucking bear? Oh God it can't be a bear, bears aren't that big*—close around the meat of his broad shoulder and then yank roughly back and forth. Chris's head snapped in rhythm to the pulling action, and he let out a scream that half deafened Eva.

He looked at her with eyes blinded by pain and reached for her with his right arm—the one that wasn't bleeding a flow of crimson all over the ruined window—and Eva pulled back, terrified that whatever had him might get her, too.

Chris reached around with the same hand that had moved toward her and smashed his fist into the thing on his shoulder. He clawed at it with hooked fingers, ready to tear the thing away from him. Whatever he hit must have been sensitive, because it let him go. His face drawn and tight, Chris pushed on the gas again, trying to escape. The cat jumped forward, and Eva let herself breathe again, barely aware that she'd been holding her breath.

They moved forward, finally, finally on their way. Chris had to go to the clinic, no two ways about that. She would be in trouble with her parents, but they would be alive, and that was worth a month or two of grounding.

And the car stopped, slamming violently to a halt as it collided with another vehicle trying to escape. This time the impact was much worse, and Eva's head bounced off the window on her side, making her see bright flashes and sink her teeth into her own tongue. Warm, coppery blood flowed into her mouth, and everything around her went fuzzy for a second. She looked over at Chris, trying to form words, but nothing came out except scarlet liquid in a wet stream.

She shook herself, forced her brain to work, despite the aching in her head. She needed to tell Chris to drive, damn it, forget everything else and just drive! But the words wouldn't form.

Chris was fighting with the gearshift. It was stuck, and his hand was slippery with blood. He cursed anxiously under his breath, looking her way, ready to say something himself.

And then the face came through the window again, this time sinking its crimsoned teeth into his cheek, his chin, and drawing together with a sickening crunch that finally broke Eva's paralysis. She shoved hard against the passenger's side door, all rational thought fading away, replaced by the primal need to run. Chris screamed, and Eva felt her heart sink, knowing he was either dead or close to it.

She pushed harder, her hand scrabbling for the handle that would open her way to freedom. With a groan of protest the door popped open, spilling her on the cold gravel and dirt. Eva didn't even bother standing up, she just pushed off the ground and into a run. Her eyes took in the shapes—there had to be a dozen or more of the black things—ripping into people she'd known and cared about. She didn't scream, there wasn't enough of her mind that was rational to allow that. She just ran, darting around obstacles as her feet propelled her forward.

Off to her right, she saw a shape that was bigger even than the ones she'd already witnessed. Eva was not short. She was tall for her age, and that was one of the things she'd always hated about her own appearance. That and her hair almost never did what it was supposed to, and she would never be as skinny as the cheerleaders for the football team. She was muscular from years of tomboying, and she sometimes wished she could reverse time and work on that during her more formative years.

But next to the thing coming her way she was a midget. It was almost six feet tall at the shoulders, and its face was as large as her whole torso. It was not, in fact, a hear, but that would have been preferable. The hound moving toward her glared from narrowed eyes that burned with a greenish light, and the breath it cast from its wrinkled muzzle glowed with the same strange coloration. It almost looked like it was breathing fire.

Eva looked at the beast, let it register in her head, and pushed herself even faster. Her long legs pumped hard, practically devouring the distance down to the main road. Her ears caught the sound of something heavy moving after her—and she didn't have to work hard to guess what that something was—even over the sounds of screams and growls. One of the screams, she knew in her heart, was that of Chris. Tears came to her wide eyes, blurring everything, but still she ran.

Her heart felt like it would explode, and her breaths came out like a blast of fire, scorching her lungs as she moved. There was a pain in her side that told her she'd pushed too far, a warning from her body to take it a little easier, but she was damned if she would listen. The monster was behind her, and she could feel it getting closer and closer.

Trees that could barely be seen in the darkness slapped mercilessly at her, like the taunting hands of vicious children, and she felt the scrapes and cuts from them as they stung her again and again.

Somewhere along the way she'd lost sight of the road, but it wasn't important; she knew she'd get home sooner or later if she kept running. Even if it hurt to move and her legs felt like someone had tied lead weights to them, she knew she had to keep going.

Then she felt the teeth slam down into the back of her calf, saw the ground leap up and slam into her as her leg was hauled off high into the air. She looked back and saw the dog-thing with the freaky eyes looking back at her, its mouth clamped firmly on her lower leg.

Eva managed to scream again, the pain forcing precious air from her tortured lungs as it ran through her nerves like a lightning strike. She hung suspended from the ground, held in the viselike prison of the monster's jaws, and she screamed as loud and long as she could. Her free leg kicked at the face of the demon, but even though she felt her heel scrape across fur and press the bone beneath it, her hunter did not let go. From behind the thing, she heard the sounds of howling. Strange, deep howls, not at all like the ones in the movies, and she saw dark shapes coming her way past the massive shoulders that almost completely blocked her view.

Eva managed one more good scream as the rest of the pack met up with her. The one that had her was huge, but the others weren't exactly small either. It didn't really seem fair, the way they all came forward, grinning through bloodied muzzles and moving slowly in a circle as she whimpered and tried desperately to free herself. She'd heard of animals chewing their own legs off to get out of bear traps—a thought she'd always found repulsive, both the traps and what the animals did to themselves—and if she could have, she'd have done the same to escape the shadowy forms that moved closer in a slow, toying progress.

Eva pulled herself into a fetal position, her hands over her head as she swung from the mouth of the lead dog-thing. One of the smaller ones came forward and snapped at her hand, taking a finger in the process, and she cried out in pain as she swung her ruined fist, cuffing the beast with what remained intact. Another came forward and took a chomp out of her side that felt like a blowtorch's caress.

Through the pain and panic of watching the things move in for the kill, Eva thought back to what her mother had always said about cats and dogs. Cats were the ones who were supposed to toy with their prey. Dogs were supposed to be quick and efficient killers. A maddened laugh broke past her lips as they finally prepared to pounce. *You got it wrong, Mom! Dogs can play with their kills, too!* They proved Eva right over the next fifteen minutes, the last ones of her life.

IX

The sound of police cars tearing past the house and up toward Old Quarry Road woke Jason Long from his fitful sleep. And Beauregard, who loved to howl along with the sirens, made the idea of going back to sleep a pipe dream. Sleep had become, frankly, something of a luxury of late, and he was annoyed by the noises. Beside him, Adrienne slept soundly, her face made innocent by the virtue of being relaxed. He looked at her and felt the butterflies attack his stomach's lining voraciously. That happened a lot these days. It was, he knew, a side effect of considering a life without her by his side and with him in the course of the day.

Despite her betrayal, Jason loved Adrienne deeply. He just wasn't sure if he could stay with her. Every time he thought of the letter he'd found, he had the same feeling he got when dropping from the top of a particularly steep hill on a roller coaster.

Everything fell except his stomach, which struggled desperately to catch up. The difference was, it just didn't feel the same when there wasn't a roller coaster under him.

He reached out one hand, stroking her hair lightly. She sighed, and in her sleep at least she didn't turn away from him. Somewhere else in the house, his children slept. And the thought of being without them in his life was, if anything, even more terrifying than the thought of being without Addy. It just wasn't right, damn it all to hell. He had played by the rules: he'd never cheated on Addy, he'd never even considered the idea seriously, and yet here he was, preparing himself to say goodbye to her and walk out of her world.

All because he'd opened a letter he should never have seen. Read lines written by his wife's hand and meant for another man entirely. He'd have given almost anything to be able to forget that damned letter.

But it wouldn't go away. It sat there like a neon sign burning on a starless night, and he couldn't help but be drawn back to it again and again.

He carefully got out of bed, moving as delicately as he could so as to avoid waking his wife. Outside, through the window, he could see the flashing lights of the emergency vehicles as they spun in the woods. Someone had done something stupid up there, he assumed, and he hoped whatever it was didn't prove fatal. But it was an idle hope. In the long run, he was certain that whatever had occurred had absolutely nothing to do with him and his.

Just as, in the long run, he knew he couldn't stay with Adrienne. No matter that he loved her. He could no longer trust her. He might be able to forgive one betrayal, but even now there was a voice in the recesses of his brain that kept offering up the possibility that she was maybe not at home while he was at work. That she was, just possibly, mind you, entertaining another man, a lover who made her feel somehow more complete than he was managing to do. And that thought hurt him deeply. And the notion that somewhere a man who was sleeping with his wife might be amused by Jason's dilemma did nothing at all to make him calmer.

It was getting bad. He tried to hide it, but he was looking at the men he knew differently now, wondering if one of them was smiling in his face and cuckolding him at the same time. He moved quietly out of his room, closing the door softly behind him and heading down the hallway to the stairs. He stepped carefully, knowing where every creaking floorboard was, and how to avoid them.

He needed a cup of coffee, and he needed to think. He wanted to scream and rage and throw things, but he knew that was the worst possible thing he could do in the present situation. Part of him still wanted to go crazy, called for him to force himself on Adrienne and make her know that she was his, to claim her like a conquest. He crushed that nagging voice every time he heard it, and he crushed it hard. He would, he had long ago decided, castrate himself with a spoon before he would ever solve an argument with a woman that way.

And the thought of hurting Adrienne that way was almost nauseating. That he could even have those sorts of notions made him feel like a criminal.

Down the stairs, moving cautiously, he tiptoed through the darkened house with instincts honed from years of making the same trip in the wee hours of the morning. Had he been anywhere else he'd likely have stubbed his toe or even tripped over something, but not here, not in his home. He knew it too well. It was a comforting knowledge, even if he knew that he'd soon have to leave the place behind.

Because, of course, Adrienne would be allowed to keep the house and the kids. That was only right. He could find another place, but there was no way in hell he would make them move, make them abandon what was theirs, too.

He blinked as he rounded the last corner between him and the kitchen. Though there wasn't much light in the room, there was some. More than should have been visible. His mind jumped automatically to the notion that there was an invader in the house, someone who had no right or reason for being there. He dismissed it as soon as he smelled the hot cocoa.

Jason walked into the room and saw his daughter. April should have been asleep, but she wasn't. Maybe she, like he, was having trouble sleeping. Maybe she knew what he already knew, or sensed it on some level. Maybe she understood that he wouldn't be around much longer.

Beau certainly acted like he knew something was wrong. He'd spent the last few nights sitting at the window and staring into the darkness, as if he were waiting for something bad to happen. Tonight he wandered from room to room like a guard patrolling the perimeter. His lip lifted occasionally in a silent threat, but when he looked toward Jason, he wagged his tail and looked almost guilty about the entire affair.

April looked up and did a slight jump in her seat, unprepared for seeing anyone. "Geez, Daddy, you scared the hell out of me." She started to smile and then covered her mouth when she realized that she'd cursed in front of him.

Jason smiled back and shook his head. "Don't worry about the word. I've heard worse. And I'm sorry, sweetie, I didn't mean to scare you." He moved over and kissed her lightly on the top of her head, smelling the shampoo and her own clean scent. "What are you doing up so late?"

"I couldn't sleep."

"Anything you want to talk about?"

April looked back at him, her face clouded by whatever thoughts might haunt a sixteen-year-old girl. "I was thinking about everything that's happened around here lately, I mean, with Stan and the graveyard and with Terri… It all just keeps going in circles around in my head."

"Well, there's been a lot going on…" He looked away, the guilt he felt at the idea of leaving slapping him deep inside his chest.

"And…" She looked over at him, and her eyes looked about ready to shed tears. "And then there's you and Mom. Dad? What's going on between you two?"

Jason Long looked at his daughter and weighed whether or not she was old enough to be told the truth. It wasn't an easy decision, in many ways she was still a child, and at the same time…he began to understand why parents often had difficulty associating with their children. "It's…complicated, April. Let's just leave it at I don't know your mom as well as I thought I did."

"Are you two going to split up, Daddy?"

"I don't know. Maybe. Maybe just for a short while…"

April nodded, and the tears that had been threatening finally started to fall from her eyes. She didn't cry out loud, but her pretty face collapsed a bit, and her eyes leaked a steady flow. Jason reached over and took her hand in his. "Sweetie, I know this is hard, it's not easy for me, either, but I think maybe I need time to deal with a few things, and I think maybe the only way I can is if I'm not here." She gripped his hand tightly and nodded her understanding, but the tears, if anything, simply fell faster. None of his thoughts about Addie made a damned bit of sense when he saw April's tears. The very idea of hurting his little angel just tore him apart inside. He squeezed harder on her hand and said words he had trouble believing until he thought of April and Stan. "It's probably just me being silly, April. And before I do anything drastic, I intend to talk everything out with your mom. I just haven't had the nerve to do it yet."

"What did Mom do that's so bad, Daddy?"

"I can't talk about that, April. I just can't."

They sat in silence for several seconds, which grew into minutes at a terrifying pace. Jason stood up, his coffee forgotten, and kissed April once more on the top of her head. "Whatever happens, April, remember that I love you, and I love Stan and your mom, too. It's just that sometimes things don't work the way they're supposed to."

Jason went back to his room and lay down beside his wife. He watched her sleeping and, despite his beliefs that it would not happen, eventually he drifted back into a deep, dreamless slumber.

Chapter Nine

I

The weekend did not bring the normal sense of relaxation to Serenity. If anything, it brought more tensions. Sometime during the night sixteen of the high school's students had disappeared, and just after two in the morning their cars were found up at The Point, along with several spots where blood trailed on the ground and where two of Elway Deveraux's hounds had managed to get themselves run over. It was anyone's guess what the hell had happened up there, but damn near everyone took it for granted that the dogs had gone feral. Deveraux had a lot of dogs, and it was not a thought that made people comfortable. It did, however, give many of the people in Serenity a sense of purpose. The damned animals had to be taken down, and they had to be taken down fast if anyone wanted to sleep comfortably again.

The very thought of Serenity's Animal Control Unit handling the matter alone was ludicrous. Bob Haskill was a good worker, and he could handle a lot, but he was only one man, and he didn't even carry anything stronger than a few tranquilizer darts. And as much as the people in town knew the constables were capable of handling most troubles, there wasn't a soul in the whole town who believed they could handle the dogs by themselves. It didn't take long for volunteers to show up. Like most small towns, Serenity Falls boasted a fair number of game hunters. They came prepared to do their best to track down and kill the animals many of them had taken along with them on hunting trips in the past.

No one who went out looking for the dogs had any doubt that they would find them, and if any of the hunters thought the whole event was going to be fun, they had the good sense not to advertise the fact.

There was only one problem with the notion of hunting down the wild pack. Enough woods to make tracking almost anything a challenge surrounded Serenity. And the dogs, whatever might be wrong with them, were cunning. They seemed to know the best ways to hide themselves, and it was a daunting task to find any evidence that they had ever been anywhere near the woods. The animals left no droppings, made no trails through the dense growth that didn't seem to fit, and were apparently very good at blending in with the scenery.

It was a long day filled with fruitless searching, and before it was over, most of the hunters would be discouraged. A few, however, knew that the dogs would show themselves sooner or later, and they were the ones who were rewarded for their patience. They were the ones who knew enough of animal nature to figure out that the best way to find the dogs was to have the animals find them.

Alden Waters, Marty Glass, and Rene Haldeman set their trap and waited patiently. They did not take the hunt as a game, which they were known to do on occasions when they were out deer hunting. They did not drink anything but water, and none of them even considered smoking a cigarette. They knew that the prey they were after wasn't deer: they were dogs, and they had a hunter's instinct all their own. Each of the men had been hunting in these woods for twenty years or more, and Alden Waters, who would be sixty years old in only another month, had almost forty years' worth of time as a hunter and tracker.

He was hardly as good as the Indians they had in Hollywood movies, but he knew about as much as anyone else of the area and was prepared for a long stakeout if that was what was needed.

The men sat perched on their platforms—the same ones they used during deer season—and they watched the woods around them. Below Alden a young pig sat tied to the tree where he had his wooden perch. The animal was already a goner, but had no knowledge of that fact as it rooted around in the mulch, looking for something worthwhile to eat. Alden had put several cuts into the animal's thick hide. They weren't the sort of cuts that would be a major problem, but they were the sort that bled more than a bit. Porky down below him was meant as bait, pure and simple. He had no illusions about the animal living through any encounters with the pack, but he knew it would probably bring them running if they caught a whiff of the blood. Assuming, of course, that the animals weren't completely sated from the people they'd torn apart the night before.

He had doubts about their being too full to eat. The kids were missing, but that didn't mean they'd all been gotten by the animals. Even with all the blood he'd seen when he found the cars and the two dead dogs at The Point, he held hopes that the kids themselves would be okay.

It wasn't a very big hope, but it was all he had.

Alden had been out only two days ago hunting around for a good area to set up camp and shoot a few deer come the fall. That was, in fact, what he'd been doing again today when he came across the cars of those poor kids. Insomnia left Alden walking at all hours of the night. But unlike the early morning hours of this day, he'd discovered corpses when he went out on Thursday morning. Not human, thank God, but still unsettling in their implications. A family of deer, not just one of them but four all told, had been torn into by what he now guessed were the dogs he'd heard about from Bill Karstens. The bodies had been savaged. Not a one of those animals had been left in any state that could have left them alive in the long run. Most of them had been, frankly, torn apart. But Alden had given a lot of thought to those remains while he lay back and tried to think through everything he'd seen, and he knew one thing for certain.

Whatever the dogs had been after, they hadn't been after food. There wasn't enough meat or entrails taken from the deer to feed a single dog, let alone a pack of them. They'd been torn apart for the sheer pleasure of killing them. It wasn't a notion that made the old hunter feel very comfortable.

Given a choice between a hungry pack of wolves and a hungry pack of dogs, Alden would have chosen the wolves in a heartbeat. Wolves, he knew, were not likely to bother with humans, contrary to the bad rap they got from fairytales and monster movies. Wolves, unless they were rabid or seriously desperate, would do everything they could to avoid men.

Dogs, on the other hand, were not the least bit afraid of people. They lived around humans and had no fear of them in a hostile situation. The newspapers were always full of stories about how one person or another had been savaged by a dog, and to the best of his knowledge, there wasn't a single valid case of a healthy wolf attacking a person. The closest you'd find in the average newspaper was an attack by a wolf-dog hybrid, and that came down to the same catch as the dogs; they just weren't as leery of people as wolves were.

And despite that knowledge, Alden had never heard of a dog attacking and killing a person for the pleasure of it. But he'd have sworn on a stack of Bibles that whatever had killed the kids the night before had been after doing just that. Killing for pleasure.

He snorted quietly to himself. *And here I thought only people did that sort of thing. Silly me.*

Alden shifted on his perch and scanned the woods, almost wishing he had a walkie-talkie for calling to the other groups and seeing what the hell was going on. But he and the boys had agreed in advance that they wouldn't risk it. If they made too many sounds, it might drive the dogs away, as unlikely as that seemed after what they'd done up at The Point.

He considered it a blessing that he hadn't heard the sounds of gunfire or ambulances coming through the woods. It made him almost proud of the local boys—most of whom he'd gone hunting with on a few occasions—that none of them took the task lightly. But he had to wonder where they all were, and if they'd encountered anything. And he couldn't help worrying about it. A lot of the volunteers were youngsters, barely out of high school themselves. And more than a few of them were there for personal reasons.

It was a small enough town. Damn near everybody out in the woods knew or was related to one of those kids.

It was personal for too many of them. Alden was afraid before it was all over, someone would get hurt and maybe even killed. That was why he was here, to prevent that from happening if he could.

Alden's knees creaked slightly as he shifted his weight. He was feeling his years in the strangely chilly weather. Still, he could wait. Waiting was what it was all about. Waiting, patience, and then the killing.

II

Stan practically had to beg to be allowed to go over to Dave's place. The walk was only about a quarter of a mile, and most of that was through streets that were populated—the area where the worries came was apparently where the farms started, as if a pack of dogs would be more prone to hide in open fields and sneak in for the kill than in say, the narrow alleys between a few of the homes. It was a logic that meant nothing to Stan, but that was hardly surprising—still, he'd had to practically beg before his mom conceded to letting him go.

And it had been worth it. Dave's family was always a lot of fun. When Stan was around Dave alone, he tended to think his friend was unique. When he saw him with his whole family was when he normally realized that Dave was just, as his father was fond of saying, "a product of his environment."

Dave Pageant came from a very large family, and most of the members of that group could be called eccentric without any stretching of the truth. To Stan, they were all delightful. Dave had a large group of cousins and actual siblings, all of whom were simply referred to as his brothers and sisters. Stan didn't know all of the details, but some time back, Dave's grandparents had been left with the burden of raising not only their own children, but those of two separate siblings of Earl Pageant. Rather than fret and fuss, they'd simply made the whole lot of them into one big group and called them all their children. All told, there were about twenty members in the household. They should have been absolutely miserable with that many people crowded into one place, but they weren't. It baffled Stan's mind, but in a good way.

Dave was almost the baby of the family. Only Tina was younger, and that was by three years. Tina was mostly just annoying in Stan's eyes. But the next closest siblings, Amber and Suzette, were an endless source of fascination for him. They were seventeen-year-old twins, with dark red hair and freckled skin and bodies that belonged in the centerfold of *Playboy*. They teased Stan mercilessly whenever he came over, flirting with him and doing everything they could to make him blush. He ate it up like candy. Right before the twins was Danny, who was also seventeen and tried to be as macho as possible. And the last sibling of actual interest to Stan was Ricky, who was almost twenty but was also slow. He was older than Dave physically, but for all intents and purposes may as well have been younger. He laughed at even the dumbest jokes and always forgot what he'd said only a few minutes before, so would tell the same bad jokes and stories to a person about a dozen times unless he was reminded that he'd already told it. Almost everyone else in the family was grown up, but they still lived at the farm, and they were genuinely pleasant to be around.

After the last few days at home, going over to Dave's was almost like getting to go to Disney World. Despite the killings—and everyone had heard about them and most everyone was miserable with grief or frustration over them—the Pageants were still happy to see him and fun to be around.

He'd been there for a few hours already, with both of the twins running around constantly and tormenting him—they were cute, and the fact that they noticed him only enhanced that cuteness—and he and Dave were out in the front yard, the only part of the property not dedicated to raising something to eat or sell. The day was winding down as far as Dave was concerned. He would be called to handle his evening chores soon, and after that he had homework. For Stan it meant going back home and enduring the strange tensions in the Long household. The idea made him melancholy, or maybe it was just the autumnlike weather. Either way he wished the good feelings didn't have to end.

Dave looked over at him with a bland sort of smile on his face. "Sun's gonna be setting pretty soon. If you're thinking of not getting your ass beat, you ought to start home."

Stan looked back at him and nodded. "Yeah..."

"Hey, don't sound so excited." His voice was dry and amused. Which, when Stan let himself think about it, pretty much summed up Dave's personality. Dave was not normally the sort to get overly excited about anything. He was also the sort who read between the lines very well. "Things starting to get rough at home?"

Stan looked at his friend for a few seconds in silence and then nodded. "Not really starting, exactly. More like been rough for a while."

"You figure they're headed for divorce?" And there it was, spelled out in black and white and just plain undeniably in front of him. Stan had avoided thinking about it, but it had been lurking around the corners and waiting for him.

"I dunno. Maybe. Probably." His chest felt all wrong, like someone was sitting on his rib cage and bouncing up and down. It was not a comfortable feeling by any means. His eyes gave that nasty sting that told him he was about to embarrass himself and cry, and he looked away from Dave while he tried his best to make the tears stay where the hell they were.

It didn't work. Before he could have done as much as stand up and move a foot away, he was crying. Almost as quickly, Dave had an arm around his shoulders and a moderately embarrassed look on his face. Stan turned toward the comfort offered and let himself go, sobbing against his best friend's chest and hugging him like there was a hurricane coming and Dave was the only tree available.

Dave hugged back, and if he was worried about anyone seeing them and maybe calling them queer or something, he didn't let it show. His big hands patted Stan on the back, and he held him and let him release what he'd been holding in for so long. Dave's glasses slid halfway down his face before Stan was done. He knew how much Dave hated it when his glasses slipped and that the boy did nothing to fix the problem—which was almost like not zipping your fly in Dave's eyes—he was deeply touched. It was a silly thing to feel good about, but he did just the same.

They sat in complete silence when it was done, and while it wasn't quite an uncomfortable span of time, it was close to it. Neither of them, despite being best friends for as long as they could remember, had ever hugged for God's sake. Stan wanted to say thanks, but couldn't think of exactly how to do it without making Dave feel embarrassed.

The seizure took that worry away.

Stan's body spasmed so hard that he almost stood up fully before arching backward and slamming headfirst into the ground, his arms and legs thrashing and beating against the ground to four different rhythms while his body twisted and writhed like a captive serpent. His teeth clacked together, and his head did its best to force itself down past the grass and deep into the soil beneath.

He didn't hear Dave screaming his name or feel the hands that tried to hold him down. He didn't see Amber and Suzette rushing from the house, or feel their hands on his body, or hear their soothing words as they spoke to him.

He wasn't really there for any of that or the things that followed. He was elsewhere...

He was with the shadows again, and for the first time he could make out details, brief flashes of color and lines that defined faces more clearly. He almost preferred the darkness. The expressions he saw were filled with rage and fury like a tornado or a forest fire. A man in dark, shabby clothes screamed something that was too muffled to make out... *Every solace green.* But it sounded like a promise of pain to come. The man's hair was overly thick and wiry, and his grin was a nasty slash across a face that was painted white. The smile did not match the way his mouth moved. All around him were people or things that made no sense. There were horses and dwarves and people who just plain looked wrong, all of them seen as shadows that from time to time revealed a part of themselves, only to fade back into the darkness.

They were angry. No, they were murderous. They didn't want to scream and rant. They wanted blood and death and violence. He smelled smoke and popcorn and sugary confections and horse shit and stranger things, though he saw nothing but the strange twilight figures moving around him.

Stan didn't dare move or draw attention to himself, not after the last time he'd been this close to the things that roamed around him. He could still feel the pain of his skin freezing, and the terror of having these creatures move through his body. He wanted to go home, to be back with his mom and dad and even his sister, away from the freakish things moving around him. He didn't want to hear their muted voices or try to understand what they were saying. He wanted to be anywhere but here.

The shushing susurrations of the shadows continued, growing louder by slow degrees, and though he didn't want to listen to the words, he felt compelled. They were saying something, and they were trying to make their point known, but it was proving damned difficult to understand them.

When he could take the whispered noises no longer, he called out to the closest form, a dwarfish thing that grinned an impossibly wide smile and hissed angrily when it noticed him. The smile—a painted red slash on pale white skin—split to bare teeth as the shadow thing looked his way. "What are you?"

Every solace green.

"What do you want from me?"

Every solace green. The thing slipped closer, and though Stan was sitting on the ground in the strange nonplace where he found himself, it looked at him from the same height. Dark, feverish eyes burned in shadows so deep they could have been the sockets of a skull. Its voice was angry and urgent, and Stan didn't know if it was trying to warn him of something or trying to threaten him. Either way, the dwarven clown scared the hell out of him.

"I can't understand you." The thing came closer, and he could feel its chill breath on his face. The awful, cloyingly sweet smell of cotton candy and rotted flesh spilled from the distorted mouth of the thing as it tried again to make its words heard.

Every solace green.

"I can't hear you. Speak louder, please." Stan's voice cracked as he spoke, and he thought for sure that he'd pee himself.

Despite his trepidation, he knew the words were important, and they were close to something he could understand. As much as the idea of really comprehending the words terrified him, he had to know. It was a compulsion after so long.

The dwarf stood directly in front of him, and he saw for the first time how withered it looked, almost mummified under the garish colors painting its face. This time he understood when it spoke. *Every so lals greem.* Stan shook his head and tried to back away, but the hands of the clown, thick, powerful hands that seemed almost too large for the small body, grabbed his shoulders and pulled his face closer until he could feel the flesh of the thing, the cold, dead flesh that seemed almost to writhe against his face. *Every. Soul. Will. SCREAM!*

All around him he heard the words chanted. And now they were as clear as crystal to his ears. *Every soul will scream. Every soul will scream. Every soul will scream and scream and scream!*

The chant continued as Stan rose shakily to his feet and started running. He had no idea where he was planning to go, but he knew he had to get away from them, from the shadows that came closer to him and started reaching with frozen hands and tearing at his body. Wherever they touched, he felt a shred of himself pulled and stretched until it ripped away. He ran as fast as he could, but they were everywhere, an endless army of angry, hateful shades. Stan screamed and tried to get away, but they were everywhere.

He stumbled, he fell, and they were upon him. Their words chanted endlessly as they covered him in their darkness, and his own screams filled the air to mingle with their whispered battle cry.

III

Charlee sat in her room, and Jessie sat beside her. They were both miserably bored. It wasn't that they couldn't find something to watch on TV, because they could. It wasn't that they couldn't talk, because they could. It wasn't even that they couldn't find something to do in the house. It was simply because they were stuck inside. That fact made what should have been a good time rather like being in prison.

It was the principle of the thing.

There was something inherently wrong with being stuck in the house when she hadn't done anything wrong. Heck, her grades were even decent for once. Her stupid brother could go outside. Why? Because he was a guy, that was why—well, okay, and he was four years older, but still.

Even now, as she and Jessie sat in her room and toyed with what they could do that would be fun—all of the usual video games and movies had magically lost their appeal as soon as Charlee realized she was held captive by her parents—her brother Dean was out in the world and having good time. It wasn't the least bit fair to her way of thinking.

Charlee sighed and moved to the window. Outside the road led east and west, and no one was taking the opportunity presented. The day was as close to perfect as she'd ever seen, with cool air she could feel through the screen that was somehow not quite as sweet for blowing into the house while she was trapped.

Her mom was downstairs and not willing to listen to reason. When Charlene had tried discussing the matter of leaving the house earlier, she'd shaken her head very slowly and very steadily and finally simply told her that it wasn't going to happen. When Charlee asked why—doing her best to avoid actively whining about the situation—her mom simply said that there had been a dog attack.

Charlee never really liked dogs—they were smelly, and they barked too much—but she still couldn't quite imagine it was all *that* bad getting bitten by one, unless maybe it was the size of that monster Stan owned. Thinking of Stan made her smile, and thinking of the time she caught him trying to walk Beauregard made her want to laugh out loud. It'd been at the end of the last school year, and Stan hadn't started growing taller than her again. They were exactly the same height, which seemed to make him crazy, like it was a contest. She and Jessie had been walking toward the schools—it was a Saturday, but they always walked around town when the weather permitted—and come across Stan and his Saint Bernard heading toward them. The big dog was eager to go forward and preferred the idea of going a lot faster than Stan had in mind. He was pulling on his leash, and Stan was struggling to keep him from taking off at a full run. Jessie, seeing the boy she liked but would never confess to liking, had called out. Stan got a confused look on his face. It was the look he normally had stuck there when anyone spoke to him. Then the expression turned into alarm as Beau started running toward the two girls, and Stan was hauled along for the ride. He made a yelping sound and dug his heels in, but the massive dog was not to be stopped. Not until he reached his target at least. Beau threw himself into the air, balancing on his hind legs, and planted his paws on Jessie's shoulders. The weight alone would probably have knocked her down, but the dog's big sloppy tongue attacking her face like an ice cream cone so thoroughly shocked Charlee's best friend that she tried backing up and ended up on the ground with the dog over her, lapping at her face like crazy. It might have been a scary situation under some circumstances, but Jess was laughing so hard and the dog was wagging not just his tail, it seemed, but his whole body. It was very funny in a warped way, funny enough that Charlee had trouble catching her breath while it was happening.

Still the idea of seeing a dog that size with a snarl on its face and trying to bite…the very notion gave Charlee the shivers.

But still, it was wrong to waste a perfect day inside when she could imagine that everyone else in town was having fun in the sun. Heck, the last good days of the year were on them. The summer break was just about to start, and that always went by too quickly, and in no time they'd have to start wearing heavy jackets to avoid freezing to death.

She was toying with just climbing out the window and getting gone. It wasn't that hard to do; she'd done it a few other times. But never in broad daylight. Never when her folks were awake, and, just to make matters worse, when her dad was out hunting for a dog. She sighed again, and Jessie looked over at her with a hopeful expression.

"Monopoly?"

"We played that last night."

"I know, but it beats listening to you mope."

"I'm not moping."

"No? What do you call it?"

"I don't know, Jess, I just want to go outside." Jessie was exasperating.

Jess sighed. "Well, maybe they got those dogs already."

"I doubt it. That would mean the day could go well."

"Are you always so pessimistic?"

"What? This is a surprise to you?"

"No, but I keep hoping you'll lighten up." It never stopped surprising Charlee that her best friend was actually opinionated when they were by themselves. It was only when they were in a group that Jessie became a milksop.

"Okay, so say I decide not to be a pessimist. How is that going to make my life better?"

"You'll be in a better mood all the time."

"No, I'll be in a worse mood."

"How do you figure?"

"If I'm optimistic, I have to expect things to go right, right?"

"Yeah…"

"So if they go wrong, I'll be disappointed. Right?"

"Yeah, but…"

"But if I'm a pessimist, and nothing goes the way I'd like, it's just what I expected. And if it goes right, it's a pleasant surprise."

Jessie looked at her and frowned, a puzzled expression on her face. "And you actually believe that?"

"Sure." Charlee shrugged. "It's worked for me so far."

"Well," Jessie sniffed the air, almost disdainfully, but not quite. "If that's the best you can come up with for a philosophy of life, it's small wonder you don't have a boyfriend yet."

"Yeah?" Charlee bristled at that comment. It wasn't like she was actively looking for a guy to hang with or anything. Jessie was just trying to push her buttons and doing an admirable job of it. "Well what's your excuse for not having a boyfriend? Can't decide on only one? Can't find one that will boss you around enough?"

Jess's head turned sharply, as if she'd been slapped. "What do you mean by that?"

Charlee could have stopped right then, knew she should have if she wanted to avoid a blowup with Jessie, but she didn't. Instead, she bared her teeth in a smile that was almost a snarl and moved ahead. "You know what I mean. You can't make a decision on your own, Jessie. You're looking for someone to make all of them for you."

"That's a lie!"

"No it isn't. You can't stand having to think for yourself. God, Jessie, every time anyone has an argument you're so busy taking both sides you forget what they're even arguing about."

Jessie shook her head and looked away. "You take that back, Charlene. You take it back right now."

"Why? Does the truth hurt?" If asked exactly why she was so busily attacking her friend, Charlee couldn't have answered. Maybe she was just sick of Jessie's holier-than-thou attitude; maybe she just felt particularly vicious and wanted to see her friend cry. Whatever the reason, she did not listen to the voice in her head that told her to stop. She kept right on going. "You can't even decide whether or not you like a guy unless you've heard five other girls say he's cute. Hell, Jessie, if a guy tried kissing you, you'd probably ask him to stop until you could find out from everyone else if it was a good idea."

Jessie stood up, her normally friendly face dark and bitter and just a little sad, and Charlee immediately felt like shit about the whole thing, "That's fine, Charlene. You just go ahead and say whatever mean things you feel like saying. I'm going home."

"Jess… I'm sorry…"

Jessie looked over at her, and her eyes narrowed ever so slightly before she answered. "Sorry because you hurt me? Or just sorry that I don't feel like letting you step on me anymore today?" She walked to the door out of Charlee's room and shook her head. "Either way, I'm still out of here, and you're still stuck."

Jess left, and Charlee sat on her bed, wondering exactly why she'd decided to beat up on her best friend. She didn't know, but it left a bad taste in her mouth.

IV

Jessie didn't walk toward her house so much as she sulked. She tried to tell herself that Charlee was just in one of her moods—they weren't frequent, but when they came up, Jess did her best to just give her best friend her space—but it didn't take the sting out of the words. Had she been a more vindictive girl, she'd have sworn off of Charlee for life. But she wasn't. So instead she pouted and walked a lazy trail toward her house only five blocks away.

She didn't want to cry, didn't want to let Charlee get to her that way, but she felt it happening anyway. She felt that irritating burning at the inner corners of her eyes and felt the flash of heat that sent a light fogging over her glasses. She stopped walking and forced the tears back through a series of blinks. She was good at stopping herself from crying. It was a talent she'd mastered over the last few years. She had to, because damn near everything made her feel like breaking down in tears.

Charlee didn't understand, couldn't understand what Jessie's life was like. Jessie didn't share what she went through with anyone. It was not in her nature. When she was very, very young her mother had told her that the best way to keep people happy was to keep your bad thoughts to yourself. Jessie had taken that to heart. You had to work and work hard to get Jessie Grant to admit that life wasn't perfect, and to date no one had ever tried successfully.

Jessie wasn't worth the effort.

Oh, she knew well enough that her parents loved her, but in the same idle way that they might love a pet dog. When she did something right they patted her on the head, maybe took her out for dinner, but after that, she was just background noise. Her dad was busy trying to pay the bills, and her mom...well, her mom was normally too busy ragging on her dad for not paying all the bills fast enough. They fought constantly, though she knew they loved each other. They never yelled at Jessie, and she supposed she was grateful for that, but still, sometimes she wondered if the yelling wouldn't have actually been better than the near silence in the house.

It was easier when she was younger. Back when she was really little, there never seemed to be any problems at home. Everyone got along just fine, and everyone seemed happier. She'd thought that maybe her dad getting the job with the quarry would help, but so far it hadn't made much of a difference. Of course, the first paycheck from the work wasn't due in until Monday, so maybe then it would change.

She'd been looking forward to spending time with Charlee. Charlee was so dynamic—that was Jessie's newest word, dynamic—and so ready to just tell the world to fuck off if it got in her way. But she was also fun to be around, unless she got into one of her moods.

Like now.

Sometimes Jessie had to work at it not to hate Charlee.

She was still lost in her dark thoughts when she realized she was being followed.

V

Lawrence Grey sat at the desk in his room, the latest Dean Koontz thriller in front of him, and looked down at the baseball diamond behind the church, just to the left of where the cemetery started. There was no one on the field today, and he found that depressing. At least he could watch other kids when there was a game. He might not be able to join them, but he could watch. Make-believe would simply have to be enough.

Saturday, that particular Saturday that is, was a bit unusual. Penelope Grey was not at home. She was out shopping in the city with her sister. Lawrence was not heartbroken to have a little time to himself for a change of pace, and the fact that he was trusted to stay on his own meant a good deal to him.

Though he had been, as ever, strongly cautioned not to leave the house under any circumstances.

Penny Grey was a good woman, and he loved her. She was his mom, after all, but on days like this, when the weather was cool and crisp, he felt like he could do without ever seeing her again. She was his mother, true enough, but she was also his captor.

All because she was worried about him. She often reminded him about his father when he said that he would be okay if he went outside. She lorded the story of his father over him as all the proof she ever needed that it wasn't a safe world for a growing young boy.

Penny and Daniel Grey had been married too young, perhaps. She was only twenty-two when they married, and he was only twenty-four. They divorced after eighteen months, and Daniel Grey left town to seek his fame and fortune elsewhere in the world. He left Penny with a substantial house payment and a bun in the oven. Daniel didn't bother with a forwarding address, and he certainly didn't bother with alimony. Penny, with her typical strength—which most agreed was more than enough for five or six people—went about her life without him. She had graduated college only a few weeks before they were married, and she'd managed to get herself work as a freelance computer programmer long before the industry really exploded. She had, as was her usual style, been prepared for the future.

That should have been the end of the story, and if it had been, Lawrence suspected he would have been a much happier kid. When Lawrence was two, his father had come back to town, and it was when he finally came around again that he learned he had a son. Penny told him he could go drown himself in the quarry when he asked to meet his descendant. They fought right there on the front lawn of the house, screaming and cursing at each other like there was no end to their stamina. The only thing that broke up the argument was one of the neighbors—Lawrence thought it was Mrs. Barrinton, she was always sticking her nose where it didn't belong, according to his mother—called the police and the constables dragged his father away from the premises.

Somewhere along the way, during his time away from Serenity Falls, Daniel must have gone through some serious changes in his life. This time around, Daniel Grey didn't take "no" very well as an answer. Later the same day, well after the sun had set, he broke into the house he'd helped purchase and tried to take his son by force. He didn't bring a gun with him; he brought a hunting knife.

Penny Grey got herself stabbed three times before he managed to peel her off of the door that separated her ex-husband from his son. Her blouses normally concealed two of the scars she carried—one on her stomach, the other on her right bicep. The last scar, the one that constantly reminded her of the conflict was just under her right eye and ran all the way to her right ear. It was deep and thick and marred her pretty face. She required hospitalization and almost a full year of physical therapy before she was back to her old self. But what she'd endured meant nothing at all to her.

It was secondary to what had almost happened to her son. Daniel Grey came within minutes of chopping Lawrence into so much stewing meat before he was found. He'd taken off and hidden himself in what he assumed would be the last place anyone would look for him: the Blackwell house. Some people apparently thought a little faster than Daniel. It was the second place after his hotel room that Bill Karstens looked.

According to what Lawrence's mom had to say about the subject, Karstens caught Daniel in the act of sharpening his hunting knife, with Lawrence pinned to the kitchen counter with duct tape. There wasn't much of a scuffle, but it ended with Daniel Grey knocked silly by a wooden baton and handcuffed. He was locked into the county jail for all of two weeks before he managed to make bond, and after that he was never seen again by anyone in the town.

But Penny Grey didn't think it was over. She didn't trust that her ex-husband would ever take no for an answer on anything again, and she wasn't taking any chances. Penny carried a handgun these days, and Lawrence was well aware of it. He was also very certain that touching that weapon would get his ass tanned to the point where sitting would seem like an exquisite torture for several weeks.

Lawrence wasn't allowed to touch anything stronger than a butter knife. His mother had become something of a specialist in the art of overprotection. It was one of the things that simply was in his life, and Lawrence had long ago stopped really thinking about it. Except, of course, when he was restless and wanted so desperately to go outside and see people other than his mother and whatever faces were on the television.

Sometimes he needed a little more than his mom in his world. Sometimes he needed to actually interact with real flesh and blood that wasn't a blood relative. Lawrence Grey was not precisely a happy kid, and he knew it.

But the world was what it was, as his mom was fond of saying. Best not to dwell on it.

He ran a hand through his thin black hair and stared at the field outside again. His eyes grew just a shade wider when he saw that this time a person was on the field. Jessie Grant was walking along, her head down and her bottom lip stuck out in a pout that made her even prettier than she normally was. He watched her walking, the way the sun caught red highlights in her brown hair and the way her developing hips moved gently in an unconsciously provocative sway as she walked.

Looking toward her, he felt his heart thud a little faster in his chest. Jessie had that effect on him. Most girls did. They were practically a foreign species. The closest he'd ever come to having a girlfriend was developing a crush on Sarah Michelle Gellar on *Buffy the Vampire Slayer*. Aside from looking at them and watching them interact on television sets, he had almost no experience talking to girls. His mom didn't count, and neither did his Aunt Lois, with whom his mother was currently shopping.

Lawrence watched Jessie walking, her pretty face screwed into a pout, and felt his skin flush and his heart go out to her. She looked like she was truly miserable about something, and he figured he knew just how she felt. He was almost always miserable about something.

He saw her slow progress across the field, saw the look of sorrow on her face, and did something he never did. He pulled on his shoes and walked outside. Setting his sights, he started following Jessie as she moved past the cemetery. He had no idea what he was planning, if he would ever get up the nerve to talk to her, or if he would suddenly freeze up and then bolt back home, but he was feeling bold, and for once he allowed himself to act on that feeling.

He liked the sensation of doing something wrong, and as he walked farther from his home, Lawrence began to smile.

VI

It was just possibly too early in the day for a drink, but the bar was open and allegedly had a grill to go along with whatever they were passing off as spirits in this part of the world. Bart Cambridge wasn't really all that particular. He was tired from too many hours on the road, and he needed a rest. So Townsley's Bar and Grill won the good old coin toss, and he pulled over into the graveled parking lot. There were already several cars in the lot, and the smell of something cooking over a wood fire made his stomach growl.

In the seat beside him, his guest passenger stirred and smiled. Bart turned away quickly. He liked the guy all right, but his smile was about as calming as raw oysters after an all-night drunk. There was nothing out of place about the man's teeth; they were a little large, maybe, but that was all. His face was normal enough that he could get lost in a crowd in about ten seconds flat. But still, when his teeth showed in a smile, it was almost like a challenge, and one that he made more as a joke than because he felt there was any sort of threat.

Bart looked at the man and nodded his head toward the eatery. "I figured now is as good a time as any for breakfast."

Jonathan Crowley climbed out of the car and flashed another grin. His eyes seemed to say that he knew it was more than breakfast Bart wanted. "Seeing as it's almost lunchtime, that seems fair."

"Yeah, well, the old stomach is starting to growl a bit…"

"Well, this one's on me." His smile spread wider across his face, and Bart felt a chill run down his spine. That smile seemed to bring back memories from his days in high school, when he was often easy prey for the jocks and the greasers both. "My way of saying thanks for the lift. Despite the man's easygoing friendliness, despite his having been nothing but pleasant on the trip, Bart almost wished he'd never stopped to give him a ride. He was creepy. His eyes always seemed to look deeper than they should, and they seemed to find flaws wherever they looked. It was like hanging around with the head librarian after having torn the nudes out of several *National Geographic* magazines. The last four hours had left him wanting to squirm in his seat while he drove, and that couldn't possibly be a good thing.

Crowley moved to look over the building, almost seeming to inspect it for flaws, and then nodded to himself. Bart followed along, trying to see what could make the wood-and-brick building worth examining closely. Finally he shrugged. For all he knew, the man was comparing it to one of his own favorite haunts.

The interior of Townsley's was pretty much what he'd expected: seedy, but with a dash of tacky neon doing its best to hide that fact. There were several fairly rough-looking men sitting around the tables, a few of them actually daring to eat the food. As they were likely locals, that was probably a good sign. Then again, they also looked like the sort who would gleefully eat cows that were still screaming in protest. They were not exactly the sort of fellas he would normally choose to associate with. Still, you did what you had to when working as a sales rep. Especially when there was serious money to be made. It had been a windfall learning about the takeover of the old quarry, and he had little doubt that the new owners would need equipment.

Crowley strolled through the crowd like he owned the place, blatantly ignoring the stares he got. He settled in at the bar and grabbed one of the menus propped up against an empty water glass. Bart followed, but he was far more conscious of the stares. The men in the room were not, in general, looking very friendly. They looked tired, and they looked irritable. Maybe it was his imagination, but he didn't tend to think so.

Following his companion's example, he sat at the bar and grabbed a menu. Despite the chilly reception, the air carried a tantalizing scent of grilling burgers that had his stomach growling. The man who owned the bar was old enough to have fathered most of the people sitting at the tables, and mean enough—if his scowl meant anything—to break every last one of them over his knee. His white shirt had the name

Reggie embroidered onto the front, just above the breast pocket on the left side. Reggie all but growled his offer of assistances—"*Help you boys?*"—and did nothing but nod when they made their orders. He made up for it by being fast with the service and offering very generous portions.

Jonathan Crowley ate meticulously. He took careful bites from his cheeseburger and fries and chewed with the same sort of care a doctor might use to perform surgery. If he derived any actual pleasure from the food, he hid it well. At that particular time, Bart couldn't have cared less. The chili he ate was just shy of paradise, even if he could feel the lining of his stomach peeling away like dead skin under a sand blaster. It was worth the pain. Still, he made a note to hit the Rolaids in his pocket as soon as he was done.

Bart was almost finished with his meal when he became painfully aware of how silent the bar had become. He was chewing happily when he first realized that no one was talking, and that the jukebox—which played an endless run of melancholy country western songs about trucks, dogs, and women in no particular order—wasn't piping out music any longer. His chewing slowed down as he wondered if he'd made some sort of hideous social blunder without realizing it, and he replayed the last few moments in his mind. Nope. Not a damned thing that he could think of. He hadn't burped, farted, or insulted anyone's lineage. Also, his deodorant was still doing just fine.

Jonathan Crowley was very calmly setting down the remains of his burger. His face was expressionless, but his eyes almost alight with sardonic humor.

"John, did I miss something?"

Crowley looked at him for a second, then his eyes shifted to a place to the right and behind Bart. Then he looked back at Bart again. "Not yet, but I suspect we're about to meet with the local welcome wagon."

Bart cast his eyes toward the mirror behind the bar. Through the grime that coated its surface, he could see one of the bruisers heading toward them. The man's reflection wasn't distorted by the mirror, but he desperately wished that it was. *Big, big man. Not really muscular, just sort of beefy in a natural-born-killer sort of way.* Bart could guess that this was the part where he had to do a song and dance or lose a few teeth to the local boy with the twisted sense of humor. He could sing and dance with the best of them, but he didn't have to like it. It was too much like the crap he'd put up with in high school.

Oh, make no mistake, he would sing and dance, just like he had in the bad old days, because the alternative was unpleasant to consider.

The last time Bart had been in a fight had been his second year in college. He'd fought with Stewart Coleman over the affections of Carrie Mickle. Carrie was a very friendly girl who'd chosen Bart over Stewart. Stewart, the quarterback of the football team—*Go Vikings*—didn't seem to like the notion that a guy like Bart who was pudgy and already starting to lose his hair, might have managed to win Carrie's affections over his own buff self. Stewie called Carrie a whore, and Bart decided to fight for the honor of a girl neither of them knew from Eve but both desperately wanted to screw.

Bart got as far as "Why, you limp-dicked motherfu—" before the hero of the football arena hit him square in the nose with a fist that seemed even larger than his head. Several of the other partygoers pulled good ol' Stewie off of Bart before the damage went any further than three teeth, a broken nose, a dislocated jaw, and four cracked ribs. Rumor came down later that Stew had been hopped up on crack cocaine. Bart didn't much care what the substance was, he was far too busy trying to recover for the next month or so.

Physically he was fine. Emotionally, he wanted to run home to Mommy every time somebody looked at him like they might be thinking of the possibility of challenging him to a fight. The fact that his mother had passed on to the next life after losing her own fight with pancreatic cancer didn't stop him from wanting to go to her. He was a coward, and not the least bit embarrassed about confessing that fact. People didn't seem to play as nicely after grade school, and the older he got, the worse they wanted to get. He wasn't taking any chances.

Bart was trying to figure how quickly he could leave Townsley's when the local version of the big bad wolf dropped a heavy hand on his shoulder. "You boys are new in town, aincha?"

The voice was pleasant enough, but Bart knew better than to think it was friendly conversation the man was after. As if to prove him right, the fingers on the man's hand squeezed a little too firmly on his shoulder. Like, firmly enough to try digging for bone under the meat and skin that covered said bone.

Bart forced a pleasant smile on his face. "Just got into town. Looks like a great place."

"Yeah? That's nice. Ever been through here before?"

Bart looked at the broad face reflected behind him. It was almost rectangular and made him think of models he'd seen of Cro-Magnon man. The guy had one thick black eyebrow over his eyes, which were about as squinty as Clint Eastwood's in one of his spaghetti Westerns. The leering smile perched over his lantern jaw made the man look about as intelligent as the average cantaloupe, albeit a rabid cantaloupe. What hair he had on his head was black going gray and looked just enough like mold growing on a rotten melon that Bart had to bite the inside of his cheek to stop a nervous giggle.

"No, can't say as I have. Neither has my friend."

"You sure about that? Maybe you were in town just a couple of days ago."

"I'm pretty sure I'd remember that."

The hand on his shoulder increased its pressure, and he looked over at Crowley to see what his one hope in hell during a fight was up to. The man was looking back at him with a serene, closemouthed smile.

Bart swallowed hard and shook his head as he raised his hands to shoulder height, the palms facing outward and away from the man behind him. "Look, I have no idea what might have happened here two days ago, but I really don't want any trouble..."

"Neither do I, buddy. Where would you get the idea that I wanted trouble?"

Before Bart could answer, Crowley spoke up. "Maybe it's the way your fingers are digging for clams in his shoulder, bright boy."

In an effort to prove that he was just as quick on his verbal feet, the local looked over and responded. "Say what?"

"I don't repeat myself. At least not right now. Whatever happened in your little piss pot town, I wasn't here, and neither was he." Crowley's facial expression hadn't changed much. He still had that vague, closemouthed smile in place. The main difference was that his eyes actually looked bored by the exchange.

The hand lifted off of Bart's shoulder, and for a second he couldn't decide if that was a good thing or a bad thing. He watched the man behind him move toward Crowley in the mirror, almost afraid to turn his head to watch the reality. He might get noticed again. Several of the other locals were looking their way and following the action. He watched them in the mirror, too. A few of them were doing more than merely observing their buddy. They were getting up, apparently to join him.

Bart concentrated on not actively whimpering.

The lowbrow who'd been ready to start something with him now stood between him and John Crowley. "I don't think I was talking to you. I think I was talking to your buddy." Oh yeah, he was quick on the sharp-tongued retorts today, boys and girls.

"And I'm pretty damned sure neither one of us was talking to you." Crowley sat up a little straighter in his seat and started to smile in earnest. "Now, run home to Mommy, before I have to teach you a lesson about good manners."

The man didn't bother trying any more verbal repartees; he hauled back his large fist and swung hard at Crowley's face. Crowley took the shot across his jaw, his head snapping back and the glasses he wore all but flying away from the bridge of his hawkish nose. It was a damned fine hit. The impact rippled all the way up the bruiser's arm and to his shoulder. It also knocked Crowley half out of his seat.

Crowley slid the rest of the way to the ground, his head lowered for a second, looking at the ground. Then he raised his face, and the smile that made Bart nervous was back, only it was broader than he would have thought possible.

VII

Mike and Amelia went into Townsley's as a sort of test. It had been over two weeks, and Mike had not had a drink. Now it was time to see if he could resist the urge, the smell, and the availability of the liquor. Townsley's was a dive, but they had everything you could want to drink and then some. Amelia was along as an anchor.

Amelia was very good at keeping Mike anchored to the right path. She was having that effect on him more and more, though he didn't like to think about the implications. He didn't want to consider that he could possibly be falling for her—though the thought kept creeping in when he wasn't expecting it—didn't want to think that he was using her as a substitute Amy—though it was a possibility that kept haunting him when he was alone—or as a replacement for dat ol' demon alkeehawl that had been his constant companion for far too long.

He didn't like the possibility that he was that weak, or that cruel. Still, the thoughts kept coming back to him.

Amelia climbed out of the passenger's seat, her face friendly but deliberately neutral. She was not there to judge, and he knew that she would say nothing at all if he decided to drink down a pint or two of his old favorites. The thought that she would accept him no matter what he did was, frankly, a bit unsettling.

She'd proved that just the day before, when he went ballistic over the grave desecration. Without even checking how much damage was done, he'd gone into an absolute fit, ranting, raving, and cursing God and everyone around him like a complete madman. It was only later, after Amelia had taken him home and all but tucked him into bed, that he discovered Amy's grave had not been disturbed. And through it all, Amelia had been patient and understanding.

And he was damned if he could figure out why.

Mike locked the doors on his old car and walked toward the tinted-glass entrance of Townsley's with Amelia beside him. Without even thinking about it, he slipped his hand into hers. They fit together very well.

Mike opened the door and forced himself to relax. Not even through the threshold, and he could feel his stomach doing flipflops as the thought of having booze available to him jumped into his skull. Amelia's long fingers gripped his own and squeezed encouragement. He stepped forward.

And was promptly knocked on his ass for his troubles. It's hard to keep your balance when 257 pounds of staggering brawler runs into you at high velocity. Mike made a sound that might have been a squawk, and then his head was smacking into the wall hard enough to make him see stars in the middle of the day. Amelia let out an indignant sound and grabbed the man who was now sprawled across him by one thick arm, dragging him off to the side. The man's only comment was a deep, faint groan.

By the time Amelia had managed to haul the man most of the way off him, Mike was standing up, his head ringing and the anger he held inside blossoming again into a proper rage. He looked toward the man on the ground and thought hard about kicking him. But it only took him a second to realize that Mitch Booker was already unconscious. Booker was a local, and one that Mike could take or leave as far as personalities went. Apparently someone in the bar decided to take offense to Mitch's normal bad attitude. Judging by the sounds coming through the door as it slowly dragged shut, either that somebody or Mitch's buddies had decided not to leave the fighting just yet.

Amelia pushed against Mike as he moved into the bar, both of them trying to adjust to the difference between the bright sunlight outside and the dim interior of Townsley's. In the semidarkness they heard the sounds of someone grunting and a heavy, meaty noise that made Mike think of a meat tenderizer slapping down on a particularly tough piece of beef. As his eyes adjusted, Mike saw that four of the locals were in the process of circling one stranger. Two more of the regulars—guys he knew from working on the house, and a few he had helped with loans when he was with the bank—were busy doing their very best to keep the man pinned in place. And lastly, one more local—Tom Hardwick in this case—was sitting on another man's flabby chest and slapping him lightly in the face again and again. Tom was talking low, too low for Mike to hear the words, but the sound of his voice was taunting and petty. Mike was a little disappointed; he'd started to believe Tom had grown out of his days of picking on people who were obviously not a match for him.

The guy being held by Butch and Bernie Howard, two of the most notorious brawlers in all of the county by Mike's recollection, was wriggling like a pissed-off sidewinder, and the brothers were hard-pressed to hold him at all. There was a lot of panting going on, and through the smells of Reggie's chili, stale beer, and cigarette smoke, Mike could almost have sworn he caught the scent of pure testosterone.

Mike cast his eyes off to the side of the conflict, even as Amelia pushed past him into the room, and found Reggie calmly talking on the phone. Reggie saw him and nodded, and Mike crossed his arms, watching the fight unfold. There was a part of him that wanted to break up the brawl, but the bigger part knew he'd have no chance at all against that many guys. It was a stupid scenario, and he hated the indecision that held him in place.

The problem was, Mike Blake didn't like to fight. He never knew when to say enough and back off. Just as importantly, he didn't want to see Amelia getting hurt in the crossfire. Groups that size didn't stay stationary when they lost control, and sooner or later the people on the sidelines got hurt. It was almost inevitable.

Amelia stared openmouthed at the crowd, her eyes going wider and wider. She focused on the strangers, her head moving from one to the other, and then she took in each of the men who worked for her with eyes that seemed to want to deny the whole sordid mess.

Reggie called out loudly, "I've called the cops, youse guys. So knock it off!"

No one paid him the least bit of attention.

Amelia put her hands on Mike's arms, just as he was deciding to at least get Tom off of the guy on the ground. The poor slob under Hardwick looked like he was having a panic attack. His face was red and blotchy, and his eyes were as round as saucers. "No, Mike. Don't. You do *not* want to get involved in this one." There was a note of panic in her voice, and he looked over at her, perplexed. "I mean it. It's going to be over soon, and you don't want any part of what's about to happen."

Mike looked into her eyes, looked beyond their shape and the infinitely dark color of them, and saw fear. He nodded and made himself stop. It was the very least he owed her, and besides, he was still more worried about her than two strangers. At least no one had any weapons.

The stranger being held by the Howard brothers leaned his head to the side, straining as if he meant to kiss Bernie on the mouth. If that was his intention, he missed by a few inches. He sank his teeth into the tip of Bernie's nose—a hard target to miss—and yanked back harshly. His mouth pulled away with a wet sound, and his lips were stained red. The look on the stranger's face was not what Mike had expected. The man was smiling as he spat something from his mouth. He looked like he was having a party. The sound that came out of Bernie Howard was something between the screech of locked brakes on a wet road and the sound of a pig trying desperately to escape a snare. "By dose! He bit op by fugging dose!" Bernie's hands flew to his face, protecting himself from any further damage instinctively. In the process he left himself wide open for the stranger's follow-through. Bernie Howard dropped like a sack of wet laundry when the man hauled off and kicked him in the back of his head. Mike winced in sympathy.

Bruce "Butch" Howard yanked hard on the arm he still had a grip on and pulled the stranger toward him, fully intent on changing the shape of the man's head. Instead of fighting against the move, the stranger moved into it, sending Butch stumbling backward with a puzzled expression. That wasn't what was supposed to happen, the expression said. That wasn't at all what Butch was prepared for. If he found the change in resistance surprising, he must have thought the laws of physics had altered irreparably when the newcomer dropped low and swept a leg across both of Howard's knees. One second Butch was staggering, the next his head was cracking into a barstool. Mike, who was having a little trouble grasping exactly how quickly the lean man had taken down the twin sons of Earline Howard, watched Butch try to regain his feet for about three seconds before simply dropping limply to the ground, unconscious. By the time Bruce settled in for his nap, his opponent was moving across the floor in a sort of sliding walk, his hands twitching just a bit as he approached Tom Hardwick.

Tom was still slapping the cheeks of the man he'd pinned. The man was looking around wildly, desperate for a way to escape. When his eyes found the legs of the other stranger moving in his direction, they grew almost panicky. The round face turned paler, ignoring the slaps Tom was issuing, and the prone victim of the Serenity welcome wagon, à la Hardwick, started praying under his breath. Mike had assumed they were friends who'd come into the bar together, but watching the pinned man's reaction made him consider reassessing the situation. He looked more afraid of the man coming at him than of the one who was literally on top of him.

"Hey, buddy." The words were softly spoken and almost casual. Especially compared to the warning cries from the locals. Tom Hardwick turned toward them just the same and caught a knee in his temple for his troubles. Tom grunted and rolled to the side, his face more enraged than wounded. The stranger backed up and let him stand, his posture saying that he didn't feel any need to hurry himself.

He even let Tom gather his thoughts and seriously consider whether or not he should continue the fight.

Behind him, a few of the others were looking ready to join in again, but Tom gestured them off with one beefy hand. Whatever bad blood had already passed was a bit too personal for Tom to want any help. Besides, he outweighed his opponent by a good fifty to sixty pounds.

The pudgy guy Tom had used as a floor mat scrambled backward away from the fight, his eyes on the stranger the entire time. Reggie was still calling for everyone to calm down, but he didn't sound like he was willing to get himself hurt to break up the problem. And outside, the sound of police sirens was drawing closer.

Mike watched on, Amelia's delicate hands the only thing that stopped him from moving forward. The sirens started to sink into a few of the brawlers, who called to Tom to break it off before the heat got too hot to handle. Tom shook his head as if to dispel the annoying sounds of their voices, and then he charged like an angry bull, lowering his head and preparing, it seemed, to ram his opponent in the gut.

The stranger danced lightly to the side and brought an elbow down on the back of Hardwick's neck. Already overbalanced by his own momentum, Tom fell forward and hit the ground face-first. Unlike the last two people the stranger had fought, Tom got back up for more. The lean man slid forward and jabbed Tom in the face with a fast right fist, and then hit him three more times with the same hand. Each impact sent Hardwick's head snapping back. Apparently four was enough. Tom didn't get back up after he fell for the second time.

Amelia's hands relaxed their almost desperate grip on Mike, but he didn't move forward. He was far too busy watching the guy who walked over to the bar and had a seat on one of the stools. The stranger was almost plain, and only average in build to boot, but he knew how to fight and did so with more confidence than most of the men Mike knew could ever muster.

Barely anyone had moved a muscle when the police showed up. Jack Michaels and Victor Barnes both looked tired and a little angry when they arrived. The stranger who'd finished the fight was smiling broadly and looking at them with amusement. The other stranger was all but curled up in a fetal position. Aside from the unconscious trio on the floor and Mike, Amelia, and Reggie, everyone else was pretending to find something interesting to study on the walls or the ceiling.

It took long enough for everything to be cleared up that Mike and Amelia actually had time to sit down for a meal. Reggie served them himself, while his line cook was being questioned by Jack. They had the chili, which, true to the bar owner's word, was wonderful. Throughout the course of the meal, however, Amelia seemed distracted and worried. She wasn't quite as all there as she normally seemed, and that worried Mike.

Just after they'd finished their lunch, Jack Michaels asked them a few questions while Victor Barnes talked to the two strangers. The short round one left a few minutes later, and the lean fighter looked over their way.

Ignoring the constables, he walked over to their table, his eyes on Amelia. Mike watched the stranger's face go from smiling to a frown of concentration. Then his face shifted again, from the frown to a look of surprise that bordered on terror. Finally, his face shifted into neutral, and he calmly placed a pair of rimless glasses on his face and looked at Amelia expectantly.

Jack looked at Amelia and asked if she had any idea what had started the fight, but she failed to notice as her attention was drawn to the stranger.

Amelia looked back, her face a cloud of worries and doubts that made her look like a teenager fretting about her first date. She stared up at the man and broke a light sweat. Mike looked from one to the other with knitted brows, wondering what the hell was going on.

After a very tense few seconds, during which time Jack Michaels finally realized that his question wasn't about to get answered, Amelia broke the growing stretch of silence. "Hello, John," she said softly as she looked at the stranger. "It's been a long time."

Jonathan Crowley looked back at her, his face darkening and his eyes—which had seemed amused throughout the fight—burning with a low, hot anger.

VIII

Some events go almost unnoticed in a town. They might be significant to a family or even to a few friends, but they remain minuscule when compared to the events that can shape even a regular day in the life of a community. Such was the case when sixteen teenagers who had been thought injured or dead all came home in the middle of the day. There were arguments, to be sure, and more than a few people were angry at having spent half of a Saturday stuck in the woods hunting for dogs that simply refused to be found.

There were people who wanted to see every last one of those kids locked in jail for pulling a stupid hoax and scaring the hell out of the community, and there were parents who grounded their teens — allegedly for life, but that sort of punishment never lasts — and there were others who listened to the story they had to tell of dogs who kept them trapped at the quarry overnight and forgave their children for the ten years they'd aged while waiting desperately for news of what had happened to their loved ones.

But mostly those were just noises, and mostly those noises all carried the same sigh of relief. Serenity had not lost sixteen children, after all. The magnitude of such a dilemma was not going to destroy them, was not going to overshadow the devastating blow already dealt the town by the desecration of the largest and oldest cemetery in all of Serenity.

And in the end, the event was barely noticed.

IX

Jack Michaels was tired. Not just the sort of "think I could use a few hours to recover from my lack of sleep" tired that he normally suffered from, but a deep tired that ran all the way through his bones and left his eyes feeling like some bastard had lined them with sandpaper when he wasn't looking. Not surprisingly, being that wiped out made him a little cranky.

The closest thing he'd had to good news in the last four days was that the kids who'd been chased and presumed killed by Deveraux's dogs had, in fact, escaped serious injury. Half of them were in the hospital right now, just for observation, but they were expected to be up and about the next day. The other half were—if the regulars who passed him such information weren't lying—already prepared to start the next football season a few months early. Something came out right, finally, as if to counter everything that was going wrong just lately.

Wrong. Like the fact that four men were suffering from some nasty bruises and bumps, and the man responsible for most of them was sitting in a cell behind him, and probably smiling. No, make that definitely smiling. He could feel the man's glee.

Just to make sure he wasn't imagining things, he looked into the mirror over his desk. The man was still sitting in the same position, his face neutral. Jack didn't like him. Something about the guy was creepy. Just as importantly, despite the stranger being nothing but proper, something about him was annoying.

Vic Barnes seemed to think so, too. He hadn't said as much, but he kept looking at the man in the second holding cell—the first being filled with his victims—and looking away whenever the man made eye contact. He made Victor Barnes nervous, and that in turn made Jack Michaels nervous.

Nervous and tired. Twenty minutes to go until Bill Karstens and Bob Steinman took over. He could last another twenty minutes, if he worked at it. Jack stretched, slid his chair away from the desk, and took a deep breath. It didn't do any good, but he could pretend that moving was waking him up a bit.

His eyes shifted across the room, looking in on the four men who sat glumly in one cell licking their wounds for all intents and purposes. Next to them in the second cell was the reason for all the wound licking. He had a split lip, but it wasn't much of a split really, just a scratch when you got right down to it. And unlike the people in the cell next door to his, he was pleased with himself. Quietly, thoroughly pleased with himself. The only thing that seemed to stop him from being perfectly content was that he had a roommate in Terry Palance, who was mostly staring at the wall when he wasn't blinking back tears of depression. Jack wanted to feel sorry for Terry, but he couldn't quite muster it. The stranger did his best to ignore the younger man.

Jack studied the man and felt himself studied in return. He didn't like the feeling. Probably because the man doing the judging remained quietly amused. That was almost as unsettling as the notion that the guy who remained casually draped over the bunk in the cell was still scaring all hell out of Vic.

The man leaned forward on the bunk, pushing his eyeglasses up the bridge of his nose, and locked eyes with Jack. "Will I have a chance to make a phone call at any point, Constable?"

"Did you have someone you needed to call?"

"Not particularly. I'm just curious."

"What about?"

"Why I'm being held in this cell, when no one has read me my rights and no one has said anything about pressing charges."

Jack shook his head. "I don't plan on pressing charges, and neither does Reg Townsley, though he'd be well within his rights."

"What a coincidence. I hadn't planned on pressing charges either. Glad to see we're all on the same page of the book here."

"And who would you be pressing charges against?"

The man jerked his thumb in the direction of the adjoining cell and nodded toward Hardwick. "Bright boy over there."

Jack allowed a slight smile. It wasn't often anyone came along who would willingly risk annoying Tom Hardwick. It was even less often that the man would take anything that even hinted at an insult without making a comment in return. Hardwick merely sat where he was, looking at the ground. "Are you saying he started the little dance session you boys had?"

"As a matter of fact, I am."

"Well, that jibes with what Reggie told me earlier. And I can't say as I'm really shocked by the idea. Tom likes to rough things up from time to time."

"How special for Tom."

"You seem sort of amused by all of this, Mr....?"

"Crowley. Jonathan Crowley."

"Do you find this funny, Mr. Crowley?"

"Only moderately so."

"What is it you find funny, if you don't mind my asking?"

"Just that I've been here before. Not in this town, mind you. But I've been in the same situation."

"Move around a lot, do you?"

Crowley shrugged. "Side effect of being idly rich, I suppose. A man gets bored, he likes to travel."

"What brings you to Serenity Falls, Mr. Crowley?"

"I was just passing through, but I think I'll stay awhile."

"Really? What made you decide on that?"

"I like the people here."

Jack walked over to the cell and unlocked it. "Well, I'm glad to see you think we're an okay lot, all things considered."

"Am I free to go?"

"Are you going to start any fights that I should know about?"

"It's not on my agenda, Constable."

"Then I guess you're free to go."

Crowley walked out of the cell, looking around the place as if it had changed from one side of the bars to the other. His gaze ran across the men in the adjoining cell, and he smiled. "It's been fun, guys. Let's try it again sometime."

"That could almost be taken to mean you want to start something, Mr. Crowley."

"Not at all, Constable. Not at all." He looked at Jack and smiled. It was fair to say Michaels didn't like the man's smile.

"Have a nice day, Mr. Crowley."

"Say, I noticed you have a bit of a stir up at the cemetery."

"You could say that."

"Any idea who was responsible?"

"Not yet, but we're working on it."

Crowley nodded, and that damned creepy smile of his grew a little broader. "Have a nice day, Constable."

Crowley left the building, whistling to himself as he went. Jack watched him the entire way, and Vic watched beside him.

"That," Victor Barnes said, "is a very, very strange man."

"Creepy sonuvabitch."

"I don't like him."

"No shit, I'd have never noticed."

"Don't be a smart-ass, Jack. It doesn't suit you."

They sat in silence for the next ten minutes. Just before their relief shift showed, Jack looked over at Victor and shook his head. "Did you say anything to him about the cemetery?"

"Nope."

"I wonder how he knew?"

"Well, it's sort of hard to miss, Jack."

"Yeah, but he said he hadn't actually been in town yet. Just at Townsley's."

"There're files all over the place, Jack. He must have seen 'em.

"That, or he's maybe been in town a little more often than he says."

"You think he did it?"

"I think it's a possibility, Vic. I think it's a real possibility."

"Think maybe he needs watching?"

"No. Just keep an ear out."

"You figure anyone in this town is gonna be talking about Jonathan Crowley?"

"Vic. I'd be willing to bet money on it."

X

Patience, some say, is a virtue. It was a tenet that Alden Waters had always lived by and one he knew for a fact to be as good as the Gospel. The sun had long set, and the wind was picking up out in the woods near the falls. His legs felt like he'd hiked about four hundred miles, but that was okay, too. Because after waiting patiently with Marty Glass and Rene Haldeman throughout the morning and into the late night, he was finally rewarded for his troubles.

The dogs came, moving with an almost eerie silence, in search of fresh meat. The young sow tied to the next tree over was just what they wanted: easy prey.

The wait had almost done Alden in. He didn't like to think about the fact that he was getting older, but his circulation just wasn't what it used to be, and he felt the cold in his joints in ways that he never had in the past. Getting old was not half as much fun as it used to be. Still, he was here, and his wait was over. Now it was just a matter of being calm for a few more minutes. Let the dogs take the bait, and all would be well.

Alden watched as they moved in, sniffing the air and crouching low to the ground as they approached. The hounds were beautiful animals, and he regretted that they had to be killed. Still, they'd gone feral, and he couldn't let them roam around tearing into anyone or anything they pleased. There were children in town who'd never done anything wrong and didn't deserve that sort of fate. Though he could think of a few people in town who probably wouldn't be missed by much of anyone if they got torn limb from limb, he could think of far more who would be.

The pig down below was making a lot of noise, mostly along the line of loud, panicky squeals. He couldn't really blame it. He nodded to Marty and Rene, who carefully took aim at the animals below and waited for him to take the first shot. Alden sighted down his rifle and breathed steadily. As he exhaled, he squeezed the trigger and felt the light kick of a bullet leaving to find its mark. One of the dogs made a surprised woof and spun hard to the left before hitting the ground and starting to make serious noises. Alden winced. He'd been hoping for a clean kill.

Before the rest of the dogs could respond, the fellas opened fire. Two more dropped, not making nearly the same level of noise, and while each of the other hunters took aim at another animal, Alden finished off the one he'd shot before. He took no pleasure from his actions, which for him was rare. He loved to hunt. But this? This was a massacre, and it felt wrong.

The sound of bullets cutting through the air mingled with the desperate screams of the pig below and yelps of pain from several of the dogs. Cordite stung Alden's nostrils and made his eyes water. Down below, the dogs bucked and snapped madly at the source of their pain while a few of the pack tried to head for higher ground. None of them made it.

And then it was over. The dogs were dead, and the pig was still shrieking loud enough to deafen anything in a ten-foot radius. Alden looked down on the bloodied remains of at least fifteen good hunting dogs and shook his head.

"I guess that's it, boys. Let's get on down and see what's what."

Rene looked at him and nodded silently. Marty let out a sigh and shook his head. "Damn shame is what it is, Alden. Those were good dogs."

"I know, Marty. But what else could we do?" He slung his rifle over his shoulder and carefully worked his way over to the rope ladder. It took him awhile to get down to the ground, and by the time he was there, both of his friends were looking the dogs over. Rene took the time to shoot one of them in the skull, his face impassive. Sometimes he thought maybe Rene liked shooting things a little too much, but the man knew how to behave himself well enough that Alden never worried about that knowledge.

Rene looked at him and nodded. "They're all done for."

"I guess that's about the best we could hope for, guys. Let's go tell it to the judge, as it were."

Alden untied the pig from the base of the tree and damn near lost a few layers of skin when it took off. He'd hoped to bring it back to the farm, but better to lose one sow than a few fingers. With any luck someone would find the poor bugger in a few days and let him know.

Rene and Marty both did a few stretches and limbered up as best they could. Watching them made Alden feel a little better about getting old. If they were feeling it, he wasn't the only one who'd been tortured by the weather and the long wait.

The wind picked up as they started toward the main road.

Alden allowed himself a small sigh and started trudging through the carpet of dry leaves.

He let his tired mind start drifting toward the fall and gave thought to whether or not he would be out here hunting when the time came around. Alden had his doubts. There comes a time when you have to figure you're about due to call it done for outside activities, and he was getting damned close if he wasn't already there. Maybe he should have been sadder about the idea, and maybe he would be in a little while, but right then and there, all he cared about was getting into bed and going to sleep.

Alden was lagging a little behind his friends and straining a bit to hear what they were saying, when the growling started. He cocked his head and listened for a second before realizing that it wasn't just the leaves blowing in the cold night or the sound of that stupid pig running around nearby. It was growling. And it sounded like it was damned close to right behind him. He started walking faster, calling out to his hunting partners as he moved in.

"Fellas? I think maybe we missed one of those dogs…"

Marty looked over his shoulder with an expression that said very clearly he thought Alden was insane. The look on his face shifted fast to one of confusion and then again into a mask of pure fear. Alden turned around slowly, almost afraid of what he might see behind him.

And immediately wished he hadn't looked.

There was a man behind him, standing in the shadows of the trees. But the man wasn't the problem. It was the dogs around him that were the cause of the alarm. The very dogs he and his friends had killed only five minutes earlier. Every last one of them was still dead, or at least they should have been. Someone had apparently forgotten to tell them that. The animals moved toward him with bared teeth and eyes that seemed to look anywhere they pleased. They moved like puppets, jerky motions that made their bodies twitch and sway as they came closer. One of them, probably the one Rene had decided wasn't dead enough earlier, had a gaping hole through its skull, and he could see the foliage on the other side of what remained.

Alden stepped backward, his eyes wide, and tried to remember how to think. His mind didn't like what his eyes were seeing one little bit, and his body felt far colder than what the wind alone should have been able to cause.

Deep inside the pack of dogs, the man stepped forward into the moonlight and away from the shadows of the trees. Alden saw his face and finally found his voice. "What? How the hell did you get out here?"

"Same as you, Alden. I walked." The smile that flashed from the familiar face was not comforting. Somewhere behind him, Alden heard Rene start making a noise that wasn't all that different from the sounds the pig had made earlier. "Now boys, hunting out of season is a criminal offense. And I'm pretty sure it isn't dog hunting season."

Marty wanted in on the conversation. He pointed a finger that Alden could just see out of the corner of his eye and all but shrieked as he spoke. "Those dogs are dead! Those goddamned dogs are dead!" Alden nodded silently to agree.

The man moved forward, shaking his head. "Nothing around here dies anymore without my permission, Marty."

"That's nuts! That's nuts, and it's not possible!" Marty was not firing all pistons anymore. The sweat on his brow, the pale color of his skin, and the wide eyes that stared at the man in front of Alden made all of that clear. Alden knew shock well enough from a few of the hunting accidents he'd been witness to over the years, and Marty was either already in that state or heading toward it at a dangerous speed.

"Be that as it may, it's true." He walked forward, and the pack of dead things moved with him. "These dogs should be dead, and yet here they are, walking along with me." He smiled. "And you know something? I'm a little annoyed about this whole situation. I have plans for these fine animals. Why, if I didn't know they'd heal up just as soon as I told them to, I'd have to be downright pissed off at you."

Rene was still making piggy noises, but his head was on well enough for him to take aim with his rifle. Alden had completely forgotten about his own weapon until just that moment. He shrugged his shoulder until the strap holding it in place slipped down from its perch into the crook of his elbow. He wasn't quite sure if he'd have it in him to shoot—the damn dogs coming closer weren't doing his nerves a whole lot of good just then—but at least it would be a little faster for him if he decided to go that route.

Rene switched off the safety on his rifle and aimed carefully for a spot right between the eyes of the man approaching. "You'll be wanting to call off the dogs, if you feel the need to keep breathing." The threat was legitimate—Alden had no doubt of that—but it sounded rather silly with the way Rene's voice was squeaking about three octaves higher than it should have.

"Rene...please...if the dogs are walking around, what makes you think a bullet or two would stop me?"

Rene thought about that for a few seconds—Alden could almost see the smoke—and then shook his head. "Way I got the math done, I'm a goner if I don't convince you to call off the dogs. I'm willing to take my chances."

Alden looked away from the men and down at the dogs moving slowly forward. They were almost close enough to touch, and he didn't plan on staying around to let that happen. He started backing away from the twitching dead things and swung his rifle into a ready position. He could think of a lot of things he'd rather be doing than taking shots at zombie bloodhounds, but he liked the idea just fine when compared to the alternative.

"Alden?" The voice was amused, and the man's face was smirking in a way that just didn't quite seem right. "Where do you think you're going?"

"I'm just getting the hell out of here. I have no argument with you, and I aim to keep it that way."

The man shrugged. "Have a nice night, Alden."

He didn't bother to answer. He just kept backing away, grateful to see that the dogs were no longer following him.

Rene turned to look at him, his eyes wide and all but begging him for backup. Alden shook his head, hating himself for being a coward about the whole thing but far more worried about living through the night.

Marty looked his way, too, but the look on his face said he was not really home just then.

And oh, he wanted so desperately to run. To turn and run and never look back. But the dogs were there, and the idea of any of those damned things being at his back was enough to make him move slowly. But only barely. The one closest to him was still looking his way with eyes that shouldn't have been able to see. By the way it crouched, he figured it could reach him easily in just a few leaps. His bladder wanted to explode when he thought about those teeth tearing into him.

Alden stopped when he felt the heated breath on his back, blowing down from above his head. He turned in time to see the biggest dog he'd ever come across in his life opening its mouth. The eyes burned with a greenish glow, and the teeth, which showed past the drawn lips of the thing, were black.

Behind him he heard the voice of the man who'd spotted them in the woods and come calling with a pack of dead dogs as an escort. The voice was gloating now, savoring the dilemma he found himself in. "Alden, did I mention that I brought along a friend?"

"Ohmygodinheaven…"

"Oh, and Alden? Just so you know, he doesn't much like hunters."

Alden stared into the face of the massive beast and let his rifle fall from hands that no longer had the strength to hold it. His bladder gave up the fight to hold back around the same time the creature leaned in closer and breathed a plume of warmth across his face.

Alden Waters turned on his heel as sharply as he could manage on the uneven ground and started back toward the pack of dead things that waited for him. The man watched on and laughed as what the locals had once called a hellhound moved after him with paws far surer that its prey's feet.

One forepaw swatted the old man across his back and sent him sprawling into the dry leaves along the ground in the woods. Alden slammed into the dirt and mulch hard enough to knock the wind out of him and stayed there for a few seconds too long while he tried to remember how to breathe properly. The thing set a forepaw on his back and pinned him like a butterfly to a collector's board. He moaned under the weight and felt his ribs threatening to break.

Rene kept the rifle sighted on the man, and the man in turn ignored him. Alden saw the polished shoes of the man as he came closer and finally crouched next to his prone body.

"Alden, it looks to me like he doesn't want you leaving yet."

"Why are you doing this?"

"Because I have to, Alden.

"Who's making you?"

"You. All of you. Everyone in this entire town." He shrugged. "Or maybe I just feel like it."

He tried to grasp the gist of what the man was saying to him, but it still didn't make any sense. Despite the pressure on his ribs, Alden tried again. "How did I make you do this? I'm just an old man."

"I know. You're one of the lucky ones."

A small desperate hope blossomed in Alden's chest. He voiced his question with an almost physically noticeable sigh of relief. "I am?"

"Oh yes, Alden. You are."

"How do you figure? I've got a devil sitting on my back, and I'm guessing you don't plan on asking it to let me go."

"Well, you're right about that." He leaned in closer, close enough for Alden to smell his Brut aftershave. "No, I mean you're lucky because you've had a pretty full life."

"What gives you the right to decide that?" Alden blinked his eyes several times, trying to fight off the fear and the tears threatening him with embarrassment. Bad enough to die if he had to, but he was damned if he'd cry like a schoolgirl when it happened.

"What gives you the right to hunt dogs in the dead of night, Alden?"

"I was trying to protect people!"

"Of course you were. Naturally. And all those deer you killed over the years?"

"I have to eat." What the hell was this? When had the man become an animal rights activist anyway?

"Well, and there we get to the real meat of the matter, don't we? I have to eat, too."

"What? What the hell are you talking about! I'm supposed to be your dinner?" Okay, that was an unsettling idea, and Alden just didn't like this turn of events. He tried to push off the ground, but the dog-thing was still resting a foreleg like a tree trunk on his back. The struggle didn't get him anything but a few more bruises and a very winded feeling.

"Something like that. Not in the way you're thinking, of course, but something along those lines."

Before Alden could respond, the air filled with the sounds of Marty screaming in pain along with a chorus of growls from the pack of animals they'd killed earlier. He turned his head in time to watch four of the hounds take his longtime friend down to the ground, their bodies jumping back after they locked their jaws on different parts of his body. Marty's sounds got louder as one of them managed to pull away a piece of skin around the size of a football. Marty bucked on the ground, flailing his arms and pounding his fists against the creatures. They shrugged off the blows like they were little more than a strong breeze.

"Ahhh! Alden! Rene! Help meeee!" Marty fought hard, trying every trick in the book, including taking a bite out of one of his attackers, but they didn't stop. They kept chewing away pieces of him and throwing them aside. Even when Rene finally snapped out of it enough to shoot the damned things, all it did was knock them over, and they rolled right back on their feet with a few new holes in their pelts.

Alden started laughing, barely aware that he was making the sound. It wasn't funny really, but it sort of was. Marty Glass screaming away as a bunch of dead mutts ripped into him, and what could he do? *Nothing*, he thought. *I can't do a goddamned thing. I've got a dog the size of a Buick sitting on my ass, and I'm busy having a nice conversation with a man who says he's here to eat me!* He laughed harder, all the while trying to make himself stop, because he was having a damned hard time getting his breath back with the black dog pinning him down. Alden pulled handfuls of leaves and mulch closer to him as he tried to scramble up and stop laughing at the same time. Marty's tortured form blurred as tears started pouring from his eyes and oh God it hurt to laugh so hard, hurt to watch that fuzzy form get torn apart by the pack of rejects form a Living Dead movie.

The ground next to him exploded in a blast of debris, and he heard the sound of a rifle firing, even over his own strained laughter. Marty screamed again, and the sound shut off halfway through, becoming a wet sucking noise. That was okay though, whatever Marty couldn't finish Rene was apparently willing to handle for him. Rene started screaming in a high-pitched shriek that made Alden think of the time his Aunt Louise had come over and felt a mouse run over her foot.

Alden laid his head back on the ground, the laughter taking more energy than he could spare, his breaths coming in frantic gulps as he tried to make himself just please, God above, please calm down. This was worse than crying ever could have been.

Some time later—a month, a century, or maybe a few lifetimes— Alden finally quieted down. By then the killing was over. Marty and Rene were silent, and the dogs were busy feeding themselves. Alden's head felt swollen, and his thoughts—such as they were—were feverish. The chill that had haunted him all day long was a thousand times worse, except where the black paw of a monster perched on his upper back. Right around there, his skin felt sunburned, which in contrast to the freezing cold everywhere else was almost comforting in a demented way.

"Alden? Are you back now?" The voice was amused and teasing. "You were gone for a while there, and I was starting to worry."

"Heh… Worry? Why the hell were you starting to worry, you fuck? It ain't like you're gonna let me out of here alive."

"Well, I've been thinking about that."

"Yeah?" Alden didn't have any doubts that he was dead, but what the hell, keep the bastard amused, and maybe he could buy an extra minute or two before the thing on his ass decided to bite his head off.

Just of late he figured he'd take every minute he could get. "What? You decided to let me live as long as I promise not to tell anyone that you're a freak of nature?"

"Oh, Alden, I'm not a freak of nature. There's nothing remotely natural about me anymore." The man's hand stroked over his brow, and Alden shivered at the contact. If the air was close to freezing, the hand that stroked his brow seemed to have gone much, much colder than that.

"Look, I don't want to die here. I just want to go home..."

"I know, Alden. Earline is waiting for you, and probably worried halfway to death by now."

"Earline don't deserve any of this. You leave her alone..."

"I've always liked Earline, Alden. You have a wonderful woman for a wife." Alden watched him stand up and dust himself off, the dark blue of his pants fading into the nighttime forest as if he wasn't there at all. Maybe he was just a figment, maybe this was all just a really bad dream...

"I'm going to let you live, Alden. The dogs have fed enough, and they're feeling much better now."

Alden craned his head up to the face that seemed miles above him. It hurt to stretch his neck that way, but it was almost worth it to see the sincerity in the eyes of his captor/savior.

"You are?" There was a desperate note in his voice that he truly hated. He felt like a man begging for scraps, and he never wanted to feel that way.

"Well, yes. But there's a condition."

"What? What do I have to do?"

"There's a man here in town. He and I are not friends. His life for yours, Alden. And for Earline's as well."

Alden listened carefully to the man's words, letting them sink into him. One life for two, one stranger for his life and Earline's. In the long run it wasn't much of a decision to make. Alden had always been a survivor.

Chapter Ten

I

Sunday morning was cold, not just cool. And the sky promised far more than clouds before the day was done. But for the present, it was merely cold.

Jonathan Crowley sat at the edge of the Powers Memorial Cemetery and watched the town go by. There was not one but two churches at the edge of the sprawling graveyard, and both of them were doing good business. Or at least attendance was good. It was maybe just a touch too cynical to say that they were only opening their doors for donations alone.

Crowley looked at the open doors of the Lutheran Church of the Resurrection and shook his head. He then let his eyes drift over to the Methodist congregation and did the same. Perhaps it was cynical, but then again, maybe it wasn't. Either way, Crowley didn't honestly care. Right now he was hunting for faces. Or at least expressions.

A fat man walked past him and looked his way for a second, the set of his mouth saying he disapproved of people leaning on the stone wall surrounding the cemetery. Crowley threw him a wink, and the man moved a little faster. A very large family came past, dressed in their Sunday finery. They looked enough alike that he assumed they were mostly an extended family. There were two young women who eyed him with curiosity and maybe a promise of a good time. He didn't wink at them. They might take it the wrong way. There was a kid with them, maybe in his very early teens, who caught Crowley's eye only because he looked at the stranger so intently. His eyes didn't just give John a quick once-over, they focused on him and drank in details. There was nothing apologetic or subdued about the way the kid stared, and he found that amusing. It was rare to find an individual who wasn't at least polite about their examination of another. That rarity became almost an impossibility when the person doing the staring was a kid over the age of four.

He stared at the boy, and the boy returned the favor for several seconds before his older sister yanked him forward by his hand and told him it was impolite to stare. She, in turn, stared at Crowley for several seconds herself, a small smile playing on her lips the entire time. He'd have bet money she was rather popular with the local boys.

The next group coming up the way made him smile. It was led by his buddy from the night before. The ape with the death wish. Tom Hardwick, that was the name. *Good old Tommy…it's nice to have a friend in town so soon after arriving.* Hardwick took one look at him and then lowered his head. Apparently he'd had enough fighting for the time being. That, or the old woman walking next to him was his mother, and he didn't much like the idea of there being a problem with her around. Crowley watched the man's eyes dart from him to the woman walking gamely next to him and nodded. There was a time and place for everything, and if Hardwick wanted another round later, that would wait until then.

Either way, it wasn't really relevant. His little bout of bar fighting had already served its purpose and let him meet the Law in Serenity. Meeting the Law was an important part of his job. He had to know if the locals had any protection from whatever was happening around them.

And there was definitely a need for protection in the town.

Something was stirring, and whatever it was would probably awaken fully in the near future. He could feel it, could almost taste it. Then again, he thought, that could just be the stink from the pieces they missed in the graveyard. The ground was still disturbed from whatever had happened in the cemetery, and the smell of dead things was strong enough to turn most people's stomachs.

Crowley shrugged and pulled an Egg McMuffin from the bag he'd brought along. He bit into it and started chewing while he continued watching the people in Serenity. What he saw failed to impress him. They were just people, and not many of them stuck out as the sort he would even find interesting to talk to.

He ate in silence, watching and waiting. Finally, the doors to the churches were closed, and the sermons began inside each of them. After a few more minutes, he felt a delicate hand reach out and touch his shoulder. He didn't turn to look. He knew who it was.

"John, can we talk?" Her voice hadn't changed in the least. Nor had her scent.

"What on earth would we have to talk about?"

"Why you're here. How you've been. What you've been doing for yourself since…"

He snorted a short laugh and shook his head. "I'm here because I've been led here. I've been me. And I'm still doing what I'm always doing, Amelia. I'm still hunting things that go bump in the night."

"You didn't come here to find me?" Oh, her voice was so hopeful, relieved to hear that little tidbit of news.

"I can say in all honesty you're one of the last people I expected to run across. Does that make you feel better?"

"I didn't mean it that way, John, you know that." And there, that slight embarrassment at being caught. That, and maybe just a twinge of regret.

"Of course you didn't. You don't ever mean to hurt people, do you?"

She was silent for a few seconds after that, and he almost let himself feel regret for the comment.

"No, John, I don't. You know that. It just happens."

"You need to learn to turn that off, before someone gets seriously hurt."

"I didn't ask for it in the first place."

"I know. That's why we're having this conversation."

"What do you mean?"

"You know exactly what I mean, Amelia." He let out a sigh and pressed his finger and thumb to the bridge of his nose. He absolutely hated conversations like this. "I mean if I thought you were doing it on purpose or being malicious about it, I'd have to hunt you down."

"You know I don't!" She sounded wounded by the very idea, offended. "You know I'd never deliberately do that to a person."

"Like I said, if I thought otherwise…"

"Besides, you can't just do what you want. There are rules…"

"You don't have to remind me, Amelia. I know the rules very well."

"Yes, I imagine you do." And there, just the right tone of regret in her voice, like maybe she was sorry for everything. He hated that. Hated that she could make him think about her feelings for even a second. That was a weakness. "Do you hate me, John?"

"No."

"Are you sure?"

"Amelia, hating you would take more effort than I'm willing to invest. I have other things to do with my energy and with my time. Do you understand me?"

"I think I do."

"Good."

"So now that you're here, what will you do?"

"Wait."

"Wait for what?"

"Someone to ask me."

"Someone to…?" He looked at her shadow on the ground, watched how it started, and then nodded. "Oh."

"Exactly. There are rules that have to be followed."

"Would it help if I asked?"

"No. Not this time."

"But why not?"

"Because you're not a part of whatever the hell is going on here. If you become part of it later, it might help, but you're not directly connected."

"How can you tell that? How can you just look at a place and tell that?"

Crowley lifted one eyebrow and finally managed the courage to actually look at her. She was, of course, as stunning as ever. "How can you do the things you do?"

"I just can. It's like walking or breathing."

"Well, then you've just answered your own question."

"You don't make any sense, you know that?"

"I'm not supposed to make sense. It's not what I'm about."

"No. No, I suppose it isn't."

They stayed that way, in silence for several seconds, neither quite looking at the other but keeping each other in their periphery. Finally, just to break the silence—and maybe to keep himself from doing something truly stupid—Crowley spoke again. "Who is he?"

"His name is Mike Blake. He's a nice man with a lot of problems."

"Aside from being an alcoholic?"

"You could tell that?"

"His eyes tended to stay in one of three places. On you, on the fight, and on the bottles behind the bar. Also, he has very fine gin blossoms on his nose."

"You're very perceptive."

"I have to be."

"Isn't there anyone else to do it? To go after the bad ones?"

"Of course there is. There are always others."

"Then why do you keep going? I know you hate it. You've told me as much. So why do you do it?"

"Because I don't like them. Because they keep fucking things up and messing people over."

"That's not an answer. You've already said there are others who would do the job if it had to be done."

"How about this. I don't trust the others to get it right. They aren't me, and I don't have any proof that they'll do anything but screw everything up and let the wrong things walk around."

"That's a little better, I guess. Closer to the truth, at least."

"Besides, what else is there for me? Love? Happiness? The right woman coming along and making it all right?"

"It could happen, John. It could if you'd let it." He sighed and looked away from her. A car rolled past, and he didn't bother to pay it the least bit of attention. "No. It couldn't. It won't. And even if it could happen, I wouldn't let it."

"You'd rather be miserable, is that it?"

"No."

"Then what, John? Why do you keep doing this to yourself?"

"You just can't leave it alone, can you?" Crowley stood up and turned to face her, his eyes dark and his expression darker. "You always have to keep picking and picking until you find out what you want, is that it?"

"I just want to help, John…" She backed away as she said it, perhaps remembering that all was not what it seemed with him. He stepped forward, not letting her get away that easily.

"I know that! I know you want to help make it better, Amelia, but you can't. You want to know why I keep doing this? Figure it out! What happened the last time I tried to have a normal life? Do you remember? You ought to have the answer to this with no problem at all; you were there."

Amelia backed away from him faster, shaking her head in denial. Crowley grinned. "Were you expecting absolution from me? Not in this lifetime, cupcake. Not any time soon." Oh it felt so good to say that to her, to know that it was tearing her up inside. Or at least he told himself that. It was easier that way.

He turned away from her and sat back down on the low wall around the cemetery. Both congregations were still inside, still praying to the same God in their own ways. Faith was an interesting luxury.

Behind him, he could hear her rapid breathing, the way she was trying her best not to cry. "Go to Mike Blake. Be good to him. Make sure he's good to you."

She left without saying a word, and he let her. There were other things to worry about for now, like the presence he still felt creeping around the periphery, waiting for something.

And like the indirect invitation that had brought him here. He knew this was the right place; he could feel it in every part of his body. And damn, it was really starting to piss him off.

"Somebody wants me here, and that's okay with me, but if somebody doesn't make it clear who or what somebody is, and soon, I'm going to be very, very annoyed."

The only answer he got was a slight breeze. Jonathan Crowley got up and started walking. Inevitably, whatever was after him would make itself known. He had all the time in the world to figure it out. That was one luxury at least. Time. Plenty of time.

II

Becky Glass's world fell to pieces at ten fifteen in the morning that very Sunday. That was when Bill Karstens came to the door and told her and her mother that her father was dead. That was, of course, utter nonsense. Her father was too big a man to ever be killed in a hunting accident.

And yet, there he was, his face solemn, his eyes nervous and sad. He looked down at her from his height and shook his head. "I'm so very sorry, Becky. Your father was a good man..."

"You're lying!" She knew what she was saying was wrong, that she would surely be punished for disagreeing with an adult, but she had to say what she knew was the truth. "My daddy isn't dead! He's with Uncle Alden, and they're hunting the dogs that scared those kids! He didn't get hurt! He didn't die!"

Officer Karstens reached out a hand and placed it on her forehead. Maybe it was supposed to be comforting, but it felt like he had a fever and was burning her. She backed away from him and ran through the house to her room, her haven. Somewhere behind her, she heard her mother cry out her name, but that didn't matter. The comfort of her bed with its array of stuffed animals was all she had. Becky threw herself down on the bed and gripped her favorite bear, Mr. Wiggles, in a death clutch.

She didn't cry, she wailed. Becky howled her grief into the worn synthetic fur on Mr. Wiggles' belly until her throat was raw and her breaths came in ragged gasps for oxygen. "It's not fair... Everything was going right for once." She hugged the bear even tighter, her mind swimming with thoughts of how much everything had changed for her at school in a short time. How, for the first time since she was born, people at school were treating her like she was someone they could talk to, instead of just whisper about when they thought she wasn't listening—or, in some cases, even when they thought she was.

This wasn't supposed to happen, and she had to make someone somewhere understand that. After twelve years of being the outsider, she was entitled to a little happiness, wasn't she?

She heard the sound of the front door closing softly, and then the sounds of her mother's footsteps walking slowly to the living room.

234 / James A. Moore

Part of her wanted to get up, to go to her mother and offer comfort, but just at that moment she was feeling selfish. She didn't want to hear her mother crying, even as faintly as she already could, and she didn't want to see her mother's tears.

Her head felt full of snot and ready to explode from the heat of her crying jag. Becky rolled over on her bed and stared up at the ceiling, her eyes focusing on nothing at all. Down the hallway she heard the sounds of her mother's grief, so similar to her own noises from before. As petty as it was—and she knew even then that it was petty—she resented her mother's tears. Her mother was supposed to be there for her, to give her comfort and strength. She wasn't supposed to be crying herself.

Becky slid out of her bed and walked over to her bedroom window. The view was of nothing but the woods where Officer Karstens said her father had died. Becky frowned and felt her lip tremble and pull down again, felt the sting of more tears threatening to escape her body. She shook her head angrily, denying them that right. All the time, all over the place, she let the tears rule over her. Well, not anymore. She had better ways to take care of her problems.

Becky Glass opened the window in her bedroom and very carefully removed the screen from its position. She knew if her mother heard her, she'd be forced to stay inside. Well, there were ways to take care of what was happening in her life, if the old stories around school were true. She'd only heard them secondhand—no one wanted to share the stories with Becky Glass; she wasn't worth the trouble—but she had heard them.

Emmy Walstrop was the one who told the story. She was talking to Jessie Grant, probably just trying to frighten her, and Becky had listened.

Emmy told the story in simple enough terms. "The thing about it is, no one knows where to find her, the witch, I mean. But they say, if you can figure out where to look for her, she'll grant your wishes. You just have to know what to say."

Well, there was a simple enough logic to that. It was a logic that Rebecca Glass felt she could follow with fair ease, too. The problem would be finding the witch, and if she was going to try that, she'd have to find someone who knew the woods pretty darned well.

That meant she had to find the old MacGruder place. Simon MacGruder made his living in the woods. If anyone knew where the old witch was supposed to be found, it would be him. He was practically a hermit as she understood it. He'd been known to tell a few stories if he was in the mood, and a few of the ones he told involved the witch that supposedly lived in the woods.

Becky set off for the woods before she could chicken out. She really had no desire to make a journey, but she had to. She had to if she was going to have a chance to—"But *they say, if you can figure out where to look for her, she'll grant your wishes*"—find a way to bring her father back. It could be argued that Becky Glass was not rational when she headed for the woods that day. It could also be argued that she merely believed in magic. At the ripe old age of twelve, Becky set forth from her house. Time would tell if she was right or she was wrong.

III

Jessie Grant sat at the edge of the hospital bed and looked down at Stan Long's sleeping body. Dave Pageant stood beside her, his face knotted with worry. Jessie wasn't really sure why she was there. She and Stan had never been close friends—that would have required her talking to him, and it was never easy for her to initiate a conversation with anyone other than Charlee and occasionally her folks. Still, Stan was a nice guy, and he didn't deserve what he was going through.

Dave told her all about the latest seizure, how he flopped like a fish out of water, and no one, no one could get him to wake up. He'd recovered from whatever it was, and now he was just sleeping. His parents had spent the whole night in the hospital, and now they were down in the cafeteria eating food. She'd heard rumors that they weren't exactly getting along, but after seeing Stan's parents together, she knew they weren't exactly even friends anymore. They hadn't actually yelled at each other, but the silence between them had been almost worse than yelling.

She was so lost in her thoughts she almost screamed when Dave spoke. "They say they think it's epilepsy, but I don't think it is."

"No? Why not?"

"I've been looking up stuff on epilepsy on the Internet. Stan doesn't act right for it."

"I don't think the Internet is gonna replace doctors any time soon, Dave."

"Neither do I. But I don't think Stan has it anyway."

"Okay, Dr. Dave, what does he have then?"

Dave squatted next to her, looking her eye to eye, and shook his head. "I think Stan's haunted."

"By ghosts?"

"Yeah."

"You're crazy. Ghosts aren't real."

"Can you prove that?"

"No, but can you prove that they are?"

"No. But I'm willing to say they are for now."

"Okay, Dave. Why do you think Stan's being haunted by ghosts?"

"He was asking me about them the other day. He said he kept hearing people talking to him whenever he had one of his seizures."

Jessie pushed her glasses back up her nose and was almost amused to watch Dave do the exact same thing, as if she'd reminded him with her own gesture. "Well, aren't people supposed to see things when they have seizures?"

"Maybe, but I don't think they're supposed to see things like that."

"Did you tell anyone?"

"Just you."

"Why didn't you tell one of the doctors?"

"Because I don't want them thinking Stan is a nutter."

"Do you think he is?"

"No."

Jessie had no idea how to respond to that. Was Stan crazy? No, probably not, at least not in her mind. She looked back at Dave and nodded her agreement with him.

"Okay, Dave, so what do we do about it?"

"I don't know."

"Maybe we could call a psychic. One of those ones that says they talk to dead people."

"A medium?" Dave frowned lightly, lost for a split second in thought. "That could get expensive. Even the ones on the phone charge by the minute."

"I don't have any money." Jessie looked away, looked at the floor to avoid being embarrassed. "Dad just started working a few weeks ago."

"I could maybe get the money together. But not a phone psychic. I figure they're all fakes anyway."

"They had a couple on a show on the Learning Channel that deals with these things, and demons, too. I taped the show for Dad, because he was too tired to watch it. I could find their names, or"—and oh how saying the words made her skin feel sweaty—"you could come over and watch it."

Dave gave that serious thought—he almost always seemed to give everything serious thought—and then nodded as a smile lit his face. "Cool. If you can get the name, I can probably get hold of them."

Within ten minutes Mrs. Long was back, looking haggard and as pretty as a model to Jessie. She hoped she could manage to look anywhere near as good when she was older, but she had her doubts. The two of them said their good-byes, and Jessie leaned over the bed and kissed Stan on the forehead. She really hadn't planned to, it just sort of happened. But she was glad she did.

The hospital wasn't really much to look at—inside or out—but it was close enough that they could walk away from the three-story structure and still get back to her house within only half an hour. Really, when she thought about it, just about every part of Serenity was close enough to get to in half an hour or less. She often wondered why so many people even bothered with cars.

Dave walked with long strides that chewed up the ground, almost as if he took it personally that cars were faster at moving than he was. But she managed to keep pace. She mentioned running across Lawrence the day before just for something to break the silence.

And as soon as she did, Dave stopped in his tracks. "Lawrence Grey was out of his house?"

"Yeah. He had the biggest smile I've ever seen on his face, too. I don't think I've ever seen him anywhere but at school before. It was kind of weird."

"I'll bet he had a smile. I just hope his mom didn't catch him outside..."

"Why's that?"

"Because she's a psycho, that's why." Dave's broad face was set in a half scowl, and he pushed his glasses back up his face as he looked at her. "Why do you think he's always stuck at home? Because he wants to be? His mom does that to him. It's like she's afraid to let him out of her sight."

"Why?"

"Well, to hear Joey tell it, she's afraid he'll break if he's hurt by someone. Said his dad stole him when he was a little kid."

"But I've heard other things, too."

"Like what?"

"Like maybe his dad was trying to get him away from her before she could do anything bad to him."

Dave looked away for a second and then sighed. "Anyway, what did you two talk about?"

She shrugged her shoulders, and watched, astonished and a little flattered, when Dave's eyes flicked to her chest for a second before refocusing on her face. "Just stuff. How much he hates math class, and he kept going on about how nice the day was."

Dave seemed to mull that over as he started walking again, that same high-speed stride that always tore up the distance between where he was and where he was going. His face got that distant, dreaming look she knew meant he was lost in deep thought, and Jessie shut up. It was hard enough walking that fast anyway.

By the time they finally reached her house, Jessie was almost winded. Dave looked like they'd just taken a casual walk through the park. He wasn't even breathing hard. Jessie checked the house and found the note that said her mom was working at the library all day and that there were cold cuts in the fridge. Her father was still on shift at the house. He was taking every bit of overtime they offered while the place was being refinished, and he was glad to get it. She'd heard him tell her mom that if he could keep up the pace for a couple more weeks, they'd be caught up on the bills. Really caught up and not playing rushing roulette, whatever that was.

Jessie led Dave into the house and walked over to the TV, searching through the half-dozen videocassettes until she found the one she was looking for. After a few minutes of fumbling around with the remote and the rewind button, she found the sequence that mattered.

Dave watched in silence, his entire world focused on the screen and the tape playing in the VCR. Jessie watched, too. She watched Dave. Funny how she'd never noticed how handsome he was before.

"I know them. I've seen them on the websites. I can get them." She practically jumped out of her skin when Dave spoke. He'd been so still she'd started thinking of him almost as a picture to look at.

"How? I mean, how do you know you can get them here?"

"That's easy. They'll come to look at the cemetery alone."

"I don't get it. What's so special about a vandalized cemetery?"

Dave smiled. "You didn't look carefully enough at what was going on out there. The graveyard wasn't vandalized."

Jessie shook her head. He was cute, but sometimes he was also really annoying. "Will you just once actually say what you're talking about?"

"The graves, Jessie. They weren't broken into. They were broken out of. Those two on your tape, Mary and Jacob Parsons, they'll come here just for the publicity they can get for proving I'm right."

He sounded so sure of himself, and Jessie envied him that quality. In all the time she'd known Dave, he'd never seemed flustered or bothered by the events in his life. She wondered how he could do that, as if it were a magic trick that he might someday deign to teach her. Assuming, of course, that she ever got up the guts to ask.

"So, how will you get hold of them? When will you get hold of them?"

"Today if I can. I'm gonna go on home and see about emailing them or maybe even calling."

She nodded, wishing she could just tell him to forget all of that and stay around for a while. Jessie didn't want to be alone. It left her too much time for thinking about things she'd rather avoid thinking about.

As Dave stood up, she tried to think of something, anything to say to make him linger for just a while longer. Her body moved without conscious thought, and she leaned forward, kissing him on the lips, even as her mind wailed into a blind panic at the idea. *I didn't mean it!*

I take it back! Oh, God, please don't let him yell at me, please don't let him yell, or laugh, or cry, or any of those things I keep seeing when I imagine kissing a boy.

Dave's lips were soft and warm and felt like magic against her own. She looked into his eyes and saw them widen a little, then saw the way they lit up and changed, and even though he didn't smile—his lips were occupied during that brief eternity—she knew he was pleased.

Jessie broke the kiss almost as quickly as she'd started it, and pulled back from Dave as if afraid he would haul off and deck her for her daring. Instead, he looked at her with a slowly growing *Aww, shucks, ma'am* grin on his face and blushed for the first time she could remember ever seeing in her life. His hand moved toward her slowly, and one finger ran from her temple to her jawline in a light caress.

Dave spoke breathlessly as he headed for the door, and she saw that his knees seemed a little weaker than usual. He groped for the doorknob with his eyes on hers and that smile drifting over his face like a ray of sunshine breaking through storm clouds. "That was nice, Jessie."

"It was?"

"Yeah. Very nice." His eyes had a look of wonder in them, painted with a little guilty pleasure to make the surprise seem even more surreal. "I've kind of been wondering what it would be like to kiss you."

Jessie blinked and felt her heart try to triple its normal speed. "You have?" And she prayed he didn't notice the shock in her voice.

"Yeah, since about third grade. Thanks." And that small smile finally broke into a broader one, the kind that lets a person count all of the teeth behind the lips. "I'll call you when I find out anything, okay?"

"Okay." She smiled back, her skin feeling too tight and flushed with warmth. Like a fever, but a lot nicer.

"Bye."

"See ya."

Dave finally managed to open the door and slip outside, his eyes on hers until the last possible second. Jessie watched him from her window as he walked toward the farm where he lived with his massive family. He walked a lot slower than he usually did, and that made her feel good. Made her feel special.

IV

Joey was sitting on his porch, reading the latest *Detective Comics*, when Becky walked past. Without even thinking about it, he called out a greeting. Becky looked up at him with eyes that were red and puffy from her earlier tears and nodded to him.

"Hey, Becky. What are you up to?" Contrary to what Becky believed about herself, not everyone in town thought of her as some sort of pariah. Joey, for instance, thought she was pretty cool, if a bit snobby. It never dawned on him that she might be shy. Shy was not a concept that fit easily in his worldview. Of all the people he knew, the only one he would have called shy was Lawrence Grey.

"Oh... Hi. Umm... I'm going into the woods to find Mr. MacGruder."

"Yeah? Why you looking for him?"

Becky looked away, and he saw the way her faced kept trying to collapse and understood that she would most likely be in tears if it weren't for her self-control. Butterflies started fluttering in his stomach, and he felt the hair on his neck rise. Something bad had happened to Becky, maybe even something that was more than bad. He rose to his feet and walked in her direction, his face showing his concern, even though his voice remained casual. "Becky? Are you okay?"

"I don't... I can't tell you, Joey."

Joey moved closer and stopped right in front of her. The look she shot him was two parts doubt and one part fear. "What's wrong, Becky?"

"I—" Her eyes dropped down to the ground, and she shifted from one foot to the other like a fidgety bird. Rebecca Glass looked back up, and Joey watched as the tears started to build in her eyes and then spill over. Her voice when she spoke again was cracked and higher than usual. "My daddy's dead."

Joey looked at her and tried to think of what to say to that. It was much worse than he'd imagined it might be. He thought maybe she'd lost something, a necklace or an earring, or that one of the bigger kids had tried touching her the way he had been warned they sometimes tried to touch boys and girls alike. He never even thought about the possibility that she'd lost anything as major as her father. That was well beyond the realm of possibilities in his world. That was beyond major; it was huge, a fuckup of epic proportions.

"Oh shit, Becky, I'm sorry."

Becky looked at him with water-streaked eyes and said nothing. There was nothing to say, really. What? She was gonna tell him it was all right?

Just because she looked like she needed it and because he really was one of the good guys in his own way, Joey reached out and hugged her awkwardly. He'd never hugged a girl aside from his mother in his entire life, and it felt wrong. It felt good, sort of, but wrong. Like stepping into the Twilight Zone and just going along for the ride. He could almost hear the theme song playing in the back of his head.

Becky froze when he touched her, her body growing rigid and her face shifting from miserable depression to stark fear before it settled on an odd combination of the two emotions. Then she hugged back, her arms wrapping around his rib cage as she drew close to him and clutched tightly against his body. It was hard to breathe with her squeezing against him, and despite the situation, the bad timing, the almost desperate sense of loss that covered her entire body and seemed to generate a cloud of sorrow around her, he felt his own body respond in an embarrassing fashion.

He'd never touched a girl in any way that could be considered intimate, and really, a hug hardly qualified, but he was very aware of her close proximity and parts of him that were certainly not equipped for a sexual encounter pretended that they were. It made the hug awkward and exciting both, and he did everything he could to ignore it and let her cry her grief onto his shoulder. *She's got breasts.* The thought came unbidden to his mind as he patted her back and felt the tears from her eyes drip onto his shoulder, along with her warm breath and the vibrations of her soft, whining cries of grief.

"Shhhhh..." He rocked her back and forth, just as his own mother had rocked him when he was young. "Don't cry, Becky. Don't cry." He almost said it would be all right, that it would get better, but he caught himself in time. He leaned into the hug, still tight enough that it made catching his breath seem an impossible task, and kissed the crown of her head softly. Despite what his lower body seemed to want, there was nothing sexual about the kiss. Merely a touch to add comfort in a time when she seemed to need comfort so very desperately. He held her that way for a long, long time until her tears finally faded away.

Becky backed up, her face pale and streaked with angry tear marks. "I'm sorry... I didn't mean to do that."

Joey stepped forward, compensating for her retreat, and hugged her lightly a second time. "It's okay. I didn't mind."

"I guess I'm not as tough as I'm supposed to be."

"No one ever is, not really." He smiled at her, and she managed something close to a weak smile of her own. It made her plain face look pretty in a sad way. "I'm really sorry, Becky. About your father I mean."

"I just don't believe it." She shook her head, her eyes wide as a deer's when caught by headlights. Then she just sort of hardened. He saw the look on her face go from bewildered grief to a stony sort of anger in an instant. "And I won't let it happen."

"What do you mean you won't...?"

"I'm gonna find her, the witch. And she's gonna make it right."

He almost told her that was a load of crap. Almost scoffed at what she said. But he stopped himself. In her shoes, he wouldn't like it too much if someone burst his bubble. So it wouldn't work. So what? She needed to find that out for herself.

Just the same, he had no intention of letting her go into the woods by herself. "Fine. But I'm coming with you if that's cool."

And just like that, the angry face was gone, replaced by a sort of dazed shock, as if he had just told her he was really a girl and had been pulling a fast one on everybody for the last twelve years. "You'd do that for me?"

"What? Of course. That's what friends do, silly. They go off into the woods and look for witches together." He smiled at the look on her face and then draped an arm around her shoulders, sort of as a follow-up to the hug. She leaned against him for a few seconds, and he had to admit he liked the feeling. Then, with a certain dread in his stomach about the idea that there *might* actually be a witch, the two of them set off into the woods.

They walked in silence, and neither of them really minded. And Becky did not complain when he wrapped his fingers loosely around her hand as they journeyed.

V

Greg Randers slipped out of his bed as carefully as he could, afraid to wake Nona. She would want to leave if he woke her, and he didn't want that. Not if he could keep her a little longer.

If he had his way, they'd be together all the time instead of just when she could be certain her husband wasn't going to be a problem. And there wasn't any way to put it other than that. Carl was a big problem. Around 265 pounds of big problem. He had Greg by almost 100 pounds, and most of that weight was in the form of meat, not fat.

He took care of emptying his bladder and then moved back into the bedroom. Nona was still sleeping, looking far too much like an angel. She was beautiful, and sometimes, looking at her, knowing she was not his forever but only for a short time, was like agony. It hurt to look at her for too long, as if she might suddenly vanish and leave him with nothing.

Greg sat at the edge of the bed, his rump near her long, elegant legs, and stared into her face. If it was painful, that was okay. It was better to look and absorb while she was here than to be without her. Even speaking on the phone—which was mostly what they could do about their feelings for each other—was better than thinking about her with Carl.

For only the second time, they'd actually managed to make love— with her it wasn't sex, it was making love, he felt he now knew the difference between the two—and as sweet as it had been, he was soured by the idea that she would not be able to stay long.

Nona shifted in her sleep and made a little sound, a soft moan that made him want to lean over and kiss her. Instead, he ran his hand over her leg in a slow caress. Her eyes fluttered, and she smiled in her half sleep. He let his hand go farther, moving under the covers to the place where her legs joined. Nona opened her eyes and smiled warmly, then let out a small gasp of pleasure as he reached farther still with his hand. Several minutes later he and she were occupied with getting to know each other better than their normal stolen kisses would allow. They spent over half the morning getting to know each other and exploring the bodies they dreamed of when they went to sleep at night.

When they were done, Greg kissed Nona's sweating forehead and tasted the salt of her perspiration. It was like the finest ambrosia to him. She snuggled close for a moment, savoring the rare moment together.

And then he opened his mouth and fucked everything up again. "I love you, Nona."

"Don't say that, Greg."

"I know, I know I shouldn't say it, but sometimes I have to."

"I don't want you to. It makes me sad." Her voice was pouty but not in a spoiled way, more in a way that said she meant it. She didn't want to be hurt by the words. Not like she'd been hurt by Carl saying them.

"I wish he'd just go away. I wish he'd never been born."

"Sometimes I do, too." He didn't let his mouth screw things up a second time. He kept shut on the subject of divorce. Carl was not the sort who believed in divorce. Carl believed in till death do we part. There was no deliberation on the subject and certainly no way to convince him otherwise. Greg knew that, because they'd discussed the matter before.

"I have to go…"

"I know. I wish you could stay, though."

"So do I." Nona rose from the bed with a liquid grace that was only one part of the hundreds of reasons he could think of to love her. He watched her with his eyes and wanted desperately to pull her back to him and never let her go. "But Carl's shift will end soon, and if I'm not home…"

She didn't have to say more. They both knew what would happen if she wasn't there when Carl came home. He'd heard enough stories about Carl's fists. He'd heard enough of the tales to make him want to sweat bullets at the idea of crossing the man. Still, for Nona he'd seriously consider it.

Did she love him as much? He didn't know. She'd never actually said that she loved him, but her gestures, her smile, and her actions made him want to believe she did with a potent desperation.

He watched her dress in silence, wanting to speak, wanting to make her stay. Knowing that he couldn't. When she was finished, he kissed her again, a long, lingering kiss that would have to hold him until she could get the time to see him again. His hand in hers, he walked her to the door of his house, which had been furnished to suit her tastes and to make her as happy as he could in the limited fashions allowed him.

He opened the door for Nona and prepared to give her one last kiss. He smiled warmly, and she in turn looked past him and toward the entranceway to his house, and screamed.

Greg turned his head just in time to meet Carl's fist square in his face. He heard more than felt the sound of his nose breaking. The strike was harsh enough to make his face go numb from the impact, and his eyes watered furiously as he staggered back into the room. His feet managed to wrap themselves around the brass coat rack near the front door, and he did a stumbling dance until he met with the wall.

Carl walked in after him, his hands balled into fists roughly the size of Greg's skull. Greg was trying hard to remember how to think, but Carl didn't seem to have that problem. He moved straight for Greg and kicked him in the chest with a size-fourteen construction boot. Something hot ran through Greg's rib cage with a breaking sound, and he groaned in pain as Nona started screaming again.

Carl looked away from Greg long enough to smile at his wife. "Don't you even think about going anywhere, Nona. Don't you even think of breathing funny." Nona looked at her husband and turned deathly pale, the color draining even from her lips.

Greg tried to stand up and gasped as the hot spot in his chest seemed to explode into something worse. He fell back against the floor, looking up at Carl, who managed to look even more impressive and terrifying than usual. Carl reached down and grabbed a double handful of Greg's arms, lifting him from the ground as if he were an infant.

"You got balls, boy, messing with my wife."

Greg didn't answer. He was too busy getting closer and closer to puking all over the front of his assailant's T-shirt. Behind him, Nona made light whimpering sounds, and he could just see the fear marring her pretty face in his mind's eye. Greg made a fist and swung it as hard as he could toward Carl. It might have been blind luck, it might have been something else. Whatever the case, he actually managed to connect solidly with his opponent's jaw.

Carl's head snapped back, and the hands holding Greg in place loosened. He managed not to fall on his face as his feet dropped to the ground, but it wasn't easy, what with the way his knees had gone all watery on him.

He'd really hoped that the punch he delivered to Carl would do some good. Christ knew it had made his fist feel like so much broken glass just afterward, but all it managed to do was make the man madder. Carl was, as his father used to say, a scrapper. Greg had never been a scrapper. He didn't like to fight.

Carl returned the punch with heavy interest. One second Greg was up and standing, the next he was staggering back against the far wall with little explosions of light going across his field of vision almost endlessly.

Maybe he was on the edge of dreaming by that point, he couldn't really say, but he would have sworn he saw someone standing behind Carl. A masculine figure buried in shadows. He could almost make out the face, someone familiar, and then the figure was gone. *Hit me harder than I thought. I'm seeing things.* Carl reached for him again, his hands out to grab and lift or maybe just start pulling the skin right off Greg's bones. The man looked capable of it.

And then Carl stopped, frozen in place for a moment with a look of utter confusion marring his features. He turned halfway around at the waist, looking for something that wasn't there. Someone or something behind him.

Greg took advantage of the distraction and kicked his right leg forward as hard as he could, planting his heel directly into Carl Bradford's testicles. The man's head snapped back in his direction as fast as a striking cobra, even as his hands went automatically toward his crotch. "You... I can't..." Greg didn't give himself time to think; he just kicked again. This time his heel caught the edge of Bradford's kneecap, and he heard a muffled crunching noise that was almost completely drowned out by Bradford's scream.

Greg felt a grim satisfaction as the man fell to the floor, clutching at his ruined knee. Carl's face was white, and his eyes were as round as saucers. Greg kicked him again. This time it was only a glancing blow, but it felt good, just the same. Nona stood off on the side, her eyes as wide as her husband's, her hands covering her mouth as if to suppress a scream.

And thinking of Nona, Greg looked down at Carl and felt himself harden to the task before him. The man was already trying to get back up, his face darkened by rage. But the ruined knee and the nauseating pain in his lower regions were slowing him down more than he might have expected. Carl Bradford looked like he was more than willing to kill Greg.

Greg felt the same way about him. The difference was simply that Greg was in a better position to do something about it. He looked over at Nona, who was shifting her eyes between the two men like an observer at a heated tennis match. When he finally managed to make contact with her, his expression asked the question for him: *Do you want him dead?*

Nona looked down at her husband, the man who had, on four separate occasions, beaten her with the skill and care of a grand inquisitor and who had on many more occasions forced her to perform her "wifely duties" for him whether or not she was willing, and slowly she nodded her head three times.

Greg looked around the living room, his head still spinning a little and his nose now starting to feel as if a hundred bees had settled into his nostrils and sinuses, searching for a good weapon. He found the coat rack that had sent him sprawling earlier and gripped it like a battle-ax in both hands.

Carl had enough time to look up and realize what was happening before the base of the unconventional weapon crashed into his temple and split his right eye open. Greg might have thought that would be enough to stop the construction worker, but he was sadly mistaken. The blow took all of the fight out of him but didn't do a damned thing to slow down his screaming and thrashing around. His size-fourteen boots kicked and slammed against the hardwood floor, and Greg almost dropped his weapon when Carl bucked hard, blood splashing from the hand that covered the right side of his face.

He was trying to say something, and his left hand kept reaching for Greg's leg. Greg danced back from the groping hand, knowing that if Carl grabbed hold of him, he was as good as dead. No way in hell would Bradford forgive him for what he'd just done. He ignored whatever words were straining to free themselves from Carl and concentrated on hitting the man again and again. His arms were screaming in protest, and his wrists felt like they were on fire by the time he'd finished with the beating.

And Carl Bradford lay dead in front of him, a large man with a pile of hamburger for a skull. He looked away from the mess he'd made and looked over to Nona for the strength to continue doing anything at all. Nona looked not at Greg, but at her husband's mortal remains and the expression on her face said she couldn't have been happier.

He felt sick and excited. He almost wanted to throw up, and at the same time, he was exhilarated by the idea that there was nothing at all to keep him and Nona apart any longer.

Nothing except the body of a man who outweighed him by a good hundred pounds. Murder had never been in Greg's plans. Not exactly an option he'd ever really considered before now. Something big was gripping his rib cage in a vise grip and squeezing like a python looking for an easy supper. *Can't panic, not now, Greg. You don't have the time to spare. You have to do something about the body.*

"Greg, what the hell are were going to do with him?" He almost jumped out of his skin. He looked over at Nona and shook his head, the sweat starting to bead slowly on his forehead and in his armpits. Nerves of steel were not one of his emotional features. Adrenaline and fear had just gotten him through a very rough minute or two, but already the former was fading away, leaving him shaky-kneed and with a serious need to take a leak.

"I don't know, Nona. Give me a minute to think, okay?"

She nodded her head, her face still flushed with an almost excited look. Then she moved over to him, her face changing to concern for him. "Are you okay, Greg? Did he... Oh, it looks like he broke your nose..."

Her hands moved up, touching his face gently, and he felt himself calming down, his mind clearing. God, even her touch was enough to make him feel more complete. "It's okay, Nona. It's not the first time I've broken my nose. Hurts like hell, but I swear if you look at my nose the wrong way, it breaks again." He might have said more, but before he could, she was kissing him. It wasn't a light peck on the cheek, either, but a full-on, face-mashing lip-lock. Just like that, the adrenaline was back in his system, but working toward a different goal. Greg had bruises on his rib cage and probably a few more on his shoulders, but that didn't matter. They seemed to fade away to nothingness in comparison to the passion he felt coming off Nona in an almost physical wave.

For a while at least, he forgot the body that lay on the floor of his front parlor as he and Nona managed to find their way back to his bedroom. Nona and Greg engaged in what can only properly be called a sexual marathon, fueled by death and violence, by the adrenaline that burned through their bodies.

Later. They could dispose of the body later. And he thought he knew just how…

VI

Charlee opened the door after the person outside knocked for the third time. She hadn't really wanted to get up and answer it, but what choice was there when her mom was off in the greenhouse, and her dad was sleeping on the couch in his den?

She swung the door inward, her face set in a typical expression of annoyance, and then saw her sister looking back at her with a broad smile on her pretty face. The main difference between Charlee and Nancy Lyons was their ages. Nancy was eight years older than her sister, stood approximately four inches taller, and had finished her run with puberty by and large. Aside from those factors, they could have been mirror images.

It took about three seconds for Charlee to register that her sister was back in town, and then she all but flew into her sibling's arms, squealing like a kid on Christmas morning. Nancy hugged her back just as fiercely, and Charlee called through the open door to her parents, letting them know that the college girl had come home to visit.

Mom and Dad came out to greet their daughter, surprised by the unexpected visit but very happy as well. After several sessions of hugs and smiles, they went into the house, Nancy answering all of her parents' questions as they went.

"Why haven't you called, honey?" Insert soft, guilt-inspiring tone here.

"I've been studying, Mom. I'm loaded on classes, and I don't have a lot of spare time after I'm done with school and work." And those words spoken with a very slight change in pitch, a minor whining noise that made Nancy sound as young as her sibling.

"Well, you could at least find the time to call, Nancy, your mom and me, we worry about you." Insert calm, placating Dad tone here.

"I do call, Dad, but the phone's always busy."

"That would be your sister on the phone with her little friends," Mom said. "I remember what you were like, always gabbing away, and I swear Charlee is five times worse."

"Mom..."

"Not now, Charlee. So, have you met any boys yet? Are you going steady with some nice doctor-to-be?"

"Mom, like I said, I barely have time for the classes and work, too. Boys are out of the question for at least another couple of years."

"Nonsense! There's always time to find Mister Right." Playful teasing sounds and maybe an edge of desperation that just didn't seem to fit properly.

"Let her alone, honey. If Nancy isn't ready to commit to a relationship, then don't force the matter." A very real note of warning. Daddy didn't want to think of his daughter with a man.

"Of course you'd say that. She's still your little girl after all." There was just the slightest edge in her mother's voice on that one, a chill that hadn't existed a few seconds before and that went away almost as quickly as it showed itself, and Charlee wondered why it was there. If she didn't know better, she'd almost think her mother was jealous of her sister. She shook off the notion as silly. What was there to be jealous of?

"Don't start that again. Of course she's my little girl. I've got two of them, and I don't want either of them growing up too fast. I'm greedy."

The babbling went on for another twenty minutes, and by the time it was done, there was an almost blissful silence in the house. Charlee went back up to her room, ready to escape from the mess. She loved her parents, but sometimes they were really a pain in the ass. She tried calling over to Jessie's place as soon as she was on her bed, but there was no answer again. Four times she'd tried, and four times she'd failed. It'd taken her a few hours to decide she should apologize to her best friend for being an idiot, and now that she had, she wanted to get it over with as quickly as possible. It was weird, Jessie not being home all day on a Sunday. She and her folks always went to church first thing, but normally they were home by one in the afternoon, latest, and it was almost time for supper already.

She shook her head and decided not to think about it anymore. She'd already left three messages, and she wasn't going to leave a fourth. It would make it seem like she was desperate, and that would never do.

Annoyed by her friend's absence, she sat on the edge of the bed and started sorting through her homework assignments. The next day was school again, and Mr. LeMarrs's class. He still had a vendetta against her, she was sure of it. Every time she made eye contact, he was looking at her with that pouty little sour expression. He was a lemon sucker, and she hated him.

Well, maybe not hated, but definitely did not like.

Hate was too strong a word, and she tried to avoid using words improperly. Her father said misusing words was like killing the American culture one sentence at a time. Who was she to argue?

Nancy knocked lightly and slipped into the room, closing the door behind her.

Charlee smiled, glad for the chance to see her sister alone, without her folks to cramp their style.

"Hi, Charlee. Have you missed me?"

"Nah. I knew you'd be back." It was the answer expected and the one she gave. It was sort of tradition. Actually showing emotion was okay, but only at the end of a visit. Whenever Nancy came home they both pretended that all was well and the change in routine wasn't really that drastic a change.

"Yeah, I didn't miss you either." Just to prove how little she'd missed her sister, Nancy pulled Charlee close in a warm hug. Charlee loved when she did that. It was rare, almost as rare as her parents hugging her.

Charlee enjoyed the brief display of affection for as long as it lasted and resisted the urge to sigh when it was over.

"So what made you come back to this dump, Nancy?"

"Same old, same old. I wanted to hook up with some friends, maybe get a little relaxing done. See my little sister and tickle her half to death…the usual." And by the time the words sank in, Nancy had already pinned Charlee to the bed, her agile fingers mercilessly assaulting the younger girl's sensitive spots, tickling her until she was on the edge of hysterical tears. Anyone else trying that sort of crap would likely have gotten a fist or two aimed at their face, but with Nancy it was okay. Nancy was special.

There was a time, distant now, when the father of the two girls had been a little too easy with the belt strap. Which is to say he'd blistered Charlee's ass to the point where it was almost impossible for her to do more than walk very slowly, and sitting down was the sort of hellish pain normally reserved for victims of the Inquisition. On four separate occasions, Rodney Lyons had taken his youngest daughter over his knee and left her hindquarters bloodied and blistered because she'd had the audacity to give him lip. The fifth time he got ready to "make her sorry she was ever born" as he so eloquently put it, Nancy had intervened.

To this day Charlee had never discovered exactly what her sister had said to her father. She saw his face go red with anger and then very, very pale while Nancy spoke to him. She saw her father nod and look her way, and that was the end of it. She merely understood that her derriere remained untortured as a result of something her sister said in hushed whispers to her father.

That in and of itself had earned Nancy her undying gratitude. That she was also pretty cool as big sisters went was just gravy. Nancy had already taught her the fundamentals of wearing makeup without looking trashy—knowledge she was not allowed to use as yet by order of her parents, but she had the knowledge nonetheless—and told her all sorts of stories about the things guys will do to try getting into the pants of unwary girls.

Compared to some of the older sisters of girls she knew from school, her sibling was a saint. That was probably made easier by Nancy not living at home anymore. They'd had more than their fair share of fights over the years. But not seeing each other every day meant not wanting to rehash arguments from the week before. It was a nice change of pace.

Charlee told Nancy all about what was happening in town—from old drunk Mike going sober to Terri Halloway getting hurt (and maybe something more, no one knows for sure, and Terri isn't talking about it) to the graveyard desecrations at Powers Cemetery and the opening of the quarry sometime next year. The last part didn't sound so great until she explained that the new owners were already paying people to fix up Havenwood and to prepare the quarry for use.

Nancy told Charlee all about school. Yes, she had a boyfriend, but he was black, and mom would never understand. It wasn't serious, but there it was, just the same. No, they hadn't gone all the way yet, and that was one of the reasons they were breaking up. Yes, she still worked at a bar after school three days a week, and no, she didn't much like it. For that matter, she wasn't all that fond of school, but she was going to make it anyhow, because the idea of coming back to town and working at Frannie's again was enough to make her feel like she had a thunderstorm brewing in her stomach.

Still, she wanted to go see Frannie. Wanted to check how everything was going with Terry. She knew him well enough to actually doubt whether or not he was innocent, and she knew Frannie well enough to know that the whole thing was probably eating the woman alive. Frannie was a hard woman to work for but a sweetheart when you weren't on the clock.

Nancy stood up after their long session of catching up and stretched her lean body like a cat, slow and sensuous. She made it look so easy, and that was a little annoying to Charlee, but only a little. Even the natural grace that Charlee knew she would never be able to match wasn't enough to take away how happy she was to see her sister again.

Nancy left the room and moments later the house, driving away in her little piece-of-crap Honda that was ready to fall apart at the first serious sneeze.

Charlee never saw her sister again.

VII

Joey and Becky walked through the woods, and as far as Joey was concerned, it had probably been a bad idea. A light rain had started, and if he didn't have a cold from it already, he surely would before it was all said and done. Joey was wearing jeans, a thin dress shirt, and a light gray sweater. The weather had been nice earlier, just a little chilly but now... His shoes were soaked through, and the weather was definitely heading down toward freezing. It was almost summertime, and that meant he shouldn't have to worry about the cold, but here he was freezing his ass off like it was Halloween; his nose felt like a block of ice placed firmly in the center of his face. One sneeze, and that sucker was likely to crack like bad porcelain and fall off.

Becky was still obsessed. They'd been out here for what seemed like hours, and the girl was as determined as ever to find the witch of the woods. Joey didn't think the witch was real, but he would have bet money that Becky wasn't going to stop until she figured that out for herself. He'd just have to wait it out in the meantime.

The clouds that had threatened all day long were only dropping a little rain so far, but he didn't think that would last. They were also working as wonderful cover for the sun. It was barely past four and already as dark as if the sun had just crashed through the horizon. So far things could possibly suck more, but he had trouble believing it. He shivered as the wind picked up and dropped frigid water down the back of his shirt and light sweater.

Up ahead of him, Becky kept plodding along, walking with a stride that would have eaten up twice the distance if she didn't have to maneuver around so damned many trees. He'd never really thought about how many trees there were in the woods, or the sheer volume of shrubs and other plants. A few months back he'd have given up completely within the first twenty minutes. The woods were too dense.

He would have given up anyway, but Becky was so determined, and the woods were no place for a girl to be by herself, even one who was as competent as she was. Besides, there was a part of him that wanted to know what was out in the woods. It was normally a small part, but for now it fed on his desire to help her deal with the loss of her father and rode piggyback on the part of him that was enjoying her company and the warmth generated by touching her hand. That part was growing, too, almost driven into a frenzy by their earlier hugs and the discovery that Becky had a nice body under all those baggy clothes she normally wore. It might have been wrong for him to even consider that in light of her loss, but his body just didn't seem to care.

So he walked through the woods, almost running to keep pace with the girl he'd never noticed until a few weeks ago and never considered as anything but another face until earlier that day. And he told himself he walked with her because she needed company right then. And that was at least partially true.

He was so lost in his train of thoughts—guilty and innocent alike—that he almost ran Becky over when she came to a sudden stop. Joey started to mumble an apology, even as he savored the way she'd felt against him, when he saw what made her put on the brakes.

Simon MacGruder's place. It had to be where the old hermit lived, because it was the only house they'd run across. It wasn't exactly the shack he'd been imagining over the years. The place had two levels, for one thing, and shacks didn't usually look like they'd survive World War Three if it ever came around. There was enough gingerbread on the house to make it look like an overenthusiastic confection, and three chimneys ran from the base of the building up its sides, spewing forth white smoke and the smell of burning wood. It looked like a very comfortable place to be, but sitting as it did in the middle of the woods gave Joey a sense that it just didn't belong there.

If Becky felt the same way, she didn't let it stop her. She pulled gently at his hand as she started walking, and Joey followed. He wondered if she got the same sort of comfort from the grip they shared as he did. Not just the comfort of thinking about being with him, but the comfort of being with someone in this place. The chill in the air seemed somehow magnified here, as if the cold that was outside his body was doing its best to creep into him and overwhelm his body's heat. Having Becky there made it tolerable, but just barely.

There are dogs out here, he thought. *Big dogs, the sort that eat little kids like me for breakfast. And just for extra kicks, there's the house out in the woods and the thought of dealing with crazy old MacGruder. Are we having fun yet? Am I really stupid enough to think that I could help Becky if something went wrong?*

The closer he came to the house, the more he wanted to pull away from Becky and run like hell. The hairs on the back of his neck were standing up on their own, and he didn't like it one damned bit.

But the moment passed, however fitfully, and he continued on, his hand wrapped around Becky's fingers. The hundred or so yards to that house seemed to go on forever, but eventually, finally, they arrived.

Without so much as a how do you do, Becky knocked on the darkly stained door of the place. The wood sounded thick, and he could barely hear her knock.

Maybe the old guy isn't there. Maybe he's out hunting or even in town, and we'll be able to call this done. From the other side of the door he thought he heard the sound of something moving, coming closer to where he and Becky stood. Joey wanted to run like mad, to get the hell out of there before there was no more chance to turn back.

"Becky, are you sure about this? I mean really, really sure?"

Becky turned to look at him, her pale face set and determined. She licked her lips and nodded, trying her best to put on a proper smile and failing. "I have to do this, Joey. I have to. But you don't."

And there it was, an out. He could just nod his head, wish her well, and be on his way. Easy as pie. Except, of course, that it is never that easy. "No. In for a penny in for a pound, whatever that means."

She smiled more successfully then, and her fingers squeezed his by way of saying thanks. Before either of them could say more, the door opened to the house in the woods.

Joey looked at the man with the intensity of a doctor studying a new and unusual form of open sore. He saw the short gray hair, the broad, open face, and realized that he knew the man they'd come to see. Not well, certainly not on a first-name basis, but better than he'd expected. This was not the face of a crazy old coot living out in a shack, but the face of the nice old guy he'd seen coming through the area for years and years. He'd passed the old guy a hundred times easily, and one or the other had always made a friendly gesture that the other returned.

That made the whole thing less sinister somehow.

Simon MacGruder looked down from his height advantage—not much of one, really, he wasn't a very tall man—and smiled. "Well, I wasn't expecting company, not on a night like this, but why don't you two come on out of the rain and have a seat." He stepped back from the door and held it open for his guests. Becky and Joey slipped inside, grateful to get out of the cold for a minute or two.

The big old house was well lit, with lamps and candles everywhere. Somehow Joey had expected the place to be dark and brooding, like something from an old sixties' horror flick. The walls of the main room were covered with bookshelves, all of which were almost overflowing with old leather-bound tomes of every size imaginable. There was no television in the room, and that was a little weird, but it made sense, seeing as the man had no electricity. MacGruder ushered the two of them in and gestured for them to sit before leaving them alone. He came back a few minutes later with a very large pot of tea and some homemade cookies for nibbling. He was dressed in jeans and a red flannel shirt, and his round, weathered face bore an expression of mild curiosity as he looked at the two of them.

"What brings you two out here in the middle of such ugly weather?" His face had the same expression as before, but he had a little grin starting, almost as if he felt he knew the answer.

Becky cleared her throat and looked at the man for moment before speaking. "I'm trying to find the witch."

MacGruder didn't laugh. He nodded his head and stared back into her eyes. "Are you sure that's what you want?"

"Yessir. I need to find her."

"Why would a little thing like you be out looking for the witch in this sort of weather?"

"I need her help, to find my father."

"I saw Bill Karstens this morning. Your name wouldn't be Rebecca Glass, would it?"

"Yessir. That's me."

Joey thought he'd hear the same words he'd said earlier himself come out of the old man's mouth. Some form of condolence for her loss. Instead, MacGruder just nodded his head slowly. "You're sure this is what you want? Sometimes she's not so kind to people who bother her. Sometimes she can be very, very mean about it."

Becky looked at him again, her eyes never wavering. "I need to see her. I need to have my dad back."

"What makes you so sure she can give you what you want?"

"Well, she's a witch, isn't she?"

"That's what I've heard, yes. But witches aren't always up to raising the dead, you know. That takes a lot of effort."

"She's the only chance I have."

MacGruder nodded his head again, lost in thought. "I'm not sure where she is, you know. She doesn't normally come around for tea. But I have a few ideas of where you could look."

"Please, Mr. MacGruder, anything you can tell me would help."

The old man rose from his seat and walked over to an old oak desk with a rolling top. He opened it and pulled out a legal pad with bright yellow pages and a felt-tipped pen. When he sat back down, it was on the chair right next to Becky's, and she leaned forward to watch as he started drawing a map. Joey leaned in as well, noticing the faint scent of Old Spice on the man as it mingled with Becky's hair. He liked the way she smelled.

MacGruder spoke again, his voice much softer than before. "This is where you are now." He drew an X on the paper before him and as Joey watched continued on detailing a map of the woods around them. "I've seen the witch on five occasions, and three of them happened right around here." He added a clearing near the edge of the falls, where the water came out of the granite and spilled across the woods to form a creek. "If I were to go looking for her, it'd be around this area. There's seven big pieces of granite that just sort of stick up like broken teeth near the water. That's the place you should try."

"Why does she go there?" It took Joey a second to realize he'd spoken aloud.

"Well, I reckon she likes it there. It's got a pretty enough view, and not too many people come around, because it's treacherous walking."

"Treacherous?"

"There's a lot of loose soil from when the creek floods, and a lot of dead trees in the area. A person who isn't cautious is likely to break a leg, or worse."

Joey nodded and kept quiet. This was Becky's quest. He was just along to make sure she didn't get hurt. The idea of walking over rough terrain in the woods held a certain perverse appeal to him, but he pushed those thoughts away as quickly as he could.

MacGruder finished drawing his map and tore the sheet of paper from the pad before handing it to Becky. "That's about all there is to it. If you want to try meeting up with the witch, there's the place where you might get lucky."

"Thank you, Mr. MacGruder. Thank you so very much."

The man looked back at her and smiled with an expression that didn't quite make it to his eyes. "Don't thank me. I'm probably not doing you any favors."

The two youths rose from their seats, ready to get on with their duties before it got any colder or wetter or darker. For Joey, the idea of going home was starting to have a very special appeal. The idea of snuggling under his covers and drifting to sleep was beginning to sound far more exciting than any more walking through the woods. Even staying in the house where they were—where it was warm and dry with a fire blazing in the fireplace and hot tea to drink, thanks very much—seemed like a better idea. One look over at Becky, and he knew that home was a long ways off yet, and that the cold weather outside, from which he was just finally recovering, was not going to wait much longer.

She said you could go, that you didn't have to go with her to the woods. She gave you an out, man, why don't you fucking take it? He knew the voice well enough. It was his. It spoke of doing sensible things and getting the hell out of Dodge while the getting was good. It made sense. He knew there were bad risks from walking around with the thin, wet clothes he was currently in, and the idea of slipping and cracking his skull open in the darkness of the woods was not adding anything at all to his comfort level. Joey was fascinated by illness. He knew more about medicine and the arts of healing than most adults aside from doctors and emergency medical technicians. While most kids were reading the latest about Harry Potter's exploits, he was online and looking over articles about first aid and every illness listed on WebMD. But that didn't mean he wanted to experience them firsthand. There were big risks with broken bones. Arteries could be mangled, nerves could be severed. Shock could set in and make it impossible to think rationally, even if he wasn't badly broken enough to make moving an impossibility. And what if something happened to Becky? What would he do then? She was actually just a little taller than he was, and just as broad across the shoulders—not that that said much, he was sort of skinny—and even he could see that she would never be thin. She had too many muscles for thin; she would likely grow up to be what his mom always called "good farm stock" when she was being cynical. She would be a strong woman, just as she was a strong girl. He, on the other hand, was never going to be a jock, unless it was playing baseball or something. He wasn't designed to be a bruiser. It was a fact. What in the name of God would he do if Becky broke her leg or something? Carry her out of the woods? The very idea was enough to make him snort an aborted laugh from his nose.

Then Becky turned and smiled at him. Just another weak little smile that said she was glad he was there. And just as fast as that smile crossed her lips, he pushed all of the doubts from his head and smiled back. He wasn't going home. Not yet at least. He was going with Becky to make sure she didn't break a leg or something. And if she did, well, he would just have to work something out, wouldn't he?

As they were getting ready to leave, Simon MacGruder told them to hold up for a minute and went into one of the rooms up the stairs of his big old house. He came back down with two heavy flannel coats that had probably not been used by him in years. He made them each promise to wear one and told them to bring them back when they were better suited for walking through the woods. Joey said thanks and took the coat, grateful for the added protection. Becky took the coat offered to her and said thanks as well, but he suspected the words were more for the directions than for the jacket.

A few minutes later they were ready to go. They took the information, the map, the coats, and a big damned thermos loaded with more hot tea along with them. If Simon MacGruder doubted their abilities, he never let it show. Joey wondered why it was that he'd been so scared of the man before. Maybe it was just knowing that he lived all alone in the woods that did it. He wasn't really sure.

Warmed by the fire, and better suited for walking into the woods, he and Rebecca walked away from Simon MacGruder's house and prepared to meet a witch. When they were away from the house, Becky leaned in close to him and gave him a warm hug. It felt wonderful, tingly and warm and sweet. Given a choice, he'd have just stayed there in the cold rain and hugged her for a few hundred more hours.

Maybe later, he thought, *after the witch scares the hell out of me*. It was all right. That hug alone—initiated by her and not by him—was enough to make it worth the trip.

VIII

Frannie Palance let out a squeal worthy of a girl half her age and ran halfway across the diner to reach Nancy Lyons. She all but knocked the girl over in her enthusiasm to hug her. Nancy hugged back just as fiercely, and a few moments later, after they'd each said their hurried hellos and how are yous, the older woman sat Nancy down and brought her a menu. Nancy knew better than to argue. Frannie remained convinced that Nancy was far too skinny and did her best to fatten her up every time they saw each other.

"Why the hell is it so cold?" Nancy shivered and patted her arms, rubbing the flesh to warm it. She was inside now, and Frannie had the heat going, but the chill still lingered. "I've been wearing T-shirts for the last three weeks at school, and I come back here and need a damned coat."

Frannie grimaced and shrugged. "I dunno, hon. I just know it's been going on for a couple of weeks now." She chuckled. "If it keeps up, I'm gonna go broke from the damned heating bills." She ran her blunt fingers through Nancy's hair and smiled. "Damn, it's good to see you."

"I heard about Terry, Frannie. Is everything okay?"

Frannie's handsome face—she could not honestly be called pretty, but she was handsome—seemed to draw in a bit, and she sighed. "I don't know, hon, I really don't. He keeps telling me he didn't do a thing to her, aside from making her walk home, and I want to believe him, but it's hard when Jack Michaels has him locked away, and Terri Halloway has been sitting in a hospital for most of the last two weeks. She just got out yesterday, for heaven's sake, and she still doesn't really look herself. Her face is the same, but I don't think anyone's seen her smile." Her eyes drifted over to the tables filled with people, and Nancy knew she was already thinking about making her rounds and seeing if anyone needed anything.

"They can wait five minutes, Frannie. I know that's hard to believe, but they can."

Frannie nodded and allowed herself a weak smile.

"So, maybe Terry didn't do anything but let her off. Is there any evidence besides Terri's word?" That sounded so damned awkward.

She knew who they were talking about, and knew that Frannie could keep up, but Nancy always thought there was something a little weird about two people with the same name dating. It made life complicated in a stupid way.

"There was evidence that she was hurt, and badly hurt...sexually. But there wasn't any proof that it was my son, just her word against his. And everyone in town knew they were dating. It's not like Serenity's the sort of place where anyone can keep a secret."

Nancy smiled and nodded. Frannie might be surprised by how many secrets could be kept, but Nancy didn't feel like being the one to enlighten her. "Well, then it comes down to her word against his. Is he going to make bail?"

"Not with my help. I can't afford to post bail for him, and I don't really know if I want to."

"What do you mean?"

"Well, when he was confronted by Jack, he ran. Nancy, when I was being raised, I always heard that only guilty people run. That doesn't really help me have any trust in Terry right now." She lowered her head, tried to avoid looking at Nancy as she said that last, as if the admission made her feel somehow guilty of a crime herself.

"Oh, Frannie. I know Terry well enough. I don't think he's got it in him to actually hurt anyone. And I don't think he'd ever do that to a woman." She thought about her father, the things he'd started doing to Charlee before she confronted him and warned him to knock it off if he wanted to avoid jail time, and then forced the thoughts away. "He's not the type. I can see him running from Jack, because Jack can make you feel guilty even when you haven't done anything, but I can't really see him raping some girl." She spoke the last in a whisper, knowing she probably needn't have bothered. Everyone in town knew about what had happened. If they didn't, they knew someone who did. It was the way things were in Serenity.

The older woman's hands wrapped around hers and squeezed tightly at her fingers for a second before letting them free. "Thanks, hon. You don't know how much that means to me. But I'm still not gonna bail him out. He hasn't said more than ten words to me since he was arrested. If he asked, maybe, but I'm not going to just pour out my savings and hope he'll show up for court."

"So use his car as bond. He can't get very far if his car is gone."

Frannie laughed. "Oh, he'd have a fit! I can just see him!" She laughed harder, almost cackling as she gasped in breaths. "Oh my Lord, but he'd be ready for a straitjacket!" It wasn't meant as a joke, though she could see how it could be interpreted that way. Anyone who knew Terry knew that car meant more to him than just about anything else in his life. He might yell at his mother or even at his girlfriend, but his words for the car were always soft.

"Maybe, but the car's still in your name if I remember right, and that way you could be sure he wouldn't go off without at least really thinking about it."

Frannie shook her head. "It's almost not worth it."

"You and Terry still fighting a lot?"

"Does the sun set in the west?"

"So let him stay there. Maybe he'll figure out how to be a little more civil to you while he's cooling his heels."

"Jack still won't even come in here. It's like he's afraid of me."

"He probably is, Frannie. He's probably thinking you'd just as soon shoot him as see him."

Frannie excused herself for a minute, going to see to a new couple coming through the doors of the diner. Hell would likely freeze over and have time to thaw again before Frannie Palance would let anyone seat themselves in her diner. It might not be enough of a crime to send a person to hell, but in Frannie's eyes it was still a sin.

Nancy made eye contact with the man who was sitting at the next booth. He had a nice face, if a little plain. He nodded a greeting in return and went back to his dinner. Watching him eat reminded her that she was hungry, and she settled on a country fried steak and gravy dinner.

When Frannie came back, she took Nancy's order and then went into the kitchen. A few minutes later she was back again, acting like nothing at all had happened. She continued the conversation from where they had been. "So what should I do about Jack? Call him on the phone and tell him to forget he arrested Terry?"

"Might not be a bad idea. Might even let him know that all is well between you two, if it really is."

"It'd be better if we slept together, but these days I'm out of practice." The words were said in a monotone, with a dry humor in the voice. Nancy knew better. Frannie'd had a thing for Jack for years. She just never got around to doing anything about it.

"I told you before; sometimes you have to let a guy know that you like him."

"And I told you before; I don't play that way. If he likes me, he can ask me out."

"I swear, Frannie, you're worse than some of the girls I knew in high school."

"Well, I've seen some of the girls you went to school with, and I think I'll take that as an insult."

"Just go talk to Jack and get it over with." She rolled her eyes toward the ceiling for a second. "It's not like you've got anything to lose at this point. You're already not talking to each other."

"I might. I just might." Which meant, of course, that Frannie would think about it for a few hours and then set it aside. It was her way. She could be stubborn enough to make rivers bend to her will, but she would never, not in a million years, actually confront Jack Michaels on where they stood in what could be a relationship between them. He might say "Let's be friends," and that would probably wreck Frannie. She would rather have the possibility than risk the reality.

Frannie got up and went into the kitchen again, coming out with three dinners on a waiting tray. She gave Nancy her dinner and moved to another table, then went to take the order of the couple who'd come in after Nancy had. When she had half finished her meal, Frannie came back to visit with her.

"The one thing I hate about this job, the only thing, is that I can't ever take a day off. I worry too much about things being done right."

Nancy smiled. "It's good to know some things never change, Frannie. I don't think the world would know what to do if you took a day off."

Frannie smiled back. "It's good to see you again, Nancy. I miss when you worked here."

"Oh, I'm not that far down the road, and I always visit when I'm here."

"I know. But it's not the same."

"Yeah, but I think I'll be coming back when I graduate, and that's only a few months from now."

"What the hell are you going to do in this town with a college degree?"

"What else? Work at the mine. I've already got a few feelers out. I think I can get myself set up with a good job."

"Well, that would be nice."

"Serenity is home to me. Where else would I want to go?"

Frannie didn't answer her on that one. She just smiled and got a distant look in her eyes.

IX

Terry Palance was not expecting visitors, and he didn't want any either. He was the very first to admit what he'd done to Terri had been wrong, but this was getting insane. Everything in his world was doing its best to collapse around him, and he was facing the possibility of spending a very, very long time in jail. The public defender, the guy who was going to represent him in court, for Chrissake, wanted him to confess and plea bargain down to a lesser offense. It didn't seem to matter that he hadn't touched her. The man just wanted it over and done with. What the hell. It wasn't the lawyer who spent time in jail if he fucked it up, oh no, it was Terry himself. Wasn't that a wonderful solution?

Somehow it just didn't work for him.

So he was minding his own business, getting more and more miserable about the entire scenario, when who should walk into the jail? None other than the reason he was behind bars in the first place, Terri Halloway.

He watched slack-jawed as she came over to his cell and stood before him. Damn, despite everything, she looked good. Her face was as pretty as ever, despite the lack of a smile, and her eyes, well, he could drown in her eyes. Terry made those sorts of thoughts go away. He was supposed to be angry with her, hell he *was* angry with her, and there was no way in hell he was going to be nice to the bitch who had him locked away in a cage.

"Hello, Terry." Her voice was soft, and the way she avoided looking directly at him was just right for making the mountain over at the desk—Barnes, that was his name—look over with a slight warning in his eyes.

"What are you doing here?"

"I came to see if you were all right." Her voice had just the right level of regret, just the perfect blend of sorrow with a dash of fear. He hated her for that. It was almost enough to make him feel like he had done something to her.

"I'm here." He gestured wildly at the accommodations. "What the fuck do you think?"

"Why are you being so cold, Terry?" She blinked several times rapidly, and he could almost see tears trying to start in her eyes, but damn it, he wasn't falling for any of that shit. She'd ruined him, and he refused to feel bad for her.

"Because I never touched you!" He stood up and moved toward the bars that separated them, his entire body bristling, his anger blooming like a fire inside him. "I never fucking laid a finger on you! What do you think they charged me with, Terri? Date abandonment? They charged me with raping you and trying to kill you! I never did that! I never would!"

Terri flinched back, her body trembling, and watching her put on the act made him want to reach through the bars and strangle her. Everything had been going right in his life, everything that mattered at least, and she pulled this shit on him to make sure he knew beyond a doubt that he'd fucked up when he messed with her. The very thought that he'd ever felt bad about leaving her behind was enough to make him want to scream.

Victor Barnes wasn't of the same mind. He moved up behind her with a speed that didn't seem possible for someone so big and crossed his arms over his massive chest. The look he shot Terry made it clear that he was treading on very thin ice. Terry got the message and backed away from the bars.

Terri Halloway looked at him with her eyes wide and tears ready to fall from them. "I loved you, Terry. I did. I just wasn't ready and you, you…" She started crying, and Barnes put a protective hand on her thin shoulder. A second later she turned away from Terry and cried on the constable's shirt. He pulled her close, staring daggers at the young man behind the bars, his eyes asking him very simply how he could have done a thing like that to an innocent girl. Despite his innocence, Terry felt like the worst sort of scum.

Barnes led her away from him, and he watched them go, his own feelings confused and distracted by what had just happened.

X

The girl was a wreck, her whole body shivered as if she'd been in a blizzard. And her tears were hot against his rib cage. She was so tiny, almost like a porcelain doll, and he wanted to take care of her, make her feel better about what she'd just been through. It couldn't have been easy facing the man who'd left her for dead in the woods, but she'd done it just the same.

She trembled against him, and Victor Barnes did his best to comfort her, a little surprised by the fact that her parents weren't along to make sure she was safe through the confrontation. "There, there. You're safe. He can't hurt you."

"I thought he was special, that he was gonna be the one for me to grow old with and have kids with and everything." Her words were muffled, and her breath was warm on his chest. His arms moved more carefully around her, and he was extremely aware of how bad it would look to anyone who came in and saw him hugging her. He eased her gently away from him and reached over to his desk for a Kleenex.

She nodded her thanks and looked at him with dark, soulful eyes that were far too old for a face so young. "Thank you."

"It's not a problem. Where are your folks? Did they drop you off here?"

"I walked…"

"You walked? In this weather?"

"It's not all that far. I-I didn't want my folks to know that I was coming to see Terry. They wouldn't understand."

"Well, I can see that, I guess. I'm having a little trouble with it myself."

"I just... I dunno, I wanted to see him, to make sure what I remembered was right. I know what he did, I was there, but it doesn't feel real to me." She looked away, then back toward him with those soulful eyes and a shy expression on her face. "I don't know how to explain it. I'm not good with words."

"Well, I'll tell you what. Bill Karstens is supposed to be here in a few minutes. When he comes in, I'll give you a lift home. Your folks would probably shoot me on sight if I let you walk."

She nodded, her face showing quiet gratitude. "I don't want to walk again. I swear I was almost having flashbacks just getting over here in the dark."

He could imagine it, but just barely. She was braver than she knew to walk through the darkness after what she'd been through. It was becoming an exercise in patience and self-control to avoid breaking the neck of the sick fuck in the other room. He'd never taken well to the idea of anyone forcing themselves on a woman. What was supposed to be a pleasurable union between two people made into something ugly and violent that left scars deeper than most people could ever know. He knew about them though. His mother, his own mother had been raped when he was still in his early teens. What happened to the pig who had done it was not a matter of public record, but Victor Barnes came from a large family with three other boys all older than him and most almost as big as he was. That particular incident was one they never spoke of, save once. His older brother Jeremy looked him in the face a day after they'd finished the task and told him matter-of-factly that no one would ever find the body.

He shook the thought away and rubbed one hand across Terri's back, a small sign of confidence in her. Then he rose and poured himself a cup of coffee, asking with his eyes if she'd like a cup herself. She nodded and gave him that little smile of hers that said thanks. *If I was twenty years younger*, he thought, *I'd be actively doing everything I could to get to know her better.* The thought came into his mind and lingered, and he wanted very much to make it go away. He'd seen enough of the world and experienced enough of it to know that nothing good could come from those thoughts. Besides which, the poor girl was recovering from a serious trauma. He would certainly not be responsible for adding to it.

Still, she was a pretty little thing, and he suspected if he wanted to, he could make her interested. Something about vulnerable girls always made him hard in about three seconds.

He shook the thought out of his head, or at least back into the animal part of his mind. He was trying to be respectable these days. That meant actually obeying the laws. It wasn't an idea that sat well, but with time, he could make it work.

Karstens showed up five minutes before his shift was supposed to start, looking as crisp and professional as ever. Vic left with Terri Halloway only a few minutes later, glad to get away. Something about Karstens always made him feel like he was in the presence of a complete slimeball. The man all but generated a field of energy that pushed any kind thoughts away. Best to leave before there was a conflict.

XI

The weather was hideous. The rain falling to the ground was cold and seemed to find new ways to slide past their clothes and into the places where they should have been warm and dry. To make matters worse, most every muscle in his body felt strained and ready to snap like an overstressed rubber band.

Greg Randers was also terrified. What if they got caught? What if the cops came along and found them in the act of savaging Carl's corpse? What if Nona suddenly decided she really did love Carl and she didn't want anything more to do with the man who killed her husband for her? What if, what if, what if.... The list of doubts was almost endless.

Nona stood near him, her body obviously feeling the cold at least as much as his was. Her arms wrapped over her chest, and she seemed to almost pull into herself physically as she shivered in the near-freezing rain.

And Greg lifted the pocketknife and slashed into the body of Nona's husband again, doing his best to make the wounds look like the bite marks of a big dog. Dogs. His little puppy—well, his and Nona's really—was gone. He hadn't really thought about Biscuit much—her name for the dog, not his—but he thought about it now as he made bloody tears into the body of a man he barely knew and hated just the same.

There was a flash of light in the distance, and as he turned to look in that direction, he heard the low growl of thunder in the nighttime sky. *Just what we need now, a good jolt of electricity. Maybe it will bring Carl back for a second try.* He shuddered at the thought. Too damned many bad horror movies. He worked the blade of his knife into Carl's cheek, just below his left eye, adding finishing touches to what managed to look like a pretty realistic series of tooth marks. Just a few more, and they could call this done. They could get back over to Greg's place and pretend that none of this had happened for a few hours, get lost in each other all over again. Sore or not, he was sure he could manage to rise to the occasion.

Murder seemed to work just fine as an aphrodisiac. Probably something to do with the adrenaline that kept pumping into his body when he least expected it. Despite being physically exhausted and mentally wiped out, he kept having erratic bursts of energy.

"There. I think that should do it." His voice sounded hoarse to his own ears.

"Oh, God, Greg, let's get the hell out of here. This place gives me the creeps." There was a tone of desperation in Nona's voice, an edge of hysteria that he fully sympathized with.

"Yeah. I've had it." He stood up, his knees protesting as he rose, and folded the blade back into his knife. It was too dark to examine his handiwork. But that was all right. No one would be able to find Carl for a long time with any luck. Almost nobody ever went into the woods this far.

Greg gave Nona a hug that was meant to comfort rather than arouse, and the two of them walked away, back in the direction of his house.

Carl Bradford's body rested against the granite outcroppings, his cold blood trickling from his remains to mingle with the rain.

From the other side of the seven large granite teeth that rose from the ground almost like petals of a dying flower, Becky Glass and Joey Whitman made their way across the uneven ground as carefully as they could. When they reached the odd formation of stones, Joey studied it in silence. Becky looked at it, too, a slow smile growing on her face.

Above them the winds grew stronger, rattling leaves from the trees and scattering them far and wide. The rains slowed down almost as if the very storm itself was holding its breath.

"Here we are…"

"Yeah. You really don't have to stay, Joey. I can handle this all by myself."

"I know."

"Then, I don't get it. Why are you still here?"

"Because I want to make sure you can handle it by yourself." She nodded her head, no longer looking in his direction. She stared at the stones.

"So, what happens now, Becky?"

"Um. I have to do the invocation."

"Okay…"

"I don't know if I can have you stay for this part."

"But I don't think you should be alone out here."

"Well then, you have to turn your back and promise not to look."

"Why?"

"Emmy Walstrop says it works best if you're in your birthday suit and nothing else."

It would have been a tight race on which of them blushed harder.

"You're kidding, right?"

"Well, that's what she said, and I'm not taking any chances, Joey Whitman!"

Joey looked at her long and hard, trying not to imagine what she'd look like naked. It wasn't easy. "Okay. I'm turning around." Damn, it wasn't easy.

Joey turned to face the woods, letting his mind wander as the rains increased again, and the wind started scrubbing the tops of the trees. His ears felt like they were going to fall off, and his nose was starting to drip as much from the liquid in his sinuses as from the rain falling on his face.

Behind him, barely even a murmur past the sounds of the wind, he heard Becky start talking, calling out to the witch. The darkness kept him from fully focusing on the trees, leaving little more than silhouettes, and even those seemed to shift and grow as the winds picked up. He listened to the almost silent request from Becky to the witch in the woods and wondered what lunacy had brought him out into the cold. His skin felt waterlogged and likely never to be dry again despite the coat he now sported.

Out in the darkness, beyond where he could see, something rustled that sounded different than the wind. It had more weight to the way it moved, and it seemed to breathe almost as a counterpoint to the rhythm of the trees and the storm that sighed around them. Something was coming closer, and the very thought sent deeper chills into Joey than the weather had managed.

"Joey?" Becky's voice was excited, trembling on the edge of something that might have been excitement or might have been fear. "Joey, can you hear that?"

"Yeah. Yeah I can." He paused a moment, holding his breath and swallowing rapidly again and again in an effort to make the dryness in his throat go away. Then he took a deep breath and called out loud enough to be heard easily over the growing storm, "Can anyone hear me?"

Something in the woods answered.

XII

The boys who desperately wanted to be the terrors of Serenity gathered together in the rain and looked up at Havenwood with expressions that showed everything from excitement to nervous dread. Marco DeMillio was looking forward to breaking in. He wanted to cause some serious hurt to the place, and he wanted to see if he could maybe get lucky enough to find the uptight bitch who lived there all alone and waiting for some companionship.

He didn't much care if she wanted company. He was in it strictly for himself. At the ripe old age of fifteen he figured it was time to finally have a little fun.

Marco figured he had long since earned a few good times. Growing up in Serenity had never been easy. His father was long gone from his life and his mother.... Well, she liked to party enough to make most longtime alcoholics look at her with pity. Janet DeMillio was known far and wide as one of the easiest lays in the area, and that reputation had done nothing to make Marco's life any easier. Like all of the guys he hung around with—all of whom had their own tales about growing up, and most of them sounded a lot like his—he'd taken a lot of crap in his short life. He'd been the brunt of a few too many jokes by the jocks and a few too many ass kickings when he dared open his mouth and tried to retaliate. Now that puberty had started, that was beginning to change.

And just recently, within the last few weeks, the changes had begun to become very evident. Marco smiled to himself when he thought about it. Not long after they'd met the man who became their secret benefactor, everything had started finally going right in his life and in the lives of his friends. It was like magic. One day they were all but laughingstocks, even when they were together, and the next, they were being taken seriously.

Well, at least they were being taken seriously by a few people. The ones who'd looked at them like they were crazy when they invited themselves to the party at Mike Miller's place. Mike was one of the popular crowd. He was handsome, he was intelligent, and he was very well off. Mommy and Daddy were out of town—on a safari to celebrate their eighteenth wedding anniversary, of all things—and Mike was quick to take advantage of their absence by throwing a party for a few dozen classmates. Mike's mistake was not inviting Marco and his friends.

When in doubt, crash. Marco and Todd Hornsby, the unofficial leaders of the group, decided that they should all attend the party anyway, and the rest of the guys agreed readily enough. There would be girls, there would be booze, and if things worked out right, they just might get lucky.

The kids at the party weren't quite cool enough to actually have the major leaguers of the school there, but they were all hyped up anyway. The gang dropped on by, and at first everything was cool. If anyone at the party was unhappy about them being there, they kept it to themselves, and that was a good thing.

Then Marco lit a cigarette, and Miller got all nasty on him. It wasn't even pot, it was tobacco, but that didn't stop the geek from getting in Marco's face. Marco took it for about ten seconds. Then he broke Mike's nose. There were a few people who screamed, and even a few who decided it was time to fight back. But in the long run it wasn't much of a battle. The Hamiltons, Andy and Perry, took over for most of the fight. It wasn't that Marco didn't have his part in it, because he did. He beat Miller black and blue and kicked him a few times for good measure. But in comparison to the Hamiltons, he might as well have been having a pleasant conversation. Andy and Perry did a sort of tag team beating on their opponents, normally focusing on one person at a time and swinging with hands and feet like there was no tomorrow. By the time it was all over, about eight teens had been bloodied and bruised in a bad way.

And the consequences for Marco and the boys? None. All it took was the promise to do it all over again if anyone talked, and suddenly everyone had amnesia. It felt good to be in control of a situation. It was exciting and even arousing.

And tonight, well, tonight he figured he could do something about that arousal. His hand reached down and patted the front pocket of his jeans. He had four condoms there. He figured if there was no physical evidence, like sperm, it was her word against theirs. He didn't want the woman in the house dead. He wanted her afraid. Knowing that she was too ashamed to report what happened, and truly, deeply scared that they would come back and do it again, that was the part he liked best about the idea.

Marty Hardwick looked over at him and grinned, his braces catching the lights from inside the house and lighting up inside his mouth. He mimed heading toward the door, and Marco nodded. It was time to have a little fun. Time to party like there was no tomorrow. But he had to remember to get what their benefactor wanted before they left.

Marco led the way, and they moved carefully toward the back of Haven wood. It wasn't likely that there would be any cops around, but there was no reason to take chances when they didn't have to. The wind and rain helped blanket their sounds as surely as the darkness hid their movements.

XIII

Sometimes life was good. Not as often as he would have liked, but Jonathan Crowley had never been all that picky when it came to the good breaks life offered. He took them when they came his way and was glad of them.

He'd spent most of the day in the town's small public library and in the Hall of Records, researching everything he could find out about Serenity and its past. Overall, it was roughly as exciting as watching mold grow on stale bread. Being bored left him edgy and desperately in need of a little workout.

And lo, as if by magic, there they were, a group of losers trying to break into the house of someone he could almost claim he cared about in some way. The thought of explaining the facts of life to the little darlings just made him feel all tingly inside. Well, at the very least, it made him happy. Tingly might be pushing just a bit.

Crowley slid out of the shadows near the front of the house, his smile stretching across his face as he moved through the cold, wet night. There was a little shit standing guard—or at least he was supposed to be standing guard; in actuality he was picking his nose and looking up at the window of the second story. Crowley moved through the increasing rain to stand beside him and waited patiently. Almost as an afterthought, he took the water-spotted glasses from his face. Why have to buy another pair if he could avoid it?

After almost a full minute spent alternately watching the kid root into his nose with a finger that probably hadn't been washed in the last week and the dark-haired kid doing his best to jimmy the lock with a Swiss Army blade, he made his presence known.

He coughed politely into his hand, and when the redhead turned to look at him with very wide eyes, he smiled broadly. "Does Ms. Dunlow know you're trying to break into her house? I mean, is this a test of the existing security system, or are you just a bunch of truly stupid kids?"

The first of the really stupid kids almost jumped out of his skin, emitting a shriek that would have done proud a housefrau from the fifties who'd just seen a particularly scary mouse.

Crowley popped him in the mouth before he could actually say anything. Hitting the kid hurt: the braces in his punching bag's face were plentiful, and the wires split the skin on his knuckles almost as easily as they chewed through the interior of the screamer's lips. On the bright side, the redhead looked particularly unconscious by the time he hit the ground, and his lack of awareness made him stop screaming.

Crowley backed away into the deeper darkness of the yard before any of the others could get a good look at him. Upstairs in the house, a light came on where the metal-mouthed kid had been staring. Apparently they'd either been scoping the place out, or they knew where to look.

The teens did what most teens do in sudden situations of stress. They started calling out to each other, and a couple of them looked ready to run. That wouldn't do at all; this was just starting to be really amusing.

"Why don't you all behave yourselves and line up nice and neat for me, okay?" They didn't listen, not that he'd really expected they would. Instead, they started looking every which way, trying to figure out where he was. He obliged them by stepping out of the darkness again, his smile advertising his amusement with the game.

Two of them got bold and rushed him. The one who'd been trying his lock-picking skills on the deadbolted back door called out his encouragement. "Get him, Andy! Fuck him up, Perry!" One of them, a pizza face with bleached blond hair, made a wild swing for Crowley's face and looked honestly surprised when his fist missed his target. John grabbed the hand that whizzed past him and pulled down and away, throwing his opponent completely off balance. The kid slipped and fell, splashing across the waterlogged lawn. The other one—this one had long brown hair that was matted to his skull by the rain—got stupid and pulled out a switchblade.

As a general rule, Jonathan Crowley didn't do more to an opponent than his opponent was willing to do to him. If it was fists alone, he could handle that. If it was weapons, he could accommodate that request just as easily. Of course, he didn't normally carry any of his own instruments of destruction, so he had to take whatever might come his way.

The kid was as bad with a knife as his friend was with fists. So Crowley took the time to break his attacker's wrist before taking his toy from him. He grabbed with both hands, spun hard to his left, and then brought a knee up into the bones just below either Perry or Andy's hand. The bones broke with a wet sound that was positively delicious to Crowley's ears. The sound the kid made as he fell down and started clutching his wounded arm was something like he imagined a pig might make if a steamroller was slowly backing over it.

The one he'd knocked onto the ground started trying to stand. Jonathan helped change his mind with a galvanized rubber heel to the back of his head. That was three down and four to go, if he'd counted properly. Crowley looked around and discovered that the last of the lot had taken the few moments while he was distracted to regroup.

The thought made his grin grow even wider. He wanted a challenge, and one on one, none of these twerps looked like they'd last five seconds with him. Crowley crouched slightly and headed toward them, eager for the confrontation. They moved, too, though a bit more cautiously.

He'd taken his fourth step when he felt something hit him in his left thigh with enough force to knock him down. Half a second after the impact, he felt the heat running down his leg and took the time to look. There was a hole there, red and wet and steaming in the cold air. It had no reason to be there that he could think of, at least until the sound of the gunshot finally registered.

It hurt, and more importantly, it was putting him at one hell of a disadvantage when he considered the four kids coming his way. Adrenaline kicked into his system like lightning, and Jonathan Crowley thought carefully about his options. Giving up was out of the question. There wasn't a one of the fine, upstanding citizens he was facing who looked the least bit likely to just forget about the whole mess. Fighting wasn't looking all that much better. He'd been shot in his leg, and the wounded limb wasn't really in the mood to pull its fair share of the weight. Running went the same way as surrendering. It wasn't going to work, not with one leg being mutinous.

But next to the other possibility, the one where whoever the hell it was who was firing at him kept on shooting until he was dead, fighting seemed like a pretty good idea. Provided, of course, he could get away from the sharpshooter in the woods.

That thought seemed to be the shooter's cue. The second bullet missed his head by half an inch.

Chapter Eleven

I

Alden Waters took aim and missed the second time. It wasn't because of the weather, which was horrible, or even the chill that was seeping deep into his old bones. It was because the man he was supposed to kill had done nothing wrong. It was Alden and his wife or the man below him on the ground. The problem was, he had no desire to hurt the man.

Alden didn't like hurting people, and he sure as sin didn't much take to the notion of murdering them. He sighed and sighted down his scope again. In the telescopic lens of his sight, he saw the wounded man rise, looking back in his direction. The brown eyes that moved in the stranger's face were calm enough to make the entire thing feel surreal to the old hunter. People getting shot at generally weren't calm about it. He hesitated. There was something about the man that was, well, scary. He had a gun with a telescopic sight, and the man he had dead in his aim was scaring him from half a football field away.

He squeezed lightly on the trigger, reminding himself that Earline's life was on the line. *He brought those damned dogs back from the dead. Just think what he could do to poor, sweet Earline. You ain't got a choice this time, Alden. You just do what has to be done and call it a day. Earline don't need to know, and she don't need to suffer from all of this. So you swallow it up, old son, and you do it right.*

The steady hand won the match, and Alden's hand was like a rock. There wasn't the slightest tremor.

And the stranger in his sights looked directly into his eye, looked and focused on him. From easily fifty yards' distance, the man saw him and knew what he was doing. Behind the man, one of the teens he'd been tangling with moved to attack, satisfied that the stranger was distracted enough to make it a safe bet.

Alden squeezed the trigger, held firm as the rifle bucked in his hand, and watched as the face that looked toward him vanished. He heard a high, shrill scream of pain and closed his eyes for a second.

It's over. There's no way he'll live through that, God above help me.

He made himself open his eyes and look. It took a second to refocus, to track what was happening. Instead of the stranger lying dead on the ground, he saw one of the boys who'd been attacking the man. There was a black stain growing from the boy's stomach. He'd shot Perry Hamilton in his guts.

Alden all but fell from the tree where he was perched. His heart felt like someone was punching it with a sledgehammer. *Oh, Lord above! How the hell can I ever fix this?* His mind wanted to freeze, and he wanted to run down and see if he could help the boy. But then he remembered the dogs. And he remembered Earline and the promise that she would suffer and die slowly.

It wasn't easy for Alden Waters to be a hard man. It went against the grain of his life and philosophies, but when Earline was in the picture, he could manage it well enough. He moved his sight carefully, looking for the man he'd shot in the leg. The boy would have to wait until after he had finished his task.

He could hear the screams of the other kids down below. They'd realized just how screwy things were, if he was guessing right. He saw them moving closer to Perry, who writhed on the ground, clutching his stomach. The steam from the wound rose up from his belly even as the darker wetness spread over his shirt. Alden felt sick.

He took several deep breaths, just like he'd done in Asia during his tour of duty. Humans just weren't the same as animals in his eyes. He hunted deer to live, and he'd hunted humans in the past for the same reason, but he never liked it.

He moved the scope around again, trying to find the man he had to kill. Nothing. The man was apparently gone, and that was both a relief and a curse. He was glad the wound hadn't been fatal, and at the same time he had to think of Earline. Despite what his conscience told him, he had to finish the job. Earline came before a man he'd never met; it was just that simple.

He checked the area again, making sure he knew for certain that the man was gone. There was no sign of him. Only seconds had passed, but that didn't mean the stranger might not be coming his way, hell-bent on revenge. Still, there was time. Fifty yards was a long trip, and longer still with a game leg.

Alden slid down from his perch, cursing when his coat caught on the jagged bark and tried to get away from him. He landed roughly, his joints reminding him that he was too old for such antics. The rifle slid from where he'd slung it over his shoulder and almost fell off his arm, but reflex made him catch it before it could hit the overly wet grass and mulch beneath him.

His breath plumed out in front of him, and he shivered in the cold. In the distance he could still hear the sounds of the kids screaming and talking in panicked tones. He started walking away, his conscience telling him to go to them, to help them, even as his common sense told him to get the hell away from the area. The constables would not take well to his having shot a boy, even a ruffian like Perry Hamilton. Even thinking of the constables sent a shiver through him.

He took two steps away from Havenwood's main building, determined to go home and wait for the consequences of failure—he'd be damned if he'd go down without a fight, but he couldn't do it. He'd missed the easy fatal shot on his target earlier, and he knew he had done it on purpose. He wasn't a brave man, true, but neither was he capable of cold-blooded murder, regardless of what failing meant. In his heart, he knew Earline would rather not be the cause of someone else's death, even indirectly. She was a good, Christian woman and would not take well to being saved from death by such foul means.

He took one more step, and finally the cries of the wounded boy were too much. His truck wasn't far away. He could get the boy to the hospital, and he could tend to his wounds before that time came. Alden Waters turned back toward the scene of his crime and sighed mightily. He had to help; there was no other way around it. He'd have to face the consequences, even if it meant he'd have to face—

The hands that grabbed his shirt felt like steel vises clamping onto him. Alden Waters felt himself lifted from the ground and thrown before he fully realized he wasn't alone. The world tilted madly, and then he was on his back, the freezing rain slapping across his face and splashing into his eyes. He wasn't sure, but he thought he'd wet himself.

Jonathan Crowley's loafered foot slammed down on the rifle in his hand, pinning the hand and the weapon to the ground. Alden heard himself scream as the bones under the rifle creaked and splintered.

"Did that hurt, old man?" The stranger looked down at him and smiled the nastiest smile he'd ever seen. "Would you like to know how much what you did to my leg hurts? Because, I gotta tell you, I feel an awful lot like giving you a hands-on demonstration right now."

"I didn't want to do it, mister! I swear to God Almighty I didn't have a choice!" His voice was trembling, and he thought that maybe his heart was trying to climb out of his chest. The stranger loomed closer over him, and the pressure on his hand increased till he thought for sure he'd black out.

"Really? Well, why don't you explain that to me before I have to get...persuasive." Damnedest thing, he was lying on his back with water running into his eyes, and he could still see each and every tooth in that grin as clearly as if it was high noon on a sunny day.

"I had to do it. I was told if I didn't kill you, he'd kill me, and he'd kill my wife!" Alden's voice cracked as he thought of Earline.

The man above him didn't even blink. He just leaned in a bit more and smiled while Alden tried his best to black out from the pain in his hand. When the pain subsided and Alden could think again, he looked up at the man and waited for any sort of response. It wasn't a long wait. "Okay. I'm game. Tell me all about your dilemma and who sent you to do me in. And make it interesting, because right now, I'm really not in the mood to be bored."

"Listen, mister, there are some kids over there, and one of them got shot while I was...while I was aiming for your head. He needs help."

"Maybe. Maybe not. I haven't decided yet." The man shrugged, his smile getting wider still. "Something about the little shit trying to put a knife in my rib cage makes me less than sympathetic."

"He's a good kid, mostly. Perry doesn't deserve to die, not like that."

The stranger reached down, lifted his foot from the rifle, and hauled Alden into a standing position. "Maybe you're right. We'll go see how the little darling is doing. Leave the rifle. Maybe you'll be less stupid without it. Not that I'm holding my breath."

He dragged Alden, limping heavily from the wound in his leg and moving faster than the hunter would have expected possible. The rain kept coming down, and all Alden could think about was how much nicer his life would be if he could just go home and pretend that none of this was happening. Being pulled along by a stranger with a seriously poor disposition—though, in light of the near-death experience he could understand that part—wasn't letting his imagination get away with too much dreaming.

They covered the distance in short order and wound up in the back yard of the sprawling old house in under three minutes. Alden wanted desperately to pee again.

The lady who owned the house was there, and so was Mike Blake. The young woman was down on her knees, speaking calmly to Perry, her voice soothing and soft. Mike had the boy's shirt open and was looking at the bloody wound while Perry whimpered and gritted his teeth.

The stranger slung Alden around and pushed him hard to the ground. Alden landed on both hands, and the one that had been stomped screamed in protest. Alden joined right along.

Mike Blake took one look at Alden, one look at the stranger, and then, face set, went back to examining the wound on Perry.

The woman looked at the man he'd been told to kill and spoke volumes about regret with the expression on her face. "Hello, Jonathan. I've already called for an ambulance."

The man looked at her with no change in his expression. His eyes looked at her, then to the boy on the ground and the man tending to him. "There's your shooter. Seems he wanted me dead by request. Just business as usual." There was no bragging in the comment, but there was an edge of happiness that made Alden wonder just what the hell he'd gotten himself into.

"What are you going to do, John?" She looked over at Alden nervously, and he felt his blood try to freeze in his veins.

"We're going to have a nice chat. He's going to tell me why he shot at me and who asked him to do it, or I'm going to pull his eyes from their sockets and leave him blind as well as stupid." He looked over at

Alden again, his smile as eager as that of a groom on his wedding night. "Isn't that right?"

Alden nodded in silence. His mouth didn't want to work right, so he left it shut. In the distance he could hear the sound of sirens coming their way. That thought scared him almost more than the man looking at him, but only almost. He wondered which of the constables it would be, and suspected he knew. The ice that had been chilling his veins started spilling into his stomach, and despite the rain, he felt hideously dry mouthed. Alden swallowed hard, forcing his tongue free from the roof of his mouth. "I can tell you who made me do it, mister, but you aren't gonna like it."

The sirens stopped at the front of the house, and flashes of red, blue, and white light strobed from the sides to illuminate the shrubs and lawn. Alden looked in that direction with a mix of hope for salvation and dread of certain damnation.

The stranger looked at him, followed where his eyes were going, and then looked back again. "Don't keep me in suspense, old man. Spill it."

Alden watched the paramedics come running around the corner. He knew them, of course, but couldn't have thought of their names just then to save his life. His eyes darted past them to the two constables who showed up. And when he saw them, he felt his heart sink deeper still.

His hand trembled as he pointed past Jack Michaels to the man walking with him. "Him. Bill Karstens told me to kill you if I wanted to live."

Even from a distance and through the dark, he could see Karstens's hand reaching for the revolver on his hip.

II

Jack Michaels was pretty sure like he'd died and rigor mortis had set in. His joints were stiff and felt swollen. His eyes were bleary, and his lungs felt filled with enough snot to serve a dozen or more people.

Corpses, he thought. *Didn't take enough precautions with the corpses. Christ only knows what the hell might be cooking in my lungs.* He coughed like a truck engine trying to start up on a cold day as they moved around the corner of the house, after the paramedics. He didn't know who'd been shot or who'd been doing the shooting. All he knew was someone got stupid with a gun. He'd had more than enough of that sort of thing lately. The bar fights were up in numbers, the domestic abuse in Serenity was getting ridiculous, and now there were people shooting each other like it was just as normal as walking the dog. Maybe he was being cynical. This was the only shooting he knew of, but he figured it was only a matter of time before it got worse.

He rounded the corner and looked on as the paramedics rushed over to the boy on the ground. He wasn't overly surprised to see that it was Perry Hamilton. The kid almost begged to get himself hurt every time he left his house. Of course, if the rumors were true—and as they were only rumors, he could do nothing about it—he pretty much left the house to avoid having his old man wale on him. A great family life, he was sure.

Mike Blake was standing up from doing what he could to tend to Perry's wounds, and the new lady in town—Amelia Dunlow—was right next to him. Seeing them together was almost enough to cause flashbacks to the past. Her resemblance to Amy Blake was beyond uncanny and moved all the way to bordering on supernatural. They looked like they were getting close, and he couldn't help but wonder what she saw in Mike. He wasn't exactly the prize of the day.

Off to the side, cowed by what had happened to Perry, the rest of the local gang of would-be ruffians stood shuffling from foot to foot and looking decidedly unhappy about being anywhere near where they were. And on the ground, not but fifteen feet away from where he and Bill were, Alden Waters lay soaking wet and looking like something a cat had been playing with a little too roughly.

And last but not least, the freaky stranger he'd dealt with two days earlier. Crowley. He was favoring one leg heavily and grinning ear to ear as Waters pointed a finger directly at Bill Karstens and said something about being threatened by one of his constables. That was not a mild accusation, and Jack didn't like it in the least.

He'd just opened his mouth to tell Alden he'd best have the evidence to back up those words when Karstens pulled his revolver and aimed it at the old man. Feeling like death warmed over, sure that he would never make it in time, he yanked his own sidearm from its holster and pointed the muzzle at Bill's head. He had no idea he could move that fast. He wondered who was actually more surprised, his second-in-command or himself.

Karstens looked over his shoulder for an instant, his eyes fever bright in the freezing rain, and then he pulled the trigger.

Alden Waters died instantly, half of his head sheared away by a bullet from the constable's gun. It was the first time in ten years that anyone had been shot by one of the constables. That sort of thing just wasn't necessary in Serenity Falls. Jack was frozen. He'd always been prepared to use a pistol if he had to. Hell, the speed with which he'd just drawn the damned thing proved that, but he never in a million years expected to do it against one of his own men, even one like Karstens.

All around him the people on the scene did the sensible thing and backed away. Several of the boys were screaming loud enough to wake the dead, and Mike Blake looked ready to actually try to jump Bill. Crowley shook his head, his eyes darting from one pistol to the other as if he were watching a tennis match.

Jack's hands were trembling, but he managed to keep them steady enough to stay centered on Bill's temple. "Have you lost your goddamned mind? You drop the weapon, Bill! Right fucking now!"

Karstens moved his weapon, taking aim a second time. The barrel pointed straight and true toward the chest of Jonathan Crowley. The man's smile practically glowed in the strobing lights reflected from the rescue vehicles.

"Jack, it's not that I don't want to follow your order... Oh, screw it, yes it is." Karstens fired four times. Jack fired twice.

Part of him was screaming deep inside even as he pulled the trigger. William Montgomery Karstens was not his favorite man, that was true. He wasn't even in the top ten, but, damn it, he'd never wanted to see the man dead and certainly not by his own hand. And there was no doubt about it, Karstens was dead. Not really possible to live with your skull caved in and your face missing. He bit down hard on the inside of his mouth to stop himself from breaking into hysterical laughter.

He was dimly aware of people screaming. It was hard to hear past the ringing in his ears. Jack made himself look around the area and tried to remember what it was he should be looking for. It finally dawned on him: the stranger was very likely dead.

He made himself focus. Nope. The grinning bastard was looking right at him, standing about two feet from where he'd been before. Damnedest thing, he didn't have any more wounds. Not a one, despite good old Bill taking four shots at him.

Then the grin faded from his face, and he looked down at the corpse of Bill Karstens. Jack did not want to look, had absolutely no intention of taking the time to look, but he did it anyway. Just in time to see Bill — good old headless Bill — start rising from the ground, parts of his skull falling away in a bloodied torrent.

Bill Karstens rose to his feet, the remains of his skull hanging loosely from his neck in a pulped ruin. He swiveled that mess over toward Crowley and then over toward Jack. From that gaping wound where his face should have been, he emitted a deep, almost thunderous voice that burbled wetly as he spoke. "I didn't think you had the balls to do it, Jack. I guess maybe I underestimated you." Bill took a slow, sliding step forward, his body trembling with the effort it apparently took to get up and walk after getting your head blown away. He pointed a heavy finger in Crowley's direction and spoke again with that hollow, vile voice that sounded nothing at all like Karstens's ever did. "I knew you'd get here eventually, Hunter. Now we can finally put paid to what you did to me before."

And Jonathan Crowley, apparently unimpressed by the display, shrugged his shoulders and grinned again. "Don't you think this would be a lot easier if you'd just tell me who you are?"

"Soon. You'll know soon enough."

The body fell down a second time, and Jack Michaels thought he heard a hissing sound, rather like water falling on hot coals. Then something—damned if he could have said just what—exploded outward from the bloodied stump of a head and expanded like a cloud of iridescent gas. It didn't stay around long enough for him to actually see just what it was. Instead, the thing that poured itself out of Bill Karstens flowed across the wet grass, leaving a scorch mark in its wake.

Crowley looked over at Jack and smiled thinly. "Like I said, nice town."

Jack had no response to that.

III

By the time the sun rose over Serenity, the worst of the rains were over with. The air was just at the edge of freezing, and the world seemed to have quieted down. Most people were just starting to stir, and it being a Monday, they were by and large not really excited about the idea of getting out of bed.

Some people wanted to go to bed more than they wanted anything else. Marco DeMillio would probably have given his right arm for the chance to close his eyes for half an hour, but it wasn't meant to be. Indirectly or not, he was part of a crime scene, and that meant he was basically screwed. And hard, at that. And, judging by the giant glaring at him from across the quaintly titled "interview room," he was likely to remain unlubed throughout the process.

He'd tried to explain that he and his friends were just passing by the old house when everything happened, but the freak wasn't willing to listen. Victor Barnes looked over at him and glowered menacingly. Marco liked to think he was pretty tough—tougher than the average jock at least—but damn, even with a happy smile on his broad face the guy was big enough to make him want to run home to his mother.

Of course, the fact that his mother was in the main waiting room was enough to make him just plain want to run. He could have taken a beating or two, but he didn't have to worry about that with his mother—maybe a few of her different boyfriends over the years, but not her. His mom would do what she always did. She would cry. They weren't crocodile tears that his mother let fall from her eyes. She only cried when she was certain that one of her kids was going to be hurt in a big way, or when one of them pulled a boner stunt like what he'd done last night.

So his mother would cry, and that more than anything else that might happen would make him feel like dog shit held out for everyone to see.

"Okay," the big constable said in a calm voice that belied the expression on his face. "For the zillionth time, you were just minding your own business, you saw the stranger come up to the house and go around the back, and then you decided to investigate what he was up to."

"Yeah…"

"Why?"

"Why what?"

"Why did you decide to investigate his walking around the place?"

"Well, he looked…shady."

"Fine. Let's get you in a holding cell, and then you can tell it to the judge."

"What? I thought…"

"Thought what? You'd be going home?"

"Well, my mom's here…"

"Yes, she is. But right now you're being held in a criminal investigation, and that means you aren't going anywhere or seeing anyone until I've had a chance to talk to all of your little buddies, one at a time."

"We didn't do nuthin!"

"Yeah. Right. Just innocent little waifs out for a stroll in the freezing rain." He didn't figure much more sarcasm could have gone into that last comment without the help of Hollywood special effects.

"Well, I have the right to a lawyer!"

"Yes, you do. We informed you of that when we took you in for questioning. Do you want one?" The giant's eyes locked on his and stared hard at him, no, through him. The man might have been listening to him speak or might have been thinking of the best way to dispose of his body when he was finished with breaking every single bone in it. Marco couldn't have said and didn't really want to ponder it too seriously.

"No…not yet."

"Good. Come with me."

He stood up, pushing the metal chair across the tile floor as he backed away from the table. Marco didn't even think about the idea of arguing with him.

In the outer area, Chief Michaels was questioning the guy they'd gone round and round with and the woman who owned the house. Mike Blake was there, too, but he didn't seem to be involved in the actual question-and-answer session. The guy who'd pretty much walked through all of his friends the night before was making himself at home, sitting on the edge of the desk and drinking a cup of coffee. He'd seen the man get shot in the leg, but if it was bothering him now, he gave no sign.

The man cast a look at him that made him think hanging close to the walking mountain would be a good idea. Five minutes later he sat in one of the holding cells, looking over to see Terry Palance occupying a corner of the room. Terry Palance, one of the big men on campus at the school. Terry'd kicked his ass a few times on general principles. Terry was very good at kicking ass. He and the rest of the jocks made a practice of it. Last night he'd have been up to returning the favor. Last night he'd felt invincible with his secret benefactor. Then he'd seen Constable Bill Karstens get his head blown off. No more safety from worries, no more protection against the cops as long as they were cautious.

Last night seemed a long, long time ago.

Terry Palance barely even looked up. If he recognized Marco, he didn't show it.

Marco sat on the hard metallic shelf that passed for a bed, not even bothering to put the thin mattress in place from where they'd rolled it up like a sleeping bag. He sat quietly and looked at the floor, fearing on a deep level that anything he said might catch the attention of the bigger kid in the cell.

He stared at the floor, wondering when it had suddenly all fallen apart again, and after they'd just started finally having fun. He managed not to cry, but it was an effort.

IV

Breakfast had been a strain. April Long had sat through it and then all but run to the bus stop to get away. Mom and Dad were both completely civil, of course, but the frost between them made the air outside feel like the hottest day in August.

She was still waiting for the bus to show up when Dave Pageant came past. Dave nodded, smiled in a distracted way, and started walking on toward the school. She nodded back and watched him as he walked. On a whim, she started walking with him. He looked over, his face showing just the briefest flash of surprise, and then he looked ahead again, walking with that gotta-get-there-now stride that ate up the ground he walked over. She was taller, and she was athletic. She managed to keep up, but barely.

After about five minutes, when she was starting to get winded and wondering if Dave ever actually slowed down for anything, she shook her head and sighed. "Will you please just slow down?"

Dave looked over at her, his calm face cracking for a second to reveal confusion.

"Sure. I'm sorry, April. Did you want to talk about something?"

"Well, not really, I just…wanted to see how you are."

"Oh, I'm fine. How are you?" Maybe it showed in her face, maybe she took too long to answer. Maybe, for that matter, it was just that Dave understood everything going on in her life better than she expected—well, almost everything. He didn't know about some things. No one else did. Whatever the case, he looked at her for a few seconds and then frowned. "That bad, hunh?"

April nodded silently, closing her eyes for a second to stop something embarrassing, like maybe a crying jag, in front of a kid four years younger than her. He put an awkward arm around her shoulder and patted her back like he was burping a baby.

He didn't say anything. He just stood there like that and let her lean on him. She imagined he was Steve, and that made it a little better for a while. After a couple of minutes, she hugged him back briefly and thanked him with a smile.

"You okay, April?"

"I guess so. Yeah."

"I'm a good listener, you know. If you ever need one."

"I know, Dave. And thanks."

Dave nodded and gave a quick flash of an actual smile. It was one of the very few times she could remember ever seeing his teeth other than when he was laughing. Dave almost never actually exposed his teeth when he smiled. He just curled his lips up.

"Dave?"

"Yeah?"

"Do you think Stan will be okay?"

"Of course he will."

"What makes you so sure?"

"He's my best friend. I won't let him be sick for too long. We've got too much stuff to do yet."

"Like what?" His answer threw her, so she felt obligated to ask for an explanation.

"Well, hell, April. He's never even kissed a girl. He can't up and die on me yet. That's not the way it's supposed to work."

"What? There are rules?"

And there he was with that same thoughtful, almost lost in concentration look that he always got when he was doing almost anything. "Well, they aren't official or anything, but yeah. Of course there are rules. There are always rules."

"Okay. Enlighten me, what are the rules according to Dave Pageant?"

Dave shrugged. "Okay...rules of life or rules to live by?"

April had to think about that one. "Rules of life."

"You've been cheated if you never have a best friend. Everyone gets at least one in their life, unless they are just too stupid to even try making friends. You get to kiss at least one pretty girl, or one handsome guy if you are a pretty girl. Brothers and sisters will piss you off one minute and fight to the death for you the next." His eyebrows wrinkled together as he spoke. She half expected to see smoke come from his ears, he was concentrating so hard. "Everyone gets away with at least three really stupid things. They might get hurt, but they don't have to die because of them. After three, anything goes. Nobody ever cooks as good as your mom, and no one is ever bigger and stronger than your dad, even if he's skinny as a rail and twice as wimpy as Lawrence Grey. There are more, but I can't figure them out right now."

"Okay." She grinned. She rather liked the rules so far. "What are your rules to live by?"

"Well, that's getting a little personal, don't you think?"

"Oh, come on, you tell me yours, and I'll tell you mine."

Dave shrugged. "Okay, but if you spread mine around, you won't be happy about it."

"Are you threatening me?"

"Not really, no. But I have my ways."

Oddly enough, she believed him. She agreed that the words would stay between them. When he started talking again, she listened very carefully. He spoke fast, ticking off the rules on his fingers. "Never lie. Sooner or later it'll bite you in the butt. Always take the blame when you did something wrong, because if they blame someone else for what you did, you'll feel guilty later. Be nice. Clean your plate. Say your prayers, but only when they're sincere. Always remember there's someone bigger and meaner out there. Never make fun of a person with an accent, and notice everyone around you, all of the time."

"Why the last two?"

"Excuse me?"

"Why the last two? Why never make fun of a person with an accent, and why notice everyone all the time?"

"Well, if the person has an accent, that means they know one more language than you do."

"What if they just have a hick accent, like someone from Alabama?"

"Okay, never make fun of someone with a foreign accent."

"What if you already speak another language?"

"Most people who speak more than one don't make fun of people who are learning another one. They already know how hard it is."

She nodded. He probably had a good point on that one. "What about noticing people?"

"What if you aren't noticing the people around you, and your one best friend ever walks right by? How would you know?"

"You have strange rules, Dave."

"Yeah, well, being normal is sort of like hard work, and I'm a lazy person by nature."

"You said that Stan hadn't had his first kiss yet. Have you?"

He looked away and then back, with just the faintest hint of a blush on his face. "Maybe."

"I thought you said you never lied."

"Actually, it's a rule I try to live by. Now and then I break them. You try, and sometimes you succeed. Besides, 'maybe' isn't a lie, it's just not a straight answer." He looked away again and then back at her. "Your turn."

"What?"

"Your turn. You said if I told you my rules, you'd tell me yours."

"Well, a deal is a deal…" She started walking, and he moved with her. It was still a ways to go to get to the school, and if they didn't get it in gear, they'd be late. "Okay. First rule: never tell anyone what you're thinking. It makes you vulnerable. Second rule: You can tell your best friend, because a real best friend will never rat you out, not when it counts. Third rule: always get in the last word. Fourth rule: do your homework, it isn't as hard as it seems, and you might need the studies for when test time comes. Fifth rule: always do what your parents say, because there's less fighting that way. Sixth rule: don't trust guys, they lie. Seventh rule: wear deodorant because nobody likes body odor."

Dave nodded as he walked. "Those are pretty good rules, too." He smiled softly for a second. "Except maybe for number six. But I'm biased."

"Thanks."

They were almost at the school when she stopped walking again, half a block from where their worlds would separate completely for the next eight hours. Dave slowed and then stopped, looking over his shoulder as if puzzled for a second. Then he grinned. "Afraid to be seen with a sixth grader?"

"No." She walked up to him, looking around quickly to make sure they were unseen. When she was confident enough, she leaned forward and kissed him on the mouth. It was a short kiss, certainly not a romantic clinch, but she felt his lips against hers for the span of around three seconds, and looked into his eyes as they got impossibly wide with shock.

When the kiss broke, she could see him trying not to be flustered. "Why did you do that?"

"Just making sure that life follows the rules with you. Just in case 'maybe' meant no."

She left him standing there, a dazed look on his face. April was pretty sure Dave was too smart to think the kiss had meant anything more than what she'd said, or she'd have never even considered it. But it was nice to see him unsettled. It was a rare thing. And if she made him happy with the kiss, that was all the better. He had, after all, brightened her day enough to make it tolerable.

V

Jason Long answered the phone on the second ring, grateful for anything at all that would break the silence between Adrienne and himself. The tension between them was like a strained nerve stretched to the breaking point, and he didn't know how much longer he could take it before he decided to lash out.

He thought about the letter, the one he'd found returned to the house, written to a dead man. He dwelled on the words his wife had written to another man, and he felt the gulf between them grow larger still. All of his life he'd wanted little more than a roof over his head and a woman who loved him as much as he loved her. Until that damned letter showed itself and he'd let curiosity get the better of him, he thought he'd found that simple happiness.

He wanted to scream. He wanted to reach out to the woman he'd married and beat her within inches of her life. He wanted to force himself on her, like an animal marking his territory. He wanted to hold her closely and make it all go away, every bad thought and every little pain.

Instead he just brooded, watching her do her best to avoid his bad mood, acting as if she'd never done anything wrong. Her confused looks of innocence only made it worse, amplifying his desire to explode.

So when the phone rang, he was quick to snap it up. "Hello?"

"Mr. Long?" The voice was deep and friendly and made him think, *Middle-aged salesman.*

"Speaking."

"This is Jacob Parsons. I'm calling regarding the e-mail you sent me, explaining your son's condition."

Jason shook his head, despite the fact that he knew the man on the other end of the phone couldn't possibly see him do it. "I'm afraid I don't know what you're talking about, Mr. Parsons."

"You sent me an e-mail yesterday, regarding your son's seizures…"

Jason shook his head again, then allowed himself a small smile. Perhaps one of the doctors was consulting a specialist? In his current state of mind, that made as much sense as anything going on in his world. "Was there something you felt you could do to help Stan, Mr. Parsons?" Funny that the man wasn't a doctor, but who the hell was he to judge?

"Well, we'd like to come examine the situation if that's all right with you."

"Certainly, by all means. Anything that can help him."

"Well, wonderful. We'll head out that way in the next few hours. We just have some equipment to pack."

The man had a pleasant voice, sounded friendly and eager to help. Jason wanted to believe he would do some good, so he agreed. But truth be told, he wasn't really following the conversation very much. He knew he should be, knew that Stan was not doing well, and that the situation was only getting worse. But as much as he loved his son, most of his mind was occupied with the fact that he also loved his wife, and she was slipping away from him. Despite what she had done, the pain and grief and bitter anger her actions had caused, he couldn't look past the thought that losing her would be the worst thing that could happen to him.

Jason said his good-byes to the pleasant voice on the phone and placed the phone back in its cradle. From down the short hallway he could hear the sounds of Addy washing the breakfast dishes. He should have been on his way to work on most days, but with Stan in the hospital he'd taken a few days off.

He stood up and went over to his briefcase, fishing inside it until he found the letter. Enough. It was time. He either confronted her and worked out something—maybe a marriage counselor or maybe divorce, he didn't know which—or their relationship was dead. There was no way around it.

He stepped toward the sounds of silverware under running water, preparing as best he could for what was next. Something cold and heavy settled into his stomach and almost seemed to feed on the idea of the coming confrontation.

Naturally, he was nowhere near prepared for what he found out.

VI

Mike Blake looked at the man sitting on the edge of the desk and wondered what it was about him that kept Amelia constantly flustered. Oh, she was hardly blatant about it, but he could see it whenever her eyes slid over his way. He knew her that well, even after the short time they'd been together.

Still, he wasn't going to let it bother him. He refused to let her past—and it was painfully obvious from the very beginning that there was a past between the two—make him do something stupid. *Besides, I have no claim on her. She's been wonderful, but there's been no talk about us being an item. If she wants to date some skinny freak who smiles too much, I'm not in any position to say anything about it.*

It sounded good, but he knew he didn't feel that way. Not really. He'd never been the type to believe in casual sex, even back in high school when he'd practiced it as regularly as he could.

Part of him was disappointed that they hadn't had a chance to actually do anything earlier, before the weirdness over at the mansion. Being with Amelia in that way was always amazing.

On the other side of the argument, however, was the fact that if they had been doing anything, it surely would have been interrupted by the gunfire anyway.

They hadn't been making love, or even having a quickie. They'd been looking over the dolls in the room that adjoined her bedroom-to-be.

The dolls that kept moving on their own.

Amelia had mentioned them to him earlier in the day, after she'd gone off to have her conversation with Crowley. While they'd been eating a cold lunch of tuna fish sandwiches—made just the way he liked, with pickles and onions added to the mix, as if she'd read his mind—she'd brought up the fact that the dolls they'd discovered together moved whenever she wasn't looking.

He'd scoffed at the notion, telling her to stop pulling his leg in so many words. She in turn had made a bet of it. They'd go look at the dolls together, and then they'd go off somewhere for an hour or two and come back. He'd agreed, and they'd looked over the dolls carefully. He was still amazed by the detail on each of the tiny figures. That each of them looked so very real, so lifelike—he half expected their hair to move in the breeze from the slight opening in the window—was enough to make him feel dizzy. He could see where the illusion of them moving—if indeed she was not pulling his leg, which he still expected was the case—could easily seem real to Amelia.

They went out shopping and spent some time at the quarry, while Amelia explained in detail the plans for properly starting it back up again. She had ambitions, that was for damned sure.

Then they went back to the house, and he saw for himself. Amelia had locked the doors before they left, making a show of it for his benefit. He'd seen her lock the doors, and he knew for a fact that she was the only person with the keys. He'd added the locks to the doll room himself only the week before at her request.

When the door was opened, the dolls had moved. Not a little bit either. Some had moved only a few inches, true, but others had relocated to different shelves in the room, and a few had even made it to the opposite wall. He'd looked around the room, wondering if anyone could have snuck in and knowing it just wasn't possible, as chills flowed through his body and covered him in gooseflesh.

They'd been talking over the possibility that there was an explanation that made sense—and failing miserably in coming up with one—when the fighting broke out in the yard.

Constable Michaels spoke up, interrupting his thoughts. For the last ten minutes they'd all been doing their own thing—which mostly meant inhaling great quantities of coffee—and it had been easy to drift into introspection. As soon as the man spoke, he made himself focus on what was going on.

"Okay, Mr. Crowley, you seem to have a lot of ideas about what's going on around here. Why don't you share them?" The constable sounded angry, or at least as close as he was going to manage in his current state. Mike wondered exactly how much he'd missed, realizing that maybe he wasn't quite as alert as he'd thought.

"Actually, I don't have much of an idea what's going on here, Officer. I just know that a lot of it isn't natural."

"Where do you get that sort of notion?"

"Could it be the headless cop who was trying to kill me after you'd blown his face away?" Crowley still had that amused tone in his voice that Mike found both irritating and unsettling. "Maybe you remember him?"

"Point taken." Michaels sighed and knocked back the rest of his coffee. "So why don't you seem bothered by that idea?"

"It's not exactly something that's new to me."

Amelia snorted softly at that.

Crowley looked her way for an instant, his eyes acknowledging her short laugh for what it was. That simple sound said that his comment was an understatement of epic scale.

"Could you explain that to me?"

"I've been known to deal with a few strange critters from time to time. Most of them needed to be reminded how to behave."

Michaels looked at him and raised one eyebrow. "And you know how to make them behave?"

"Well, it's a learning process."

"What makes you a specialist in monsters?"

"Might be my degree in parapsychology. Might be my willingness to do a little research to find out what the problem is." Crowley leaned back a bit on the desk, his eyes peering over his rimless glasses at the constable with a look that was both amused and condescending. "Maybe it's just my willingness to see what's right in front of me."

"What do you mean?"

"Know a lot about your town, do you, Constable?"

"I know how to get around the streets."

"Okay, here's another one. Have you figured out the pattern to your recent grave desecration yet? I have."

Michaels frowned. "What pattern?"

"Well, not all of your graves were…rudely disinterred. A lot of them were, but not all of them. Can you guess what the unmolested sites have in common? Go on, guess." His smile showed no maliciousness in that moment, merely amusement.

The constable sighed. "Please, Mr. Crowley. I'm really not up to this. Just humor me and let me know what's going on."

"Spoilsport." He shrugged his shoulders. "All of the graves that were left alone had one thing in common: the people buried there were murdered."

"Excuse me?"

"All of the graves left alone contained the mortal remains of murder victims." He paused, thinking for a moment. "Actually, I'm making assumptions about three of them, but it makes sense in light of all the others."

"What brings you to that conclusion, Mr. Crowley?"

"Research, Constable, research. I got bold and daring, and I checked the newspaper files at the *Serenity Sentinel*. Funny thing about headstones, they give dates. Funny thing about dates, they usually can be found in newspapers." He shook his head. "You'd be amazed how few people use that sort of information to their advantage."

"You'd be amazed how few people have time to look into that sort of thing when they actually have to work for a living." The words were harsh, but only because the constable was feeling guilty.

"Yeah, sucks the way that works. What do you know about Serenity's history?"

"What they taught us in school." He shrugged. "History's never been really big on my list of favorite subjects."

"Really? Pity. Your little town has an interesting history. Did you know, for instance, that the founding father of Serenity was an amateur witch hunter?"

"Can't say as I did. What's that got to do with anything?"

"He only ever hunted one woman. He tortured a confession from her and killed her. Nice man."

"Interesting, but the same question. What the hell's that got to do with anything at all?"

Crowley shrugged. "Maybe nothing at all, maybe everything. All I know is that this town has a history of violence that dates back all the way to when it was settled."

"Yeah, and so does every other town in New York and most of them in America, for that matter."

"Oh, there's violence everywhere. It just seems a little like this town is preoccupied with it."

"You sure a certain tussle you had the other day isn't just making you a little sensitive to the idea of violence?"

Before Crowley could answer, the phone rang. Michaels snatched the receiver from the cradle before it could ring a second time. He spoke softly, and while he was talking, Mike looked over at Crowley to find the man looking back at him with an unsettling intensity. It was almost a minute before either of them looked away. Mike hated that he was the one who blinked first.

Crowley leaned toward him, his mouth curled into an amused smirk. "You don't like me, do you?"

"Should I?"

"That's up to you, isn't it?"

"I suppose it is." He looked at the man again, weighing his words carefully. "I don't know you well enough to like you or not. First opinion, you think too much of yourself."

Crowley laughed, his eyes showing genuine amusement. "Really? Well, that's refreshingly honest of you."

"How nice of you to think so, I'm sure." If his voice was a little dry, that was only to be expected. He was being civil solely because of Amelia. He did not, in fact, like Jonathan Crowley. There was something about him that almost immediately grated across his nerves.

"Go on, tell me more. What else is it about me that you don't like?"

Amelia made a sort of cautionary noise, a hum that said without words that this could be a bad territory to go into. Mike chose to ignore it. "I don't like your smile or the fact that you always seem to have a reason for smiling." He thought about it for a second. "You remind me of a schoolyard bully, only without all the added muscle."

"You'd know a lot about schoolyard bullies, too, wouldn't you Mike?"

"What do you mean?"

"I've been reading the papers over at the library. You can get a lot of information out of small-town papers. You don't look much like a bully, but you had your day, didn't you?"

"Well, the difference is, I got over it. What's your excuse?"

"Maybe I'm just a big kid at heart."

"Or maybe you're just a bully who never figured out how to stop being mean for mean's sake."

Crowley shook his head, grinning again. "You're entitled to your opinion. It's wrong, but that's okay." He stood up, stretching his lean body, and Mike noticed that Amelia watched. He reminded himself again that he had no claims to her, nor any right to be upset by the gesture. But it wasn't easy.

Jack Michaels got off the phone, shaking his head. "Well, looks like you're not the only one who thinks something's gone sour in Serenity, Mr. Crowley."

"Really? Who else decided to get a clue?"

"Couple of parapsychologists and specialists have decided to take a look at one of the local boys, see if he's possessed or some such."

Crowley's head craned around, his eyes alert and focused completely on the constable. "And do these people have names?"

Michaels looked at him with a dazed expression, and when he spoke again, his voice sounded just slightly off. "Jacob and Mary Parsons."

"Really?" Crowley's voice took on a purring quality that Mike found unsettling, more so when he noticed Amelia out of the corner of his eye, and how pale she'd suddenly become. "Well, that *is* special. Such a lovely couple."

"Am I mistaken, or is that sarcasm in your voice?"

"Well, it isn't exactly sincerity now, is it?"

"What do you know about these people that I should know?"

"They aren't exactly adept at doing what's made them famous. They're just good at faking it."

"They aren't real ghost busters?"

"They aren't anything but charlatans."

"I'm having a little trouble believing that your word would mean much, Mr. Crowley."

Crowley actually looked surprised. "Why would that be, Constable?"

"Mostly because whatever it was that made—" He paused for a second and swallowed hard enough for his throat to make a clicking sound. "That made Bill Karstens get back up off the ground seemed to know you, and he called you Hunter, not Crowley."

"Hunter is more like a title, much like Constable."

"Why would Bill Karstens call you by a title?"

"Bill Karstens didn't call me anything. Whatever possessed him did."

Jack Michaels leaned over his desk, his eyes set and staring hard at the man who so casually leaned on the edge of it. "And what might that be, Mr. Crowley? What on God's green earth possessed him?"

"I haven't the foggiest idea."

Michaels did his best to stare the man down, but it didn't work. The constable turned away first, and that in turn made Crowley's grin spread even wider on his face.

"I have a dead officer, a dead local, and a handful of teenagers on my hands, Crowley. And then I have you. Most of them I can probably figure out how to handle, but you are an exception. What am I supposed to do about you?"

Crowley stood up, stifling a yawn. "Whatever you feel you have to do, Constable. But whatever it is will have to wait. I'm tired, and I'm going to get some sleep." He started walking toward the entrance to the building and stopped long enough to regard the constable. "And whatever else you do, I might recommend getting a little rest. You look putrid."

Michaels didn't stop him from leaving.

A moment later, Amelia's hand reached out and touched the constable's arm gently. "He's right about you not looking your best, Jack. You really should get some rest."

The man sighed and looked down at her hand on his arm, then down at the desk in front of him. "I know. I just don't know if I can spare the manpower."

"You won't do anyone any good if you're in the hospital, Jack." Mike was almost surprised to hear his own voice. He hadn't really planned on speaking. Finally the man nodded his head, accepting defeat.

"I'll do it, but I don't have to like it." He groaned for a long moment and shook his head. "Hell, even a nap will have to wait."

"Why's that?"

Michaels looked at him and then looked at the ground. "Because I have to tell Maureen Karstens that her husband is dead."

"Take a nap first, Constable. Even a short one. If you try speaking to her now, it will only make matters worse." Jack looked at Amelia and then nodded. A moment later he did it again and then stood up.

Amelia rose with him, her every gesture making it look like she was helping an invalid as she walked with him toward the door. Mike watched from where he sat, not certain exactly what he was feeling anymore. The last few hours had stretched on and on in his mind, and mostly, he wanted them to contract back down to normal. Hours, as a rule, should not feel like days. Hell, that was why he'd started drinking in the first place, wasn't it?

Thinking of alcohol was not precisely wise just then. He wanted desperately to get ripped and call it a night. That wasn't necessarily the best thing for him to be contemplating at nine in the morning.

VII

Charlene Lyons looked at Mr. LeMarrs and shuddered inwardly. She'd forgotten all about the test today. More importantly, she could tell by the way he was looking at her that he knew she wasn't prepared. His fat face was gloating.

Charlee wanted to slide under a rock and hide, but she knew it wasn't going to happen. There were some things that simply couldn't be escaped, and this was one of them. LeMarrs looked right at her as he handed down the sheaf of papers that would be passed back to her and then those behind her. Somewhere along the way she'd be expected to put down the right answers if she wanted to pass his class. It was that last part of the equation that was causing her grief.

She let her eyes move around the room one last time, taking in the faces of her fellow students. None of them looked thrilled about the test, except maybe for Lawrence, and really, he was just trying not to let her see him looking at her like he always did. Becky wasn't there. She frowned a little at that. It wasn't like Becky not to be at school. They weren't exactly tight friends, but not seeing Becky was sort of like not having the clock on the wall. It belonged there, and its absence made her feel funny.

Charlee was brought back to the present by the stack of test papers Alan Berry handed back to her. She did her best to smile a thanks she didn't feel and took one, handing the rest to Joey behind her. Joey took them, his eyes barely acknowledging her.

Rule number one: Lawrence always looked at every girl and smiled hopefully, doubtless knowing that the best he could hope for in return was a smile. Rule number two: Dave always smiled that little half smile of his and winked at the girls and guys alike. Sort of like he was saying the whole thing was just a joke and one that he found really quite funny. Rule number three: Stan always blushed when he looked at a girl, which was sort of cute but a little weird. Rule number four: Joey always made eye contact and held it for a few moments, like he was trying to look deep into them and figure them out, and he always, always smiled.

The day was getting weirder and weirder. Bad enough that Stan still wasn't there, but now Becky was gone and Joey wasn't looking like he was searching for the meaning of life in her eyes. She was beginning to not like this particular Monday. One look at the test paper confirmed it. Yep, this day was going to suck.

Behind her, Joey Whitman looked at his test and felt nothing. His hand lifted the pencil and started writing, ignoring the questions on the paper completely. The words, if words they were, were not in English, and the characters that made the words were not letters of any alphabet used since the time of Babylon.

Almost forty minutes went by in complete silence, for the quiet sounds of people reading aloud to themselves and the occasional sniffle brought on by the cold weather. When she was finished, Charlee set her paper facedown and looked at her desk.

Five minutes before the end of the class, Mr. LeMarrs walked up and down the aisles, collecting the end results. He came from behind Charlee, but she couldn't have missed his heavy footsteps if she'd tried. When he stopped walking, Charlee closed her eyes, dreading some nasty comment about her abilities. He liked making nasty comments. It was his specialty.

No one could have been more surprised when the nastiness was directed at Joey instead of her. "What exactly is this, Mr. Whitman?"

"It—it's my test, sir."

"I know it's your test, young man, but these are surely not the answers you want me to grade, are they?"

Charlee looked around, watching Joey's face carefully. He looked confused and a little panicked, which was pretty much the way anyone looked when LeMarrs started in on an attack. "I don't know what you mean, sir."

LeMarrs waved the test paper in Joey's face, and even with the paper almost sideways to her, she could see that something was very wrong with his answers. "I *mean* there isn't a single number anywhere on this paper, young man, and as this is a math class, one expects numbers somewhere along the way. I *mean* that I also expect written answers to be in English, not in ancient Egyptian or whatever this is supposed to be." She was still stunned by a man that size being so amazingly prissy, but at that moment, Charlee found nothing at all humorous in his behavior. "Maybe this is a joke, Mr. Whitman. But if so, I am not laughing." He looked toward Charlee for a second. "As I'm sure Ms. Lyons will tell you, I do not have a sense of humor." His words came as a barrage, not as a discussion, and the effect left poor Joey — who was never in any sort of trouble — looking rather dazed.

"I didn't—"

"Didn't what? Want to pass my class? You're certainly doing an excellent job of failing this test, young man. I wonder how your parents will feel about your shenanigans if I decide to call them and let them know about this. Or perhaps I should have Mr. Wortham make that call while you're waiting in his office."

"You do whatever you have to, Mr. LeMarrs, but stop waving that damned paper in my face." Joey Whitman also never, ever cursed in front of adults. It just wasn't done. And the very notion of anyone actively speaking out against LeMarrs was genuinely ludicrous. The only exception was Dave Pageant, who normally managed to be the exception to most of the rules. Every student in the class, even Lawrence, who always sat ramrod stiff and facing the front of the class at the first sign of trouble, turned and looked when Joey made his opinion known. Several of them even made shocked noises.

LeMarrs reached out his big hand, grabbing Joey's biceps and wrapping his fingers completely around his arm. "What did you just say to me?" His voice couldn't really be called properly menacing; that was like trying to be intimidated by the sound of Mickey Mouse having a fit. It just didn't work. But his size was another matter. And Mr. LeMarrs had broken the cardinal rule that all teachers followed: He'd touched a student in a hostile way. There was nothing disciplinarian in his grip on Joey's arm. The hand that held him was squeezing with a fierce, crushing force, and Joey responded by bleating out a noise like squealing brakes.

"Get your fucking hands offa me!" Joey swung his free hand around in an arc and slapped the teacher's knuckles with enough force to make the flesh shake.

Charlee watched on, her jaw hanging open, as LeMarrs pulled his hand away from Joey's arm, the test papers spilling from his left hand to rain down across the linoleum. His face looked as shocked as hers, and that, too, was just plain wrong.

"You don't ever touch me, fat man! Not ever! If you touch me again, I'll see you in jail!" Joey stood up, flying from his seat like a jack-in-the-box on heavy doses of crack cocaine. His eyes were wide and glassy, and his teeth were bared in a snarl that was positively frightening.

It took LeMarrs only a second to recover, and when he did, his whole head turned red with anger; forget his cheeks, baby, his whole head went crimson. "That's it! You can take yourself down to Principal Wortham's office right now, young man. I'll see you expelled before I'll take this sort of monkey business from you!"

"Fuck you!"

Not even Dave, who was always, always in trouble of some sort, had ever considered speaking that way to a teacher. It just wasn't done. There were rules you could bend, and some you didn't even consider messing with. Using the *f* word was beyond a no-no. That was moving into the sort of trouble you avoided at all costs.

This time, when LeMarrs's hand came toward Joey, it was higher up, and it wasn't trying to grab. He'd have surely slapped Joey's head off his shoulders if Dave hadn't interfered. Somehow the biggest kid in the class had moved from his desk and into a position to actually prevent things from getting beyond bad. His arms—so big when he stood alone, but thin and frail next to the teacher's—whipped out and wrapped around LeMarrs's arm, stopping his swing from connecting.

The force behind the wild swipe was enough to drag Dave along until he almost collided with Joey.

The teacher's broad face went through a sort of wave of emotions. He'd been furious that one of the kids would dare to speak to him that way, and he'd had a brief look of satisfied triumph on his face when he started swinging, but it changed quickly into something like terror, wide eyes and all, just before Dave blocked his shot.

Dave's voice wavered nervously, a dancing jitterbug in his throat that made him sound all wrong. "Mr. LeMarrs? Maybe you better just go get Mr. Wortham to handle this?"

All the anger had drained out of LeMarrs, who was now as pale as a ghost and sweating heavily. He nodded dumbly at Dave, his eyes looking weird and almost teary. "Yes. Thank you, Dave."

He looked down at Joey, his flabby face almost slack, then he moved toward the door. "Everyone please take their seat."

Dave motioned Joey to sit down, then gathered the tests on the floor, carefully rearranging them before he finished gathering the rest from the other students. Most everyone sat at their desks, facing forward, almost afraid to move. Even Joey seemed cowed by what had happened.

Charlee was about to ask if Joey was okay, when Dave leaned over between them. He looked at Joey, his face almost unreadable. "Sign this, now."

Joey blinked, then nodded, doing as he was told. Dave held his own test in one hand, a blank test on the desk in front of his friend. He spoke out the answers to the test—and Charlee knew she'd not failed, but not exactly done fabulously either, just by listening to the answers and remembering what she'd put down—and Joey wrote them quickly, both of them looking toward the open hallway door from time to time. When Joey was done, Dave put the tests in order on the big stack on the teacher's desk.

Then he looked at the class. "Nobody hit anyone, okay guys? Mr. LeMarrs never hit Joey; Joey never hit him." His eyes turned on Joey behind his glasses and he stared hard. "Joey just said a few bad words, and no one gets fired and no one gets expelled."

Everyone knew the score: LeMarrs was a mean, small-minded man, but he was also a nice guy sometimes. He might yell at them one day and the next bring cookies to the classroom because he remembered it was someone's birthday. He was an adult, and that meant he obviously had a few gears loose. But he wasn't the worst thing they'd ever had in school—that would have been Mrs. Brown, the third-grade history teacher, who never ever spoke to anyone, but instead screamed at them—and he didn't deserve to lose his job because Joey had been a weenie. And Joey, who was about to at least get suspension, didn't deserve to fail the test because his mind was off somewhere else. Even if he did, everyone liked Dave Pageant. They listened more for him than for either the teacher or the student involved in the fight.

Dave sat against the edge of LeMarrs's desk, looking out at all of them until Wortham showed up with a very nervous-looking teacher in front of him. Just as they entered the room, the bell rang shrilly. Charlee gaped, hardly believing everything had happened in only five minutes.

VIII

Mary and Jacob Parsons pulled up in the parking lot of the Westerfield Medical Center and climbed out of their rental car without ceremony. Mary carried her purse in one hand and a small dictation tape recorder in the other. Jacob carried a small camcorder in his left hand, leaving his right hand free.

Mary Parsons dressed in a simple, elegant blue business suit. Her long auburn hair was down, and her wide eyeglasses showed warm brown eyes to the world. She was dressed to look as friendly as she could without removing the slight authoritative edge that she sometimes had to expose in order to get the job done. Jacob dressed in a nice shirt, a tie, and blue jeans. They exchanged glances as they headed for room 315 of the medical center. They were here to do work, and they were both prepared to make the most of whatever they discovered. Most of the trip down from New Hampshire had been spent in discussion of their latest book. If things worked out well, this would be one of the final chapters in the third volume of their *Possessions and Visitations* series. If it was a good enough book, their agent was hoping to work them into a weekly cable television series.

The Discovery Channel was always looking for new angles, and with ten very successful books on the paranormal under their collective belts, the couple was ready to move on to bigger and better things. At thirty-five years of age, the schoolteacher-turned-psychic was ready for the big time, and Jacob, just a year older, was ready to join her.

They didn't introduce themselves to anyone. They just casually strolled through the building's hallways until they reached the place where they wanted to be. Aside from the boy lying in the bed watching the television, the room was empty.

He was a good-looking kid, but not looking his healthiest. He was too pale, and there were circles dark enough to look like bruises under his blue eyes. His hair was a dirty blond color and looked like a bird's nest on top of his head. He barely noticed when they stepped into the room.

"Are you Stanley Long?" Jacob led the questions, his voice warm and friendly, while Mary listened and tried to get a feel for what was going on. It was too easy to bury yourself in the hopes that the case was legitimate, too easy to fall for a scam set up by someone who wanted to disprove what you knew was true. For that reason, Mary always scoped the place out as carefully as she could while simultaneously listening to her husband's gentle interrogations.

The boy looked over at the two of them and nodded weakly. "Do I know you?"

"I'm Jacob, and this is my wife Mary."

He nodded. "The Parsons. I saw you on TV just last week."

"We've been on the television a few times, yes."

"You wanna make me into one of your stories?"

"Well no, not exactly." Jacob blushed lightly, his wide, friendly face casting a guilty look for half a second. "We want to help you."

"Yeah, but I bet there's money in it somewhere."

"We don't charge to help you, Stanley, we just want to see if we can figure out what's making you sick."

"Dead people are making me sick. They won't leave me alone." He said it so matter-of-factly that the statement sent shivers down Mary's spine. "You make them go away, and I'll be fine."

"Why do you think dead people are making you sick, Stanley?"

"I think they want to eat my soul. Or maybe take my body for their own, but they won't fit." He looked over at Mary and smiled slightly. She smiled back, looking at his handsome face and hoping that they would be able to help him somehow. At that age, he was supposed to be playing games and daydreaming about girls, not sitting in the hospital looking so lost and alone. She'd never had kids, couldn't in fact, but there was a maternal streak in Mary that was very, very evident on the cases where they dealt with kids.

"Stanley."

"Stan. Call me Stan, please."

Jacob nodded. "Stan, when did all of this start?"

"Right after I drowned."

"Yes, your father said something about that in his letter. You never had an experience before that?"

"No sir." He tilted his head, as if he were listening to something. "No, that's not right. It was right before I drowned. Me and Dave were at the old house near the quarry, and we saw a ghost."

Jacob nodded quietly, trying to figure out the next question. Mary leaned in closer, her hand touching Stan's. "Tell me about the ghost, Stan."

"He was old, and mean, and I think he was Blackwell's ghost. The man who owned the quarry. He killed his whole family before he killed himself." He looked into her eyes, his gaze penetrating, too intense and…haunted to belong on a little boy who was just starting to think about puberty. "He was creepy."

"I'll bet." She gave his hand a squeeze and let it go. Jacob leaned back, letting her ask the questions now. "Do you think the ghost caused this?"

"No. I think it was when I drowned. I heard sometimes that happens to people with near-death experiences. They come back different."

"You're a very smart young man."

Stan shrugged and blushed enough that his face almost had color again.

"Do you see the dead people all the time?"

"No. Mostly when I'm sleeping, but now and then when I'm awake."

"Do they say anything to you?"

"Sometimes. Sometimes they say stuff, but it's hard to make out."

"Try to remember what they say for me, can you do that?"

"'Every solace green.'"

She shook her head. "Doesn't make much sense, does it?"

"I said it was hard to understand..." He looked disappointed.

"Well, if you really are hearing the dead, they're talking from a long ways off. It's not like a phone call."

"I wish it was. Then I could hang up on them."

Mary nodded. She'd never heard of a case like this one—except maybe for that movie from a few years ago—and it intrigued her.

"Well, maybe we can fix this so you don't have to hear them anymore."

"The doctors haven't been able to do it." Spoken like a true twelve-year-old. He was disappointed by the failures, and judging by his sickly complexion, he had reason to be.

She reached out and patted his hand again, ready to call it quits for the time being. They needed to research the possible causes, and the boy needed his rest. Before she actually touched him, his hand whipped up and grabbed hers in a crushing grip.

Mary Parsons sucked in a breath as the fingers of the boy's hand sank deep into her flesh, bruising and making bones creak. His voice, when he spoke, was not his own. "They're coming back. You can't stop them, you can only suffer if you stay." Stan Long's eyes fluttered, and the heart monitor he was strapped to started making radical, loud beeping noises as the lines of green on the black display field went crazy. "They'll take you, too, Mary Parsons. They'll take you down with them!"

Jacob calmly reached over and tried to pry the boy's fingers from her hand. His efforts were in vain. The grip was like an iron bear trap on her hand and wrist. Stan's head turned toward him, his neck muscles standing out like wires under his skin. "It's already too late for you, Jacob. You're a dead man walking." The boy's face changed, the muscles moving in ways that just were not physically possible, distorting his visage and making him look much older. His lips peeled back in a grin that sent shivers through Mary. "You're gonna be joining them in the darkness before this week is over, Jacob Parsons. You'll die and leave poor Mary all alone."

Jacob made a wheezing sound that probably meant an asthma attack was on the way. Mary tried pulling her hand away and was successful this time. Stan Long's young body arched up, bowing in the center until his legs and buttocks were off the bed, his full weight on his neck and his feet. For all the world he looked like someone was electrifying him. Mary backed away, worried about him, about her husband, and about her own sanity. She'd never in all her years seen anything like it.

Something cold touched her, moved through her away from the boy and then out of the room. Gooseflesh slithered over her body, and her hair stood on end. Stan Long crashed down on the hospital bed like a lifeless doll, his heart monitor slowing down to a less insane level, though not quite normal.

Mary looked over at her husband, who was staring at the boy with wide, wet eyes.

"Mary," he said, his voice as frightened as his face. "I think we might just have a situation here."

She nodded, not trusting her voice to actually work.

IX

Greg woke up to a dream come true. Nora, beside him, sleeping sweetly, her soft breaths blowing on his face. Someday he hoped to make it a regular part of his daily routine.

His body was still pleasantly sore from their lovemaking sessions. His bladder was heavy with the need to pee, but he held off, just enjoying the feeling of waking up next to her. He knew he'd have to get up soon, but for the moment the discomfort was a mild thing.

Back when he was a freshman in high school, Nora had been a senior and on the cheerleading squad. He'd watched her back then just like almost every other guy at school had. She was a beauty. She'd never noticed him, but that was to be expected. He was a freshman, after all. He spent the remainder of that school year heavily in lust with a girl who was, in every imaginable way, inaccessible.

Then in January of this year he met her, really met her, for the first time. He'd seen her around, normally on the arm of some strapping local football hero or seeing a few friends when she was back from going to college. She'd smile when she saw him, but it was just the sort of smile you give to someone you've seen for years and never met. That changed when they were both waiting in line at the bank on one of those occasions where there was only one teller and an impossibly long string of people stood before them. He'd been waiting as patiently as he could, which was very difficult, when he heard her speak behind him. Her first words to him were simply: "Do I know you?"

He made her guess where they'd met, and after about twelve guesses, she figured it out. By the time the line was finished with the two of them, they'd discussed a few of the people they both knew and then decided on a late lunch. By the time lunch was done—just a quick meal at Frannie's, but it wound up being a two-and-a-half-hour-long quick lunch—he'd decided he'd made a new friend.

They talked about everything. He heard the stories of how Carl, who'd seemed like such a wonderful guy when they'd started dating, suddenly became a tyrant after they married. She'd told him about how she'd tried to leave him, and how he had made his point about that not happening by "marking his territory" as he liked to put it. After beating her—carefully, leaving no marks that could be seen—he'd forced himself on her, being deliberately cruel and violent. It'd taken her a week to finally be able to sit without wincing. Just to make sure she understood her position, Carl sometimes came home and forced himself on her again. Normally after a rough day of working as an electrician and then drinking with his buddies. Nona wasn't allowed to have buddies. No one around to tell her how stupid she was for staying with him.

It wasn't until almost a month later that they first managed to have a physical encounter. It should have been awkward. He knew she was married, knew exactly who her husband was and that Carl would likely tear his arms off and beat him to death with them if he was caught. But it wasn't awkward. It was everything he'd ever read in a *Penthouse Forum* letter and more. When they were finished, both of them pleasantly exhausted and sated, she'd rolled over and rested her head on his shoulder, asking why it was that she hadn't met him first.

He had no answer to that, but that, too, was okay; it had been a rhetorical question.

On Valentine's Day he'd given her a small choker with a heart-shaped pendant. She acted like it was the biggest diamond she'd ever seen and hugged him with a sort of desperation that was both a pleasant surprise and frightening in its intensity. She lamented having nothing to give him—Carl was in charge of the money, and the very idea of spending any frivolously was enough to make her pale—and almost cried when he told her she already gave him more than he'd ever dared hope for.

And now, for the first time since he'd seen her in high school, he knew that was true on more levels than he'd ever expected. They had to be cautious, careful not to make any moves that were too blatant, but the one obstacle that had stood between the two of them being together and happy was gone.

Murderer! You sick, twisted fuck! You killed a man and took his wife! What the hell do you think your parents would say if they were still alive?

They could be together. Six months from now, maybe eight, people would understand when she left that shit hole she'd been forced to live in and moved in with him properly. And if the neighbors had anything to say about it, they could kiss his ass. They could be discreet until then. It wasn't all that hard.

He rolled over, his eyes studying her perfect face. The girl next door was now in his bedroom, with him. As she opened her eyes and looked at him, a small, loving smile forming on her lips, he wondered what he could have ever done to deserve being this happy.

———

Elsewhere, deep in the woods where something had answered a young girl's prayers the night before, Carl Bradford's body twitched. His mind could hardly be called his own, but that was okay. His nerve endings screamed with agony, a conflagration of pain that made every experience he'd ever had seem trivial in comparison. Once, not long after he'd started working as an electrician, he'd set his hand on a live wire, unaware that the man he was working with was doing a voltage check. The current had frozen him in place, unable to do more than jitterbug wildly while his nerves screamed. He'd gotten second-degree burns inside his hand and arm before it was over. He'd spent two weeks doped up on drugs that left him stupefied but still in excruciating pain, barely able to move his hand from the inflammation. After that he'd spent another month sweating through physical therapy and sometimes crying tears like a baby as he tried to make all the muscles work the way they were supposed to.

That had hurt a lot.

This was a hundred times worse.

But it was okay. His skin moved slowly, wounds on his flesh twisting and stretching until the cuts pulled themselves shut and sealed, leaving cold, white slashes where there had been exposed meat and gristle before. Torn ligaments and tendons, already victims of rigor mortis, creaked under dead flesh as they snaked back together. And every single movement brought new waves of nauseating, debilitating anguish. His nerves did a systems check that left him spasming, his pale lips drawn back in an inverted grin. Then his lungs kicked in, taking huge, gasping draws of air into flesh that was already atrophied and waterlogged from spending time in the freezing rain of the last twelve hours. He coughed a dubious reddish fluid from deep in his lungs and rolled over onto his stomach, his joints aching with every movement and his body shivering from more than merely the cold of the morning.

But it was okay. It was all right and dyn-no-miiite! No pain, no gain. He opened his eyes, and pupils that shouldn't have been able to see anything registered light in a level that made him feel like someone was shoving hot fireplace pokers into his skull. He'd have screamed if his lungs would have allowed it. Even closing his eyes didn't help. It was the nerves, he was certain of it. They just weren't prepared to work again. He'd read or heard something about how once nerves died they tended to stay dead. He could understand why. Nothing sane would want to go through this without a really good reason.

But it was okay. Birth was supposedly traumatic, and he guessed rebirth was worse. Besides, he had a reason.

"N... N-Nona."

He crawled slowly upward, standing on legs that wanted to go every way imaginable except the right way. There was a breeze blowing, but it wasn't enough to make him sway as much as he did. The pain was slowly fading away, leaving the memory of the pain like a trail through his body.

"Nona." Carl Bradford allowed himself a smile that felt off kilter. Nothing was working just the way he remembered. The thick gauze of his death had been peeled away from him, but not without leaving a few scars, it seemed. "Nona, darling, this time you've pushed me too far."

His steps grew more confident as he walked, muscles and motor functions relearning what should have been easy, but relearning quickly. His fists clenched and unclenched next to his legs as he walked slowly back toward the town where he'd been born and raised, lived, married, and died.

"No more mister nice guy."

X

Dave Pageant met up with Jessie as she started away from her final class of the day, falling into stride with her. Jessie saw him, and her heart sped up a bit. She was a little worried that maybe he wouldn't want to talk to her, or worse, would laugh at her or say something after she'd kissed him yesterday. All through the school day, she'd expected to hear snickers or snide comments about the whole thing. And for just as long she'd both dreaded and hoped for the moment when she would see him again.

"Hi, Jess."

"Hi."

He leaned in close, his words for her ears only. "You look very pretty."

She didn't think a blush could come to her face that quickly. And for the second time in all the years she'd known him—which was her whole life—she saw *him* blush.

"Thanks." She knew her smile had to be absolutely huge. She was surprised that every person in the hallways wasn't staring at them, but they were just going on like it was no big deal, and so she kept walking.

They walked together, moving over to her locker, where he leaned against the next one, looking at the people going past and nodding to a few. Aside from the red flush across his skin, he was looking pretty chilly. "Cool as a cucumber," as her daddy liked to say. "You didn't call me, about Stan, I mean." She added the last quickly, not wanting him to think she meant about the kiss she'd stolen the day before, though that was really more on her mind than Stan was right then.

"I wanted to, but I didn't get a response to my e-mail." He shrugged. "Maybe when I get home tonight."

"Oh."

"So, what are you doing now?"

"Just going home, I guess."

"Oh."

"Why?" Did that sound too eager? She hoped not, but she wasn't really sure.

"Well, I was thinking about going over to see Stan again. Make sure he's doing okay." He looked at her eyes for a few seconds, then looked away. "I was thinking maybe you'd like to come along."

"Oh. Okay."

His eyes looked around at the rapidly emptying hallways. "So that means you'll come with me?"

"Sure. I just have to call my folks first, so they don't worry."

He nodded. "That's cool." He swung his backpack over one shoulder, almost like a girl's purse, though there was nothing at all feminine about the gesture. "I saw Stan's sister this morning."

"Yeah? How's she doing?"

"She's sort of weirded out about the whole thing." He shrugged again, looking away for a moment and then meeting her eyes. "She cried a little bit, and I gave her a hug, and we talked about God and stuff."

"She's that bad, hunh?"

"Yeah, sort of like when my cat died and I was wigged for a week. Only, Stan isn't dead, just sick."

Jessie nodded, closing her locker and frowning a little petulantly. But only a small frown. It just didn't sit right, him talking to Stan's sister. She was a very pretty girl, and though Jessie had absolutely no right or claim to Dave, she wanted to. Thinking about April Long, who was as tall as Dave and pretty enough to be a model, and comparing herself to the older girl, Jessie could see where getting a hug from April would win out against a kiss from her. It wasn't a comforting notion. She slipped on her thick winter coat as they left the building and stepped into the gray afternoon. Lawrence's mom was already there, waiting for him. She nodded curtly to them and then brightened as Lawrence came out the doors behind them.

They chatted about the day—yes, Joey got in trouble, and no, it wasn't all that bad. Mr. LeMarrs had a bad attitude going, but it wasn't like anyone got shot or anything. Then Dave moved closer in, his face inches from hers as they walked toward the medical center to see Stan.

"Can you keep a secret, Jessie?"

"Sure."

"I got a kiss from April."

Jessie felt her skin grow cold, even colder than the weather should have caused. "Y-you did? Why?"

"We were talking about things people should do before they died. I told her Stan couldn't die yet because he'd never gotten a kiss from a pretty girl." She knew Dave well enough to understand his logic, which should have scared the hell out of her but didn't. She nodded. "She gave me a kiss, just in case anything bad should happen to me."

"Oh."

He stopped walking, his eyes on hers, the lenses of his glasses doing nothing to reduce the intensity of his stare. "I wanted to let you know."

"Why?" She could feel that damned sting back behind her eyes, the one that said she felt like crying. She wasn't going to let that happen. Here she'd been thinking that Dave had liked the kiss, and now he was telling her about a kiss from an older, prettier girl. And that hurt, dammit, even if she didn't want it to, it hurt. It was embarrassing and even a little cruel on his part as far as she was concerned.

"Well, because maybe she would tell someone, and you would hear about it from them, and that would be wrong." He looked away from her, his face flushing again. She wanted to run away from him, but didn't. She didn't want him to see her cry or anything else that would give him ammunition to tease her with later. "And, because I wanted to make sure you knew about it from me instead of from someone else. It wasn't a kiss like you and me had."

"It wasn't?" Here it came, the punch line to the joke that would leave her wanting to curl up and die, like she didn't already. She blinked fast several times, making good and damned sure that those tears of hers stayed away.

"No. I mean it was nice, but it was like a thank-you kiss. For being there when she needed someone to talk to." He moved in front of her and put one hand at her chin making her look up into his big blue eyes. "I wanted you to know that, and I wanted to tell you I liked your kiss better."

"You did?" She looked up at him, her eyes wide, the very concept that her kiss could even come close to being measured against a girl like April was puzzling. That hers was liked better than April's was beyond comprehension.

He leaned down, putting his lips to hers and kissing her softly. After half a second to let that sink in, she kissed back. His lips seemed even warmer in the cold air, though she couldn't figure how that was possible when her own nose was feeling like an ice cube. Their kiss was longer this time.

"Yeah," he said when the kiss finally broke, however reluctantly. "A lot better."

Jessie smiled again, her lips feeling tingly where they'd made contact with his. "Thanks."

He stole another quick kiss from her, just a peck, really, but it was nice, too. "Don't thank me; you started it." If there was a teasing quality in his voice, it was not a harsh one, nor meant to be cruel.

They started walking again, Jessie's step keeping up with his, though he walked with that same fast stride he always used. "Hey, Jessie?"

"Yeah?"

Dave looked over at her, his face uncertain and maybe just the littlest bit scared. "Is it okay if, I mean, can I tell people you're my girlfriend?"

She couldn't say words just then, so she nodded instead. As they walked again, the wind picked up and sent shivers through both of their bodies that had less to do with the cold than with the idea of being boyfriend and girlfriend. Somehow their hands wound up locked together and stayed that way for the rest of the trip.

XI

Jonathan Crowley met up with the visiting Parsons at Frannie's Donut Hut, which was the only place he'd found in the dumpy little town—aside from a dozen different fast-food joints—that actually served good food at a reasonable price. He liked it immediately. He did not, however, think much of the Parsons. She looked like a librarian trying not to look like a librarian, and he looked like a used car salesman on vacation. The only good point about the entire situation as far as he was concerned was that both of them looked like they'd just swallowed something cold, slimy, and possibly squirming. He knew it wasn't the food that brought about those looks, and that meant the two of them had actually had an encounter of some sort.

Maybe if he was lucky, they'd learned an important lesson in the process. The thought brought a quick flash of a smile to his face. He could hope.

Mary Parsons was doing her best to appear calm, which was not something she seemed capable of at the present time. Jacob Parsons looked like he was both on the edge of a panic attack and simultaneously ecstatic about something. Crowley figured one loud noise would probably have given the man a coronary on the spot. He wished he had an air horn to help Parsons along his way.

It was petty, true enough, but he just didn't like the two of them messing in things they liked to think they knew about. He also didn't like that they were doing it for a profit.

Still, he didn't do or say anything. He merely watched them and ate his meal in relative silence. The two of them kept whispering to each other, and he listened to snippets of the conversation. Some kid named Stan was having seizures at what passed for a hospital locally. He made note of the name and put it in his mental to-do list. Right now he was taking a short break from the research he'd been doing at the offices of the *Serenity Sentinel*, Not the most original name he'd ever heard for a newspaper, and he used the term kindly. Like most of the small towns he ran across, the paper was one half fluff and one half sports news. Now and then, just to spice things up, they actually had a story or two that was noteworthy. But in Serenity Falls, it was what wasn't written that normally seemed interesting. There wasn't a whole lot written about murders in the town, just as an example. And normally when it was there in the paper, it was on the fourth or fifth page and buried under a few community announcements. That was a rather interesting little tidbit in and of itself. Not surprising, not when you considered that damned near everyone in a town this size would have heard about it beforehand, but interesting just the same.

The "happy" little couple was still whispering, but they were roughly about as quiet as a herd of rutting rhinos in an echo chamber. They'd have had to work to actually be louder. He listened. Not that he really cared what they had to say—no one had yet invited him to the party, and that meant that he was just sort of listening to avoid the boredom. If he kept telling himself that, the frustration factor wasn't as bad.

Jonathan Crowley did not like waiting for something to happen. He liked getting into the middle of things and bringing a little order back to the world. Most of the time he could count on a phone call or a letter to invite him into the fray, but this time around he was just sort of stuck in idle waiting for anything worth noticing to happen and for that magic turn of words that would let him get involved.

In the meantime, he now knew more about Serenity Falls than any living and sane person should have to endure. The founding father of the town was just shy of a Nazi when it came to control, at least from what he could gather. The people who were with him apparently liked getting their routines given to them by the fruitcake who'd been in charge, and if he was reading between the lines as well as he figured he was, ye olde towne founder was very fond of boffing other women. He sent half of the men in town off for one reason or another, and the odds were pretty damned good that he'd paid visits aplenty to lonely wives who needed a good man to keep them company. It was something of a mystery as to whether or not they actually wanted the

company, but Crowley figured most of them gave it up for fear they'd
be seen as witches after the first of the lonely wives' club decided not
to play by the old bastard's rules.

And this man was celebrated as a local hero.

He was pondering this fact and chewing on a piece of potato from
his Yankee pot roast, when he noticed the Parsons looking over in his
direction with vaguely puzzled expressions. He looked back, leaving
his face deliberately blank, give or take the mastication of tuber in
gravy. Hell would freeze over before he would approach them first.

He had his principles, after all.

He drank back a sip of coffee, his eyes on the two worried faces that
looked over in his direction, and resisted the urge to tell them that
pictures last longer. His eyes met first Jacob Parsons's watery brown
eyes, and then the hazel orbs of Mary Parsons. He decided she was
attractive in a way, and suspected she was probably the sort who liked
to dress in leather and scold her hubby with a cat-o'-nine-tails. She just
had that sort of look to her. He had no problem seeing her in nine-inch
heels with her hair yanked back in a severe bun.

It was Mary who finally got the nerve to approach him. She walked
delicately, almost like a deer approaching a watering hole. He figured
one good, loud *"Boo "* and she'd have bolted for the door with all
pretense at elegance or sophistication shattered.

Out of a mixture of curiosity and mercy, he did not go boo. Mostly,
it was curiosity.

"Excuse me," she said, her voice nervous enough to make him have
to stifle a grin. "But would your name be Jonathan Crowley?"

"Guilty as charged. And you would be Mary Parsons. What can I
do for you today?"

She sighed with relief, her face relaxing enough to let him realize
that she was, indeed, rather attractive behind her deliberately no-
nonsense attire. "Thank God."

"Whatever for?"

"I'm sorry?"

"Never mind. What can I do for you?"

She leaned in close, her eyes wide and her brow wrinkled upward
in a way that showed her age. Next to her husband she was positively
young in appearance, but he knew she was in her thirties at the very

least. Worry made her age far more apparent. "I don't know how to say this..."

"Try being direct. My lunch is getting cold."

She looked at him for several seconds with an expression that said she knew he was being deliberately cold and that there was nothing she could do about it. "Are you the same Jonathan Crowley who dealt with some unpleasantries in New Haven two years ago?"

"Yes, I am. To answer your next question, I know what sort of work you do, and we are in related fields. Now, what can I do for you?"

"I need your help."

"What with?"

"It's...we're on a case, Jacob and me, and I don't think we can handle it alone. Would you be interested in taking part in the investigation?" She looked positively terrified to be speaking with him. Not for the usual reasons, but because he had a solid reputation in her chosen field. Okay, a nearly legendary reputation, truth be told.

"Are you asking for my help?"

"I just thought..."

"Are...you...asking...for...my...help?" He spoke slowly, as if she just might be an idiot. The flash of anger in her eyes told him she was not at all happy about the way he put that question.

"Yes."

"Fine. I'd be glad to."

She pulled back, eyes wide and face puzzled. "Just like that?"

"Sure."

"But you don't know what we're dealing with."

And now he grinned, and the look on her face stayed much the same, but her face grew a shade or two paler. "Don't be silly. Of course I know what you're working on." He took a leisurely sip of his coffee. "Why else would I be in this town?"

"I... How did you know?"

"Let's not worry about that. I'll tell you what. Why don't you take me to see your friend, Stan, over at the hospital. You can fill me in on the specifics while we're headed over there."

She nodded, apparently not trusting her mouth to make any sensible comments. Crowley rose from his seat, tossing a twenty down on the table to cover his bill. He stretched and sighed, feeling his muscles relax for the first time in days.

They were on their way five minutes later, and Jonathan Crowley smiled to himself as they made the short car ride. It was nice to finally be able to get serious about work again.

XII

Dave Pageant and Jessie Grant stared down at Stan in his hospital bed and knew despair. He'd looked much better the day before. Stan had been pale then, but now he looked like someone with a sick sense of humor had whitewashed every available spot where skin showed. His breathing had not sounded so wet before, nor had his body seemed so thin.

Dave had a look on his face that said he wanted to cry, which was not at all an expression anyone was used to seeing on him. It was a look Jessie wanted desperately to make go away. *If wishes were dollars, I'd be a millionaire.* Jessie had a lot of wishes; she just knew better than to expect them to come true. One wish she had was for Stan to get better. He was a nice guy, if a little flighty, and she liked him. The nice ones were always the ones who went through this sort of stuff. It never seemed to happen to someone like Andy or Perry Hamilton. Not, she decided, that she wished them any harm. She just wished they'd stop being so nasty all the time.

Stan was whispering in his sleep. His pale lips moved frantically, but only in the smallest increments. Whatever words he was saying sounded urgent, but even leaning in close, they couldn't make out what he uttered. The sounds that came from him were little more than hisses.

"What's he saying? I can't make it out."

Dave shrugged. "It could be almost anything."

The voice that came from behind them was almost jovial but still sent a shiver down Jessie's spine. It just seemed wrong for anyone to be that cheerful in a hospital room. "I think he said, 'Visiting hours are over; the doctor is in.'"

They both turned and looked at the man in the doorway. He was dressed in dark blue Dockers and a turtleneck that matched. He was average in almost every way, from his brown hair to his brown eyes and average face. But he was intimidating. Looking at him, Jessie felt like someone caught in the act of setting fire to the school by the principal.

The man smiled, and Jessie felt a deep-seated fear crawl through her body. Dave must have felt something like what she did, because he backed away a couple of steps.

"Hi, kiddies. I'm here to see Stan. What I have to say to him is strictly between the two of us. That means it's time for you to leave."

Dave looked at the man for a few seconds, his face as calm as ever, and shook his head. "Who are you, and why should I care what you want?"

"I'm a specialist."

"No you aren't."

"Really? What makes you say that?"

"I saw you the other day. If you were a specialist, you'd have already visited with Stan."

"I remember. You were on your way to church."

"Yeah, and you were picking grave mold off of headstones."

"Actually, I was sitting on the wall of the cemetery. The picking was just to keep my hands occupied."

"If you're a specialist, what's your specialty?"

"Paranormal relief for the spiritually challenged."

"Uh-hunh."

"No, really, it's what I do."

"Where'd you get your degree?"

"Which one?"

Jessie watched the interplay between the two of them, her eyes darting from one face to the other as they bantered back and forth. She couldn't decide if they were actually arguing or having a good time just faking it.

"The one that makes you a specialist in spiritually challenged paranormal medicine."

"Actually, it's a doctorate in parapsychology."

"I've seen a lot of shows on parapsychology. You weren't in any of them."

"I don't like to be a glory hound. I leave that to the financially challenged paranormal doctors."

Dave looked at him dubiously. "You don't look so rich to me."

"You don't look smart enough to understand what financially challenged means, but there it is."

"Okay. I'll give you that one."

"Good. Now get the hell out of the room, kid. I want to have a talk with Stan in private."

"Nope."

The stranger looked at Dave for several seconds, and while she could see by the way he was standing that Dave was not having fun with the examination, he didn't back down. "You're an annoying little thing, aren't you?"

"I've been called worse."

"I'm sure you have."

"I don't think I trust you. That means I don't think I'll leave you alone with Stan."

"I don't care what you think, you little twerp. Get the hell out of here."

"Or what?"

The man's smile grew broader, and he leaned in closer to Dave, who was having trouble keeping his voice steady. "I'll make you leave."

Dave started to say something back, and then his face went blank, like someone had cut all the muscles that made his mouth and jaw work, and he nodded. "Okay."

Dave stepped past Jessie without even looking at her. He walked out of the room, while Jessie looked on, baffled by his reaction. Dave never backed down unless he was convinced that he was wrong. It normally took a lot of convincing.

Jessie looked at the stranger, who had turned his gaze to her, and very carefully moved away from him, skirting the wall until she could reach the door. She felt his eyes on her the entire time and worried for a few seconds that he might try attacking her. His smile was rabid, and the look in his brown eyes, even hidden behind his rimless glasses, made her think he wouldn't mind biting her and taking out a chunk of flesh. That thought was enough to get her running.

She found Dave in the hallway, blinking his eyes and looking a little stunned. He looked over at her and squinted. "Did I just leave the room because he told me to?"

Jessie nodded, her eyes wide and worried. "Uh-hunh."

Dave looked at the doorway to the room and started toward the opening. Before he made it there, the door slammed shut.

Dave tried it a few times without success and looked back at Jessie. "How'd he do that?"

"Do what?"

"How'd he jam the door shut?"

"Maybe he locked it?"

"No. He couldn't have."

"Why not?"

"It's a hospital, Jessie. They don't have locks on the doors leading to the patients' rooms."

"Oh," she said. After a few moments of silence, she moved closer to Dave. "So what do we do now?"

Dave looked at her and then back at the door. "We go find a doctor. I'm not letting that creep mess with Stan."

There was only one problem with Dave's plan. It involved getting the attention of an adult. Sad fact of life: adults seldom take notice of children that aren't their own. It took almost ten minutes to make someone actually pay attention to them, and then there was the matter of just how urgent the problem might be. When they were done explaining the situation, the nurse they finally managed to get to listen to them scowled and placed meaty hands on even meatier hips. She insisted that they wait away from the room and then started moving in that direction, a large woman whose very steps seemed to make the floor of the building shake.

They sat down in the waiting area closest to Stan's room, sitting not in the chairs but on the tile floor. After they got as comfortable as they could on the cold linoleum, Dave's hand reached out and gripped hers loosely. She liked the way his hand felt, warm and strong, with a few calluses. The nurse was in plain view from where they sat, and they watched her as she tried to open the door to Dave's room, and as she finally gave up and moved with a strange rolling gait that seemed only to occur in truly large women. She moved much faster than Dave would have imagined possible.

Dave noticed an older couple sitting down the hallway in the waiting room proper. He pointed to them and told her they were the Parsons, the people he'd called on to come help Stan.

"Maybe they asked the creep in there to help them." Her voice sounded doubtful, even to her own ears.

"Maybe, but if they had to go to a guy like that, they can't be very good at what they do."

"Why?"

"'Cause that guy looks more like he should be teaching history classes than like he should be exorcising whatever got into Stan."

On the other side of a door that couldn't be locked, but was, they heard the soft sounds of voices talking in hushed tones. Then they heard silence. Before too much time had passed, they heard screams.

XIII

Jonathan Crowley looked down at the boy and knew right away that something was seriously wrong with him. Aside from the lack of color—he was as white as a new sheet and about as active—the kid's eyes were darting everywhere under lids closed almost desperately tight. He twitched almost constantly, and the parts of him that didn't twitch looked like they were giving the idea serious consideration.

He scanned the medical charts set at the foot of the bed and read the notes as carefully as he could. There wasn't a whole lot to go on. Every test the local doctors had tried came back negative, which was a good thing, but not very helpful.

He placed one hand on the boy's brow and closed his eyes. There was something going on deep inside, beneath the skin and under the bone. Something decidedly wrong was happening to Stan Long, and he decided it was time to discover what that something was.

"Wake up, Stan."

Stan Long's eyes shot open, and he looked over at Crowley with the sort of alertness that said he was fully focused on the man beside his hospital bed. Beside him his heart monitor continued on without any change.

"I'm awake."

"Good. My name is Jonathan. I'm here to help you if I can. Why don't you tell me what's been going on."

"I've got something wrong inside my head. The doctors think it's epilepsy, but I don't."

"What do you think it is, Stan?"

"I think there's people crawling around inside me."

"Really? What sort of people?"

"Dead people."

"Well, I can't say it'd be the first time I heard of such things without lying."

Stan smiled wanly for him at that.

"What makes you think they're dead?"

"Because they keep taking from me."

"Taking what?"

"I think they're maybe taking my soul. Or my life force, whatever you want to call it."

"Well, that's possible, too, but not something you run across every day."

"I don't know what else to call it." Stan shrugged, and the attention he'd been giving to Crowley seemed to fade out a bit. He was tired, and he was weakened by whatever was happening to him.

"Well, I don't think it's epilepsy. I think maybe you're a little closer to understanding what's going on than your doctors are. Which isn't to say that they're wrong, so much as they can't see what the problem is."

"What *is* the problem? Why are they messing with me? I didn't do anything to anyone." His voice hitched a bit toward the end, and his eyes watered.

"I don't think they're doing anything to you. I think you're just able to see them. And if you can see them, then they can see you." He ran his hand over the boy's forehead, felt the seething energies deep within his pale skull, and smiled briefly down at the boy. "If they are dead people, and I tend to think they are, then they've been waiting for someone like you for a long, long time."

"What do you mean?"

"Well, Stan, you're living in a strange little town. Most places I've been to have ghosts. Places that are supposed to be haunted. Do you have anything like that around here?"

"Yeah, Havenwood."

"Places like Havenwood." He nodded at Stan and ran his fingers through hair desperately in need of a good washing. "The thing is, Stan, I haven't felt any ghosts around here."

"Do you normally? Feel ghosts, I mean?"

"When I want to… No, when I need to." Crowley closed his eyes for a second, thinking back on the many times in the past when he'd needed to feel the spirits of the dead around him. Sometimes they were only faint whispers. Sometimes they did so much more than merely make noise. Despite himself, he felt a shiver run through his body. "Let's just say I can normally find a ghost when I need to and leave it at that. The thing about it is, I can't feel them here in this town. I've read up on Serenity, Stan. Want to know what I found?"

"Sure." He didn't really, but it was the polite thing to say.

"Serenity Falls has a penchant for murder, Stan. Your hometown has probably had more murders per capita than New York City and Jersey City combined."

"Um… What's a per capita?"

"It means when you compare numbers. If there's been one murder for every hundred people in New York City, then in comparison it should be the same for Serenity or even less. It isn't."

"One out of a hundred people in New York is murdered?"

"Well, that number's maybe a little high, but that's what per capita means. It's a way of averaging these things out."

"And we've got more murders on the average than they do in New York City?"

"Yes."

"And that's bad?"

"Well, it isn't exactly the sort of thing you want to brag about. It means a lot of people around these parts have been murdered. More than is the average for a town this size."

"So that means there should be more ghosts?"

"Something like that. But I can't sense them or see them or hear them. That's weird. Trust me."

"So why can I hear them?"

"Well, that's what I'm trying to figure out. And I think I might have the answer, but I need you to confirm a few things for me."

"Okay…" The boy sounded rather doubtful, which, under the circumstances, made perfect sense.

"Have you had a serious fever lately? Or maybe a close call where you got hurt?"

He nodded, his hair tickling across Crowley's palm. "I had to get CPR a few weeks ago. I almost drowned after seeing a ghost at Havenwood."

"What did you see?"

"An old man threw a head at me."

"Well, that's not something you see every day, now, is it?"

"No." The boy laughed a bit; it was weak, but it was a laugh.

"Okay, Stan. This is what I think I've got figured out. You had a near-death experience. Sometimes people going through that claim they can see or hear the dead afterward. I know that sounds weird, but there it is. I tend to think of it as getting your radio dials adjusted. It's like when you have the accident, whatever it might be, the wavelengths you work on are changed. When that happens, sometimes they change so you can see things that most people can't or won't see."

"So my radio dials have been reset for dead?" If the kid's eyes had been any bigger. Crowley figured they'd have just popped out of their sockets and rolled away.

"Something like that."

"How do I set them back?"

"Well, that's where it gets tricky, I can probably help you with that, but it's not going to be really comfortable."

The kid looked at him dubiously. "Does this involve touching me in weird places?"

"What?" Crowley blinked, taken completely off guard by the question. "Good God, no!" He calmed himself. The world had changed a lot over the years, but maybe sometimes the changes were for the better. At least the kid had the good sense to worry about that sort of thing. "I've got my hand on your forehead, that's the only place I need to touch."

"Okay. Just checking."

"Understood."

"What kind of not really comfortable are we talking about? I mean, pulling a tooth not really comfortable or getting kicked in the balls not really comfortable?"

"Well, probably the latter of the two. Are you always this blunt?"

"How often do you have a stranger come and tell you he's gonna make you all better but it might hurt a lot?" The kid's eyes were sharp and shiny against his pasty white skin.

"Point taken. Okay, kid, here's how it works. If I do it right, everything goes back to the way it was. That's a big if, because your mind might decide it likes being tuned in where it is. Anything I do to you will be temporary if that happens."

"And if you do it wrong?"

"Well, if I guess wrong, it's possible that you're actually possessed by one or more dead people, and they might take it personally that I decided to kick them out."

"Can a ghost really hurt a person?"

Crowley thought about a few times in the past when he'd made the mistake of angering the wrong entities from beyond the grave. "More than you ever want to know, Stan. More than you ever want to know."

"Why do you know so much about ghosts and stuff?"

"I tend to think it's best to know what you're facing whenever possible. I've done a lot of research."

Stan pondered that for several moments, his face almost blank. "So if ghosts are real, what about all the other stuff, like Bigfoot and the Loch Ness Monster?"

"I can say with great sincerity that I've never met either of them."

"Have you seen other monsters?"

"Oh yes. Many."

"Which was the worst?"

"Close your eyes, Stan. I'm going to try to make you better now." Some questions were best left unanswered, and that last one, as far as Crowley was concerned, was close to the top of the list.

Stan Long closed his eyes, and Jonathan Crowley did the same. Under his breath he muttered words not meant for human ears to hear, and he felt the jolt of energies that ran down into his hand and into the boy's scalp.

Stan arched up into the air again, another seizure, but this time caused by doorways in his perceptions being shut rather than opened. His lips peeled away from his teeth, and his face was set in a rictus of pain that made him look almost rabid.

And then Jonathan Crowley was blown out of his seat as easily as if King Kong had backhanded him. He felt himself thrown, felt the wall slam into his shoulder and back as he did his best to twist away from the worst of the impact. It was damned hard to breathe when someone had squeezed all the air out of his lungs, but he did his best and was able to gulp down air after a few seconds. His trademark smile did not show itself: there was too much at stake, including the life of a twelve-year-old boy.

When he could see well enough to look around again, Stan Long was standing up on the bed, his legs spread wide and his arms hanging loosely at his sides. The look on Stan's face told Crowley that while someone was watching him, it was not the boy he'd been touching a few seconds before.

"What do you want here?" The sound that issued from the boy's mouth came from dozens, maybe even hundreds of sources.

"You can get out of the boy, for starters. Then you can give me a reason not to blast all of you down into Hell."

"He is our vessel. He is our conduit back."

"Back from where?"

"The darkness."

"No, I don't think so. He's not really equipped to carry a whole bunch of extras."

"How did you summon us?"

"Old parlor trick I learned while playing poker."

"Do not mock us!"

"What? I'm supposed to cower in fear instead?" Crowley shrugged. "Not really my cup of tea." That didn't stop his knees from wanting to shake or make his heart stay steady in his chest. He was fairly certain he was dealing with the souls of some very, very pissed-off dead people, and he'd never taken well to having to handle mob scenes. Mobs tended to get angry en masse, and that was never a good thing.

"We have no argument with you. Don't make us decide that you need to be punished." It was just wrong, damn it, hearing those voices coming from such an innocent little face, even one that was currently spraying spittle.

Why couldn't it just be another all-powerful entity out to cause grief? They're easier to deal with. "Listen, here's the situation. I know you're all angry, and I'm sure you have your reasons, but this isn't going to work. You're killing the kid you're trying to work through, and it's my job to make sure that doesn't happen."

"Why?"

"It's what I do. I stop the bad monsters from making mincemeat out of the nice little schoolkids. We all have our jobs; that's mine."

"Who are you?" Stan's mouth sneered, but his eyes remained blank.

"Who are you?"

They didn't seem to like answering questions nearly as much as they enjoyed asking them. Most of Stan Long's body was exposed as the kid took a flying leap at him and tried very hard to drive a fist through his chest. Crowley slid out of the way, cursing how slowly he moved and the pain he realized was burning through his shoulder and rib cage. Already the itch was there, trying to work on mending him, but it took time in most cases, and he moved like a man as old as he really was. The boy was wearing hospital-issue booties and slid like a dog on a freshly waxed floor, scrabbling madly to stay on his feet. It would have been funny in some cases, but Crowley wasn't much in a mood to laugh.

He couldn't very well fight back without striking against Stan Long, and he didn't exactly feel comfortable about the whole notion. Two screaming little brats had recently died in a conflagration meant to take him out, and while he hadn't exactly been fond of either of them, he hadn't wanted them dead, either.

Guilt, even minor guilt, really put a downer on his day. It was so much easier when there weren't kids involved. Stan took his moment of contemplation in stride and swung an upholstered chair at his head. Crowley didn't quite manage to duck the second time around. His glasses went far off to the right side of the room, and his skull did its best to follow. Dark swirls did their best to take away his sight, but he shook them off and moved himself into a proper fighting position. Screw the twerp, whatever wanted to hurt him so badly was going down, and damn the consequences. He could always justify whatever happened by remembering that there were more lives at stake than his and Stan's.

He kept reminding himself of that fact as the kid came closer, swinging a solid wood chair like it weighed maybe as much as a baseball. The next swing at him was lower, but he managed to get out of the way. The kid's body emitted a howl of rage that shook the windows, and Crowley backed away, searching for the right angle to clear out the unwanted guests and leave Stan alive.

"You want to leave the kid alone. Trust me on that. Leave him, and your…existences will be a lot easier."

Stan moved like a scalded cat, heading straight for him with little or no concern for his own safety, arms swinging wildly. He should have looked comical, a scrawny prepubescent charging at him, but he didn't.

Crowley punched Stan Long in the face with a roundhouse that sent him backward and dropped him on his ass. His nose looked wrong, his lips were swelling quickly, and there was a slow trickle of blood streaming from his right nostril. The kid had looked better, and he'd also looked a whole lot less angry.

From outside Crowley could hear someone trying to turn the door handle. He said a word, and the door was blocked. He'd barred it before, but a little extra precaution never hurt. And as an added measure, he barred it against anything in the room leaving in that direction. Too many people who might make suitable, if unwilling, hosts for what was in the room with him. It would take an army to actually open the door unless he wanted it open. Someone small slammed against it anyway, determined to find out what all the noise was about.

Stan came at him again, and despite the pain he knew would cause, he spoke words long forgotten by humanity again. This time the effect was far more severe.

Stan Long fairly flew backward, his mouth stretched wide enough to make the skin tear slightly at the corners of his lips, his whole body arched back and straining. Crowley knew the kid would be in pain for a week after the two seizures he'd had but maybe this would keep him alive at least. If the fall didn't kill him. Stan slammed into the wall hard enough to dent the plaster. His whole body shook and bounced, and he screamed loud enough to rattle the windows.

They came out of him, streaming like a torrent of ice through the air, vague, blurred figures that writhed around each other like debris in a tornado. The temperature in the room plummeted, frost formed on the window in an instant, and the clothes on Crowley's body stiffened in the arctic chill. The seething, swirling column of figures hovered in the air above Stan Long's body, as vague as warm breath on a cold morning. The distorted, wavery mouths of the figures opened in a scream of rage that was loud enough to make Crowley want to cover his ears.

They weren't at all pleased with what he'd done. As a unit they tried to force themselves back into the boy's body. They were repelled, scattered and blown apart by the attempt. Like water knocked aside by a rock, the luminescent forms gathered back together again, shifting constantly around each other, scrabbling to the surface of the cloud they formed. They were together, but they were not unified.

But they faked it pretty well. A few of the misty shapes led the charge toward Crowley, and the rest took the hint and followed quickly. A swarm of angry spirits took aim and tried to force their way into him, hell-bent on revenge or just possibly a new body.

Crowley smiled. He knew what they were up against.

It took them a few seconds to catch on, moments when they were doing their very best to penetrate beyond his physical self and trying their best to push his consciousness out of the way to make room for their own. The human body could hold so very much if given the chance, could play host to enough energy to allow them their vessel, their means of reaching the goal they all shared.

For one brief instant their minds overlapped with Crowley's, For one minuscule fragment of time they became aware of what he was, what he felt, and what he could do. He, in turn, caught glimpses of what they were and their own agendas.

That fragment of time was more than they could bear. The energies—call them spirits, ghosts, revenants, they had once been human beings—backed away from what they saw and did more than that. They fled from the area, drawn back to the prison they'd escaped so very briefly. They had managed to escape once; they would try again.

Crowley saw them flee, saw them swim through whatever currents they managed to find and stream out the window, their passage freezing the glass to the point where it cracked and threatened to shatter.

He looked down at Stan Long's body where it lay, spotting the signs that told him the kid was still alive. Then he knelt down close to him and pressed his lips to the boy's ear, whispering softly. The pounding on the door was barely a distraction, but it was annoying, nonetheless. He lifted Stan into his arms and settled him on the bed. He had to work fast to get everything done, but he was used to that.

XIV

Lawrence Grey sat in his room, as he so often did, and looked out over the baseball field. The day was dreary and cold and overcast, but he'd still have paid money to be out there instead of stuck in the house. He'd gotten away with sneaking out two days earlier but feared he'd never manage it a second time. For one thing, his mother was at home, not out with her sister. For another thing, Lawrence was not used to the idea of disobeying his mother. It didn't sit well with him.

But, oh, my, how nice it had been. Sitting with Jessie and talking like a regular kid, actually being around someone other than his mother and his aunt and not getting in any trouble for it. The thought of it was like a fantasy that had come to life, however briefly. He wanted it back again. He wanted the freedom to come and go as he pleased, like all the other kids he knew. It wasn't that much to ask, was it?

Lawrence looked out the window and watched a couple of kids from his class getting together. There was Joey Lawrence, dressed in a thick winter coat the color of the midnight sky. His thick blond hair blew in the wind out there, and his face was ruddy from the cold. The person joining up with him was Becky Glass. She was a shy one, which meant that now and then she actually managed to smile and wave when he looked her way. She was nice. She was pretty. Like almost all of the girls he saw at school, Lawrence liked her.

Becky looked up at his window—another thing he was used to, like they felt the need to see if the loser was looking down at them again from his throne of losers—and waved. Because he liked the idea of any human contact more than the idea of being alone, he waved back. Becky smiled, and a second later Joey was waving at him, too. *Wow, a doubleheader; you don't see those every day.* He allowed himself a smile in return, and it grew wider when Becky's gesture changed from a wave to a *come join us* sweep of her arm.

He felt a warm flash move through him at the very idea of being invited anywhere. It was followed a few seconds later by the cold, heavy reality of his situation. To get out meant slipping past his mother, which was rather like sneaking into Fort Knox. He opened his window, feeling the chill of the outside air rush in and past him. Becky was almost twenty-five feet below him, and only ten or so feet away from the house. She and Joey had moved closer as they waited.

"Come on out, Lawrence. Come join us." Oh, those were words he'd longed to hear for so very long. He backed away from the window for a second, afraid he might actually cry or something. His eyes managed to sting a bit, but he was able to hold the waterworks at bay.

"I can't. My mom won't let me go out."

Becky looked up at him with her eyes bright and smiled. "Come out anyway. It's time to have fun for once."

Lawrence found himself nodding. The very idea of going out and having a good time with friends was enough to almost hypnotize him. His mind whirled around the possible ways to leave the house without being caught. There weren't many he could think of that he hadn't been caught trying some time in the past. It was not a good situation for him to be in.

But he didn't really question it. He knew he was going to leave the house. He knew it as surely as he knew his own name. The question of how was answered easily enough when he heard the sounds of the shower starting. His mother had one of her headaches, and those normally meant a long hot shower to help her relax. Luck had decided to be his friend for a change of pace, and he in turn decided to take full advantage of it.

He waited for three minutes, until he was certain that she was in the water and probably lathered up, and then he bolted for the back door. Caution made him slip out as quietly as he could, resisting the urge to just slam the door and run. Becky and Joey were outside in the cold, looking at him with smiles.

Joey patted him on the shoulder. "Glad you made it."

"M-me, too."

Becky reached over and took his hand in hers, the smile on her face enough to make him feel warm and fuzzy. "Let's get out of here. We want to get you back before you can get in trouble." Her hand was almost burning hot in the cold air, but it felt good. "We just want to show you something." Was he crazy, or did her words sound like they held the promise of something more than show-and-tell? He thought for all of a second and decided he was crazy. Either way, he wanted to see whatever it was she wanted to show him.

Lawrence shifted from foot to foot, part of him already afraid of what his mother would say if she found him outside, most of him wanting to go off with Becky and Joey. Well, to be honest, with Becky. There was something about her that was different, something he couldn't define, but that attracted him like a moth to a flame. Dangerous, yes, but so very, very bright at the same time.

In the end there was really no choice. Lawrence chose to escape his prison, if only for a short time. He let Becky lead him away from his house and looked back once to see what so many others had seen before: the window from which he looked out at the world. It was a lonely pane of glass on the back side of the house.

They didn't go far; they didn't have to. The area around the baseball diamond was thick with trees. Even stripped of most of their leaves by the storm the night before, there was plenty of cover to stop anyone from seeing them. "What did you guys want to show me, Becky?" He managed to say the words without stuttering, but it wasn't easy. Talking to girls wasn't easy for him; boys either, for that matter.

"I just wanted to give you something, Lawrence." She moved closer to him and he felt his heart start thudding like a bass drum. The pulse was fast and hard and ran through his entire body. He was about to ask what when she planted her lips against his.

For as long as he could remember in his short life, Lawrence had wondered what it would feel like to be kissed by a girl. Not a peck on the cheek or a smack on the lips, but truly, genuinely kissed. Her lips were soft and warm, a perfect counterpoint to the cold. Her breath across his skin was as soft as a lover's caress. The feel of her body against his, even through several layers of clothing, was like magic.

It was a wonderful feeling, better by far than he'd ever imagined.

It was also the last sensation he ever knew before the force hiding inside of her tore his soul away and made itself comfortable within him. Lawrence Grey closed his eyes and died in a moment of contentment. What took his place opened its eyes and smiled lovingly at Becky and Joey.

Children made such good pawns...

Chapter Twelve

I

Mike Blake settled in behind the desk that was now his and felt a bit of awe at the notion. He'd had a smaller desk back at the bank, and a smaller paycheck. And that, he'd long since accepted, was supposed to be the highlight of his business life. The best he'd been hoping for when he'd started working at the house was enough to help him pay his bills and slowly crawl out of debt.

And now, this. All of this. All of this, and Amelia, too.

He was happy again, and the thought scared the hell out of him. Maybe he was getting paranoid in his old age, but he didn't think so. Happiness, allowing happiness, that was the sort of thing that could screw you up.

Still, the feeling wouldn't go away. Whenever he thought about the strange warm glow he'd forgotten all about, he merely had to look over at Amelia, and his doubts blew apart. Was it love? He wasn't certain, but it was at least a strong infatuation, and that would do in a pinch.

Amelia looked at him with eyes that were even prettier than usual because of the smile on her face. She looked like a kid at Christmas, despite the fact that she was the one giving out the gifts. "Do you like it? The office I mean?"

"Of course I do. But don't you think it's a bit…excessive?"

"No, silly. I think it suits you."

"I feel like I'm playing make-believe in my father's den."

"Really?"

"Yeah, but it's a nice feeling."

She moved over to him and leaned against the edge of the desk. "I hope so. I like it when you feel nice." Her leg slid up against his in a delightfully flirtatious way. "But then, I think you always feel nice."

Mike felt himself blush, which was rather an unusual sensation for him. He hadn't been much of a blusher at any point in his life, but Amelia could do that to him. He wasn't quite sure how, but she could. "That's not a good way to coax work out of me..."

"No real work to be done for a few more days..."

He ran his callused hand up her calf and to her knee, tugging her closer to him. "Well, in that case..."

Amelia got that little half-teasing smile on her face and slid forward. She was about to kiss his mouth when the entire house shook. It wasn't a light vibration but more like a sonic boom detonating directly over the roof of the sprawling old mansion. The few pictures she'd placed on the refurbished walls slid and rattled, and several of the windows shivered enough to make him worry about them breaking.

Amelia lost her balance and fell into him, her body pressed against his in a way that he didn't really mind at all. He placed his hands on her shoulders to help steady her, and she smiled her thanks. By the time she'd righted herself, the shock wave had ended.

"Okay, that was different." He looked around the room, checking to see if there was any damage. There was none that was visible.

"If I didn't know better, I'd almost think that'd been an earthquake."

"What makes you so sure it wasn't?"

"Do you honestly think my father would have purchased the quarry without doing some serious surveys of the land first? It just isn't probable to have an earthquake here."

"Why not?"

"Solid bedrock, except for a few places where the waters move underground." She smiled. "And those aren't likely to cave in; they're filled with water."

"Well, it did get cold, maybe the water froze and made the bedrock shift."

"Maybe it's old man Blackwell's ghost, telling us we shouldn't make whoopee in his house." The smile on her face made light of the comment.

"Maybe he should mind his own damned business." He grinned back, once again running his hands over her calves.

"Maybe he should," she said as she slid into his lap. Even fully clothed, she felt like a perfect fit against him. Somehow she managed to wrap her legs around him, her knees resting against the armrests. Her mouth did wonderful things to his neck that left him completely and utterly distracted, but in the nicest possible way. She ground herself against him slowly, and he responded very quickly.

His hand was sliding into her blouse when he heard the first whisper of his name. Mike did his best to ignore it, his body and mind in complete agreement that taking Amelia on the desk or anywhere else for that matter was far more important than any possible distractions.

"Mike...Mike...help me..."

The sound finally got to him enough to make him force his eyes away from Amelia's face. He looked over and saw Amy, his Amy, standing at the other side of the room. She stood with her arms wrapped around her chest, shivering, her bare flesh almost blue with cold. Her eyes, her sweet, wonderful eyes looked at him with such an expression of misery that he felt his heart break as surely as it had the morning he found she'd been murdered.

Mike looked at Amy, his heart almost stopping before it suddenly started slamming frantically against his rib cage. He tried to speak, but his mouth could only hang open and emit a weak gasp of shock.

Amelia must have sensed that something was wrong. She stopped kissing his neck long enough to ask him if he was okay.

Mike couldn't answer her. He was fixated on the figure across the room, so very much like the woman straddling him and yet so frighteningly different.

Amy moved closer, her legs not really taking her forward so much as she simply seemed to drift in his direction. Mike felt himself moan deep in his chest, the sound drowned out by his own thundering pulse. Amy reached out a hand, her eyes begging him to come to her, to touch her and protect her from something horrible.

"Mike, please make it stop. I can't stand it any longer..." And oh, Lord above, her voice was a brand across his mind, a searing, agonizing scream of grief that sent shivers running through his entire body. He couldn't catch his breath. He simply couldn't make his lungs draw in air. His eyes were frozen on Amy, even as she came closer and closer, until she was on the other side of the desk, her face almost a mirror of Amelia's, though the expressions were completely different. Amelia looked at him with worry, while Amy looked at him with such sorrow, such infinite sadness that he wanted to weep, even as he wanted nothing more than to reach out to her and comfort her, steal away whatever it was that left her so wounded.

"Mike? Honey? What's wrong?" Amelia's voice spoke softly, her concern as obvious as her unexplained attraction to him.

But counterpoint to her voice was Amy's fearful tones. *"Mike, it's happening again. Please make it stop... Make it stop...make it stop, make it stop, make it stop!"* Her voice rose in fear, her eyes looked to him, begging him to save her from whatever it was she felt happening.

And then he saw it take place. He saw the violation of his wife in vivid detail. There was no one but her on the other side of the desk, but he saw the wounds that suddenly lashed across her body, jagged cuts that gored away her porcelain flesh, tearing her perfection into shreds. He saw every wound as it happened, peeling her skin away in small ribbons, carving her perfect breasts apart and stretching her nerves like delicate roots being torn from the ground of her body.

And even as Amelia tried to get his attention, tried to make him respond to her queries by waving her hands before his eyes, he heard Amy's long, drawn-out shrieks of pain and damnation. He heard his wife's voice calling to him, begging him to make it stop.

He watched Amy die before his eyes and, somewhere along the way, it was just possible that he lost his sanity.

He watched Amy die, and then he knew nothing but darkness, and the silence that kept him was bliss.

After a time, who could say just how long, he allowed himself to think again, to see Amy's sweet face in his mind's eye and to remember the touch of her hand in his, the press of her lips against him. He allowed himself to think of the faint scent of lilac on her skin when she came from the shower and into the bedroom the two of them shared.

He let himself remember her laughter and the soft sighs she made when he'd satisfied her. He remembered the way her eyes always lit up when she smiled, and the way she was always embarrassed when a movie got to her and made her cry real tears for imaginary characters.

He let himself remember her, and all that he loved about her, both her good points and her bad. And he tried in vain to take away the memory of her body being torn away from her sweet, magical soul.

And then he awoke to Amelia's face above him. Her eyes were red from crying, her skin pale as if from shock. Behind her, towering almost like an oak tree above him, was Jonathan Crowley. The light of the day was long gone, and the man's face was hidden in shadows. Still, he sensed amusement in the expression he couldn't see. Or he thought he did, at least. Just at that time he could barely make sense of his thoughts well enough to know what was real and what he was imagining.

Amelia leaned down and kissed his face gently, somewhere between five and a thousand times. He pulled her closer in his arms and held her tightly.

When they finally broke their embrace, Jonathan Crowley reached down and helped him to his feet. He would have liked to feel indignant about the offered help, but frankly he needed it. He could barely manage to stand once he was on his feet.

Crowley helped him to the couch in the living room of Havenwood, and Amelia brought him coffee. She asked him a dozen times if he felt all right, and he answered positively on each occasion, though in truth he wasn't sure of much of anything just then.

When she had finally decided that he wasn't going to have another episode, she sat next to him on the couch, taking his hand in hers and squeezing tightly. Jonathan Crowley watched the entire display without saying a word. When it was done, he pulled over one of the high-backed chairs that sat nearby and settled into it with the grace of a cat.

The man leaned forward, his brown eyes glittering in the light of the single lamp that burned in the room. His face was calm, almost sedate. Not at all the smirking expression Mike was used to seeing. "Tell me about your wife, Mike. Tell me everything you know or think you know about how she died." It wasn't a request; it was a demand.

"What?" He frowned. He didn't want to talk about her death, not now, not ever. He wanted to think of her at peace. "Why do you want to know about Amy's death?"

"Why else? Because I want to catch her killer."

Mike started talking, slowly at first, and then faster to try to get past the painful parts. Crowley listened, never saying a word.

II

April Long lay on her bed, her body curled into a nearly fetal position, her mind drifting almost feverishly over the last twenty-four hours. Everything had almost seemed like it could maybe start going right. Stan had been improving, and the doctors spoke of letting him come home; her parents had been actually civil a few times, as opposed to merely quiet; Terri had come back to school, and if she was acting a little differently, that was to be expected. Everything should have been getting better, because enough had turned into shit just lately to make her want to scream.

And then she came home yesterday to find her father waiting for her in the family room. He sat on the couch and leaned back against one armrest in a way that told her it was going to be a rough session. He always managed to look more casual than usual when he was going to unload with both barrels.

So, knowing she'd done something wrong, she sat down on the other end of the couch and looked his way sheepishly. It was best not to speak until he wanted her to. She'd learned that lesson a long time ago.

He handed her a worn, folded piece of paper, and she took it from him, completely unaware of what lay hidden within it. His words were calm and cool, and each one of them sent shivers through her. "I found this a while back. It was a returned letter. I thought your mother had written it until this morning, when I finally confronted her about it." He paused, and April unfolded the paper slowly. She recognized her own handwriting instantly, and when she saw what she'd written, she knew she was in deep, deep trouble.

"I—Daddy, I wrote this a long time ago..."

"I know. You were what? Fourteen at the time, April?" His voice was so calm, so sedate, and she knew there was trouble coming, knew he was just a single slipup away from exploding.

Was she supposed to be ashamed? She wasn't. She'd loved him. Even if he'd been old enough to be her father, she'd loved him. And he'd loved her. She knew he had, knew it with all of her heart and soul. But she couldn't very well say that, could she? Not without getting herself in trouble even further than she already was. Hot tears burned her eyes, and she blinked them away before they could spill.

"I was fourteen when it started. It stopped just before he left town."

"I read that letter, April..." His face was turning red, and she saw him close his eyes, force himself to take deep breaths and slowly, oh, so slowly, calm down. "How many times did he touch you that way?"

"Just once, Daddy. I swear it. Right before he left town, because I wanted...I wanted him to remember me." The words were lies, but the feelings were true. She felt the tears come again, and this time she did not stop them. She closed her eyes and started crying, remembering her lover's face and the way he'd always made her feel like she was the most important person in the world. Oh, just thinking about him hurt, started the eruption of butterflies in her stomach and the damned feeling of falling away from herself.

When he'd gone away she'd burned her only two pictures of him. She didn't want to remember what he looked like or how he smelled or the touch of his body against hers. She'd wanted to hate him instead. But she couldn't. In the end she wrote him a letter, a few pages of notes to him to let him know that she would always love him, even if he was never going to come back to her.

And then she got stupid and actually mailed the letter, even knowing that he had moved, that the address would do no good. She hoped and prayed that it would be forwarded to him and that he would have a final reminder of her.

She never thought it would come back to the house. Never imagined that her father would open the letter meant for the one man in the whole world who meant more to her than he did.

He reached out to her, her father, the man who'd always been there, always taken care of her. His hand reached out, and she felt his thumb brush away her tears with a touch as delicate as a feather. When she opened her eyes and looked at him, she saw not anger but a deep, painful grief.

She cried all the harder for that and held out her arms and felt him pull her closer as she finally let herself cry for all that she had lost when her first love left town and took her innocence with him.

How long he held her was something she didn't know. She cried herself to sleep in her father's arms and woke up the next morning feeling as if a burden had been lifted from her.

And then as the day progressed, the burdens multiplied. For a few brief hours she'd thought all was going to be better, but it wasn't working out that way at all. Though the details were sketchy, something had gone wrong at the hospital earlier in the day. Stan was recovering nicely, was doing very well, in fact, but the stress was still there. Both her mother and her father were feeling the stress, too, and if there had been any easing of the tensions between them because of her unpleasant and unintentional revelation, both of her folks were hiding it damned well. They still spoke to each other in overly polite terms and with faces that had strained smiles on them. She could practically hear the grinding of their teeth.

Their tensions were not making life at home peaceful. But far worse was that she now knew she was the cause of those tensions—perhaps peripherally, perhaps not, depending on perspective—but one way or another, she was at the heart of the problem. It was her sleeping with an older man and then writing the letter that came back that was the root of the trouble. Her father hadn't said that. He didn't have to. She knew. He'd thought her mother wrote that letter. Her mom, with another man…it wasn't even a possibility, but then, until yesterday the idea had seemed more plausible to her father.

Jason Long was not a man of action. That was a simple fact of life. He was to cautious what King Kong was to big, hairy apes. On a few occasions, she and Terri—well, Terri, but she'd laughed along with the comments—had cracked jokes about what he might be like in bed: normally the end result was both of them giggling about him being as hot and erotic as a Vulcan during a debate. It was sort of easy to imagine him calmly explaining what he was about to do in the sack, and it was funny. Or at least it had been at the time. Now it wasn't funny at all. Because he wasn't very good at being an emotionless being, apparently. He let it all sink in, and he stewed over that letter he was so certain had been written by his wife. Not just a little, either; he fretted and worried and grew distant.

And Mom? Well, Mom was enough like April that she could guess what was going through her mind: her husband had been thinking she was cheating on him. He'd been thinking it for months on end, and he'd never said a word. But April had seen the looks on Adrienne Long's face; she could imagine the doubts that sat in the back of her mind and grew stronger and stronger. How could a man who claimed to love her not trust her enough to actually ask her about it? With one stupid question everything could have been solved.

There was a rift growing between her parents, and the more she thought about it, the worse she felt. That gaping wound in their relationship was wholly her fault. There was no denying it. Oh, she could look to her father and claim that his weakness, his lack of the guts to actually confront his wife was the problem, but she knew better. It would have just come to a head sooner. The end result would have been the same. At least as far as she could figure. Perhaps with more experience in her life she would have seen things differently.

She fidgeted with her sheet, thinking about how fucked up her world had become. It wasn't getting better. That was just an illusion. Nothing had been right since Stephen left. *There, I finally said his name. It doesn't hurt all that much. Not more than it would hurt to saw my arm off anyway.* She doubted anything would ever be right again.

It's easy to blame her youth for the way she felt. April Long was only fourteen when she fell in love with a man twenty years older. But that was almost too easy, and certainly not at all an accurate assessment of the facts. Emotions do not care about age. They care about being noticed and nourished. If what she felt for Stephen Wilkins wasn't the dictionary definition of love, it was as close as she'd ever come, and it hurt to think about him. Hurt to remember his touch, his sweet, special smile, and the way he laughed at her stupid little jokes. It tore her up to remember how he treated her not as a kid or even as a teenager, but as an adult. He didn't condescend to her. He didn't roll his eyes when she said something; he didn't feel like he was having to suffer through her company. He didn't, *no he hadn't*, ever felt the need to leave the room when she was irritable or just having a bad day. He had never once treated her like she was a natural disaster waiting to happen.

He was always happy to see me. He always liked being with me, even when I wasn't good company. He maybe even loved me as much as he said he did.

April felt the tears start again, and she let them flow. It didn't seem to take much of the burden from her soul to cry, but it helped a little bit. It took the edge off at least.

Downstairs, almost as a counterpoint to the storm of feelings washing through her, she heard only the silence of her parents' lack of communication. Outside, she heard Beau start barking and baying at something. His voice called out with a strange sort of sadness to it, and she thought for a second that at least the dog understood how she felt.

Then the tone of his barks changed. He stopped sounding lonely and started sounding like he was calling out a warning to stay away. He sounded both menacing and frantic, his voice shifting upward in octaves and a lower, deep growl coming from him at the same time. But that wasn't really possible, was it?

No, she didn't think a single dog could make both noises simultaneously, so she looked out her bedroom window to investigate. She looked down and to the side of the house where Beau was normally chained to the post her father had placed there years before, back when he was a puppy and the very notion had seemed ludicrous. The big old amiable Saint Bernard was still chained to his metal post, the heavy links of his leash straining as he leaped again and again toward something just out of sight. The post was actually bending, and that was something April would have thought almost impossible. She would have never guessed that the dog had anywhere near that much strength. Even when she was walking him and he saw a squirrel—his favorite animal to chase—he never gave any indication that he was anywhere near that strong. It was like he knew the family members wanted him to behave, so he just sort of played at giving a run at the rodent of the day.

But now whatever waited just around the corner was not only making him want to give chase, it was apparently pissing him off. She'd never in her life seen Beau with his teeth bared that way, never seen him strain so ferociously against the binds that held him. She started to get up, ready to go down and see what was bothering him so much, but a tiny voice told her that might not be a good idea. Beau wasn't acting at all like himself. She thought about that movie *Cujo*—it was easy to laugh when it was a big dog on TV; it was a whole different story when the big dog was in your yard and looking ready to, say, eat a car or two.

And then she saw the source of Beau's sudden defensive warnings and understood: there were other dogs on his property, not just a few, either, but a big pack of them. She tried counting the animals and gave up when they totaled over a dozen. Instead of trying her luck, April reached for her phone extension and called the constables' offices on the speed dial.

"Constable Barnes, how may I help you?" The voice was deep and amiable, and April all but panicked when she heard it.

"Constable, there's a pack of dogs outside my house, they're starting to circle our dog, and we need help now!"

He read her address back to her and confirmed that it was, indeed, the right location. Then, warning her to stay inside, he promised they'd be there as soon as possible. April thanked him and hung up the phone, moving over to the window. It looked like a standoff of some kind, with the pack doing a slow creep toward Beau, and the massive Saint Bernard in turn lunging at the ones that got too close, driving them backward.

April ran down the stairs quickly, wanting to let her folks know about the troubles. She needn't have bothered. Her father was carefully loading his shotgun with hunting shells. His face was grim and a little pale, his hands shaking a bit, but he was calm. His hands were sure enough to load the red cases into the weapon.

"Daddy, I called the police already. They're on their way. Maybe you should wait for them to get here."

He nodded. "I will, but only if those dogs stay away from Beau. I'm not going to leave him out there to get torn up."

Adrienne looked ready to go out there with only her bare hands. She'd always been the one to gripe the most when Beau did something wrong, and the first to spoil him rotten with snacks at the table. It was the way she was, the way she'd always been. Now she was ready to go through the porch door and kick the bejeezus out of several very mean-looking dogs. April was just about ready to help her, too.

From a long distance away, she heard the sound of sirens, a faint, muted warble that still managed to make it through the sounds of growls from outside. The sound seemed to spur on the pack of dogs, making them bolder, as if they knew their time was limited. They moved in closer to Beau, whose barks sounded strained and breaking as much as a nervous boy's voice during the height of puberty.

The chain that held Beau in place was taut, his full weight thrown against it until he was almost standing upright. The links vibrated with every thrust of his body, and April could swear she was seeing spaces between a few of them. The links were starting to break apart, and if Beau got free, there would be a massacre.

"Daddy… I think Beau's gonna break free…" She barely recognized her own voice. It wavered drastically, and she felt a strong urge to pee. "Oh, God, Daddy, he's getting loose!"

Beau slammed himself against the chain again, and this time she could see the links stretching. There was no way the police would make it in time. The hounds moving in on Beau were getting braver, almost as if they were deliberately taunting him. Each time he coiled himself up to spring again, a few of the dogs would lunge in close, snapping at his legs, and then scurry back as soon as he made his move toward them. It was like watching a sadistic gaggle of children picking on a man in chains: they were all smaller than him, but they were vicious and cruel in their taunts, and he was severely handicapped by the leash around his neck.

Beau fell back from his latest failed leap, and April moved toward the door, screaming her dismay as two of the dogs moved in faster than before, their teeth bared and their jaws snapping. One of them managed a mouthful of fur as Beau got back up, and then they backed away again.

Her father moved past her, pushing open the sliding glass door and aiming his shotgun at the pack of dogs. April wanted to scream again but couldn't seem to gather the breath to manage the feat.

Everything exploded at once. Her father pulled the trigger on his twelve-gauge rifle: the sound of the shot was loud enough to half deafen April. Beau flew up and out from the post again, this time going farther than he had before as the chain finally surrendered to his repeated attempts to escape.

One of the dogs flew backward, almost as if someone had yanked at an invisible leash around its neck. A plume of dark, reddish-brown filth exploded away from the dog's body as it was lifted from the ground.

Beau didn't merely land on his paws; he landed on one of the bigger dogs on his paws. Just over two hundred pounds of very irate Saint Bernard slammed into the bloodhound with enough force to send them both rolling across the lawn, and Beau fairly wrapped his jaws around the smaller dog's face, shaking his body and head violently, even as they landed and rolled. He drew back from the animal with a sizable flap of its muzzle between his teeth, and the other animal rolled away until it could regain its feet.

Neither of the wounded dogs stopped. One rose weakly back to all fours, with a hole large enough for her to put a hand through showing clearly in its side. The other, raw, wet muscle- and-sinew-covered bone exposed to the air, snarled and headed straight for Beau like a heat-seeking missile after a fireball. Beau was ready, his bloodied fangs bared in a savage grin and his body low to the ground, prepared to pounce.

One on one, he might have been okay. But the rest of the pack wasn't willing to sit back and let a single member have all the fun. They charged at him like a single beast with multiple heads, moving over the family dog, swarming him like vermin in a feeding frenzy. One second Beau was standing like a lion ready to hunt down a gazelle, and the next he was buried under an undulating mountain of fur and teeth.

April screamed again, finally finding her voice, even as her father pulled the trigger a second time. The air thundered, and another of the pack did an acrobatic flip from its position, this time trailing a ruined leg in its wake. It growled and snapped at the wound but showed no sign of feeling the injury. The beast seemed inconvenienced, not mortally wounded.

From somewhere deep in the swarming flesh that covered him, Beau started making a sound like nothing she'd ever heard before. It was a high-pitched shrieking wail of agony, broken into desperate barks. April felt her heart fall and her skin creep along her back and neck as it goose-pimpled. She felt her own face draw up into a mask of dread and saw one of the dogs lift its bloodied muzzle, snapping at warm flesh that bled far brighter than what any of the pack members had spilled from their injuries.

Jason Long roared a challenge of his own and moved out of the doorway into the yard, his shotgun aimed at the pack that tore into Beau. He pumped the action and pulled the trigger—his entire torso vibrating with the violent kick of the weapon each time—then did it three more times. The sounds were enough to make her ears hurt, but April wanted to cheer when she saw the dogs struck and thrown by each blast from the weapon. Part of her thrilled to watch them fall, and part of her wailed to think of poor Beau, whose screams were more heart-wrenching than anything she could ever remember.

Her father fired three more times, and then he pulled the trigger on an empty chamber. The look on his face would have been funny if not for the fact that he was now out in the yard with the pack of monsters that was on top of poor Beau. Right then, there was nothing funny about it at all, and it got even less humorous when five of the dogs turned and moved his way in a fast lunge.

Jason Long pulled the trigger three more times, his face first puzzled and then completely terrified. He flipped the shotgun in his hands, grabbing hold of the barrel and wincing from the heat of it, as the first of the dogs leaped for his throat.

Babe Ruth would have been proud of the way he swung his makeshift bat. His entire torso and body weight were behind the swing. The dog's whole body snapped hard to the left as the butt of the shotgun landed on its face. Had he been a second later, the animal would have torn his throat away.

The next dog didn't wait for him to catch his balance but instead body slammed him in the ribs and sent him staggering. The animal crashed down over him, its legs spread wide and its face only inches from his. Jason Long screamed, his eyes wide and his face panicky.

April screamed with him, and her mother screamed, too.

III

Tom Norris sort of liked the man next to him, when he wasn't being mildly terrified of him. Victor Barnes was an amiable sort of giant, but his sheer size intimidated. Tom wasn't used to being intimidated by much of anything. That was one of the reasons he became a constable in the first place. Not a big man himself, he was, in all honesty, a little too much like Barney Fife for his own comfort. He wasn't quite that thick, didn't try to flaunt his authority—and when he caught himself doing it he curbed the tendency as quickly as he could—and never took it for granted that a badge made him any tougher than he would have been without it. No, it was more that he was built like Don Knotts and had the same sort of hound dog face. He was comfortable enough about his looks and knew he could handle himself in a fight, but there was still something about a man as big as the one next to him that made him just a little happier to be carrying a firearm.

There was also something about the way Barnes carried himself that made him feel just a little less confident. It wasn't just that he was a big man—which he was—it was that air of confidence that only comes from long years of dealing with combat situations. He'd seen a few men come back from Korea and Vietnam with that sort of quiet swagger. It was a predatory way of walking that wasn't exactly a challenge so much as it was a signal not to fuck with the person using it. Barnes had that sort of stride. So did the freak from the bar fight, but with John Crowley it *was* a challenge, hell, even a taunt.

But at the present time it wasn't Vic's size that was scaring Tom. It was his driving skills. They'd all been properly worried about the damned dogs making a comeback around the area. Despite the hopes that the animals might have moved on, the feral pack was still around and apparently had no problem with the idea of moving through a neighborhood.

Barnes was all but hunched over the wheel of the truck he drove around in, his eyes moving everywhere around the area while Tom gave him directions. Tom had both of their shotguns between his legs, with the barrels pointed at the windshield. The safeties were on, but just to be safe… He didn't much like the idea of getting his head blown off.

Barnes looked over at him, his deep voice more tense than usual. "I can see them. Hang on to your ass."

Before Tom could even ask why, or spot the pack himself for that matter, Barnes wrenched the steering wheel hard to the right, sending them over the curb and off the road. The heavy tires on the truck caught wet grass and slipped a bit before gaining traction. Tom let out a squawk of surprise and then grabbed hold of the dashboard with one hand. There was a damned steep hill behind the two-story house they were heading for. It looked like it would be perfect for sledding down in winter and little else.

Tom squawked again when he saw Barnes aiming the massive truck straight down the grassy slope. "You're gonna get us both killed!" The truck skidded heavily, Tom's vision blurring from the vibrations and jostling.

"Not right now, Tom. We've got dogs to kill first."

The entire truck started into a nasty slide down the hill, gravity and the slick lawn fighting against the tires' traction. Barnes fought and cursed the slide, aiming the truck at the house below, and finally Tom saw why. There were over a dozen dogs down there, and they were not hanging around for scraps. They were hunting. Fresh meat for a kill, and one of the people there was already down.

Jason Long was trying to crawl away from one of the animals, crab-walking backward as the creature snapped at his face. It didn't look like he'd been chewed on yet, but it was only a matter of seconds.

Victor Barnes hissed obscenities as the truck slowed, yanking the wheel aiming at the larger pack. The dogs started to scatter, but a few were too slow. Two of them were crushed under the tires of the vehicle as it came to a stop. Their yelps and shrieks were an unholy sound, and Tom felt ill. They were only animals following their instincts, and he hated to see them killed.

On the other hand, he hated the way they were looking at him a lot more. He pushed one of the shotguns at Barnes and cocked the other. His face set in determination, his lips pressed together and his jaws clenched tightly. Barnes almost tore his door off the hinges getting out of the truck. He roared loudly and fired a shot in the air. The dogs, even those that had been looking elsewhere, turned sharply toward him. They returned the growled challenge and moved toward them like a rabid wave of fur.

Both men aimed and fired, aimed and fired, aimed and fired, knowing full well that their lives depended on moving fast. Jason Long ran back to his house, the dog having forgotten him for the idea of taking on a new challenge. Inside the house, April and Adrienne Long were teary-eyed, screaming for him to move faster.

Tom kept firing, though a sick, heavy dread began filling him. The dogs kept getting back up. That wasn't possible. They were dead, shot to hell and back, bleeding a brackish fluid that had more in common with motor oil than with blood.

Barnes was out of shells and went for his revolver, screaming like a berserker. One of the dogs took a leap at him and sank its fangs deep into the meat of his forearm, savaging at the flesh and snapping bloodied jaws together like a hyperactive Cuisinart. Barnes swung his entire body around, taking the dog through the air until he rammed it into the hood of the truck.

Tom looked down as he felt something pulling at his leg. He let out a scream of his own when he realized it was one of the dogs still pinned under the truck. He leaped backward and unloaded four shells into the head of the undying thing, vaporizing the flesh and leaving a thick, foul-smelling puddle of ruined bone and fur in his wake. That one stopped moving, but it wasn't really a good sign. He'd used the last of his shells.

"Oh shit." He was out of ammunition, and the rest of the dogs were looking like they still wanted a fresh meal. He felt heaviness in his bladder, and for a moment the idea that he might piss himself took most of his fear of the pack of hunting dogs out of his mind. *Bad enough to get ripped apart, but what the hell would Mom say if she found out I hadn't changed my underwear like she always told me to?* He started giggling, hysteria taking hold of his common sense, and he made himself stop with an effort. Wild laughter wasn't going to get him out of this situation.

He pulled his pistol, desperate to find a way out of the deep shit he was in. In the truck, the radio crackled out a query, but he couldn't hear just what it was. He was a little too busy trying to stay alive to care. Victor Barnes looked over his way and then back at the dog that refused to let go of his arm. His face was red, his body sweating heavily, and a large wet stain was spilling from around the place where the broken, bloodied, and still-savage mutt was chewing on his arm. "Get inside the house; protect them."

"No way to get to them!" The dogs were between the constables and the doorway to the house. He figured he could make it over there if he had a tank, but that was about it.

"Just do it, Norris! Get the fuck out of here!"

"Where the hell am I supposed to go, Vic?" His voice shook hard, and he wondered in a distant way why the animals didn't just get it over with and attack. They were circling around and around, like they were looking for an opening, but there was nothing stopping them that he could see. "I don't really think they're just gonna sit here and let me walk on by!"

"Then take the fucking truck!" Barnes swung the dog on his arm up into the air, his muscles corded from the effort, and then brought it down again, this time hard enough to break several bones. The thing stopped attacking and let out a muted yelp, letting go of the constable's forearm and quivering. Just then, with a look of rage on his face, Barnes looked scarier than the dogs.

He was going to argue with the man anyway. There was no way in hell he was trying his luck with the pack, and no way he was going to leave his fellow officer to handle them all by himself, either. But then the decision was taken out of his hands. He heard a sharp, piercing whistle come from up over the hill, past the deep furrows the truck's tires had cut into the lawn. As one, the pack turned their heads, looking in that direction, just the same as Barnes and Tom himself.

The dogs turned without another sound and loped up the hill.

A few of them still looked intact, but most shouldn't have been capable of any sort of motion at all. *You sick fucks should be dead! You should be lying down and gathering flies!* Norris watched them leave, his pistol all but forgotten. He should have been running after them: they were a threat to the community, and they were right in front of him. But he couldn't. His stomach felt twisted in knots, and his legs were wobbly in the worst possible way.

He looked over at Barnes and shook his head. Then Tom Norris took three long steps away from the blood and ruin at his feet and fell to the ground, vomiting up his last meal from Frannie's. He heard Victor Barnes climb back into the truck and answer the radio, but the words didn't make any sense. Nothing was making much sense in

Tom's world, where dead dogs weren't supposed to attack people, and cops responded to emergencies and stopped the bad guys.

The only thing he could do was hold himself up as he continued to dry heave. The only thing he could think about was the fact that he should have been dead, should have been torn limb from limb by the dead things that wouldn't lie still and, damn it, play dead properly. They'd stopped because they'd been called away, and they'd listened to the summons.

And the thing about that fact that bothered him the most was that it meant they were under someone's control. They weren't just a pack of hunting hounds gone feral. They weren't even just a pack of dogs that wouldn't die. They were a pack of dead dogs that were being told what to do by someone.

He wanted to get up and follow them, to find out who was behind the insanity and why. It was his job, dammit, and it was what he was supposed to do. But instead he crouched there on his hands and knees and shivered as his stomach tried to force out any contents it might have missed.

Something was making dead things get up and walk.

What else can it do? he wondered. *What else can it do, and what are we gonna do if it gets serious about tearing some people up?*

He wasn't sure he really wanted to know.

IV

Jonathan Crowley kept looking through the police files, his feet up on the desk and his face grim as he read over the details of Amy Blake's murder. There were photos, naturally. They were in black and white, with a few color ones thrown in for contrast apparently.

Looking at them almost made him feel sympathy for Mike Blake.

But they made him feel for his dead wife a lot more.

He closed the files and rose from Jack Michaels's comfortable chair, then slid the file back in where it belonged in the filing cabinet. Around the corner he could hear the one prisoner in the place moping around in his jail cell. The jock kid who'd been his cell mate for half a day.

He walked back over to the lockup room and leaned against the doorframe, looking over at the teen, who was sighing with all the drama he could muster.

"What's the matter, Junior? They forget to feed you?"

The kid looked at him with a sulky face and shook his head. "I didn't do anything to anyone. I don't deserve to be in here."

"Really? There's normally a reason for locking people up, kid. What are they blaming you for?"

"They're saying I raped my girlfriend and left her for dead, but I didn't, man. I never fucking touched her."

"That's a heavy accusation." He walked closer. Something about the kid made him curious, like he didn't already have enough to keep him busy. He was suddenly willing to play twenty questions with some little twerp who thought with his smaller head. He sighed inwardly and moved closer. "So tell me what they have on you and why you think you're not guilty of anything."

The kid looked at him and shook his head. "I don't need anyone else telling me I'm a monster, thanks anyway."

"You have something better to do?"

The kid glared some more and finally shrugged his shoulders.

"I took her out on a date. That's all. We went out to the movies and we had a good time. I didn't want the good times to end, and I might have gotten a little grabby. But I stopped when she told me to."

"Really? Hardly seems like a jailable offense. What else did you do?"

The kid shook his head and finally looked down, shamefaced. "I told her she could walk home. That if she wasn't going to put out, she wasn't worth the trouble." He told the rest of the tale as best he could, leaving out a lot of the details.

"And then somebody raped her?"

"Yeah."

"And you got the blame for it?"

"Yeah."

"Seems like you maybe deserve to be punished, sunshine." Crowley moved in closer still, a scowl on his face. "You don't really seem like the sort who needs to be walking around anyway."

"I know it was wrong, okay? Jesus! I didn't want her to get hurt! I love her!"

"Sure you do. You love her enough to dump her on a road and let her walk home. That's special of you."

"But I didn't do it! I never wanted her to get hurt!" The kid was crying. Not big tears, but a few. Crowley didn't have it in him to care. But then, he seldom did.

"So let me see if I've got this right. You dropped her off on the road, and she got raped and dumped in the woods. And what did you do when you found out she was missing?"

The kid looked at the ground again.

"Did you maybe tell the police what happened?"

"No."

"Did you think to even call her place and see if she was home?"

"No..."

"What then? You waited around to see if someone would casually mention she was dead?" He leaned against the bars of the cell, looking down at the prisoner with raw contempt in his voice and on his face. "Oh, I know, you waited at home and hoped she'd come crawling back to you." He shook his head when the kid started crying some more. "You weren't even man enough to call the cops anonymously and say where you last saw her. How long did you say she was gone? Two days? A week?"

Crowley walked away, his hands clenched at his sides. He stopped after a few steps.

"Do you really think you deserve to be treated like anything but a killer or rapist? You left her to walk home, and then you sat in your little bedroom and felt sorry for yourself when she didn't come running back. You're disgusting."

"Hey, fuck you!"

Crowley stopped in his tracks, tilting his head to the side. He turned slowly back to face the kid in the cell and walked back.

"I'm sorry. I didn't quite hear that. What did you just say?"

"I said, 'Fuck you!'" The kid was up against the bars of his cell, his face tear-stained and angry. "Who are you to judge me, anyway? Who the hell do you think you are?"

"I'm your better." He leaned in close, until his face and the boy's were inches apart. "I'm everything you should be. I've never left a girl stranded by the side of the road, and I've never once cowered in my room waiting to see if she was all right. It's called accountability. Even if you didn't rape her, you left her where it could happen. That makes you a weak little shit in my book."

"What? You never did anything you regretted later? Is that it? You're so fucking perfect that you never did anything wrong in your whole life?"

Jonathan Crowley thought back to his past, a long, long ways into his past, and he shook his head. "Not like that. Never like that. Anyone I hurt deserved to get hurt." It was a lie. There had been times when people who didn't really deserve to suffer wound up wishing they were dead, and in a few cases they got their wish, too.

It was regrettable, it was something he hated, but it was also a cold, simple fact. Sometimes people got hurt, and sometimes there was nothing he could do about it. But the rest was true. He'd never abandoned someone who needed his help, not unless they'd deserved whatever they were getting, and even then it was a rare thing.

Crowley leaned back his head, suddenly not wanting to be quite so close to the kid. "Let me put it another way, cupcake. If you'd been a man about it, if you'd just taken her home and used your hand instead of leaving her on a dark road, you wouldn't have any of this to worry about. She'd be safe at home, and so would you. There're always consequences to your actions. If you really are innocent, it'll all wash out."

Crowley turned and walked away, filing the name of the girl, Terri Halloway, in the back of his mental list of names to be researched. The list just kept getting longer and longer. Everything in the whole damned town seemed interconnected. That was to be expected, naturally; it was a town after all, and that meant everyone knew everyone else to some extent, but this was getting ridiculous.

He sat down at the constable's desk again. Pondering the implications of the markings on the corpse. The skin had been folded over, and the characters didn't work. They weren't complete. The lines and markings looked for all the world as if someone had made them with half of the surface skin covered with paper. He knew them, or at least he thought he knew them, but it was hard to tell with portions of each and every marking missing.

"It's half a puzzle or less." He tapped his fingers on the top of the desk, only idly noting the lack of any sort of staff on the premises. That was a bit odd, but not so unusual that he was worried. He took one look at the police force in Serenity and knew it was too small to handle much of anything at all.

So when the phone rang, he reached out and answered it. "Serenity constables' offices. How may I help you?"

"Hello? Yes, please, I need help. It's my husband. He's been missing for two days now, and I'm starting to get really worried."

Oh, and whoever she was, she was good at it. He could hear the careful modulation of her voice, the way she made it sound just exactly nervous enough. The caller ID on the screen showed the name, address, and phone number, all of which listed to the same man: Carlton Bradford. His fingers danced over the keyboard, typing in the name to see if there was anything more on him on file. The computer monitor in front of him flickered a few times and finally brought up the information. Carlton Bradford had seven previous arrests to his name and also suffered the unfortunate middle name of Maurice. His wife's name was Nona. "This is Nona Bradford, is that correct?"

"Yes, that's me."

"Ms. Bradford, when was the last time you saw your husband?"

"I saw him the night before last. We had dinner, and then he went off to shoot pool with some of his friends at Townsley's. He never came back, and when I called the bar, they said he hadn't been in at all."

Crowley jotted a quick note to himself to check out Townsley's. There was always a chance she was lying through her teeth about calling over there, and it wouldn't take long to find out. "What did you have for dinner that last night?"

"I'm sorry?"

"Dinner. What did you have for dinner the night your husband disappeared?"

"I—I think it was Salisbury steaks."

"What sides did you have?"

"I'm sorry?"

"What did you eat with the Salisbury steaks?" He spoke slowly, as if to a rather slow child.

"Um. We had peas and mashed potatoes."

"You're sure about that?"

"Yes."

"Okay. When did you eat?"

"Around seven, I think."

"And when did your husband leave the house?"

"Just after we ate, so I guess around seven thirty."

"And that was the night before last?"

"Yes."

"Why did you wait so long to call us, Ms. Bradford?"

"Well, because you're supposed to wait at least a full day, I thought."

"Is your husband in the practice of not coming home?"

"Well, no, not often. That's why I called."

He looked at the screen and smiled to himself for an instant. Her husband had been in jail no less than four times for disturbing the peace and drunk and disorderly. There was a typically grainy picture of him, and, as he finally noticed, there was a link to a picture of the little missus as well. He followed the link, opening her police records. She had a speeding ticket, nothing more. But she was a pretty enough woman.

He'd noticed that just the other day, when he saw her holding hands with a man who was most decidedly not her husband. They didn't hold hands like friends or relatives. Their body language said they were far more intimate as he remembered.

"I'll pass the information along, Ms. Bradford."

"Um. Thank you."

"Have a nice day."

Crowley hung up the phone, his mind trying to go over every nuance of what the woman had said. She was lying about what happened with her husband, he was certain of that much. Her responses were just a little too slow, and her voice was too nervous for the circumstances. Hell, reading between the lines on his police record it was obvious they weren't exactly a close couple, but adding in the rather intimate gestures with the other man in her life, it was easy to see that Ms. Bradford was hardly going to call the police when her husband was away.

At least not unless she had reason to believe he wouldn't be back anytime soon.

Crowley stood back up, moving away from the desk and the chair, but only after jotting a quick note to the constables. It wasn't really his problem to handle; it was theirs. Still, he felt that tingle in his scalp that told him it might end up as his problem soon enough. He was getting a lot of tingles since he'd come to Serenity Falls, and he was beginning to think they were all connected.

There's a pattern, but it's all out of order. None of this is adding up yet. He walked out of the constables' offices and out into the light of the afternoon. The cold was enough to make his teeth chatter. *I need more pieces to the puzzle. Then I can work this all out.*

There were more people out now than he'd seen since the last Sunday when everyone went spilling into the churches in the center of town. He could see the churches from where he was, not far from the strip of buildings that housed most of the smaller stores in the town. Off in the distance, behind the stores, he could just make out the shape of the school and the cemetery that cut it off from the majority of the town. School was out, and there were kids everywhere, most coming past the graveyard to reach the town proper. He watched them, really watched them for the first time since he'd gotten to town. Most of them seemed to only be going through the motions of daily life, but there were a few who were acting…off. Most of the kids were heading home with mixed expressions: some were glad the daily labors were over, others looked like they dreaded the idea of returning to their homes. Some were making jokes and cracking wise with their buddies, and others walked alone, heads down, with their every movement showing signs of submission and defeat.

Business as usual, in other words. Schools were notoriously filled with happy kids and miserable ones. There were pecking orders being established, and many of the people in those ranks either were at the low end or thought they were. It would be years before any of them really knew one way or the other where they stood in life. Right now they were just testing the waters and trying to figure out the rules. A few would catch on early; most would slowly decide how to live within the rules of their peers, their families, and their societies; and a rare one or two would either excel or go postal and kill a few companions before they were done.

That was growing up. It sucked and it was wonderful, and if he tried very, very hard, he could remember a few brief details of his own time at their age. And a lot of the time, Crowley envied them their youth, but just as often he felt a deep, lingering pity for the shit they'd be dealt. Mostly though, he ignored them. He didn't like kids. They were too unpredictable.

Just at the present time, three of them were walking slowly past where he stood, doing their best to watch him without being noticed. There was a kid who would, barring unforeseen incidents, grow up to be a jock, or at least have the look of one. Richie Cunningham with blond hair and muscles. There was a second young man who looked like a mortician in training. He was dark-haired, gaunt, and pale. He looked like he'd perhaps smiled a total of five times in his life. Worse still, Crowley would have bet good money that the poor bastard's mother still dressed him every day. His clothes were too neat, and his shoes should have been set aside for the Sunday best. Odds were good the kid wasn't allowed to have anything that resembled fun.

And then there was the girl with them. She wasn't pretty, exactly, but the way she walked, the way she moved, and even the way she looked at people exuded a sort of sexuality that should have been ridiculous on a girl who was barely entering puberty. Should have been, but wasn't. He looked around the area quickly and saw that several men and younger boys noticed it, too. Not in a conscious way, but in the way they responded. Their eyes lingered, some of them even puffed up and walked taller, as if trying to gain her favor.

It was ludicrous.

Her eyes met with Crowley's, and he looked at her closely, staring. There was something almost familiar about her, but he was damned if he could place it. Whatever that something was, it wasn't physical. It was mental. Another vibe that didn't fit with the pieces of the puzzle around him.

She smiled, her eyes challenging him, seeming to understand what was going through his mind. *Can't figure it out yet? Does it bother you not knowing? Does it make you want to scream?* Oh yes, whomever it was that was inside the girl's body—and he had no doubt that something other than a mortal soul was in there—was someone or some thing he knew. She smiled again and abruptly turned away.

But the boys continued to stare at him. And he returned the favor. Light blue eyes and dark brown ones locked with his, and he shifted between them, trying to read what was going on in the pubescent heads of the two. They wore exactly the same expression on their faces, a look of contempt that blended beautifully with a hatred he could almost feel coming off them. Whatever they felt, he knew inside that it was personal, and that made all the difference.

Whatever they are, they're supposed to be one being. That's why I couldn't sense it earlier. It was hiding. And now, it's letting me know it's here. And that means...

Crowley stepped back from the two twerps, watching their expressions change and grow darker. "I've been set up."

He turned just as the first of the screams started. He actually looked in the direction of the shouting just as the growls began. And there they were, the rotted snarling pack of hounds he'd heard people talking about. They were dead, that much was painfully obvious, and they smelled even worse than charnel houses he'd run across in Europe toward the end of the Second World War. The people on the sidewalk were moving fast, clearing a path for the pack of fang-snapping corpses, and in a few cases shrieking very loudly as they moved.

Crowley thought about doing the exact same thing for about half a second, and then he did it. There were a lot of dogs, and they were after one thing as far as he could tell. That one thing being a sizable chunk of his ass. It was not, by his standards, a very remarkable posterior, but he'd grown rather attached to having it around over the years. Also, while it was true he would heal from almost any sort of supernatural injuries that didn't really wipe out his body, it *hurt* to get torn open.

Hurt like mad.

So he ran like mad, his feet carrying him past the other runners as he raced to get away from the pack. His reward was to hear the pack start snarling and snapping even more. "Not good, not good, not good at all..." He risked a look over his shoulder and saw them coming. And damn, they looked mean. The good news, sort of, was that they were chasing after him exclusively. The bad news was exactly the same as the good news. And was there a cop around when he needed one? Of course not. How ridiculous.

Crowley darted down the next intersection, moving fast to the right and listening as the dogs came after him. They were gaining, and there was really very little he could do about that. He had to get to Amelia's place if he wanted to finish this the proper way. Proper meaning with him still breathing as opposed to him being food in so many dead stomachs.

Two blocks. I just have to make it two more blocks. I should have kept the damned things with me!

He reached into the pockets of his jeans, trying to remember what he'd shoved into them this time. There was a handful of stones in his left pocket, and a collection of coins in the right. The coins would have to do.

He looked over his shoulder and saw the leader of the things straining forward as it ran, its muzzle only a few inches from his backside. He pinched one of the coins between his thumb and forefinger and snapped it toward the animal with his wrist. His aim was true, and the quarter slapped into the cloudy left eye of the hound, exploding into its skull.

Dead or not, it still felt pain and still needed to see. The thing sprawled flat, rolling and shrieking as it shook its head, trying to dislodge the source of its new agony. The ones behind it kept coming, and Crowley kept running as fast as he could, sorting through the remaining change for a few pieces large enough to cause damage. He cut around the corner at the edge of the next block and found himself on the road leading toward Havenwood. *Where the hell did I get the idea it was only two blocks? It's a damn sight farther than that.* The road was right there, but the house itself was still almost a quarter mile away. *Why the hell can't anyone ever live somewhere that's convenient? Why can't the people I want to see ever be in the next building over, or just down the street? Why do they always have to be on the other damned side of town?*

He flicked another quarter behind him, but the dog jerked its head to the side, and he missed. That left him with a handful of pennies and dimes as his most lethal projectiles.

I'm not gonna do it. I'm not gonna let it out again. I won't, I won't, I won't...

He wanted to do this on his own. He wanted to stop them without having to reveal himself completely. He didn't want to remember what he hid from himself and from everyone else. Better by far to pretend, to at least have the illusion of a normal life.

Still, the dogs were getting really, really close, and he didn't want to think of that sort of pain. And then he smiled. Up ahead the trees grew together in a nice, thick canopy. He pushed himself harder and bolted across the street, moving into the darkness of the woods.

Not surprisingly, the hounds followed, more than happy to tear him apart in the trees instead of in the street. He smelled their stench wafting over him as the wind shifted and heard the sounds of their heavy bodies moving through the fallen leaves as they stormed across the ground.

It took an effort not to laugh.

He hit the closest tree at a full run and used his momentum to start scrambling up the bark of the oak, finally managing to grab a branch just before gravity could demand he fall all the way back down to Earth. He scrambled like a monkey until he could perch on the top of the branch, his hands holding the tree's trunk. His fingers lost a few layers of skin as he clung desperately, but he smiled when he saw the animals down below, jumping and trying to get high enough to reach him.

"Sorry, fellas," he panted as he spoke. "I'm not just ready to play fetch with you. But I will be soon." He hung there for a few seconds, waiting until he had some sort of even breathing going again, and then he stood up on the branch, testing it for strength. It was solid enough.

Down below the pack was watching him with dead eyes, moving around the base of the tree and, no doubt, hoping he would slip and fall. Crowley looked toward the next tree over, a good ten feet away, and grimaced. He could try to leap it—and just maybe succeed—or he could try moving out on the branch and practically walk over. Walking would be easier, but the branch got thinner as it went along. They tend to do that.

He looked down at the animals again. They hadn't lost any interest in him yet. Crowley took a deep breath and ran hard and fast down the length of the branch, then hopped to the next tree, his feet never coming close to losing balance. The branch he landed on, however, made a nasty cracking sound and almost dropped him before he reached the trunk. Not good, very bad. The pack moved with him, tracking along to the next tree with far less effort.

He was trying to think of another comment to make when the bones in his right hand shattered. Jonathan Crowley bit his lip and managed not to scream when he looked over and saw the damage. A rock was sticking out of his hand, looking all too much like a bird's egg resting in a nest of blood and gristle. He felt his knees grow weak and clung desperately to the rough bark as he looked away, trying to find the source of the pain.

And there he was, the blond kid he'd seen earlier. The little junior jock, looking at him and cocking back a second rock in his slingshot. His face was almost blank but for a slight smile.

"Hello, Hunter. It's so nice to see you again."

Crowley shook his head, forcing himself to flex his hand and jar loose the golf ball-sized lump of granite that stuck between and through the bones. The grating of broken meat and torn nerve endings made him want to faint dead away. The world grayed out a few times before it finally came back to solid focus for him. He shook his head and made himself lock eyes with the little shit.

"Do you want to just get this guessing game over with and tell me what I did to you already? Frankly, it's getting old now."

"Still with the false bravado? Even now, when I finally have you?" The voice of a nice, happy preteen called back to him, and the kid stepped closer. He kept the stone firmly pinched between finger and thumb, the elastic band on the weapon stretched taut.

"False my ass. When I get down from here I'm going to beat you to death."

"You'll only be hurting my host. I'll get away from you and do it all over again. Maybe this time I'll take over the girl you came here to see."

"Oh that would do you a lot of good." He smiled, feeling the itching burn of the wound in his hand starting to heal. There were a few benefits to being Jonathan Crowley, and that was one he depended on a lot.

"She means something to you, doesn't she?"

"Not really." He shrugged his shoulders, grinning at the look of surprise on the kid's face.

"Then why are you so determined to get to her?"

"She's holding something for me."

"What?"

Crowley grinned. "Let me go, and I'll show you, sunshine."

"Not likely."

"Hey, you never know until you try."

Crowley crouched low and then launched himself away from the tree, using the already weakened branch as a springboard to the next one. He almost missed, almost fell down to the dogs below. The rock the kid fired his way shot past his ear with a whistle as it cut through the air.

"I mean it, kid, I'm gonna put a serious hurt on you when I get down from here."

The boy ignored him, looking for another rock worth using. The dogs moved under him again. Crowley didn't waste any more time. He flexed his right hand a few times, feeling the broken flesh protest, and then he ran the length of the latest branch, looking at his next available tree even as he positioned himself. It was almost twenty feet to the next tree. With the closest branch, he could shave off maybe seven feet. That only left thirteen or so, with a pack of dogs and a trigger-happy brat just waiting for him to fall.

Crowley took the first three steps toward the next tree and felt the branch give out under him with a wet, cracking noise. The ground came up very, very quickly. The dogs were even faster.

V

Mike Blake was looking out the window of his new office when the commotion started. He'd been thinking again—an annoying habit he couldn't seem to break of late—and he'd been wondering about what he felt for Amelia, whether it was more than merely strong affection and if love was a real possibility. The biggest problem, and ironically the main thing that had first attracted him to her, was her close resemblance to Amy. How could he know if what he felt was wishful reflections of his lost wife or true, genuine feelings for the woman who looked so damned much like her?

It wasn't fair to stay with her if the ghost—figurative in this case, as opposed to the literal specter he'd already encountered—of his wife was going to become a serious problem. He thought about the vision of Amy he'd experienced only the day before and shivered. Two years since she'd died, two years since he'd first tried to drown his sorrows, and he had only just managed to accept that his Amy was dead and would never come back. He'd started getting on with his life at last. And then the ghost.

It was one thing to lose her, another to realize that she might not be as dead as he thought. Or, at least, that she was not resting in peace, or waiting for him in Heaven if such a place even existed.

These were the thoughts that refused to stay in the back of his mind, the ones that kept haunting him when he finally became conscious of the sounds outside. The sounds of dogs growling and barking and the sound of a child's laughter.

He might have ignored the noise outside had it not been coming closer to him. Annoyed by the sounds that were distracting him from his useless soul-searching—well, useless from his perspective, as he could never seem to find any reasonable answers—Mike stood up from the desk and looked out the window toward the woods.

And saw Jonathan Crowley fall from a tree and into the pack of dogs that had surrounded his perch. They were a good ways off, easily fifteen yards or more, but he recognized Crowley without any real trouble. Something about the man just stood out and made missing him almost impossible once you'd met him.

Crowley hit the ground, and Mike drew in a sharp breath as the pack of animals around the man attacked.

Mike didn't like Jonathan Crowley. It was just exactly that simple. He did not like him, and he doubted that he ever would or ever could. But it would be a cold, bitter day in Hell before he'd watch a person get torn apart by dogs without at least trying to do something about it.

There was no conscious thought in his running from the ground floor of the house and out the door on the side that led to the woods. He just did it. Along the way he grabbed a piece of lumber still sitting at the side of the house from when most of the rebuilding had taken place. It wasn't the easiest weapon to handle, but the two-by-four would do the job in a pinch.

"Yaaaaah! Get outta here! Get! Scat! Run!" He yelled at the top of his lungs as he ran, and felt a slight stitch start in his side almost immediately. He wasn't in the shape he'd been in when he was married, and two years of heavy drinking had taken more from him than the last few weeks had put back.

Up ahead of him, he saw the pack writhing in a wave of fur and thought he might be catching glimpses of Crowley's figure under all of them. It was almost a sure thing that the man was dead. If the dogs were half as fierce as he suspected, he couldn't think of anyone who would last even a minute.

Mike cranked back the makeshift club and charged forward, a part of him annoyed by the lack of reaction from the dogs, and most of him very, very grateful for that very same lack of reaction. They were some scary-looking things, and far worse up close. *They're dead. Every last one of those things is dead and still moving! What the hell am I doing going toward them? I should be hiding in the house.* Still he ran, and when he reached the first of the dead things, he cut loose with his wooden club and struck it hard across the side of its head.

The impact ran all the way up to his elbows and left his arms aching. He wasn't thrilled about the pain, and he was even less happy about the way the animal turned its broken skull and roared at him. It did not growl, it roared.

Mike backed away as the thing started snapping at him and lurching drunkenly away from the rest of the pack. One eye on the monster was clouded over and looked roughly toward the ground. The other eye looked right at him, and the teeth under it, already bloodied on Crowley as best he could figure, gnashed the air with a promise that they would soon know his blood as well.

He hit the damned thing in the head five more times to make sure he was getting his point across. He was screaming all the way through it, and seriously considering peeing his pants. His arms weren't sure if they wanted to be numb or scream in agony, and they were trying to do both at the same time. He swung his weapon again, ready to make it count. The dog opened its maw and clamped its teeth down on the seasoned wood, soaking up the impact like it was nothing.

Then it bit the two-by-four in half, losing teeth in the process. Mike let out a yelp that was mostly surprise and stumbled backward until he felt his heel hook on something. The ground tilted madly, and suddenly he was on his ass.

And that big dead dog? Why, it was munching on the remains of his lumber as it moved closer, teeth bared and ruined face wrinkled in anger. It roared again, and he felt the cold, rancid breath coming from its mouth, along with a few toothpicks worth of wood.

"Nice doggy...ni-ice big, dead doggy. Mikey was just kidding around..." Oh and didn't he sound so sincere, with his voice cracking like he'd made it back to puberty. Why was he out here again? Oh, yes, he remembered now, to save Crowley from the pack that was probably feeding on his remains.

"Yeah, Mikey, that ought to keep the bad thing away from you." The voice was horridly strained, but he recognized the tone in Crowley's words well enough. The man sounded amused. Mike was shocked enough at hearing Jonathan Crowley speak at all that he looked away from the monster coming toward him and sought the source of the snide comment.

He looked past the damned animal just in time to see Crowley wrap his bloodied arms around its neck and pull back with a savage wrench. The dead thing looked almost comically surprised as it was hauled backward and away from him.

Then he saw Crowley clearly, felt a cold dread rush through him. The man was bleeding, torn and ruined. Skin fell away from his body in long strings, clotted, ugly messes of muscle were exposed, in a few cases leading down to the white of bone that even the gore couldn't quite hide. His clothes were all but gone, and his hair was matted with the crimson stains of his own body and those of a few corpses. The parts of his skin that were still intact were also covered with a heavy coating of ichor. Crowley held the dead, writhing thing in his arms, and Mike watched on as one of his hands reached into the open chest cavity of the beast and started working itself deeper and deeper into the ruined torso. The animal wasn't roaring anymore, it was yipping in pain.

Jonathan Crowley did something with his hand and the hound just collapsed, as if someone had pulled a plug from its power source and knocked it out of commission. He let it fall to the ground and pulled his fist from its insides as it fell. There was something rotted and black clutched between his clenched fingers. A second later he dropped that as well.

Mike looked up at the man and shivered deep inside at the smile he saw there. He enjoyed it. Covered head to toe in the evidence of the violence he was experiencing, and he reveled in it. The expression on Crowley's face was the same as he'd have if someone told him a very funny and slightly dirty joke; Mike wanted to scream at the notion.

He might have said something about it, too, but Crowley turned away to face the rest of the dogs. It was only then that Mike Blake realized he'd been holding his breath. There were four of the beasts left, and only two of them were able to stand. One of them tried to charge Crowley, lurching sideways even as it moved forward. Mike watched the man drive his fist into the back of its head amid a series of noises that would haunt him for the rest of his days. They were wet sounds, all too much like the ones two people locked in a sexual encounter might make, and blended with them was the distinct sound of breaking bones and tearing flesh. The dead dog finally stayed dead.

The last of them looked at Crowley with something almost like fear and tried to run away. He didn't give it that chance. Despite his wounds, the man Mike had come into the woods to help started running after the animal, and when he fell upon it, Mike closed his eyes, trying not to see or hear the resulting carnage.

When he opened his eyes again, Crowley was standing over him, looking down with that same nasty smile on his face. "You okay there, Mikey?"

"Yeah. That was, um, that was disgusting." His voice quivered a bit, and he felt his lunch wanting desperately to escape the confines of his stomach.

Crowley looked away, his eyes searching the woods as he flexed his hands a few times. They were bloodied, his hands, just like the rest of him. "Comes with the territory."

"What the hell were they?"

"Dead dogs, Mike."

"But they were moving."

"Like I said, it comes with the territory."

"Why were they after you?"

"Maybe it's because I've been nosing around and trying to figure out who killed your wife, among other things. Maybe it's because I've done that sort of thing in other places, and something I dealt with before took it personally."

Mike rose to his feet, grateful that Crowley didn't offer to help him up. "We need to get you to a hospital."

Crowley shook his head. "Nope. I just need a shower and some new clothes."

"You're bleeding all over the place, Crowley. Don't be stupid."

Crowley smiled at him, his eyes amused. His voice was weak and strained, and it was obvious that the wounds that he'd suffered were agonizing, but still that tone of humor and sarcasm mingled with the grating sound of his words. "Aww...is that concern I hear in your voice, Mikey? I'm touched, really. But all I need is a shower. Seeing as Amelia's got one over at the house, I think I'll take one, too."

Crowley started walking, one leg dragging slightly and leaking blood. He moved almost as stiffly as the dogs had before he came along and tore them apart. Mike followed, still too freaked out to really put up much of an argument.

VI

Mike and Amelia sat in the living room, discussing the latest from Amelia's visit with her father. It hadn't been a long trip, only a few hours, but there had been a lot to cover. First and foremost was the use of available funds. According to Amelia at least, her father approved of the budget Mike'd laid out for her the night before. That was a good thing. Amelia might be calling the shots on getting the quarry going again, but she had to answer to her father, and he was the one who controlled the company.

Jonathan Crowley was upstairs, sleeping like a log. Mike had almost passed out when he saw the man come out of the shower with only a few scratches left to indicate that he'd ever been hurt. Crowley had just winked at him and said, "A good constitution makes up for a lot of sins, Mikey." Mike just stared, mouth hanging open, as the man sauntered into Amelia's bedroom. I'm taking a nap. Don't wake me."

An hour later, Amelia came back. He hadn't mentioned Crowley to her yet. She was in too good a mood for him to risk ruining it. He'd have to soon, though. She might not take well to a man sleeping in her bed. Then again, she seemed more than fond of Crowley. He brushed the thought away as quickly as it popped into his head, but it kept trying to creep back into his skull.

"So," she said, stretching in a way that seemed as sinuous as a cat, "the good news is, we're all set to go. All we have to do is keep everyone busy until the permits are in order." She reached out and took his hand in hers. The touch of her skin on his was as electric as ever, and he wanted nothing more than to kiss her as deeply as he could. "And I was thinking we could get in a little quality time between now and then, Mike." She smiled warmly and, as if she had read his mind, leaned up to be kissed. "I want to spend a lot of quality time with you." The kiss was as sweet and delightful as he'd expected. Each kiss from her was.

The sound of a door closing upstairs made them break this lip-lock. Mike flushed a bit, looking at her with a slightly guilty expression. "Did I mention that your friend Crowley is over?"

Amelia smiled, amused by his discomfort. "No…I think that little tidbit of information slipped somewhere along the way."

"He had a run-in with some dogs earlier…"

"Dogs?"

"Well, I think they were dogs. They looked a little like dogs…only not so living."

"Ah." She lowered her eyes for a second, then looked back at him. "You seem to be taking all the strangeness around here pretty well."

"Yeah, well, I just keep telling myself it's a side effect from giving up booze, and it makes everything a little saner." He flashed a smile at her to let her know he was kidding.

Crowley's voice came from the top of the stairs. The man was wearing fresh clothes, though Mike had no idea in hell where he'd managed to get them. What he'd had on when they came through the front door earlier was mostly in shreds and bloodied beyond repair. He moved with the brisk stride of someone who was in a good mood and happy to be where he was. His smile said he was in the mood to break someone's balls. "You gave up booze? Why would anyone want to do that?"

"Well, we came to a mutual understanding. I wouldn't drink it anymore, and it would let me have my life back."

Crowley raised one eyebrow a little and looked at him for a few seconds before deciding not to pursue the issue. "Amelia, where have you been hiding?"

"I had to see my father about some business." Her voice sounded oddly subdued.

"Really?" Crowley moved closer with a gait that was pure predator and a smile that said he liked toying with his prey. "How is the old man? Is he keeping his nose clean?"

"Yes, Jonathan. He hasn't...done anything like that for a long, long time."

"That's good to hear." He leaned against the arm of the couch on her side, his arms crossed over his chest and his brown eyes glistening with amusement. "That's very good to hear. Because, Amelia, I don't want to have to see him again. Is that clear?"

"Yes, Jonathan. It's very clear." Again, her normally cheerful demeanor was subdued to the point of nearly being extinguished. She shot a look at Crowley and then turned away fast, as if seeing him was too much for her eyes to take.

"Did you give him my message?"

"Yes."

Crowley put a hand on her shoulder, and Amelia almost jumped. Mike looked toward the man, ready to tell him to back off, and was caught by the brown eyes behind the wireless glasses. His gaze locked onto Mike and held him, almost seemed to drain him of any energy for arguing. "That was sweet of you, Amelia. Did he have anything to say back?"

"Only." She swallowed, and from the corner of his eye, he could see that she'd gone pale. "Only that he burned them. All of them. And that he doesn't know of any others, but that he hasn't been looking for them, either."

Crowley's hand on her shoulder patted down on her skin twice, and he released her, his eyes breaking the magnetic contact with Mike's own. Mike realized he'd been holding his breath, though he hadn't meant to.

Crowley leaned in closer, his mouth almost touching her perfect ear, her dark hair brushing his cheek. "Now, just one more little thing. What is it I'm feeling in your room?"

Amelia shuddered, taking in a sharp gasp of air. "I wasn't trying to hide them, Jonathan. I just didn't think they were important." Her voice was on the edge of panic. Mike stood up, ready to defend her from the man beside her.

"Of course you weren't." His voice fairly flowed with sarcasm. "There's nothing behind the locked door that I would find of interest, now is there?"

"Jonathan, please, I—"

"That's about enough of the bully tactics, Crowley." Mike's voice sounded funny to his own ears. He wasn't used to being authoritative. It wasn't usually in his nature anymore. It hadn't been for a long, long time. Maybe that was changing.

"What's the matter, Mikey?" Crowley's smile stretched wider on his lean face. "Afraid I'd do something to hurt Amelia? Don't be. We're old friends."

"I don't know what your game is, mister, or why you feel like you have to be an asshole all the time, but you leave off with giving her the third degree, or I'll kick your ass."

Amelia's hand reached out, almost like she was going to try to stop Mike from moving forward. "Mike, no..."

Crowley flowed up from his sitting position, shaking his head. "You don't want to get in my way, Mikey. You really don't."

"It's MIKE, *Johnny*. Not Mikey or sunshine or any of your other pet names. My name is Mike." He pushed a little against Amelia's hand, part of him quailing at the idea of taking on the man in front of him and part of him desperately wanting to knock the smile from Crowley's face.

"Fair enough, Mike." Crowley shrugged. "Now let's get something clear, shall we?" The man moved forward, his body stopping a millimeter from the hand that Amelia held out to stop him. "I'm not here to make you comfortable, or to take your girlfriend away from you, or even to kick your ass, as appealing as that last one is to me. I'm here because there's something going on that needs fixing, and because I was asked to fix it."

"Then why don't you get it done and go away?"

"That's exactly what I plan to do, Mike." He stepped forward, a casual stride, nothing aggressive. "But, you see, it's a little harder to handle that when I don't have the information I need to assess the situation properly. Would you like to come upstairs and see what's in that room?"

"I know what's in there. Wooden dolls."

Crowley smiled again, his eyes challenging. "Is that all? Are you sure?" He looked hard at Mike, and suddenly Mike felt like a bug under a microscope. "Are you really, really sure that's all they are?"

"Jonathan, please."

Crowley reached out and placed one finger to Amelia's lips, silencing her with the simple gesture. His eyes never left Mike's. "Why don't we all go up there and have a good, long look. I bet there's more to those little wooden dolls of yours than you know."

"Fine. Have it your way. Show me what's so special about them."

"That's a deal, Mike."

Crowley turned fast, moving up the stairs with that casual saunter of his that set Mike on edge. Mike looked at Amelia, who was in turn looking at him with eyes that were desperate for him to please, God, behave himself. He nodded and offered her a hand up. She took it, squeezing his fingers urgently, a silent communication that said *Thank you* and *Everything will be fine.* He wanted to believe her. He just wasn't sure if that was possible. He walked up the stairs after Crowley, his heart beating harder than he cared to admit.

Up into Amelia's room. The room where he'd first gotten to know her. Crowley ignored the enormous oak bed that was the centerpiece of the entire place. He paid no attention at all to the entertainment center that covered the north wall with all of the best possible electronics. He moved past the vanity where Amelia kept more fluff than makeup and went straight to the room that Mike and Amelia had uncovered, their shared secret revealed to a man Mike could easily hate. His even being in the room felt like a violation.

Crowley looked back at him with that smile of his in place, and Mike wanted to spit at him. Instead, he held his own while the man gripped the door handle and swung the door open to reveal the doll room.

Mike looked at the tiny figurines, his eyes appraising them. They were as remarkable as he remembered, and, as before, they had moved of their own volition. There was one doll, tiny as the rest and dressed in a gown that looked almost like Amy's wedding dress, that he looked for each time he entered the room. When last he'd seen it, the doll had been on the second shelf on the right side of the room. Now it was in the windowsill, and the arms were in different positions, almost as if she were waving at someone.

Crowley stepped into the room, and Mike heard a sound that he hadn't expected, almost like the hissing of a snake in the distance.

The dolls moved. Not a little, not imperceptibly. They moved openly and with as much energy as he would expect from a group fleeing Godzilla. They ran away from Crowley, trying their best to hide in the room that contained nothing but them and the shelves where they were positioned. Their faces were small enough that he could barely register them in the first place, and still he could see the terror on those minuscule features.

Mike stepped back, shaking his head in denial. Dead dogs were one thing; he could rationalize that as maybe them just being rabid and very, very dirty. But the dolls, they shouldn't have been moving. They shouldn't have been able to do anything but sit in one spot and gather dust. He'd held several of the tiny figures in his hand, felt the careful craftsmanship and attention that each had been given. They were beautiful and nearly lifelike, but there was no way they could move. No way they could be alive. He stepped back again, shaking his head and making noises in the back of his throat. *Nossir... Not at all possible. Not the least bit possible. Absolutely against the rules. I don't think I like these dolls anymore. I really, really don't think I do...*

Crowley reached out his hand and caught the wedding dress-clad doll on the windowsill. Mike thought for sure he would pass out when he heard the tiny scream of panic that came from its mouth. He moved across the room, the doll held out before him, and raised it until its face and Mike's eyes were at the same level.

"Do most dolls do this, Mike?" His voice was a whisper, barely audible, but still louder than the shrieks of panic coming from the figurine.

Mike looked at Crowley for a second and then turned his attention to the figure in the man's hand. The world faded away until it became as small and focused as the figure in Crowley's palm, and Mike felt his vision blurring. Damned if the doll didn't look exactly like his Amy, dead these last two years… The floor punched him hard in the side of his head, and then there was blackness.

VII

Crowley grinned down at Mike Blake as he lay on the floor. He set the screaming figurine down on the windowsill almost gently. "You know, Amelia, for a tough guy, he's sort of a wimp."

"Jonathan…" Her voice was one part whimper and one part plea for help, and Crowley knew she hated herself for even making a noise along those lines. He didn't really like making Amelia feel bad—well, no more than he liked making anyone feel bad at any rate—but he grinned just the same. She looked at him, her pretty face showing heavy exasperation. "Maybe you should try being nice to someone for a change, Jonathan. He's had a rough time for the last few years."

"Yeah? And that makes him special because…?"

"You're impossible, you know that, don't you?"

"Said the woman who shouldn't be walking the face of the Earth…" He looked away for a second, checking to see if macho man was conscious yet. He wasn't. "Besides, I was nice to him. I haven't hit him even once, and you know how much I dislike people calling me out."

"That's not what I meant, and you know it." She knelt down next to Mike and ran her fingers through his thinning hair. "Mike is a nice man. He doesn't deserve what you're putting him through. And not hitting him because he has an opinion doesn't qualify as being nice, Jonathan."

"Sure, he's a peach."

"Don't patronize me."

"You're the one who says he's a nice man, and I guess you'd know better than me." Crowley squatted next to her. His eyes looked over Mike on the floor and he sighed. "Still just seems a little strange to me…"

"What seems a little strange?" The tone of her voice told him she wasn't in the mood for any games. That didn't stop him from playing them.

"Well, the little figure I picked up and showed to him looked an awful lot like you, and from what you've told me, that means it's probably a figure of his wife."

Amelia's eyes left Mike and moved up to stare back into his own eyes. "And?"

"Just seemed a little strange that she only really started screaming when she saw him."

"She screamed a bit when you picked her up."

"Not to the same extent."

"What are you saying?"

"I'm not saying anything, Amelia. I'm just making an observation. Seems strange to me that the little doll that may or may not have a direct connection to his dead wife would be so panicked by seeing him."

"You don't think he had anything to do with her death, do you?"

"Who am I to say? I'm just looking for answers."

"I don't think he's capable, Jonathan. Not of murder or anything like that." But, oh, there was that little hesitation in her voice, wasn't there? Just a little catch, while she tried to decide if it was a real possibility.

"What do you think he's capable of? Throwing tantrums in the graveyard? Drinking himself into a stupor?"

"That's not fair!" Oh, now he was in trouble. She was upset about that last comment.

"Why not, Amelia? He's done both."

"And you've never lost your temper, Mr. Crowley?"

"I have on more than one occasion. I just didn't need a drink to help me get started."

"He hasn't had a drink since I've been here."

"I know."

"Then why did you bring it up?"

"Because Mikey here is in the process of waking back up, and I want him good and riled."

"Why?"

"He's so cute when he's pissed off."

"You're impossible."

"Thanks for noticing." Crowley stood up with the same fluid grace that he always did, not a joint or ligament giving the least bit of protest. Mike's groans were substantially louder. "Well, welcome back to the land of the conscious, Mike."

Mike Blake looked at him with bleary eyes and blinked. Whatever he saw when he looked at Crowley wasn't very pleasant. He turned his eyes toward Amelia instead and smiled when he saw her.

Amelia, on her knees and looking straight down at him, smiled warmly and ran her delicate fingers over his brow. The moron was eating up the affection like candy.

"Well, I can see you two want some alone time." Crowley moved away, looking back at the room full of dolls. He reached out and grabbed one before it could react, holding it loosely in his hand. The way it moved was more than a little repulsive, but he'd felt worse. "I'll be on my way, but first, Mike, how about answering one more question for me?"

Mike didn't look like he wanted to answer any more questions, but he seemed to like the idea of Crowley hanging around even less. "Sure."

"There was a boy in the woods with me, when I was running from the dogs. Real cute kid, around twelve or so, rather athletic, blond hair, blue eyes. Any idea who he might be?"

"There's lots of kids who look like that." His voice gave him away. He had one in mind.

"Humor me, Mike. Give me the first name that pops into your head."

"Joey Whitman."

"That sounds about right. Where would I find the Whitman place?"

"Why are you after Joey Whitman?"

"Those dogs? The ones that tried to eat me? They were following his lead."

Mike told him where the kid lived. "So what's next?"

Crowley looked at Mike and smiled. "Well, I want to have a chat with Joey. And I want to look into a few things that need to be investigated." The smile left his face. "I meant what I said before, Mike. I'm going to find out who murdered your wife."

"Why is that so important to you, Crowley?" The idea of the man doing anything at all that related to Amy was unsettling, though he couldn't have said exactly why.

"Because I think whoever murdered your wife is up to something in this town, Mike. The dogs were just a warning. Now it's time to find out what's really going on in Serenity Falls."

Mike had no answer to that, and neither did Amelia. Crowley left the building a few moments later, and they watched him go.

Whatever was happening in Serenity Falls, Mike suspected they'd have an answer soon.

What he didn't know was whether or not that knowledge would come with a price too high to pay.

About the Author

JAMES A. MOORE authored more than forty novels. The first decades of his career focused on his love for horror, as seen in many novels including the critically acclaimed *Fireworks*, *Under the Overtree*, *Blood Red*, and the Serenity Falls trilogy. Later, Jim earned a reputation as the "prince of grimdark fantasy" with his hugely popular Seven Forges series as well as the Tides of War trilogy. The author loved collaborating with other writers, most frequently with Christopher Golden on the Bloodstained Worlds trilogy and with Charles R. Rutledge on the Griffin & Price series, among others. Nominated for the Bram Stoker Award twice, Moore won the Shirley Jackson Award for co-editing *The Twisted Book of Shadows*. He first came to prominence as one of the principal world-builders involved in the World of Darkness from White Wolf Games, most famously Vampire: The Masquerade and Werewolf: The Apocalypse. At the time of his passing, Moore left behind one completed solo fantasy novel, as well as completed collaborations with Charles R. Rutledge and Mary SanGiovanni. Plans are afoot to bring those to readers soon.

Bibliography

NOVELS

The Black Stone Bay Series
Blood Red (with "Blood Tide"
Blood Harvest
Bloodlines

The Bloodstained Series (w/Christopher Golden)
Bloodstained Oz
Bloodstained Wonderland
Bloodstained Neverland

The Chris Corin Series
Possessions
Newbies
Rabid Growth

The Chronicles of Jonathan Crowley
Under the Overtree
Writ in Blood: Serenity Falls, Book One
The Pack: Serenity Falls, Book Two
Dark Carnival: Serenity Falls, Book Three
Cherry Hill
Smile No More
Boomtown
One Bad Week
Where the Sun Goes to Die

The Griffin & Price Series (w/Charles Rutledge)
Blind Shadows
Congregations of the Dead
A Hell Within

The Seven Forges Series
Seven Forges
The Blasted Lands
City of Wonders
The Silent Army
The Godless
The War Born

The Subject Seven Series
Subject Seven
Run

The Tides of War Series
The Last Sacrifice
Fallen Gods

Gates of the Dead

Standalone Novels
Deeper
Fireworks
Harvest Moon
The Haunted Forest Tour (w/ Jeff Strand)

NOVELLAS
Dear Diary: Run Like Hell
Homestead
The Wild Hunt

SHORT STORY COLLECTIONS
Slices
This is Halloween

Curious about other Crossroad Press books? Stop by our website:
http://crossroadpress.com
We offer quality writing
in digital, audio, and print formats.

Subscribe to our newsletter on the website homepage and receive a
free eBook.

www.ingramcontent.com/pod-product-compliance
Lightning Source LLC
Chambersburg PA
CBHW030805260626
47169CB00001B/203